William Clarkson

Christ and Missions

SALZWASSER
VERLAG

William Clarkson

Christ and Missions

Reprint of the original.

1st Edition 2023 | ISBN: 978-3-37514-609-2

Verlag (Publisher): Salzwasser Verlag GmbH, Zeilweg 44, 60439 Frankfurt, Deutschland
Vertretungsberechtigt (Authorized to represent): E. Roepke, Zeilweg 44, 60439 Frankfurt, Deutschland
Druck (Print): Books on Demand GmbH, In de Tarpen 42, 22848 Norderstedt, Deutschland

CHRIST AND MISSIONS:

OR,

FACTS AND PRINCIPLES OF EVANGELISM.

BY THE

REV. WILLIAM CLARKSON,

LATE MISSIONARY TO INDIA, AUTHOR OF 'INDIA AND THE GOSPEL,' ETC.

'THE LORD SHALL SEND THE ROD OF THY STRENGTH OUT OF ZION; RULE THOU IN THE MIDST OF THINE ENEMIES.'—*Psalm cx.*

LONDON:

JOHN SNOW, PATERNOSTER ROW.

IPSWICH: J. M. BURTON AND CO.

MDCCCLVIII.

CONTENTS.

CHAPTER I.

INTRODUCTION.

PAGE

The records of Missions a Supplement to 'The Acts of the Apostles.'—Modern 'Apostles' and their 'Acts.' —Evangelism and Proselytism distinguished.—Apathy of several Classes of Christians relative to Evangelistic work.—Study of Missionary Records urged.—As involving highest Personal Interest.—As adapted to promote practical Religion.—As affording Incentives to Glorify God.—As a means of furthering the Evangelistic Enterprise. . 1

CHAPTER II.

FORMS OF HEATHEN WORSHIP.

The World: in what conscious relationship to God and Christ?—Answer Two-fold.—The worship of the Heathen.—Man-worship in its several forms.—Devil Worship: its Principle — Prevalence — Characteristics. — Creature Worship: — Pantheism. — Other Forms.—Idol Worship.—Multiplicity and Variety of Gods.—Influence of Idolatry.—The Heathens who have no worship.—Conclusion. . . 30

PAGE

CHAPTER III.

THE MORALS OF HEATHENDOM.

Heathens' Violation of God's Law.—Identity of the forms of Heathen Iniquity.—Universality of Evil.—Intenseness.—The sins of Heathendom: What do they bespeak?—Summary.—The specific forms of Heathen Degradation the result of Moral Debasement.—Heathenism never dies out.—Positive Provisions for its Perpetuity.—Absence of everything remediative within itself.—A power ab-extra needed.—Not civilization—Nor Secular Education—but the Gospel. 58

CHAPTER IV.

THE FUTURE STATE OF THE HEATHEN.

What are the Heathen before God?—Issues of Evil are Certain.—General sentiment of Christians defended.—Heathen Depravity an insuperable Ground of Christian Solicitude.—The question transferred to the region of facts.—Are the Heathen saved *from* sin in this life?—Hopeful cases.—General question not affected.—Scripture statements.—Conclusion.—An objection answered.—Application. . 87

CHAPTER V.

THE SEVERAL FORMS OF ANTICHRIST.

The Jew: his opposition to Christ and Christians.—Infidelity. — Worldly Spirit. — Strong grounds of Hope.—Mahomadans: Their spirit towards Christ.—Their relation to Missions: Offensive and Defensive. — The Moslem's future. — Corrupt Christian Churches.—Characteristics of Apostacy.—Special aspects of Opposition to Christ.—Spiritual Lies and

PAGE

Counterfeits.—Church of Rome.—Other Churches.—Moral Relations of the above Classes. Appeal to a Spiritual Church.—Hope for Jew and Gentile only in the Economy of Grace. . . . 116

CHAPTER VI.

MODERN APOSTOLIC MISSIONS.

Missions:—Their Moral Force.—Their extensive Range.—WESTERN AFRICA:—Madeira.—Coast of Senegambia and Guinea. — First Converts. — Introduction to Inland Countries. — Prospects. — SOUTHERN AFRICA: Early Labours.—Onward progress.—New Era.—EASTERN AFRICA:—Abyssinia.—Exploratory Journey on the Coast. — MADAGASCAR: — Human Co-operation excluded. — The Agency of Christ conspicuous. 145

CHAPTER VII.

MODERN APOSTOLIC MISSIONS.

LANDS OF THE BIBLE — A Pioneer's Statement. — Formation of Armenian Churches.—Chain of Missions.—Interesting Facts.—Elements of Encouragement. NESTORIAN MISSIONS: Their Success. — DESERT REGIONS. — INDIA: A Sphere Well Known — of Multiplied Labours — of Faith and Patience — of Triumphs—of Hope. . . . 173

CHAPTER VIII.

MODERN APOSTOLIC MISSIONS.

ASSAM.—BURMAH: Its Associations.—First Era.—Second Era.—Third Era.—SIAM: Its Past and Present.—CHINA: Its Religious History.—Missionary Plans.

PAGE

—Chinese Character.—Mission Results.—Special Work at AMOY.—China's Future.—INDO-CHINESE ARCHIPELAGO: An Arduous Sphere.—A Few Successes.—SOUTHERN SEAS: Former Condition of Inhabitants.—Night of Toil.—Work of Jehovah. Methods of Divine Procedure.—Native Evangelists. —Christianized Islanders. . . . 214

CHAPTER IX.

MODERN APOSTOLIC MISSIONS.

AMERICAN INDIANS:—Interesting Associations.—Adversities of past Missions.—Present Missionary Operations.—Phases of Missionary Life.—Blessed Results. —The Indians' Future.—Indians of South America. —WEST INDIES:—Unique Experiment.—Trials of Early Labourers.—Negro Conversions.—Fruits of Emancipation.—GREENLAND AND LABRADOR:—Peculiarities of the Work.—Progress.—AGGREGATE RESULTS OF MISSIONS:—The Work Progressive.— New Phases Developed. . . . 241

CHAPTER X.

OBSERVATIONS ON THE PHENOMENA OF MISSIONS.

Principle of Selection of Stations.—Expansive Spirit of Missions.—Appositeness of Locations.—Unity of Evangelistic Means.—Oneness of Results.—Dark side of Missions.—Lack of Success.—Appeal to Facts.—Qualifying Considerations.—Missions dependant on *Command.*—Comparison with Apostolic Missions—With the Progress of the Gospel at Home.—Expenditure of Material and Life.—Answer.—Nothing Lost to God—Nor to the Individual—Nor to the Cause of Evangelization—Nor to the Church—Nor to the World.—What is Lost. 258

PAGE

CHAPTER XI.

CHRIST IN THE MISSIONARY 'CALL.'

Analsyis of the Phenomena of Evangelism.—Prerogative of the Glorified Christ.—Bearing of the Individual 'Call' on the Formation of Missionary Societies.—Objects of the 'Call.'—Manner of the 'Call.'—Principles on which Men have Embraced Missionary work.—Obedience to Command:—Moravians.—Carey.—Judson.—The highest Expression of Self-consecration.—Recognition of the Glory of the Work:—Rhenius—Mylne.—Compassion for Souls:—Johnson—Knibb.—Relative Usefulness:—Macdonald—Grant.—Christ in the Operation of all these Principles.—Counter Supposition.—Summary.—'Call' of this Book. 281

CHAPTER XII.

CHRIST IN THE MISSIONARY CHARACTER, ENDOWMENTS, AND COURSE.

Sympathy with God:—Its Developments—Christ its Author.—Sympathy with Man:—Its Origin in Christ.—Gifts and Graces.—Christ keeps his Evangelists from 'The Evil.'—Missionary Discouragements—Christ Sustains.—Fiery Trials—Christ Upholds.—Joyous Experiences of Missionary Life.—Christ in them.—Missionaries 'the Glory of Christ,' in their Mission and Character.—Honour Conferred by Christ on the Church. . . 313

CHAPTER XIII.

CHRIST IN THE 'EFFECTUAL DOOR' AND SUCCESS OF MISSIONS.

Christ's Providence for Missions—In Missions—Spiritual Results from Christ.—'Manner of Entrance' of the

PAGE

Truth. — Agency of Christ therein. — Converts' Apprehension of Christ. — Dying Experiences. — Christ the Author of such Faith.—Converts' Character.—Source in Christ.—Pentecostal Effusions.—North Americans. —Negroes.—Bechuanas.—Fingoes. —Armenians.—Nestorians.—Cingalese.—South Sea Islanders. — The Spirit of Christ. — Concluding Remarks. 347

CHAPTER XIV.

EVANGELISM IN ITS RELATIONS TO CHRIST.

Recapitulation.—Christ in Missions prosecutes his own Mission—Secures the Objects of his Redemptory Work—His Travail and Glory.—Christ in Missions an Encouragement — A Rebuke — A Motive. — Missions to be prosecuted for Christ—In the Mind of Christ—Under Christ. — Promise Fulfilled. — Conclusion. 375

CHRIST AND MISSIONS.

CHAPTER I.

INTRODUCTION.

The Records of Missions a Supplement to 'The Acts of the Apostles.' —Modern 'Apostles' and their 'Acts.'—Evangelism and Proselytism distinguished.—Apathy of several Classes of Christians relative to Evangelistic work.—Study of Missionary Records urged.—As involving highest Personal Interests.—As adapted to promote practical Religion.—As affording Incentives to glorify God.—As a means of furthering the Evangelistic Enterprise.

THE vision of prophecy has been sealed up. None can open the prophetic roll to add to its contents. All we can do is to interpret that which is written. 'The testimony of Jesus'—the inspired biography of the God-man—is also closed. None dare nor can add to the features of his divine portraiture. The history of Christ is now incapable of extension. Not a single incident may be annexed to it. No thought may be enunciated as his, no words may be put into his mouth. His 'life' is already completed in all its parts, and the whole is divine. No touch, nor finish, nor ornament, nor grace, is lacking. We have the perfect historic development of a perfect life. The 'memoir' can receive no fresh material; no 'remains' can supplement the evangelistic records.

Further—the Law is also perfected. In God's code of divine precepts, as delivered to us in the Bible, none dare introduce a single statute or command. Words that shall never pass away have been inscribed on enduring tables. Not a jot, or tittle, may be added to the inscription, or erased from it. 'The law of the Lord' is perfect in its letter and its spirit, its principles and its sanctions. To add to it is to mar it. There is no room for appending to it the commandments of men.

But while 'the Law,' and 'the Gospel,' and 'the Prophets,' are complete, there is another portion of God's revelation which is receiving continual accessions. We mean the history of Christ's self-revelation in the church; of his working *in*, and *by*, and *with* his ministers. The original memoirs of apostles and prophets are in an unbroken line supplemented by other memoirs. Holy lives and devoted deaths in the sacred cause of evangelization—great things dared and accomplished for the holy child Jesus—these are filling up from age to age, and from year to year, that which remaineth of 'The Acts of the Apostles.' In the great evangelistic work, Paul is succeeded by a Paul, Peter by a Peter, Philip by a Philip, Stephen by a Stephen. Jesus himself appears in his servants, evolves the same characters, produces the same moral phenomena, and works the same class of results.

The Spirit of holiness, and wisdom, and love, and

soundness of understanding, by the 'same effectual operation,' originates and sustains the same ministrations.

As though to signify this, the inspired historian did not wind up his record, nor formally close it. He knew that his 'treatise' was but the prelude of the future history of the Spirit's operations in the world by other holy men; that his 'acts' were but the first of a successive series which should extend along the track of time till the consummation of all things. He therefore finished his story by no climax, nor appended to it an 'Amen.' Never was a more unfinished document than 'The Acts of the Apostles.' 'And Paul,' says the historian, 'dwelt two whole years in his own hired house, and received all that came in unto him, preaching the kingdom of God, and teaching those things which concern the Lord Jesus Christ, with all confidence, no man forbidding him.'

Here is evidently the breaking off of a divine tale, which another is to take up; a thread woven in the yet unfinished woof of ministerial records, whose ends others are to take up and weave into the fabric. His history unfolds incident, but evolves no plan; fills up detached outlines, but gives no map. In this closing sentence are no finishing strokes of a vast history such as we find in the great secular historians of the rise and fall of empires, no expressed satisfaction with a work as once for all completed. He makes an abrupt pause, allowing for further evolutions of the Divine mind in the Church's history, and the unfolding of further events, as yet hidden from ages and from generations, but which time shall make manifest. Other pens must be employed. The scroll of which he has written a few lines will have to be written within and without, and by multitudes of writers of every possible variety, yet manifesting the unity of truth. A 'Finis' will be appended only when the last act of a wonder-working God in the persons of his apostles has been recorded, and the history of the Church finished.

Subsequent writers dare not, indeed, claim a like infallibility for their Scripture with the great historian, nor equal impartiality of judgment, nor the same unswerving fidelity to truth. Yet though untaught by inspiration, they have given, in the spirit of truth, a solemn testimony, and their 'Acts,' as recorded, have stood the test of human criticism as authentic, and, as a whole, will doubtless stand the scrutiny of the criticism of an all-revealing fire 'on that day.' From the first age of Christianity till now, there have been apostles; those sent by Christ for the evangelistic work, bearing the original commission, and possessing the qualifications for its fulfilment, though neither inspired nor endowed with miraculous powers. There are their 'Acts,' works of faith and love in winning souls from the heathen mass; passive endurances by those strong to suffer, energies put forth by those strong to labour, all originating in, and sustained by, a spiritual fellowship with the Lord Jesus Christ.

The records of such 'Acts' are found scattered over the whole period of the Church's history, and are written in most of the languages under heaven.

The author's object in this work is to illustrate them in connexion with the Evangelistic Missions of this age. The history of those missions is fraught with such acts as we have specified. Those who perform them give evidence that their apostolate is not 'from man,' nor 'by man,' but by 'Jesus Christ and God the Father.' Their striving is manifestly according to the working of Christ, which worketh in them mightily, and the results they accomplish are by virtue of his working with them by signs following. Though more than eighteen centuries separate us from the times of those peculiarly called 'apostles,' our age is yet apostolic. The 'ends of the world,' which have come upon us, are the years of the right hand of the Most High.—Nothing would seem more demonstrable than this. Some have but just passed from our midst, and others yet survive who can say to multitudes of converted heathen, in the language of Paul, 'The seal of our apostleship are ye,' and to whom those multitudes respond, 'In Christ Jesus you have begotten us in the Gospel.' For such we claim, without presumption, the credit of an apostolic mission, and in fulfilment thereof, apostolic action, power, and principle. To refuse this claim is to falsify the credentials furnished by Christ, and to incur his censure, 'He that despiseth *you* despiseth *me*, and he that despiseth me despiseth him that sent me.' To ignore their 'acts,' is to be blind to the developments of God's power and grace in the history of a redeemed world. It is to evince less judgment than was exercised by the magicians of Egypt when they cried, "This is the finger of God."

By the definition we have given, we have distinguished evangelistic 'Acts' from the efforts of a proselytism incessantly put forth by heathen and so-called Christian missionaries. To proselyte is human; to evangelize is divine. To work for self is from self; to work for Christ is from Christ. Attempts to convert minds, to instil dogmas, and to subjugate will, are spontaneous to human nature. Efforts to convert souls, to implant faith, and sanctify will, have a Divine origin. There is no mind which does not seek to multiply itself, and reproduce its own likeness. There is no dogma of faith sincerely embraced, which does not seek to secure the subjection of others. Thinking, feeling, sincere men, must proselyte. It is a mistake to suppose that Christianity is the only system which seeks to propagate itself, and which has its organized missionary staff. Thoughts, and creeds, and convictions, are propagated from mind to mind, and from age to age. Man persuades man, and is persuaded by him. The mind is rare which elaborates religious dogmas. The authority is only occasional which establishes religious practices. The mass receive them when proselyted to them. The zeal of the religious proselyter is proverbial. It is a principle that has characterized most ages, and has controlled the history of the world. Religious systems that have become effete may indeed cease to proselyte. They have scarcely sufficient vigour to defend themselves. They can spare none for aggressive efforts, as the decaying tree has no sap to spare to put forth fresh shoots. All that age has left it is wanted to supply the existing branches. But these systems owed their original power and influence to direct suasive efforts.

In mere proselytism, therefore, there is nothing of the Divine. The apostles of a system may be messengers of Satan. They may be impelled by a spirit of fanaticism, 'hot from hell,' or by a strong desire to assimilate others to themselves in sentiment and practice; or may be urged on by the lust of ambition—the hungerings and thirstings after a present or posthumous fame.

India affords the most striking illustration of these remarks. Buddhism was the greatest missionary institution the world ever saw—an unparalleled system of proselytism. Centuries ere the apostles of Christianity had received their mission, the sectaries of Buddhism had entered on their work, not by units, but hundreds, and had enrolled their converts in myriads and tens of myriads.

Neither the snowy range of the Himalayas, nor the typhoons of the seas of China and Japan, nor the black waters of Birmah, nor the reputed whirlpools which render a voyage to Ceylon unspeakably terrible, were sufficient to deter the missionaries of the new sect from most arduous journeys and weary voyages. They were not daunted by the violence of the barbarism which they met with in eastern islands, nor the more consolidated opposition of organized government and compact priesthoods. Thibet and Tartary, China and Japan, the Indian Archipelago, Siam, and Birmah, were the scenes of protracted labours and wonderful successes. Religious zeal opened up a highway which had never been explored for either commerce or conquest.

Asoka, emperor of India, the Constantine of Buddhism, whose monuments still exist, convened a great missionary assembly. He consecrated his own son to the work, and received the appellation 'Relative of the Faith.' The new system overruled the worn-out religion of the Vedas, suppressed Hindu caste, and abolished the exercise of the Braminical priesthood. The zeal of the new sect provided monasteries, established hospitals, erected temples, or made excavations in the solid rock to serve as repositories for the images of Buddha. The relics of Buddhist missionaries have been recently excavated from the tumuli which formed their sepulchres. We find inscriptions containing the names of the missionaries, of the countries that were visited, and the number of the converts of the respective fields of labour. The amazing results afford us a lesson of zeal apparently superhuman in energy, although entirely human in principle. And will not such zealots, we ask, rise up in judgment and condemn the thousands of a purer faith in our own land, who, with infinite motives to propagate their religion, are yet inert and apathetic?

Braminism was diffused partly by conquest, but also by proselytism. When force could not avail, the utmost accommodation was made with refractory systems. At this remote period it is still possessed of sufficient vitality to proselyte when an easy occasion offers. The wily Bramin or wandering Gosäi, holds up to the rude aboriginal, who has left his mountain home, or the Assamese, whom he deigns to visit on their richly luxuriant coast, the supremacy of Vishnu or Mahadéva, or binds on him the sacred necklace, and whispers in his ear a few initiatory words of sacred meaning. On securing a convert, he has gained an accession to the honour of his divinity, and increased his own resources of sustenance.

Mahomedanism is, by rule and principle, a vast proselyting system. Every Mussulman is by profession a proselyter. The means which are employed, as of Divine prescription, are indeed compulsory, but where force cannot be used, the true believer will seek to proselyte by reasoning and suasion. They are ever and anon converting pagan tribes in the north of Africa. They receive under their protection, on the condition of their embracing their faith, the poor negroes of western Africa, driven from their homes by the slave hunters. They are not idle in the islands of the eastern Archipelago. Occasional conversions are made from the Hindus and Pariahs of the present day. The power of charms, the virtue of some departed saint, the efficacy of certain votive offerings, or the flattery and good will of the community, with promises of some sensual gratification, are the principal powers which operate on the convert. When he is gained, his conversion is paraded and festivities are observed. Mahomed has obtained another trophy. The social power and influence of Mahomedans are increased.

Ancient Judaism was not destitute of proselyting zeal. The Pharisee went down to Arabia, or crossed the Mediterranean to Alexandria, or visited the Greek islands, and laying hold of the African, or Roman, or Greek, or Arabian, told him of Pharisaism—a law of works that would bind God himself, a system of ceremonies that would win heaven. He secured his convert; but beguiling him by lies, setting before him a false righteousness, and, it may be, a corrupt practice, he made him twofold more the child of hell than himself.

Romanism has laid claim to the divine in its Missions, and calls them in an exclusive sense apostolic. Would that we could accord the claim. It knows not what spirit it is of. Wherein any of the missionaries of Rome may have had an element of what is Christ-like in them, even a drop of the unction of the Holy One, we are in sympathy with them, and accord to them a share in apostolic acts; but the system, as it stands out before us in all its wide-spread ramifications, seems to us human, not to say in many respects devilish. It is, like Buddhism, a gigantic system of proselytism; but it is of the earth, earthy—not of the heaven, heavenly. We see in Romish missionaries neither the spirit nor power of the apostles; we witness in their operations no apostolic methods or appliances, and we behold no spiritual results. Romanism breathes out fire and slaughter, rather than peace and love; imprints a form, rather than inscribes a truth; diverts from particular phases of heathen error, rather than converts to Christian truth; allows the devils that possess an unregenerated nature to remain, or, casting them out, leaves the mind so vacant, so unfurnished with good, and so unadorned with grace, that other devils worse than the first come in and occupy their places, so that the last estate of the converts has been worse than the first. Converts are enrolled as loyal to the Pope, rather than obedient to Christ. They are attached to ecclesiastical systems rather than introduced by faith into the inheritance of saints in light. Whether we look at their Missions past or present, in India or Paraguay, China or Angola, we find the use of compulsion, if needs be, as at Goa, by all the devilish machinations of an Inquisition, or a wicked accommodation to the prejudices and idolatries of the people, or specious lies and abominable trickeries. No Bible has been given, no Christ revealed in his spirituality, no vital faith secured, no holiness implanted.

If we follow the Jesuit to Tahiti, we find him perverting men's minds from the Bible, corrupting their morals by encouragement of obsolete sports, and their faith by presenting to their religious homage others than Christ.

If we follow him to Syria or Turkey, we observe him plying his arts among the Eastern Churches; using the powers of the world that is, rather than of that which is to come; inducing the change of a name, the substitution of an authority, the observances of a calendar, the introduction of a form. Allowing, where needs be, the retention of traditional distinctions, in which the Eastern Churches pride themselves, Roman proselytism is satisfied if the Greek, or the Armenian, or the Jacobite, attach 'Catholic' to his name. If this be done, the ends of the mission are secured; the number of the Catholics is increased, additional weight is cast into the scale of political power, fresh argument is furnished for the all-comprehensiveness of the Roman Church, fresh glory is secured to the hierarchy, new honour accrues to the Propagandists. Meanwhile, hearts are left unsanctified, consciences unwashed, minds unenlightened.

'Acts of Apostles' are distinguished from all these, and innumerable other agencies, by clearly defined characteristics. Their origin is from above. The moral courage to perform them is a divine inspiration; the energy to work them out is of the Holy Spirit. Their aim and end are directed to Him who is the

Alpha and Omega of the gospel. Their character is essentially evangelistic, consisting of preaching Christ, revealing his gospel, offering his reconciliation. Their spirit and temper are, 'pureness, knowledge, long-suffering, kindness, the Holy Ghost, love unfeigned.' The means by which they are wrought are, 'the word of truth, the power of God, the armour of righteousness on the right hand and on the left.' The circumstances which attend them are 'afflictions, necessities, distresses, stripes, imprisonments, tumults, labours, watchings, fastings.' The true apostle lifts up his banners in the name of God, and he has also 'the Spirit of God.' He seeks not his own glory, but the glory of Him that hath sent him. He speaks not of himself, but as He who hath sent teaches. He enjoins not by his own authority but that of Him who ruleth. He seeks not to add to an existing community in order to exalt it in the world's estimation, or that it may exercise an increased social or political influence, but to add to that heavenly assembly, all of whose members are heirs of the inheritance of Christ. Evangelical missionaries, as a body, are not actuated by an 'esprit de corps,' but by individual allegiance to one Lord, and a sense of responsibility to Him before whose judgment seat they must stand. Their means are the application of truth, with a conscience void of offence. Their aids are the demonstration and conviction of the Holy Ghost. The issues of their work are found in renewed hearts, purged consciences, amended lives, love to

God the Father, and the Saviour, and love to all saints.

Wherein Protestant missionaries, actuated by a sectarian spirit, or lacking spiritual force, may at any time fail to exemplify this spirit, and, as far as in them lies, to secure such issues, they come short of the apostolic character, and their 'acts' are defective. It is only in this way that missionaries of any name can make their calling and election to an apostle's office sure, and obtain an apostle's reward. We point not, therefore, as the full expression of apostolic acts, to educational and scientific results, as connected with our Missions, great and striking as they may be, nor to the substantial proofs of civilization in reared villages or towns, delightful as are these oases in the desert, and appreciated by the world itself. These may, or may not, exist. They may, or may not, follow in the track of the apostle's work. They are, if realized, the indirect results—the flower, not the fruit. The 'acts' are to be known by the creation of a consistent discipleship, the enlightening and sanctification of the soul, the gathering of holy churches, the raising up of martyrs and confessors—man saved—God glorified.

The records of such 'acts' are to be found in the missionary documents of our evangelical Christendom. We hear of them from the missionaries themselves, and from their witnesses. The world itself is forced to testify of them. And yet how limited is the range of their influence, how little are they sought out, how little known, how little felt and appreciated when known. The burning bush of evangelical Missions, how few are there to draw near and look at it closely. What a large section of professing Christians is as yet unattracted by those very 'acts,' whose records are being lodged in the archives of heaven, into which angels desire to look. How inadequate is the interest in Missions evinced by Christians generally, in their social gatherings, or private and family life. How little is the spirit moved, the heart affected. They have eyes, and ears, and sense, for other objects of interest; but these fail where interest is most concentred. A great work is going on, but it meets the observation of only a faithful few. Christ fills the temple of the universe with his train, but multitudes of professors scarcely see the skirts of his glory. God is calling his sons from afar, and his daughters from the ends of the earth; but these scarcely hear the call, or mark the obedience which one and another renders to it. The dew of Christ's youth—the converts of his faith—glistens in the sun; but they are not dazzled by the sight. Souls fly as doves to their windows; but the sound of their wings strikes not the ear, nor fixes the gaze. The cloud of new-made witnesses of Christ moves over them; but they look not up nor see Him who dwells therein. We are constrained to say that, while many souls are in earnest, the church, as a whole, is apathetic on the momentous subject of Missions. To a great portion of it may be addressed the burning words of rebuke uttered to Israel: 'I work a work in your days; a work which ye shall in no wise believe, though a man declare it unto you.'

The apathy of some arises from secular pursuits and worldly engrossments. They haste to be rich; to build, to plant, to add house to house and land to land, to make to themselves a name in the earth. What heart have they for the concerns of Christ's kingdom?

We would enjoin on all who from worldly causes are indifferent to Missions, to entertain doubts as to their own Christianity. Are you Christ's? Then are Christ's interests yours. What affects him affects you. With the affairs of his kingdom you and yours are bound up. If you can be indifferent to what is his, where is the evidence that you are his? If any man have not the spirit of Christ, he is none of his. But the spirit of Christ is the spirit of Missions, the spirit of converting men, and renewing them in God's image; and how is your Christianity consistent with a systematic neglect of these processes, as exemplified in the work of Missions? Prove that you are Christ's by your interest in his work and identification with it. We doubt the profession in the absence of such fruits.

Other Christians are drawn away by pursuits and studies lawful in themselves, but allowed to be too engrossing. Science occupies their leisure, or antiquity engages them by its objects of research, or political events challenge their attention, or party interests engross their time. How can they give themselves to study missionary movements, and throw into them their time, talents, and influences?

We would intreat such, independently of the claims of the study of Missions as Christ's own work, to consider their intrinsic interest. We would meet you on your own ground. Do you love science? Here is a science of the order and method in which the Godhead acts in the redemption of lost souls; of holy principles on which those men act who are wise to win souls; of the motives which influence human hearts, inducing repentance and faith. Do you love art? Here is a consummate art whereby the cold marble forms of humanity are made instinct with the breath of spiritual life, the foul and loathsome are made fair and beautiful, that which is old as Adam becomes new as Christ; whereby men dead in trespasses and sins are quickened into a holy existence, and the graves yield up their dead. Do you love history? Here is a history whereof God is the author, and his own acts form the subject matter, all of whose events are pre-ordained, and whose issues are eternal. A history of battles between principalities and powers, and spiritual wickedness in high places, and the good soldiers of Jesus Christ; of victories and spoils, multitudes delivered from the worst of thraldoms, enjoying redemption in its earnest *here*, and awaiting the purchased possession *there*. A history, the subjects of which are called to be *saints*, and introduced into the household of

God; whose heroes shine as the stars for ever and ever. Can you ignore this element of history, or rather, this all-comprehensive history? Do politics engage your attention? See in Missions the politics of a kingdom that cannot be moved. He on whose shoulders is the government, who is King of kings and Lord of lords, makes his subjects willing in the day of his power, and rules them by love.

Even the politics of this world cannot be disassociated from Missions. Some parts of the world, as Turkey and the islands of the Pacific, are now undergoing great political changes as the issues of missionary labours. Those who were not a people become such. Former outcasts from the family of nations now take their places in the great fraternity. The unknown rise up into notice and challenge respect. The socially weak become strong, the refuse of the people become refined. As in the past, so in the future, the history of nations will be modified by the silent but potent influences of modern Missions. The gospel, as the energy of the Almighty, already sets up and pulls down, plants and roots up.

There are other causes of a far different nature which divert interest from Missions. Some eminently pious Christians, weaned from worldly pursuits, are too engaged in the study of prophecy to observe the actual times and seasons of Missions. The future has to them an attraction beyond the present. Christ's kingdom is to them all glorious as it lies in a distant, or approaching era, while the actual and present are ignored. That scene around which the mist gathers, or which is shrouded in darkness, draws off mind and heart from that which stands out in the bold relief and vivid light of clear fact. What Christ will do at his appearance and his glory causes them to ignore what Christ is doing. The kingdom of God diminishes in interest if it at all come with observation. The Lord Jesus, fulfilling his promise of his universal presence, is now with his disciples in their evangelistic work, and works with them even to the end of the world; but many students of prophecy are tempted to look away from his actual manifestations to a more or less distant future. Surely prophecy is best studied in the light of history, and best interpreted by a knowledge of present facts. The Lord's future is best illustrated by his present dealings. May we not more accurately judge of the glory into which he is to enter, by that visible transfiguration whereby he now shines all glorious in the persons of holy converts? How can we better substantiate our sincerity in praying for a kingdom to come than by noting and giving thanks for a kingdom that is come? Shall we not show our appreciation of a kingdom that is to be established by taking heed to that which is in the midst of us? It may well be doubted whether exclusive attention to a prophetical kingdom is not one of the blinds of Satan to divert Christians from the historical kingdom. Does he not, by keeping them ignorant of its grand stirring facts, detach them from engaging in its actual movements, and throwing themselves into its furtherance?

We proceed to urge a few general considerations in favour of an increased study of the evangelistic work.

We would first of all remind the Christian reader how peculiarly the cause of Missions is his own, not merely on account of his intimate relation to Christ, whereby what is his belongs equally to the believer, and whatever affects him, whether of joy or sorrow, loss or gain, affects those who are attached to him, but by virtue of a direct personal interest. Truly, with emphasis, may we say to the Christian, with regard to the sphere of Missions, 'All things are yours.' All the new relationships into which grace has introduced him, all the new affinities which grace has constituted, all the new aspirations to which grace gives rise, all the eternal prospects grace has set before him, conspire to make Missions a concentred object of personal interest and regard. The missionaries who go forth are *his* messengers. The converts are *his* also. Do Missions gather the sons of God from the world?—they are *his* brethren. The family of which *he* is a member is enlarged, and its joys enhanced by every accession. Are they introduced into the inheritance of the 'saints in light'?—they are *his* fellow-heirs, with whom he is to enjoy eternity. On the other hand, are there any disasters, defections, apostasies?—they injure *his* cause. Are there any losses, trials, persecutions?—they are of *his* fellow-members, with whom, and for whom, he cannot but suffer. His future glory is bound up with theirs. His anticipations of heaven will be all the more joyous from his knowledge, however partial, of those who are gone before him. The 'better land' is receiving one and another occupant from every tribe, and people, and tongue, with whose histories he is conversant, and whose very entrance into glory he seems to have traced, from an intimate acquaintance with the records of Missions. Is it nothing to him that he will there meet with 'babes,' in Christ as well as 'fathers;' the first fruits of an Eastern continent or a Southern isle, as well as the matured fruits of his native land? Will not eternal glory be all the more glorious because shared by a Leang Afa of China, or a Krishna of India, or Rafaravavy of Madagascar?

Further, we are assured that the study of Missions would promote the interests of a practical Christianity. Love to all saints is one primary element of piety. How much is this increased by the study now urged. Whilst love becomes deepened, as a principle, by repeated exercise, it becomes expanded by the multitude of objects. The man who knows Missions best loves most. By the medium of solid information as to their trials, sufferings, and spiritual developments, he sympathizes with the converts to Christ; his heart goes forth to them. His affections go beyond a pale, a sect, a nation. He embraces all the children of God scattered throughout the world. He sees not *a* Church, but *the* Church. He substantiates within his soul the oneness of all who are in Christ.

As Christian love is promoted by an acquaintance with Missions, so all the virtues and graces may be confirmed. There is no exercise of mind and heart towards God and man but may derive strength from the same divine study. It would do much to make the man of God perfect in every good word and work, and shape out a Christ-like Christianity. He can best see his obligations to his Lord, and his duties to man, illustrated by what others render. Devoted lives are fitted to give an inspiration to his own. Hallowed footsteps will induce him to follow. Where is such abundant scope for study of every virtue, and every grace, as in Missionary Biography?

Where is holy principle more conspicuous than in those who went forth originally at their Lord's command, when even Christendom itself doubted of their wisdom, and foreboded vain results? Where is faith to be found stronger than that of those who now go forth like Abraham, not knowing whither they go? Where is fortitude beyond that of the missionaries called to fight against a great sea of afflictions? Where is perseverance to be found exceeding that of those who sow, as it were, on bleak rocks, and look by hope only to the harvest? Can a Christian study these things, and not be changed into the same image and obtain the same qualities?

Again, how encouraging and stimulating are the

recorded examples of Christian converts! How fitted to revive our home Christianity. To the doubting and feeble-minded we would say, Behold the assurance of faith of recent converts; their 'joy unspeakable and full of glory,' while they believe in Him whom having not seen they love. To the selfish, unsteady, and inconsistent Christian we would say, Behold the steady perseverance of multitudes, their self-denials and sacrifices. To those whose love waxeth cold, we say, Witness the love of many recent converts to one another and the Lord. If heart speaks to heart, how must we be affected by the addresses of kindred hearts from the converted children of heathendom. Many a lesson may be carried home to the heart, which sermons and books have been unable to impress. Many a principle thus illustrated may find a deep lodgment, and more practical issues, than have been attained by all past study and most strenuous endeavours.

Nor would the interests of doctrinal Christianity fail to be subserved by the same means. Those will possess the most enlightened knowledge of scriptural doctrines who have studied their bearings on human hearts in the widest ranges, who have traced the specific influences of truths on those who receive them, who have observed the unity of spiritual effect of the word in the greatest possible diversity of human circumstances. Who knows the doctrines of depravity so well as those who are acquainted with the facts of depravity in the unevangelized races of men? Who so firmly grasps the doctrine of the Holy Spirit's agency, as he who has found that in its absence men do not turn to the Lord, and whose conversion, when they do turn, is manifestly the result of his convincing power? Who has so large a view of justifying faith as he who has seen the peace it imparts to sin-burdened souls—and the fruits it produces?

Would that our preachers would make Missions their study, for the very purpose of enriching their discourses. Doctrinal truths would be rendered by the preacher or essayist all the more luminous when viewed in the light cast on them by Christian experiences gathered from the various sections of regenerate humanity.

We would, further, urge the study of Missions on every devout spirit, as a means of increasing in the knowledge of God and as furnishing incentives to glorify him.

God is known by his works. His attributes are revealed in his operations. The Son knoweth him directly and intuitively. Man knows him only by revelation. The works of the Lord are great, sought out of all them that have pleasure therein. But the works of grace are pre-eminently glorious, and the special subjects of study by saints. But those works are conspicuous in the sphere of Missions. They present scope for the varied exhibitions of divine attributes. His wisdom, as revealed in the church, called out as every member is from unregeneracy, and brought in by wondrous operations, is so manifold as to be the object of study 'to principalities and powers in heavenly places.'

To men and saints, therefore, who have more peculiar interest in these things, we would say, 'Behold God himself in these apostolic records. Witness the developments of his providence, the manifestations of his wisdom, the exercises of his power, the riches of his grace. He is making all things new—shaking not only the earth, but the heavens also.' Again, are we seeking to know the Son of God? We behold him in Missions. For in them we observe the signs of his presence, the way in which he fulfils his promises, the gifts he bestows, the conquests he effects. In the evangelistic work, also, we witness the operations of the Holy Ghost. We learn from it how he opens hearts and testifies to Christ, by what influence he makes willing, by what process he renews and brings into a living unity the diversities of human nature. We see him washing and sanctifying by the word, and sealing on all who are Christ's the one unerring family likeness. Those may best appropriate the 'fellowship of the Spirit' whose acquaintance is deep with his operation on kindred hearts.

Ignorance of Missions, moreover, entails defective glorification of God. The abundant grace which is recorded in them, would, if known, through the thanksgiving of many, abound to the glory of God. He that offereth praise glorifieth God. But who can sound his praises so loud as he who traces the wonders of his grace in the deliverance of souls? Who can give thanks to God so earnestly as he who hears of the newly implanted faith of others, and of their love to all the saints, and knows that they have a hope laid up for them in heaven? Who can pray so earnestly as he whose solicitude is on behalf of the immature converts to Christianity, 'that Christ may dwell in their hearts by faith,' that they may be rooted and grounded in love, so as to comprehend the heighth and depth of the love of Christ? A Christian studying the history of redeemed souls is brought nigh to God in his sublimest emotions and most disinterested affections. Around a company of Christians, intently earnest to see the glory of Christ in Missions, are heard angels' voices, 'Glory to God in the highest; on earth peace, good will toward men.' Nay, the Redeemer himself is seen in their midst.

Paul's life was a perpetual sacrifice of praise and prayer to the God of our Lord Jesus Christ in connection with Missions. How blessed, were the life of Paul multiplied in believers. Then should we see them fulfilling their functions of a royal priesthood, offering continually spiritual sacrifices of a sweet smelling savour; hastening to know what the Lord is doing on earth, consulting every record with an interest far exceeding that which the world possesses in secular movements, converting their knowledge and discoveries into prayer and praise—

prayer drawing down blessings which inspire praise, and praise reflectively encouraging to renewed prayer; spending the time of social converse in talking of the excellency of Christ's kingdom and the glory of his power; having always in the social meeting and in the family circle a burden of prayer and a meed of praise; rising above the present gloom of this world's history, and entertaining hallowed anticipations of a glorious future, when the kingdom shall be given to the saints of the Most High and the whole earth shall be full of his glory; having their own daily path irradiated by the light thrown on it by the experiences of others, modifying their private solicitudes by their intenser interest in the trials of their brethren, and enhancing their own joys by sympathy with the joys of redeemed ones. Oh, when will the church at large put on such strength, and clothe herself with such light? Why should not believers now begin the song of heaven, and placing themselves in sympathy with those who are being gathered in, say, 'Thou hast redeemed *us* to God by thy blood'? Then would the church on earth indeed be a fit type of the church glorified, and her hallowed engagements resemble those of heavenly assemblies. Meanwhile, what loss does God sustain in being robbed of his meed of praise, due for all his wonderful works in redemption day by day from the heathen world; and what loss do saints sustain from such robbery—loss in their own souls and in direct communications from God?

We challenge a study of evangelistic records for the sake of wisely and efficiently prosecuting the work of Missions. It is often said, 'Knowledge is power.' This is deeply sententious in relation to this subject. It *is* power of the highest kind—the power which Israel had, and whence he derived his name—power with God. Knowledge would increase interest and sympathy, and would inspire prayer. Deep solicitude would lead to God's throne, for labourers, for aid, for blessing. And the answer would come down in the strengthening and reviving and expansion of Missions. But knowledge is power in another sense. If there be a history of Missions, it must be fraught with all-important lessons, must be rife with facts, and charged with principles. Who then so wise for the future conduct of Missions, as he who is most conversant with the past? Clearly to discern the track along which Jesus passes in the conquest of the world, and to know with certainty the path where he is not to be found; to learn by experience the peculiar culture on which the rain from heaven falls, and that which is scarcely moistened by a drop; to mark the circumstances under which the heavenly wind bloweth, so as most readily to meet its first breathings; these objects of knowledge are of unspeakable importance in conducting the economics of Missions. Without possessing them, we may sow vanity and reap confusion. Guided by them, we rectify the past, and apply ourselves with renewed confidence to the future. We exercise the wisdom alone available to win souls from the heathen world. We place ourselves in the way of blessing. Increased knowledge will usher in a new career of missionary labour.

Let, then, missionary literature be more cultivated and more encouraged. Let the 'periodical' be found in every Christian's house, and 'news of the churches' be deemed the noblest subject of research. Let increased information be given at our monthly prayer meetings, and God's work among the heathen form the topic of conversation in our families and at our social meetings. Especially let the Christian pray 'in secret,' and if he stretch not forth his hands to God, with a map outspread before him, as M'Cheyne has suggested, let it be because on his own heart, as well as that of God, the world is inscribed, and its wants and woes are unfolded to his view.

CHAPTER II.

FORMS OF HEATHEN WORSHIP.

The World: in what conscious relationship to God and Christ? — Answer Two-fold. — The Worship of the Heathen. — Man-worship in its several forms.—Devil worship.—Its Principle,—Prevalence,—Characteristics.—Creature worship—Pantheism.—Other Forms. — Idol worship. — Multiplicity and Variety of Gods.—Influence of Idolatry.—The Heathens who have no worship.—Conclusion.

THE gospel, of which our missionaries are the heralds, as a revelation, makes known 'God the only true, and Jesus Christ whom he hath sent'; as an announcement it says, 'God was in Christ reconciling the world unto himself'; as a message, it beseeches men in Christ's stead, 'Be ye reconciled unto God.'

In what conscious relationship then to these infinite personalities does the world stand? What acquaintance has it with God? What apprehension of Christ? The heathen portion of the world ought to have, and may have, some consciousness of a relationship with God, the Creator whose works are manifest, but can have no apprehension of Christ. This can be possessed only by those who have heard of him, and formed an estimate of his claims, as Jews and Mahomedans; and by those who have nominally received him, as the corrupt churches of eastern and western Christendom.

The answer to the question we have proposed will open up to us a two-fold subject:—first, the state of heathenism; and secondly, that of Judaism, Mahomedanism, and corrupted Christianity.

First. What do the heathen know of God? The King eternal, immortal, and invisible—he who is 'over all, God blessed for ever'—who is above all, and through all, and in all; for whom are all things, and by whom are all things;—does this glorious, adorable Being stand out in any sense or degree before the heathen mind as a living person, possessing absolute perfection, remote from all comparison, the Creator, Governor, and Judge of men?

This question can be best answered by a consideration of the actual forms of worship prevalent among the heathen. Worship is the expression of the religious life, the embodiment of religious sentiment. It is the mind's apprehension of an outer object, the going forth of the heart towards it. The worshipper strives to make the object of his worship a centre for his soul, a terminus for his being. His thoughts and interests, hopes and fears, cluster around it. The entire man is revealed in that which he worships. He is changed into the same image. In the case of imaginary deities he also changes their image into his own. His own character is moulded by their worship, and again he moulds them by his own character.

The nature of heathen worship will, therefore, best explain the aspect of the heathen mind towards God. If there be anything God-ward in the affections, we shall detect it here; or, if there be aversion from God, it will likewise reveal itself here. The elevation of one pole is the measure of the depression of the other. By knowing what and how a man worships, we can discern the relative position he occupies to God. The worship of the heathen world may be thus classified:

I. Man worship. II. Devil worship. III. Creature worship. IV. Idol worship.

I. *Man worship.*—The strong tendency in human nature to worship itself is fully developed in heathendom. That which needs in all states of society a constant restraining power is unchecked among the heathen, and is therefore widespread and virulent. Man displaces God by man. He reduces him to nothingness by making himself the 'all in all.'

Buddhism, the religion of more than three hundred millions, is a vast system of man worship. It does not indeed worship men, as Pantheism does, but man in the highest reputed form, that of the sage, the sole divinity. The contemplative man, divesting himself of passion, denying and renouncing nature, forgetful of himself and others, and ignoring all isolated existence, by means of mortification and abstraction becomes Buddha, or the partaker of nigbán, extinction of being. There have been several such. More or less are worshipped according to the prevailing form of the religion. Temples are raised to the last Buddha. Statues of a hundred feet high are cut out of the solid mountains, and his images are multiplied.

Priests are his retinue. His reputed relics are above all things sacred. Mausoleums are built for them. His tooth is guarded like a precious jewel. The impress of his foot is divinely revered. This is man worship. There is no deity involved in the existence of Buddha. He is not God. He was a man, a veritable historical personage. Man by a prescribed method may become Buddha.

In Thibet and other regions Buddha has his earthly representative. The deified sage is beyond human apprehension, and is himself beyond all capacity of knowing his worshippers. The people, therefore, make a substantial living man the object of their supreme regard. The Lama, 'priest and king,' is worshipped with divine honours.

This form of man worship is at an extreme distance from the worship of God. It bears towards him the most malignant aspect, being based on the exclusion of a proper divinity.

First. The Buddhist denies God as an independently existing Person. He says, all that is, and has been, and will be, is from eternity. To him nature is the only independent being, if, indeed, that may be termed so, which is dependent on the necessity of its own being, and the fixity of fate. The Buddhist does not simply ignore God. He has entertained the idea of God, weighed it, found it wanting, and discarded it. Arrogating to himself the omniscience of that Deity whom he denies, he makes the non-existence of God a scientific principle. He has professedly spelt out the hieroglyphics of nature, and extracted the meaning of all its glorious symbols, but has learned from them nothing save the formula—'There is no God!' He has scanned the processes of providential agency and moral government, and analyzed the complex affairs of human society, and to him the great lesson of the whole is—'There is no God.'

Again, the Buddhist denies God as Creator. There has been, he says, no such act or process as creation, no fiat of the Almighty; all that is, is of itself, and by itself, and for itself. He has heard that, in some systems of philosophy or religion, God and Creator. are interchangeable terms, and he deliberately denies both the one and the other;—No God—no Creator. On one occasion the author had been proclaiming the great Creator to a small company of Hindus. One of Buddhistic faith, a carpenter, asked him how he knew there was a Creator. He took out his watch, and presenting it, asked how he knew there was a maker of it? 'Of course, from the design evinced.' 'In like manner you should believe in God, from the marks of his power and wisdom in his works.' 'But,' replied the Buddhist, 'we have had experience that watches are made by artificers, houses by builders; but we never had any experience of a world being made.' Thus unconsciously had the Hindu peasant struck upon the argument thought so redoubtable by the Scotch metaphysician.

Further, the Buddhist denies God as Governor among the nations. Fate is the supreme governor.

Necessity is the absolute law. Actions will of themselves work out their own issues. Effects will succeed their own causes. The wheel incessantly goes round. No power has put it in action; no power avails to stay it. There is constant motion, but without progress; ceaseless change, but without a blessed issue; a dreary road, but without a goal; a hill without a summit; a depth without a bottom. The universe is without a plan.

We may indeed wonder how a people with such a faith, can retain their social existence. But first of all, special attention is rendered by Buddhism to the theory of morals, and the most strenuous attempts are made to rear a fabric of morality, though without a foundation. Again, as if to make amends for the absence of faith in a personal Deity, other doctrines are introduced. Though there is no governor, yet, by the necessity of fate, punishment is said to follow crime 'as sure as the cart-wheel follows the movement of the ox.' So absolute is this fate, that in Buddhism there is no remission of sin. Its consequences will track the perpetrator above, below, now, for ever. Buddha himself had in his exalted state to expiate crimes in former births.

Thus have the foundations been laid of a certain morality, and a class of sanctions affixed to virtue and vice. The professors of this faith are enabled thereby still to retain their atheism, without losing all social institutes, and severing all bonds of morality. The system could not otherwise have long existed, and the east would have found, as the west has experienced, that society becomes disorganized without the belief of a God, and would have hastened to recall its pristine faith. But as it is, there is a complement made up in their religious faith, and certain elements are introduced to supply the fundamental defect. The social community is thereby saved from wreck and ruin. Can this be a mere human device, or has it originated in the prince of this world, who hates God, and desires to rob him of his glory?

The Buddhist, in denying God as a governor, disbelieves in him as a rewarder of them that seek him. According to him, all existence essentially involves change and misery, inasmuch as its primary law is destruction and reproduction. Existence therefore, as such, is an evil. There is no such existence as an endlessly happy one. It is impossible that any being should be a partaker of it; much less can he impart it to those who trust in him. The only divine state is nigbán, the negation of existence, the loss of being, the absence of all self-consciousness. Such was attained by Buddha. Such is the supreme object of human pursuit. Thus, Buddhism, viewed from every point, is atheistic.

It is often said, there cannot exist a nation of atheists. The impossibility has been hitherto assumed as an axiom. Previous remarks may have tended to explain the anomaly. Concerning the fact there can be no legitimate doubt. Missionaries of Western India, conversant with the language of ancient

Buddhism, and intimate with the priests of Jainism, the modern form of Buddhism, assure us that both the ancient and modern system are atheistic. 'The Buddhist writings,' says one,* 'are before us, and their fundamental principles are intelligible only on this (the atheistic) interpretation of their substance. The Jains are living amongst us, and those of them who are initiated into the mysteries of their system, glory in the avowal of this tenet. One of their principal Jatis, or priests, lately told me that the secret in the proposition 'Ishrar nasti' ('God is not'), is regularly communicated by him to his disciples in the third year of their studies, when they evince ordinary intelligence. I hold in my hands a regular challenge by a learned Jati of Central India, confidently calling on all theists to engage in discussion with him on this very subject.' A writer on Ceylon says, 'Neither in the discourses of the priesthood, nor the practice of its followers, is either the name or existence of an eternal first cause recognised in any portion of their worship. Judson of Birmah calls Buddhism 'a system which owns no living God, and counts immortality a curse.'

This religion, indeed, has been modified according to the character of the people who have adopted it, the influence of collateral religions, and the lapse of time, but whether in Birmah or Nepaul, it is essentially the same, exclusive of a proper deity.—Whether we go to Ceylon and converse with a Cingalese

* Dr. Wilson of Bombay.

Buddhist, or meet in the streets of Canton with a Chinaman of the same faith; or, crossing the western range of the Himalayas, converse with the Thibetian in his monastery built on the shelving ridges of the hills; or repair to Birmah, and in the streets of Ava sound the religious tenets of the yellow-robed priests of Buddha; or to Siam, and under the shadow of its monarch talk with the votaries of Gautama; or to India, and distinguishing the Jains with their numerous deified sages, from the Hindus, ask them to reveal to us their faith, we find them all agreeing in one great principle—the destroyer of all principle—that nature is all in all, that there is no personal deity, no presiding intelligence, no judge of quick and dead.

Would to God that this fact, so patent to all conversant with the subject, produced its due impression on the Christian church. The fact is beyond controversy that millions are living and moving on this earth, denying the God in whom they live, and move, and have their being, essaying to live 'without God,' expecting to die 'without God,' and to live for ever 'without God;' or if they attain the summit of hope both for gods and men, namely, an extinction of being, then are they in such a realization pre-eminently 'without God.' All that there is of intellectual, thinking, reasoning mind, in Buddhist society, is against God. All that there is of the emotional—of hope, or fear, or love—is averted from him or directly opposed to him.

What an amazing fact that there should be such a

world as to deny the God who made it. And, further, how amazing that those who know God should be so little affected by such denial. Well may we be moved that we are so little moved. It might be expected that the mere announcement of the fact would strike every Christian heart, and force men to the rescue of such benighted people; that one and another minister, or candidate for the ministry, would imploringly say to God, 'Here am I,' and appeal to the church, 'Send me,' that they might bring back some of these haters of God to the knowledge and love of him. A single atheist in a village at home would be marked, and his name become a by-word. A small circle of atheists would be the reproach and terror of a neighbourhood. Society at large would shrink from them, and bid their children beware of them as plague-infected souls. Let us think, then, of a race of atheists, of more than one continent covered with them, of towns and cities filled with them, of homes tenanted by them, of a succeeding generation now being trained by them. A third of the world is in principle atheistic. Every third man would argue for atheism. Every third man is, if consistent, living out atheism. Myriads say, not merely in their heart, but with their lips, 'No God.' They not only practically, like the rest of mankind, deny God, but with all the precision of language, and all the definitions of philosophy, and in many cases, with all the virulence of hostility, say, 'No God.' Let us think of the four millions of

Buddhists of Siam, with the despotic monarch at their head, an absolutely powerful priesthood, and immense endowments. Let us glance at Japan, with its millions professing this faith, which it received from India centuries ago; of Tartary, Thibet, Nepaul, Ceylon, and, last of all, of China, a great portion of whose three hundred and sixty millions are Buddhists. What multitudes of lifeless souls, of godless spirits, of enemies to God! Among how many living men is this dead faith to be found! How many souls has it destroyed! In how many is it yet working death, and, unless the gospel be sent, in what generations yet to come will it continue to do so!

If we examine the state of mind of Buddhists relatively to the gospel, we are affected with their extreme hardness of heart. It would seem as though the heart became obtuse in the ratio of the intellect being sharpened in these religious metaphysics. This hardness is the veritable product of Buddhism. There is a hardness arising from the absence of all soothing influences, all subduing principles in the religion itself. The mind recognises no Creator, no Father, no Ruler, no Providence; discovers no will of a determining mind, no wisdom of one who 'worketh hitherto,' no love nor condescension, nor providing care, nor protecting power; feels no bosom on which it can repose, no justice to which it may appeal, no mercy which it may supplicate. Fate is a thing irresistible, suffering is by necessity. Sin has no remission. Guilt offers sacrifice in vain. There is, therefore, a wisdom in hardness of heart. The soul is thereby rendered less sensitive of time's vicissitudes, earth's sorrows, and eternity's woes.

There is also a hardness of heart arising from the habitual defence by Buddhists of their peculiar doctrines. Buddhism is an antagonistic system. It originally opposed Brahmanism. It still challenges opposition, and declares its fundamental principles impregnable. When Christianity presents itself, the Buddhist's heart becomes hard beyond comparison. Its virulence is excited. He *will* not believe. Every active principle of the soul rallies in defence of long cherished principles. The pantheist is bewildered amid his metaphysical subtleties, but the Buddhist is obdurate. 'My mind is very decided and hard,' said the Birman teacher of Judson, after he had been explaining Christian truth, 'and unless you tell me something more to the purpose, I shall never believe.' This is the ordinary language of Buddhists. The Buddhist emperor, in his palace at Ava, had no sooner read the first sentence of the tract which the Christian missionary had just put into his hands, containing the simple eternal truth that there is 'one God,' independent of change and mortality, than he dashed it contemptuously to the ground. The author has frequently preached to Jains, the Buddhists of Gujarat, and has always found them inaccessible to truth, full of pride and arrogance, and replete with self-righteousness. Compared with them, the Hindus are teachable.

Buddhism is, as we have seen, the most consolidated

form of man-worship. Other minor forms exist in all parts of heathendom. The repute of wisdom or sanctity, or the exhibition of power and magnificence, alike constitute to the heathen a claim to divine honours. If their senses are dazzled, or their imagination is charmed, the heathen who know not God cannot forbear to worship the object by which they are affected. There is the worship of the religious teacher and priest. The Chinese build temples to Confucius, and present sacrifices to him. The emperor, his magistrates, and other officials, unite in the ascription of divine honours to the great teacher and political essayist of China. Priest-worship overspreads India, and, like the corrupting carcase of Leviathan, taints the air with its foul odours. It is one of the heavy curses which have fallen on its people, corrupting their morals, and often breaking up the sanctity of domestic life. Brahmans and Gosais, Gurus of names we cannot compute, are in very deed worshipped. The water in which their feet is washed is called the elixir of immortality. To some, temples are erected, and prayers and offerings presented. The reality of such worship will appear from the following prayer, which is now offered up to a religious teacher in Gujarat, who thirty years ago lived and died among the people.

'O Swaymee Narayan, thou art the spirit of the imperishable Brahm. Thou art the god of gods. By thy commands the sun and moon and stars remain in the heavens. By thy command the earth remains. Thy glory is like that of Sesh and Sarasvatte. I am not able rightly to describe it. In this world with my mind, body, and wealth, I will serve thee. By thy help I have found the true religion, and will never forget it. For many ages I have wandered in the sea of mortal births, and until thy word reached me, I suffered much. I was born a tree, and was cut down with an axe. I was born a beast, and suffered much from hunger and thirst. I was born a reptile, and a bird, and was killed by the hunter: and in many other births I suffered countless pains. In this way I have wandered through many births, and did not know thee. At last I was born into this world (or present state of being). Here by thy great mercy I have met thee, and by obeying thy instructions, who art the lord of my life and my true relative, I shall not again be born. Thou art my chosen deity; never leave me. Thou art the foundation of my life. By thee I shall escape this salt sea of existence, and enter upon the place you appoint me: I have confidence in no other.'

Again, there is the worship of the monarch or hero. In China, the emperor is worshipped as the son of heaven, the embodiment of divine power and majesty. The Burmese and Siamese worship at the golden feet of their emperors, and adore them as gods on earth. Some African tribes worship their chief, and know no God besides or beyond him. They lavish all their possessions freely at his command, and live or die as he wills. Before the missionary Moffat had entered amongst the Matabele, Moselekatse, their chief, knew no God greater than himself, and his people recognised him as the sole divinity.

It is the character of all these forms of man-worship that they alienate the mind from God. The worshippers, filled with pride and self-sufficiency, glory in man. Having the delusive consciousness that they have with them 'the great power of God,' they care nothing for God himself. They are satisfied that there should be no God, save one in their own form, and shape, and moral resemblance. They feel no need of, and have no desire after, the living and true God. In a certain village of Gujarat, given up to this form of worship, Christian teachers could not even find an entrance. The people were so mad after their human idol that they would not hear any who questioned his divinity.

A modification of man-worship which is almost universal is that rendered to spirits of ancestors. To the Chinese mind, paternity is tantamount to divinity, and deceased parents are worshipped as a part of divinity. No object is so sacred to them as the ancestral tablet. No rites are deemed so important as those which relate to the spirits of the long line of progenitors. In India the most sacred annual festival is that devoted to the manes of the dead. The Hindu ceremonies, however, are conducted with the idea of ministering to the wants of the dead, rather than as acts of worship, and are considered as helping and consoling them in their disembodied state. Cakes of wheat, or balls of rice and sugar, are given to them for food. They are called to accept them, whether 'they be dwellers in stone, or trees, or birds, or beasts.' The heathen of semi-civilized India unite with the barbarian negroes of Western Africa, or the Fijis of the South Seas, in offering human victims to the recently deceased husband or chief.

II. *Devil worship.*—This superstition underlies most of the other more refined religions. Like the primitive rocks in geology, it is found here and there rising above and overlapping religious faiths and forms, some of which are directly antagonistic to it. The darkness and miseries, personal distresses and calamities, which are in the world as the result of man's sin, are referred to a power or powers of evil. On these every individual is dependent for exemption from suffering, and it is therefore policy to propitiate them by sacrifice, or flatter them by prayer, or persuade by offerings, or even force by threats. Evil may be considered as one or as many, residing in, and emanating from, a central person, or indefinitely multiplied. It may be embodied in a fallen angel of light, or may dwell in the lowest form. It may reside in disembodied human spirits, or in spirits superhuman and infrahuman. It may be considered as acting by itself, or by instruments which imagination can make infinite, holding in subjection and using hosts of powers, and principles, and influences. Nature may be deemed under its control, the whole range of being—every class of circumstance. Omnipresence, and an all-extended action, may be attributed to it, or a mere local authority. The higher the intellect, the nobler the embodiment of evil it makes for itself, till the dwarfed intellect of the African embodies it in something most contemned. The lower also the moral state, the more diseased the imagination, and, consequently, the more complete its sway over the soul, till, at length, to the disordered nervous apprehension, a devil breathes in every blast, rides on every wind, has an utterance in every sound; and air, and earth, and sky, are filled with perpetual revelations of the evil. Thus two beings, or two principles, are recognised by this superstition as dividing creation, providence, government—the one good, and the other evil. The theory is found in the Manichæan religions, especially in that form now extant among the Guebers of Persia or Parsees of India; but the practice is found rife and virulent in some of the South Sea islands, in Western Africa, and among the American Indians. Amongst apostate religions we are inclined to think this is of earliest origin, if not primeval. It is generally found amongst the aboriginals of a country, and the most ignorant masses of mankind. More elaborate systems have tried to cast it out, but in vain; there are traces of it existing everywhere. The third person of the Hindu triad is undoubtedly the devil, formerly worshipped by the aboriginals, and adopted into the Brahmanical system. The female demons whose worship is allowed by the Brahmans all over India, have the same origin. The 'devil' could not be 'cast out' by Brahmanism; he has therefore been admitted as a constituent of the divinity. As now represented, he stands out as the very likeness and image of Satan. He wears a necklace of human skulls, and has in his hand a goblet filled with blood. His very name is Bhuteshvar, Lord of Devils.

The Bhils and Ghonds of the Indian forests, the hill tribes of Assam, worship the evil spirits, which haunt the gloomy recesses where they dwell. The Hindu mother worships the small pox or cholera which threatens to make her motherless. The African reverences the murrain of his cattle. The New Zealander, before his conversion, worshipped the evil one. The Parsee frightens or drives away demons by noises, or scrubs his body by various ablutions for their expulsion, or places a dog before the dying to guard them from the assaults of Satan. The Indian hedges around his dwelling to keep the demons out. The African drives them away with torches and discordant instruments, and pursues them for miles after they are considered to have decamped from the villages.

This devil-worship has its devil houses, its devil dances and devil feasts, its wands and utensils, its symbols and hieroglyphics. It has also its demoniacal possessions, for which there are appropriate exorcisms by threats, or fire, or whips. There are oracular impulses and utterances. Every one may be a votary or presiding minister of this superstition, which has no professional priesthood. The man inspired with the evil genius becomes a living oracle, foaming, raving, uttering rhapsodies. This worship brings in its train a legion of superstitions, incantations, mutterings, and charms. It has its army of wizards, and witches, and conjurors. Not only the religious, but the entire life, domestic and social, is occupied with personal precautions against evil, by charms, amulets, inscriptions. Craven fear for self, and hatred of others, are the upholding principles of this worship. Its prayers, when self is concerned, are craven and abject in the most debasing degree. There is no prayer for blessing, but against a curse. As regards others, prayers are imprecations, supplications are made an engine of destruction. The hands are outspread only to draw down evil. Malice finds scope in machinations against the property or life of enemies by spells and incantations.

'There is one good, that is, God.' The aspects of this worship relatively to him need no comment. The worship of God and the worship of devils are the two opposite poles of the religion of men. The measure is that of the distances between light and darkness, good and evil, benevolence and malice. Those who practise this dire superstition do not acknowledge God the sole governor and dispenser of good and evil; but give another being, and that an evil one, a throne and dominion. Although they may speculatively recognise the former, the benefit of the recognition is destroyed by the overpowering dread they have of the latter. The reverence of the good is absorbed by fear of the evil, which becomes as exclusively the object of worship as though there were no good in existence. The evil strikes their senses, affects their imagination so vividly, and sways the whole being, that the good is ignored, and treated as impotent. Devil worshippers dare not worship the God of benevolence, lest the maliciousness of the evil one should visit them with some heavy affliction. This difficulty has often presented itself in the history of Missions. In the south of India a Hindu father has often feared to send his children to a Mission school, lest the evil one should smite the family with a curse. When a child has been seized with sickness, the parent has resorted to the missionary, and cast the responsibility on him.

Satan has thus established his dominion, and in his own name. The god of this world has actually instituted his own worship, and the world is willing to render it. If he is elsewhere by sufferance, he is here as by right and title. All are called by his name. If he is the god of this world in its general mass, he is the tutelary deity and sovereign of this portion of it. If he is acknowledged by some as a prince for the gratifications he dispenses, he is by these acknowledged as such for the woes he is able and ready to inflict. Satan tempted Christ by offering him kingdoms. He tempts these deluded ones by merely threatening evil. These worshippers expect no enjoyments from him. Their highest good is exemption from harm—sad wages for a sad service. He has raised his own standard of revolt, having his own heraldry, and, as such, his servants rally around it. There is here no form of an angel of light, no veil, no mask—all is open and undisguised. Words which Milton puts into the mouth of the fallen archangel become the symbol of each man's creed,—'Evil, be thou my good!' What a triumph for Satan thus to girdle the earth with a zone of far wider limits than the ecliptic, and reckon all within it as his own, comprising all grades of intellect, from the Parsi of India to the Bushman of Africa. The ambassadors of God amongst such a people have to cast out Satan by the finger of God. Their work admits of no parleying, no compromise. They intrude, as it were, into his kingdom, breathe his air, confront his servants. Whoever treads on his territory must indeed expect to contend with principalities, and powers, and spiritual wickedness in high places.

III. *Creature worship.*— The Pantheist is a creature worshipper on the largest scale. He is so by principle and reasoning. He dares do actually what mankind does virtually, render homage to the creature. His philosophy and religion both shut him up to a universal service. He makes, indeed, a choice, but the choice is arbitrary, and involves treason to the neglected portions. He worships creatures, not in detail merely, but in the mass; or, rather, there is no creature in the sense of aught involving a creator. That which is, is God, and an object of worship. The mass is divine; every atom of it is divine. The whole world, with every grain of it, is an object of religious service.

He does not, like the Buddhist, deny that God is, but he says, God is everything that is, and bows down to the universe of matter and of mind. Others with less comprehensiveness worship the creature in detail. They have not sufficient mind to apprehend the whole. They choose specific objects. This form of worship is universal, and most cherished. It affords scope for every taste, indulgence for every passion, variety for every fickleness, till, as of old in Egypt, a bird or an onion receives divine honours. Creatures clean or unclean, beautiful or ugly, useful or noxious, with symbolic import or without it, intelligent or brutish, animate or inanimate—from the sun shining in his strength, to the clods of the valley—from the lustrous stars of heaven, to the mould of this earth, which, in India, receives the appellation 'mother' and is honoured as such—from the ocean to the rivulet—from the banyan tree to the small tulsi plant—from the snow-white elephant, adored by the Siamese, to the rat of the Hindu, or the mantis before which the African bends—from the eagle to the small humming bird—from the rhinoceros to the tortoise—receive as divine objects, the reverence of men's hearts and hands. No possible qualities disinherit any visible object, of men's worship. As a general rule, the more debased the quality, the more popular the worship. The more remote in attributes from the Great Creator, the nearer do men draw in reverential homage. Objects are worshipped either for their own qualities, as exciting hope or fear, or as being inhabited by certain spiritual beings. The Samoan, as well as the Hindu, worships creatures most common, as divine, because his tutelar deity dwells therein. The Hindu worships the alligator in the pool, and feeds it, till it becomes tame. The African does the same. The Hindu throws his 'first-born' into the jaws of the shark; the negro also reveres and feeds it, though not with the fruit of his own body. Thus do men conspire to change the glory of the incorruptible God into an image made like to corruptible man, and to birds, and four-footed beasts, and creeping things.

Creature worship, it is evident, precludes the worship of the Creator, who is 'God over all, blessed for evermore.' As far as the heavens are from the earth, so far is it from the worship of God. The distance between the corruptible and incorruptible, the dependent and the self-existent, the created and the uncreate, the ephemeral and the eternal, is the measure of the distance of the worship of the creature and the Creator.

IV. *Idol worship.*—As the gods of polytheistic faiths are generally represented by idols, this term is here used to comprehend the worship of individual deities. Amongst them are divided, as it were, the several works of creation, or providence, or government of the world.

There are gods, in their several ranks and degrees of rule, presiding over the departments of heaven and hell, to whom may be referred all the blessings of human life, and on whom are dependent all human circumstances. All, indeed, that centres in the Divine Being, or emanates from him, is parcelled out amongst myriads of fictitious gods. There are gods of the heavens above, and the earth beneath, and the deep that lieth under; of the clouds and the rain, the thunder and lightning. There are gods of health and sickness, of weal or woe, births, marriages, or deaths;

tutelar, or vindictive. These gods have their several presidencies. There are gods of the hearth or wayside, of land or water, of forests or hills; home gods, and village gods; river gods, sea gods; gods of the barge, and boat, and ship. They have their patronages. There are gods of trades and professions, vices and virtues, fame or infamy, of thievery, and murder, and adultery. Some gods are for the individual exclusively, others have a more extensive patronage: in China the emperor has his gods, and the great ones theirs, and the people theirs. They dwell in the air, or earth, or sea; are enshrined in brutes and birds, insects and plants, blades of grass, or shells, or stones. These gods must have their history, and therefore create a mythical literature. They have their pedigrees, and 'lives,' and 'memoirs,' their birthdays and marriages. These originate festivals, which are the delight of families, fill a town with joyous tumult, and furnish occupation for days.

Amid such a multitude of gods there is no room for Him who says of himself, 'Is there a god beside me? I know not any.' Polytheism excludes the worship of God the only true. It supplants him by introducing myriads in his place.

The religious spirit destitute of God still further learns to attach itself to images of the objects revered. The likeness of things above, and of things beneath, must be created that man may point to it and say, 'This is my god.' Images of the real, or ideal, must be formed. Old myths must be attached to them, or, if themselves recent in their being, they must be made the basis of new myths. The heathen then become mad after their idols; dwindling down from the colossal forms which are cut in relief by the Buddhists of Western India from the Trappean rocks to the small hand gods of the house, varying in character from the fine significant Assyrian forms to the most debased and unmeaning imagery of a Hindu temple.

This image worship creates a host of ministers and attendants, chiefs and subordinates, to deck and undeck, to lull to sleep and awake from sleep, to wash and dress. In the absence of life and motion, dignity and majesty, there must be created their mock semblances, and the idol must have a courtly retinue to wait on godhead; *wives* must be provided for these so-called gods, and marriage ceremonies, uniting flesh to stone, must be performed.

This idol worship, further, like a great capitalist in the market, gives rise to a multiplicity of labour, and maintains its host of artificers. To supply the demand, there are in requisition the smith and the mason, the carpenter and the jeweller, the statuary and the painter. Trees are cut down and carved stones are dug from the quarry, ores are melted in the fire. The tongs and hammers, the plane and compass, are brought into requisition, and gods are cast or moulded, made or mended. Shops and warehouses are then opened with their precious wares, and gods are bought and sold. Pedestals and niches are sought out. Incantations are solicited and paid for.

The idols are placed in their divine seats, and prayers go forth from multitudes, 'Deliver us, for thou art our god.' Then are to be seen idols in the market and the field, the corners of the streets and by the way-side, in palaces and hovels, in closets and courts, under the palm tree, and in the rock, till the 'land is full of idols.' Human reason is insulted, and the Divine Majesty is profaned.

A remaining section of the heathen world is destitute of all religion, and has no worship. They may recognise the superiority of departed ancestors, of translated heroes; they may admit the occupants of other dwellings than the mere surface of this earth; but they have no thought of a being, or beings, on whom they are dependent, and from whom they derived existence. Such are many of the Southern Africans and Australians. In such minds the genuine idea of a creation's God has to be formed. They are intellectually, as well as morally, without God; yet not in the same sense as the more refined Buddhist, for they have never entertained the idea of God. In their case the missionary lacks all common ground of reasoning. They have not the traditional knowledge of others, which, though perverted, may be a subject of appeal. They are without even those perverted ideas of divinity found elsewhere, and which may be rectified. There is nought in the mind to which, by any laws of affinity, the great idea of God may attach itself. The shepherd of Horeb, when commissioned with a message to his people, asks by what name he should represent

Jehovah to the inquiring Israelites. He is told to make him known to them as the God of Abraham, of Isaac, and of Jacob. He had thus a key furnished him to their understandings and hearts, whereby he might unlock their secret consciousness. This is just what is wanted by the missionary to the class of heathen now treated of. He needs something whereby to reach the inner man. But he cannot find it. The idea of creation is absent. It is far too abstract ever to have been entertained. No idea of Providence is found in that dark soul. It is not in sufficient unison with outward appearance, and inward experience, to have suggested itself. The idea of rule and moral government is absent, as too uncongenial and self-condemning, to have been originated by the heart, or entertained, if suggested. The religious sentiment needs to be created. It would seem as though the man needed not only to be morally regenerated, but in his whole mental constitution born again. The understanding is as untaught as the heart is untrained. They are, in all respects, like to atheists, save—and the distinction is an important one—that they have never denied God, inasmuch as the conception of him has never existed in their mind.

From all that has been remarked, it is evident that the several forms of heathen worship are inimical to God, and that those who engage in them are enemies to God. If, placing ourselves on the high stand-point of Israel's great prophet, we ask the heathen with holy indignation, 'Have ye not known? have ye not heard? hath it not been told you from the beginning? have ye not understood from the foundations of the earth?' some will reply in terms of defiance of the Holy One, others will answer us by pointing to their array of false gods, while others will, by a vacancy of expression, indicate that they have no apprehension of a question that challenges the knowledge of the Supreme.

CHAPTER III.

THE MORALS OF HEATHENDOM.

Heathen's Violation of God's Law.—Identity of the forms of Heathen Iniquity.—Universality of Evil.—Intenseness.—The Sins of Heathendom, what do they bespeak?—Summary.—The specific forms of Heathen Degradation the result of Moral Debasement.—Heathenism never dies out.—Positive Provisions for its Perpetuity.—Absence of everything remediative within itself.—A Power ab-extra needed—Not Civilization—Nor Secular Education—But the Gospel.

If the worship of man is the expression of the soul, his moral conduct is the expression of his worship. The soul stamps its likeness on its worship; worship stamps its likeness on the outer conduct of life.

We have found the aspect of heathen worship to be inimical to God in his being and perfections. Let us now ask what is the aspect of heathen life towards him in his law and commands. We can but infer an equally hostile character. Corrupt worship must, by necessity, induce a corrupt life. Evil systems, however dead in themselves, must, if living in men's minds and hearts, work out evil. Their influences on the life must be in correspondence with their own nature. If the individual spiritual life is by them alienated from God, the moral will partake of the alienation. We have seen that the religious sentiment is depraved; the moral practice will partake of the same dye. If the higher life be debased, the debasement must extend to the lower.

Every negation of God in thought, or word, or deed; or the supplanting of him by other gods which are no gods; or the ignoring of him; whilst it debases man as a religious being, corrupts the moral sensibilities, and that inner corruption reveals itself in outward acts, and reproduces itself by them. A man's religious sentiment creates his affections, and affections create character, and character shapes out all the detail of his social and individual life—the cause producing the effect, and the effect reproducing the cause; and thus, in a perpetual cycle a corrupt religion produces corrupt morals, which in return increase the corruptness of the religion. With our knowledge of heathen worship, we might justly expect the morals of heathendom to be corrupt. And how fearfully do facts justify the expectation. Let us look, even from a distance, at the heathen world, and glance at the actual forms of heathen life which dare show themselves under the blue heavens and the shining sun—the godlessness of spirit, unrighteousness of principle, pride, falsehood, sensuality, of the more civilized heathen; and again the peculiar, unearthly and inhuman forms which are developed in savage heathen life; and we shall be constrained to admit that heathenism, in its moral aspects, is as opposed to the character and law of God, as it is in its worships to his being and perfections. That law may be engraven on stone or on fleshy tablets; may be inscribed on the conscience or be a traditional sentiment; may be uttered and echoed by social life; may have come down from generation to generation, by means of the family organization; but whencever it be received, and however clear or dim its characters, the law is transgressed—consciously and unconsciously—always in its spirit, mostly in its letter, in its whole length and breadth, and by the entire compass of heathen society. The first part of the decalogue is, as we have seen, violated by false, depraved worship; the latter part cannot be inviolate.

Why should we specify heathen transgressions? Rather let us not speak of them. 'Eternal silence be their doom.' Let no page be needlessly blotted by them. The testimony of the sacred Scriptures with all its boldness is exact, with all its amplitude is precise. All facts brought to light, all missionary experiences, are so many verifications of the master sketch of the first apostle of the Gentiles. A few words of his have indelibly stamped on an eternal record the characteristics of the whole heathen world. The whole expanse of Gentile history, from his era to the present, is but the filling up of his bold outlines. Heathendom has undergone vast political changes; it has even changed its gods and worships, rites and ceremonies, but its corrupt morals have remained. All that characterized Corinth and Rome, are to be found in Canton of China, or Benares of India. There are degrees and shades of heathen iniquity, but the gross substance is the same. The veil may be more or less specious which covers the evil, till, in savage life, all is found undisguised, and shame, the last hope of social life, and the last guard of domestic purity, has utterly fled; but still, underneath all, lies rank corruption. There are, indeed, depths below depths, and some parts of heathendom have sunk lower than others. In the more enlightened countries also there are a few sins—and they are *very few*—which are reprobated, and a few sinners who would not dare reveal themselves. There are also, we rejoice to say, not a few of what are popularly called virtues, and which do much to redeem humanity, showing that it is still humanity, though a fallen and corrupt one.

But where is the Gentile community of which, if viewed in the light of God's character, and will, and law, it may not be said 'corrupt are they'? The eternal moral code is mostly reversed, and men act as if they had a command to fulfil its opposites. Heathen life is made up of sins; sins against law, written or unwritten, of the ancients or the moderns, intuitive or traditional, the utterance of the individual moral sense, or of the aggregate conscience of mankind; sins against self, against humanity, against God, the ordinances of earth and of heaven; sins varying in form and character according to the degree of culture, and the stage of civilisation, from that of the bland deceitful Brahman of India, to the Dyak of Borneo; yet all having in them the deadly element of opposedness to all that God is, and all that God has ordained; sins 'secret' and 'presumptuous,' yet not so secret as that those who commit them fear the light of day, nor so known to be presumptuous as that they fear wrath on their account; sins of thought and imagination, which need not retain an airy shape, but boldly embody themselves in deeds; sins against God's truth, against his purity, against his justice, against his benevolence; sins which check mercy and hasten justice; which make us wonder that wrath is staid. Earth groans under the pressure of human guilt. The promise alone keeps back the universal destruction, and allows 'seed time and harvest, cold and heat, summer and winter,' to continue. Moral corruption is the mark whereby this planet, which is more full of heathenism than aught else, must be distinguished by the angels of heaven who may take cognizance of it.

A few remarks may illustrate a subject, which, however painful, needs to be apprehended by the Christian reader.

First, we are struck by the identity of the moral evils of heathenism. The heathen, as a section of mankind, are more comprehensive of varieties of humanity than any other. Yet the most opposite states of society, the greatest diversities of physical and national characteristics, the utmost divergence of origin, and stock, and family, are not sufficient to produce essentially different moral phenomena. No heathen people can boast over another portion of heathendom. The same general developments of evil are current, and in a wonderful extent the same particular evils are found, indicating the jealousy with which humanity asserts its own identity, and the certainty that inward depravity will, under similar circumstances, lead to the same acts and habits. Those who would claim no other affinity with each other, must admit an identity of crime. Those who are separated from each other by the utmost geographical limits, draw near and embrace, on the ground of oneness in sinful customs. There is a unity of sin which binds together the separate parts of heathendom. The Hindu Rajput female, with all her delicacy of training, her gentle habits, and nobleness of family, slays her new-born child just as the Chinese woman, or the wife of the New Zealander. The devil-worshipper in Africa performs rites to secure the death of his enemy, while the Hindu pays his priest to mutter his incantations for the same end.

The selfish Hindu, tired of the responsibility and expense of an aged parent, exposes him that he may perish. The Caffre or Bechuana leaves his aged mother with a calabash of water, and a few days' meal, to perish in the jungle by wild beasts or starvation. The Hindu digs a hole for the leper,* who has become a burden on society, and buries him alive, or casts him into the waters or fire, while the Polynesians adopt some similar plan of getting rid of the

* Such practices are now prohibited in India by the British Government.

deformed and useless. Hindu widows are cast alive on the funeral pyres of their deceased husbands, and the widows of the Fejean chiefs are strangled, whilst hundreds of slaves are immolated on the tombs of kings of Dahomi or Ashanti.

Further—the universality of evil in every heathen community is worthy of our attention. Evil in principle and habit spreads through the mass of society. The whole head becomes sick, the whole heart faint. Sins, like the spots of leprosy, spread till they cover and corrupt the whole social body. All are alike, though not equally infected. Sins in a Christian country kindle indignation, and a protest is made against them. Society arms itself to cast out the particular criminal. He sees a whole people point at him, and often chooses death rather than life, to avoid social reprobation. Not so in the heathen world. There is an absence from society of all elevated moral feeling. The sins of the individual are not taken cognizance of as crimes. The conscience of society, at any time, is but the sum of the consciences of each and every member, and if the individual conscience be corrupt, that of the aggregate must be also.

Where each man depraves the sense of the community, there can exist no outward purifying power. There are no embodied institutes of righteousness, no models of virtue, to shape and control individual sentiment. Heathendom has not two classes of society, distinct from each other, the righteous and unrighteous — the former checking the latter by positive moral efforts, and by force of influence and example, serving as a beacon in the dark night, or as a day-star guiding through winding paths. There are no righteous, no godly, or truthful. All, indeed, are not equally unrighteous. There are distinctions, but they are of degree, not of kind. There is not a righteous class standing out in bold relief from the wicked, serving as a nucleus around which the well-disposed, the thoughtful, the inquiring may rally, illustrating the blessedness of righteousness, alluring to an imitation.

In Christian countries the righteous form a distinct class, of whom all may take cognizance. These are the salt of society—the good leaven diffused through the whole mass. They form a standard of appeal. They sustain the code of morals—they illustrate as well as teach God's law. They are the 'ark' in which it is deposited, as well as the priests by whom it is read and expounded. They keep the wicked in check, and prevent the overflowings of the ungodly. They create a public consciousness of good and evil, instilling into the evilly inclined fear and shame, recalling to the law when violated, bringing back to the standard when a departure has been made from it. In spite of all these influences, visible and invisible, direct and indirect, single and accumulated, the righteous are often as Lot in Sodom or Abraham in Canaan. What a mass of iniquity is found in the streets of so-called christian towns, and how vitiated are private morals. Let the reader then imagine the state of heathen society where no such counteracting principles exist, where the theory of morals is scarcely propounded, and where it is never practised by any section of the community. In such a case, society destroys rather than saves the individual. If there be any one differing from the rest, any soul seeking after purer morals, a holier life, he is at the best as Socrates before his judges. A heathen seldom finds himself rebuked by his fellows. No withering scorn drives him from an evil course. No melting pity softens him to alter his course of life. There is no silent example that makes him fly from the presence of righteousness as more than he can endure, or haste to conform himself to it. Society is of one make, cast in one mould. Iniquity is not confronted, sin is not challenged, untruth is not questioned. None of the brethren who have sold Joseph need fear the reproof of each other; all have had a share in the foul contract. The adultress need not fear being stoned, as every one whose office it is to execute the law is tainted by the same crime. Which of the Cretans shall charge his brother with falsehood, or which of the Spartans shall arraign his brother for theft? Fear is not awakened where all are more or less chargeable with the guilt. Remorse is not excited where each neighbour is a perpetrator of the same crime. Shame is not aroused when the same spots are found on all. Each one affixes his seal to the specific iniquity, and makes it current, till the false becomes unquestionable, and that which is most abominable is unchallenged. 'Evil' by being popular, becomes 'good'; 'bitter' from being universally tasted, becomes 'sweet;' 'darkness' from the fact of overspreading all, becomes 'light,' till at length opposites exchange places, and confusion itself becomes confounded. Then do the wicked triumph in their prosperity and discard the fear of the Almighty. Evil thus diffused is aggravated. Unlike many other things, which, by being diffused through a mass, become weakened, sin acquires intensity from the space over which it travels, and the number of minds it pervades.

Men, finding they may sin with impunity, grow bold in it. One grade of iniquity leads to another. Habits go beyond themselves from very satiation, and make those bound by them seek out new inventions. Being past feeling, they give themselves over to work iniquity with greediness. Evil becomes rank, luxuriant. There are few hedges to break, and few vipers to bite. Pit-falls are not guarded nor fenced. Each sin advances to its utmost limit; each corruption takes its deepest dye till it assumes the very blackness of hell. Malice goes through all its stages till men can force themselves *to eat* the enemy they have killed, for undoubtedly excessive hatred, not hunger or fleshly appetite, is the parent of cannibalism. Falsehood is urged to such an extreme, that men lie in sheer wantonness. In India and China the natives speak lies 'on the right hand and the left,' lies to conceal facts and to make them known, to substantiate the truth and to controvert it, with and without a reason, for and against self-interest. False oaths are bought and sold in the market places of India, as any other article. Filthy language is carried so far as to form a staple article of speech, making the lips the very portals of the grave, and the throat an open sepulchre, filling a volume with its vocabulary. Filial selfishness can go to the extreme of leaving parents to die. Social pride can be urged to such issues as to murder the newly-born infant to obviate the expense of a sufficiently dignified marriage. The spirit of selfish arrogance can go so far in a family or tribe as to immolate innocent fellow-creatures on the tomb of the departed, and soak the clods under which the dead lie with the blood of the living.

There is in heathenism a self-abandonment, a yielding up of the soul to evil influences. The flesh has its lusts, and the mind likewise. Both triumph over the man. There is no spirit effectually striving against the flesh. The flesh dominates and leaves the spirit bleeding in the dust. But worse still, there is an abandonment by God. As the heathen have given him up, he gives them up. The secret but powerful restraints he imposes on men, in their own moral constitution, those checks and hindrances in providence which he lays on the path of many a sinner in our own land, those strivings no less effectual because they cannot be defined, those stirrings of the soul and shakings to its centre, whose origin may not be directly traced, but which have their no less blessed effects—where are they in the heathen mind? If they do exist, in what a feeble degree! The Divine complaint of the sins of the heathen is, 'Their cry is exceeding great.' And this intensity goes on, as with the Amorites, till the cup of iniquity is full, and periodic judgments descend which remove the refuse, and for a season purge the land of its worst scum and filth, and make the heathen themselves acknowledge, 'There is a God that judges in the earth!'

There is a further consideration which challenges our attention. Christian society is moved at the hearing of the more flagrant forms of heathen iniquity. We have long been conversant with a few of the outstanding and overshadowing evils, and we learn to reckon certain cardinal sins as the characteristics of heathendom. But an important question arises, Whence these flagrant evils? what do they bespeak?

That which arrests the attention is not the most terrible. There is something worse underneath. In knowing the sins of heathendom, we only know part of the subject. We should also consider the sinfulness whence they spring—a sinfulness not only belonging to their original nature, as men, the descendants of Adam, but as superinduced by a series of transgressions. As a succession of acts constitute a habit, so a series of habits constitutes a nature—a second nature, intensifying the corruption of the whole man

—and this second nature has become consolidated, till the individual is twice 'sold under sin.' Evil thoughts, murders, adulteries, fornications, thefts, false witness—all of which characterise the heathen—these defile; but how full of defilement must be the heart whence they all proceed. The burning lava is dreadful, which like a fiery sea submerges plains and villages; but what of the volcano whence they issue, or, still more, of the subterraneous fires of which the volcano is but the vent and passage? So, to take a few sins as illustrations, infanticide is fearful; but what a selfishness and heartless soul does it bespeak, what violations of nature's instincts, what a destruction of moral sentiment! The sin is dreadful; but the sinful sentiment and habit of mind which must have been required to originate and sustain it in a whole society of men and women—how dreadful is that! What hardening processes must the mind have passed through to obtain such a habit of obduracy.

Cannibalism is awful; but how awful the devilish hate and malice which gave it birth. The lying habits of the heathen shock us; but how false the nature which has constituted the habit. How must it love falsehood. How must the inner man be conversant with it, so that all the delights of the soul are in lies, and the food and air which nourishes it is untruth. The Hindu devotee challenges and receives divine honours, saying literally, 'I am God; worship thou me.' We are amazed and indignant at the blasphemy, but how intense must be the self-righteousness and arrogance which gave birth to such a delusion.

The Khoonds of India sacrifice children, to sprinkle the blood of their yet reeking flesh on the ground they have ploughed. We are shocked at the cruel custom, but how deep must be the *selfishness* of such a nature, when the only motive of the cruelty is to make the ground fertile, so as to secure a good harvest. Missionaries in western Africa have been assured by mothers that they at times avoided their own sons, lest they should kill them, in order to have their service in another life. What unspeakable selfishness must exist, to occasion such a fear.

And further, these gigantic evils, of which we do hear—what a multitude of minor evils do they overshadow, of which we do not hear. And what a soil it must be that supports them all—the wide-spreading upas and the rank underwood. What poisonous saps, what noxious juices, must be given out by the heathen heart to maintain such a produce, from age to age.

And again, society itself—the social mass living together—how corrupt must it be to bear such iniquity, not to purge itself from the foul blot, and cast out the unclean thing. We would that Christians would ponder this. Instead of being amazed at the outer and visible, let them think of the inward and invisible, so as to receive due impressions of the evil, and inquire more earnestly what they shall do for the heathen.

We draw this part of our subject to a conclusion.

The apostle said of the Gentiles, 'They know not God.' It was to him an indisputable fact. He does not stop to prove it. The above remarks will serve to make his statement unquestionable as regards the Gentiles of this age. Their worship, in its philosophy, its spirit, its rites and ceremonies, proves it. Their conduct in its entire range also proves it. They are 'alienated from the life of God through the darkness that is in them.' They are also 'enemies in their minds by wicked works.' The understanding has not apprehended him. The idea of him has no definite place in the mind. Thoughts of him do not enter into the mental economy. The eternal God, the all in all of creation and providence, the source of law and the fountain of judgment; the historical Deity who gave them a name, and a place, making of one blood all that dwell upon the earth, appointing the bounds of their habitation, who has borne with them, tried and proved them, visited them with rebukes and sufferings—he is not even intellectually known by them. Much less do they know him with the heart. The intellect may have some shadowy perceptions of him; but the heart has certainly no affections towards him. Light is only discerned by light. Truth alone apprehends truth, love only comprehends love. Holiness can alone apprehend holiness. But they are not of the truth, that they should know the Truthful One; nor of the light, that they should know the Father of lights. They have no love, that they should know Him who is love; nor purity, that they should know the Holy One.

The malice and falsehood of the Jews were sufficient to draw from the holy Redeemer the solemn rebuke, 'Ye are of your father the devil.' What a full application have these words to the heathen, and what stress have they when thus applied. The heathen are, by a false worship, apostate from God, and by departure from his law, morally degraded. They have lapsed from their primeval estate, have gone far from the original standard, and all the other specific forms of degradation we witness are only so many different symptoms of their fundamental moral degeneracy.

We witness a physical degradation of many of the heathen races — stunted stature, compressed or receding foreheads, disproportioned limbs, ill formed and ill set shapes; in some an expression that is hideous and terrible; in others, features that evince a vacuity of all intelligence.

And all these, we are told, are so many different cases of defection from the original type of man. But we cannot fail to discern that these departures from a physical type are also expressive of departure from a moral type. This physical degradation acquires its chief significance, and most terrible woefulness, from the moral causes which have directly or indirectly induced it. Moral processes, secret but sure, have, in the lapses of time, produced these physical results which force themselves on our attention. Physical deformity is, in a great degree, the effect, as it is the symbol, of moral deformity. That repulsive aspect which makes the beholder shudder, tells of repulsive habits, descended, it may be, through generations. Those features developing the animal rather than the man, flesh rather than spirit, reveal the carnal mind, which has come down from father to son, and tell us how far the heathen have departed from God.

We find the heathen also politically degraded. Multitudes are not reckoned among the nations, not deemed worthy of being called a people, but treated as savages, as 'brute beasts, to be taken and destroyed,' rather than as men, with whom may be held terms of amity. India and China, the two most exalted specimens of heathen civilization, retaining largely what they inherited from their forefathers at the dispersion of Babel, how have they been humbled, at many periods of their existence, by rapacious conquerors, and at all times crushed by the iron hand of despotism. What has their history been but that of dynasties raised and cast down, cities sacked and villages wasted, fierce irruptions of bold races, as marauding hordes, or disciplined armies—of lands depopulated, homes desolated, hearths profaned. And even when by such fearful means a government has been established, how often has it been to sell justice, to rob the people, to protect the guilty, to oppress the innocent. The history of heathen Asia, from the age of Assyria until now, has been a comment on the words, 'Their sorrows shall be multiplied that hasten after another god.' But the worst element of degradation such as this, is that it is but the rebuff and casting down of the Almighty, because of their departure from him, and is one of God's lessons forced on mankind, that power and rule depart from those who have left their God, in order that children may rule over them. Having committed treason against the King of kings, their own rights and liberties are sacrificed, protecting power is withdrawn, and the rod of the oppressor, or the whip of scorpions, becomes their portion.

Again, what vast masses of the heathen are socially degraded. Look at a great portion of the African race, from age to age hunted like wild beasts, enthralled, bound, sold into slavery, expatriated. This very slavery bespeaks the servitude of sin—their own, that of their progenitors, as well as that of their betrayers. They are a people robbed and spoiled, because they have first robbed God. Independently of this actual slavery, look at the virtual slavery of vast masses of the heathen. What position do they hold—at what social value are they rated? They are counted as nought by their social superiors, subjected to mere caprice, living or dying according to the will of some despot. Millions are constrained to move at the fiat of a governor, whether to dig canals, or make roads, or to wait in service. How alien to heathen life are the ideas and habits of liberty and just independence. Everything dear to man—life, property, family—how are they subject to the caprice and rapacity of a chief, a judge, a monarch. By the side of civil slavery is found spiritual despotism. The priestly and the civil powers, mutually conniving and helping each other, bind the people, as with chains of iron. Both, with unsparing rapacity, rob them of their hardly earned subsistence. The priesthood is the more powerful, inasmuch as it adds to the terrors of this life those of that which is to come. But all this degradation is chiefly terrible, because arising from the fact, that having broken fealty with the Governor among the nations, they are abandoned by him to internal disorder, oppression, and misrule.

The social degradation of woman, also, so common in heathen lands, is but the measure of woman's guilt, herself sustaining, by example and influence, the very institutes which corrupt man, and keep her debased. How degraded are the heathen, also, in their domestic institutions. Heathenism has no home, nor domestic comfort. In some places we find polygamy corrupting both man and woman, depraving families and deteriorating the race; and occasionally we meet with an institution of an opposite kind—the woman herself becoming the paramour of many husbands. When monogamy does exist, how slender is the marriage bond—how faithless, oftentimes, are the conjugal vows. This home degradation, bad in itself, is chiefly so as bespeaking the fact, that when there is spiritual adultery, domestic order and harmony cease. The door is wide open to domestic treachery, and reliance may no longer be placed on chastity and faithfulness.

Lastly, the righteous judgments of God seem to bear testimony to the sins of the heathen, overtaking them in their persons, their families, their property, their civil and social estate.

What terrible diseases overtake the heathen, like those which God laid on Egypt, from the black leprosy consuming the extremities of the sufferer, till gradually every limb drops off, or the white leprosy, making the victim white as snow, to the incurable gangrene. Many are the sick who lay helpless by such 'pools' as are to be found in heathendom, but no angel comes down to trouble the waters. What a mass of suffering in Gentile life arises from this cause—in the absence of all alleviating care and medical appliances.

Further, what an amount of physical want and wretchedness do we find in heathen countries! To those who subsist by hunting, how often does the chase fail to supply needful food, and families linger out their existence. How frequently are the pastures of the nomades dried up, and their cattle and men are wasted from the drought. The people of China, the very extreme of heathen civilization, press closely on all the supplies of nature and art, for means of subsistence—the dregs of the population eating offal and every unclean thing to sustain life. And, notwithstanding all care, yet how frequently famine overspreads a whole people. Though, as a general principle, God maketh his 'sun to shine on the evil and the good, and sendeth rain upon the just and unjust,' either that law is suspended, or men are, from indolence or want of forethought, unable to adapt themselves to the fluctuations of seasons. Famine ensues, that impoverishes whole races, and destroys multitudes. Families leave their paternal homes and lands, and migrate where corn is found, even though it be into Egyptian slavery. Parents sell their children from want of bread. Islands have been at times depopulated by it, or a small starving remnant has left its own land in a frail canoe to seek sustenance elsewhere. And pestilence comes in to divide the spoil with gaunt famine. The plague often breaks out on idolatrous festivals, from the corruption induced by large masses congregating without ordinary means of health, and sanitary precaution. It sweeps over a populous country with a virulence that testifies whence and for what it has come, depopulating whole districts, till the grass grows in the dwellings of man. 'Verily, God is terrible among the heathen.'

We close this chapter with a consideration of deep import. Of this heathenism we cannot say, as did the apostle of Judaism, 'That which decayeth and waxeth old is ready to vanish away.' No. It is indeed in decay, and it has waxed old, but heathenism never *dies out.* If ever destroyed, it must be by a power foreign to itself. If one form becomes extinct, it has the power of reproducing itself in another. It is like the banyan tree of India, whose parent stem may die, but it shoots down its branches far and wide, which themselves become parents of others, and thus, if unchecked, would cover a country or a continent. Heathenism may change its gods, its ceremonies, its philosophies, but itself never changes. Its essential nature is an unchanging one, ever developing itself in new as well as in old forms of faith and practice. Its decay is but the beginning of new life in another form. Its very corruptions feed and nourish it. It waxeth stronger with evil, and more vigorous with iniquity.

There are two considerations which would warrant our expectation of the perpetuity of heathenism, viewed from a mere human stand-point. The first is positive, arising from its own nature and influence. The second is negative, arising from the absence of everything remediative within itself. It seizes hold of the human mind and makes it like to itself, and therein has a bond for its perpetuity. Like a large river, it cuts out for itself deep channels in the very heart of society, through which it may flow undisturbed. How thoroughly is childhood pre-occupied with all that is heathen. Almost the first utterances of children are the names of their gods, often blended with lies and obscenity. Parents making a mock at sin, stain the sweet lips of unconscious childhood with words which, in a Christian country, would make even the dissolute blush. The child's first imposing sights are connected with idolatry. In India a boy's first studies are in connection with false gods. The Hindu scholar writes the name of his god ere he frames a letter, and invokes him ere he begins his task. Children's pleasures and sports are bound up with idol feasts. The cannibals of Feejee put human flesh into their children's mouths to make them brave. The boys make a pastime of cannibalism. Thus is the future man trained for this life and that which is to come.

Especially is womanhood on the side of evil. She who was first in the transgression still abides such. The corner stone of heathenism, if not its foundation, is its influence over the female heart. That very religious tendency which, directed towards truth and holiness, is one great stay and charm of Christianity in our midst, is made, by Satan, a stronghold of falsehood and impurity. Woman's influences, which in all states of society are powerful, are all on the side of heathenism. Her sensibilities, always keen, chiefly uphold it. The religious spirit, perverted from its design and abused, expends itself on idolatry, and encircles itself with its associations. Personally, she more than others worships; she more than others upholds the worshippers. Companies of women repairing to the temples with offerings are a common sight in India. Who is it that supports priests, washes their feet, worships them? Woman. She chants the praises of the gods with a feminine intoxication of passion, which still further inspires the men and encourages the priests.

Moreover, by being the early teacher of a new generation, the moulder of its mind, the former of its tastes, the inspirer of its genius, she is, in a double sense, the upholder of heathenism. Who teaches the child its earliest lesson of worship, and bids it bow down to the idol? Woman. Who takes the child when sick and offers her vows at the shrine of some god or demon, and when it has revived, takes the child that it may personally fulfil the vow? Woman. Think of it, ye mothers at home;—your sex in heathen lands is not only degraded by superstition, but is most efficient in the degradation of others. While you are supine in your Christian circles, they are earnestly training the succeeding generation in all the evils of heathenism. Think of it, ye daughters of British Israel, and resolve to uplift these degraded ones, that they may not only save themselves but others also. Be encouraged to exert your peculiar influence for their good, and by evangelizing and educating them, you will more than half destroy the vile religions of the age.

On the other hand there is within heathenism no direct remediative dispensation. When there is no specific for a raging plague, we expect those stricken to die. When there is no bread, we expect famine to waste its millions. 'Where there is no vision,' says the prophet, 'the people perish.' Heathenism starves the soul, and within its domain there is no supply of food. It wounds, and there is none to heal; it kills, and there is none to make alive. What facilities does the heathen possess of escape from heathenism? How can he deliver himself from its dread influences? What moral or spiritual power is within its compass to make him good?

What sanctifying energies are at work to make the heathen holy? There is an inner blindness of the understanding and the heart; there is also in correspondence an outer darkness. The light which is in them is darkness, and that intense; but there is an outer gloom that is its counterpart. The circumstances of heathen life, how unlike those of people dwelling in gospel lands, who, though themselves blind, live in an atmosphere of light and grope at noon day; to whom in their ignorance is yet revealed the knowledge of God and righteousness. In this case, the inner and outer evil have an awful correspondence—and as we have before seen, they are of each other the cause and effect. The outer gloom intensifies the inner darkness; the inner darkness reflectively increases the outer gloom. The absence of truth, of exemplars and motives to righteousness, serves to beguile the understanding and to deprave the heart. Again, the beguiled intellect and depraved heart still further tend to drive truth away from the dwellings of men, and reduce the standard of righteousness. Thus, heathen circumstance vitiates heathen mind and character, and they in return make outer circumstance still more adverse. If there be any appetency for truth and good, nothing outward is at hand adapted to it. If there be any aspiration after anything high and noble, the world in which it moves meets it not. The systems which the inquirer does know pervert the exercise of his faculties, and misguide him in his researches. If he ask for truth and goodness, there is no response, or a false one.—Terrible ordeal for a human soul, which, even in the presence of light, with its natural love of darkness, remains bewildered and undecided. How great must be the darkness when all around is pledged in a conspiracy to thicken it; where there is no 'perfect law of the Lord to convert the soul'; no 'sure testimony to make wise the simple'; no 'right statutes of the Lord to rejoice the heart'; no 'pure commandment of the Lord to enlighten the eyes'; no 'fear of the Lord to cleanse'; no 'true and righteous judgment of the Lord to warn'; no agency to cleanse from secret faults or keep back from presumptuous sins. No long train of prophets and teachers rises up early and testifies to righteousness. No Isaiah appears to bid the heavens hear, and the earth give ear. No Jeremiah to rebuke princes and people in the gate. No Ezekiel to unveil and denounce the yet greater and greater abominations. No Daniel to kneel and pray in arrest of judgment. No son of Zacharias in the wilderness of heathenism breaks the stillness of ages by the rousing cry, 'Repent,' or directs to the Lamb of God. No gentle voice as of Jesus, cries, 'The kingdom of heaven is at hand.' No lawgiver sits on the mount and proclaims the law and principle of blessing. No messengers 'two by two' cast out devils, and proclaim glad tidings. The stillness of ignorance abides from age to age. The monotony of error is unbroken; no soul is awakened from the deathliness of sin. All are as spell-bound. The wise and the prudent confound others and are themselves confounded. The blind lead the blind, and both fall into the ditch. Among all their counsellors there is not one to guide. Sect after sect arises. Theories, and systems, and institutes succeed each other in weary round, without any central truth. If some arise who can look nearer at the sun of truth than others, they become themselves dazzled and blinded. If they call on others to gaze likewise, they are themselves mistaken for the sun itself, and their disciples in deifying them forget the truth it was their mission to teach. The founder of purer morals dies, and in the worship which is rendered to him by his disciples, the moral system is forgotten, and often degenerates into a lower form than that from which they have been rescued. Thus, on positive and negative considerations, heathenism has, in itself, a principle of perpetuity. The strong man of heathenism armed, keepeth his palace and maintaineth his goods in peace. He has seized the citadel. He has closed every way of egress. He has secured every outpost. His scouts are placed far and wide to tell of any foreign approach. Every rising from within is suppressed. If heathenism is to be shaken it must be by a power from without. It is true, it may have become effete, having on it the decrepitude of age and its hoariness. Centuries may have enfeebled it, but of itself it will never die. It will only change its form. The phases through which it may pass are infinite. In India, Védism is succeeded by Buddhism, and Buddhism by a restored Brahmanism, which assume the new form of Puranic faiths, which again give way to local superstitions. But amid all, heathenism still remains. Such is its natural history everywhere.

It must, then, be destroyed by a power foreign to itself. Its darkness must be dissipated by an outer light; its iniquity can only be purged by some purifying extrinsic power. Where is that power to be found? Not in Western civilization. An Archimedes did not save Greece, neither can a Stephenson save India. We see no more in a railroad to destroy heathenism in China, than there was in Rome's military roads to convert her from Paganism. Civilization, when it encroaches on the domains of barbarous heathenism, extinguishes it by destroying the people among whom it is found. Backwoods are only tenanted by the civilized driving before them the savage denizens. Towns arise on the borders of lakes only when their former tenants are scattered to other homes, which are no homes. Western civilization introduced among the Eastern, already possessing their own peculiar type of civilization, fails to regenerate. A double class of vices is often produced by a mixture of the two races, and the Oriental's last estate is worse than the first. The Parsis of Bombay surround themselves by all the luxuries of Britain's metropolis, and yet worship fire. The Baboos of Calcutta imitate European manners, and yet keep the feast of Durga, or perform puja at the New Year.

Nor will heathenism recede before mere education, or instruction in moral lessons. Greece was saved from her abominations neither by the wisdom of a 'divine Plato,' nor a righteous Socrates. Aristotle left her where he found her, 'in the arms of the wicked one.' Neither Cicero nor Seneca regenerated their country.

What failed in the West will not be successful in the East. The best type of mind, and in the most healthful class of circumstances, failed to be renewed by all the civilization which existed in Greece or Rome. The inferior type of Asiatic mind, and amid Asiatic influences, the worst conceivable for truth and righteousness, will not be regenerated by the secular knowledge Europe can impart.

There is only one power that can subdue heathenism—that of Christ—the mightier than the mighty; and that power must be brought to bear by the ministers of the gospel. The grace of God that bringeth salvation must appear and be recognised. A mercy that triumphs over sin must be revealed to them. He who spoils the spoiler, and sets free the captive, must be made known in the ministry of the gospel, and then, and not till then, will heathenism fall to rise no more.

CHAPTER IV.

THE FUTURE STATE OF THE HEATHEN.

What are the heathen before God?—Issues of evil are certain.—General sentiment of Christians defended.—Heathen depravity an insuperable ground of Christian solicitude.—The question transferred to the region of facts.—Are the Heathen saved *from* sin in this life?—Hopeful cases.—General question not affected.—Scripture statements.—Conclusion.—An objection answered.—Application.

An inquiry concerning the heathen yet remains. We have found them wretched in their individual life, without a centre for the soul, given up to the sway of evil, agitated by divers passions, and distracted by fears; unhappy also in their social, and often in their domestic life. What are they in the life that is to come? We have investigated the aspects of the heathen towards God. What are God's aspects towards them? We have seen what they are in their own darkness. What are they in *his* light? This is the inquiry of the Christian, jealous for God, and also jealous for man, desiring the glory of his Lord, but also longing for the happiness of his fellow creatures. These people and tribes are justly interesting to us as ethnologists, desirous to trace their origin, the centre whence they started, the root whence they sprang; or, as linguists, tracing the affinities of their languages, and the historical facts which such affinities mark out; but it is as Christians that they transcendantly interest us. When we view them as moral and responsible souls, in their vast aggregate of numbers, and immortal destinies, they assume an interest which absorbs all other interest. There arises a thought that overpowers thought, a solicitude that outweighs all other solicitude, a question that puts a stop to other questions, and which is the terminus of our past inquiries—What are the heathen before God? What is *his* moral estimate of them? How do they stand before him now, anticipatively? How will they stand before the Judge of quick and dead? This is the question for Christians to ponder. God forbid that we should propose it in the speculative spirit of him who said, 'Lord, are there few that be saved?' We should take up the subject, not for speculation, but for truth, and duty, and action. Some avoid the inquiry as incapable of solution, dismiss it from their thoughts if it is ever suggested, and settle down in the fixed sentiment that it is beyond human investigation. The suppressed inquiry alters not gloomy facts, but it does hinder needful Christian exertions. The blinking of the question diminishes not one iota of the dread reality of the state of the heathen, but it does check the efforts which might alleviate it. This forced silence is a sullen treachery to the best interests of heathendom. It is as possible to say, 'Peace, peace,' when there is no peace, for others as for self, and the consequences are as disastrous. We virtually shut the door of the kingdom, by imagining that men are entering it, when they are going down to the chambers of death. We may have a lie in our right hand, regarding the salvation of idolaters, as idolaters have in reference to the power of their idols.

Were the issues of evil as uncertain as the origin of evil, we should not propose this inquiry; we should choose silence as wisdom. But whilst the one question is lost in uncertainty, and has been reiterated for centuries fruitlessly, the other has in it a moral certainty and a solemn fixedness. If there be such a thing as moral government and human responsibility—if evil be a dread reality—if we do not adopt the Brahmanical theory that evil and good are the same things, interchangeable words, mere human developments without any moral character—or rather, alike developments of the Godhead within; if it be a thing opposed to the character of God, hostile to his government—by its very constitution, as well as the Divine decree, precluding happiness, incapacitating its subjects for it by an equally moral and physical impossibility, and rendering its bestowal utterly inconsistent with the divine perfections—then are its issues a plain subject of human knowledge and conviction. And this knowledge, it is evident, is bound up with action. Uncertain view on this point must serve to relax the knees already too feeble, to keep hands suspended that should be uplifted in prayer, or stretched forth in vigorous action.

Arguing from the moral responsibility of the heathen

as an indisputable axiom, and from a moral government, as involved in the being and character of God; viewing on one hand the multiplied facts of heathen depravity, and on the other, the statements of Scripture, direct and indirect, explicit and inferential; regarding such depravity both in the mass and in detail;—the multitude of Christians have entertained the conviction, that the future state of the heathen is 'without hope.' 'The heathen are perishing'—such is the solemn language in which Christians have expressed their forebodings of the heathens' future, and rouse one another to exertion. It is the sentiment of our missionary hymns—often sung too thoughtlessly—of our missionary platforms, and the purport of missionary sermons, and the burden of our prayers. These words have made many a Christian heart bleed, and many a bosom sigh. They have moved the entire man, and served as an irresistible incentive to action. They have, however, proved repugnant to many minds; have awakened doubts and kindled controversy. Are the words, then, too expressive, or are they just and scriptural? Do they embody a dogma of a rigid sect, or do they express an awful truth, as demonstrable as the nature of the case will allow?

By an error in one direction, we may dishonour the Governor of the world and the principles of his government; by an error in the other, we may let the heathen alone in their condemnation, without putting forth the efforts that might have saved them.

The writer has pondered the subject at home and abroad, in the study ere he became a missionary, and amid the crowds of idolaters with the Bible in his hand and heathen nature before him, and he dares not shut out from his own mind the conviction that the general voice of Christians on this solemn subject is but the echo of the Scripture, the expression of fact. He would state in this chapter the direct and indirect grounds of this conviction.

The Scriptures tell us in general terms that 'the wrath of God is revealed from heaven against all unrighteousness and ungodliness of men.' Now these are the two comprehensive principles that are embodied in all the outward sensible forms of heathen life. They tell us that in the day when God shall judge the world in righteousness, 'tribulation and anguish will be rendered to every soul of man that doeth evil.' But, as we have before seen, evil is the very staple material of heathen life. They tell us that 'as many as have sinned without law shall also perish without law.' In addition to general statements, the Scriptures mark out specific sins and habits as objects of Divine wrath, and as tending to exclude from the kingdom of heaven. 'Be not deceived: neither fornicators, nor idolaters, nor adulterers, nor effeminate, nor abusers of themselves with mankind, nor thieves, nor covetous, nor drunkards, nor revilers, nor extortioners, shall inherit the kingdom of God.' Now these are the very classes which form the great material of heathen society. Not that each heathen has attached to him all the criminal characteristics of these classes, but that some one or more do cleave to him so as to constitute his fixed character. Can a *friend* of the heathen, in the face of such scriptural statements on one hand, and patent facts on the other, forbear to entertain most solemn forebodings of their future destiny?

And here we acknowledge that our chief forebodings for the heathen are not on account of their ignorance, in *itself* considered. That might, indeed, well excite our fears, for, first, we find that ignorance of the physical laws of the world does not save those who transgress them. They visit themselves in terrible penalties equally on those who wilfully and unconsciously violate them. The laws that prevail in the moral world also if infringed, are equally unsparing. Certain acts may be committed without the knowledge of their evil; sinful habits may be contracted in ignorance of their tendencies, yet are they not allowed to go free. Ignorance saves none from the divers penalties which the Divine Being has attached to law in this world. We might, therefore, if really solicitous for the future of the heathen, entertain fears that infraction of the divine law, which undoubtedly brings down misery in this life, might lead to dire evils in the life that is to come. The 'few stripes' with which he who knew not his master's will, yet did that which was worthy of stripes, will be smitten, are quite sufficient to excite the apprehensions of those who are solicitous about the future state of the heathen, and who, with the anxiety of love, as distinct from the apathy of indifference, are desirous to know the worst, that they may obviate it, as far as in them lies. Nor in forming an estimate of the future of the heathen, from the fact of their ignorance, should we be unmindful that ignorance is alike the parent and the offspring of evil—the cause and the effect; that it originates many of the vices, and sustains them when once in being; that it alienates the soul from the 'life of God;' that ignorance and true virtue are incompatible; that a darkened understanding produces a vitiated heart; that a mind without truth, is always conjoined with a heart without righteousness; that knowledge and goodness are essential to each other, neither having an independent existence. An immense amount of ignorance is doubtless itself a form of depravity—sometimes manifestly traceable as such, at other times forcing itself on our conviction by strongest inferences—and having this nature, is, like all other forms of depravity, of a condemnatory character.

Still, we repeat it, our chief solicitude for the heathen is not on account of their ignorance, save where it is wilful, and darkness, as such, is accepted rather than light. They might be ignorant of the God who made them, the law he has made for them, the heaven he has provided for the righteous, the hell which is prepared for sinners—and this ignorance might be their misfortune and their woe, rather than their crime. It is not even the fact of their not knowing the Saviour that excites our fears for their salvation.

We can conceive of them as not knowing the Saviour, and yet an imputation made to them of his righteousness. Their not knowing him would certainly involve no guilt, where he had not been proclaimed, and if there were a heart directed to God, a broken and contrite heart, seeking forgiveness and the Divine favour, we should find no difficulty in admitting the application to them of the blood of sprinkling, a comprehension of such penitent souls in the covenant of mercy, a bringing them within the range of that wondrous reconciliation which was effected on Calvary, and the benefits of which are secured by the Intercessor in heaven.

Our supreme solicitude for the heathen is on account of their depravity. This is a ground of fear no mere reasoning can take away, nor appeals to our feelings, nor arguing from general speculative principles of the Divine government, nor references to our moral sense. We are constrained to say that God's thoughts and God's ways often contravene our 'moral sense,' that his 'government' is often beyond our á priori imaginations, and that this opposition between the Divine in fact and the human in theory may hold good in this specific case, where error conceived by us will be irretrievably detrimental to our heathen brother's everlasting welfare. We repeat it, the sins of heathendom seem insuperable grounds of its condemnation. This appears an axiom. Yet like many first principles, it needs to be distinctly apprehended. The heathen are often 'pitied,' and in our hymns we even tell God to 'pity' them. They are called 'poor' heathen, and are viewed almost exclusively as objects of compassion. Far be it from us to draw off compassion from them. We would have every Christian heart filled with it to overflowing; but it is evident that pity is only one emotion which the case warrants, and that not the commanding one. All sin is wretchedness, and challenges pity; but all sin is guilt and challenges indignation. In viewing them as merely objects of compassion, we may forget that their sins provoke the jealous God to wrath, and involve them in condemnation. It is heathen depravity, with the guilt it involves, that makes us tremble for the future of the heathen—depravity, deeply ingrained into the whole nature, that has made their religions wicked and sometimes diabolical, and stamped itself on all their rites and ceremonies; that has stood the wear of ages and the shocks of time; that has become so certain and fixed a part of the human economy that it stands out before the heathen with all the prestige of fate, and is deemed irresistible, bound up with each individual's destiny, and the whole course of mankind, as much as the revolution of seasons is with the physical economy of the globe;—depravity that has worn out peoples and tribes, and yet maintains its vigour, destroying yet destroyed; that has stood proof against voices of the day and of the night, the revelations of God's eternal power and Godhead in his visible works, the testimony he has given of himself in fruitful seasons, the teachings of their own understandings and the monitions of their own consciences—the occasional lessons of some from among themselves, whose inspiration has made them almost prophets; —depravity that has in some cases outlived all hereditary knowledge, all earliest and latest warnings, all holy instincts of nature, all normal feelings of humanity; that has survived and still braves all the judgments of God and all the traditions of judgments. It is this depravity, we say, that makes us fear. It meets us on every hand. We cannot hide ourselves from it, nor does it hide itself from us. It meets us wherever we move, and from whatever aspect we view the heathen, from the cradle to the grave. It lays hold of our moral vision in the same way as a towering mountain fixes the gaze of the traveller in the plain, in whichever direction he may move, until he is wearied with the sight, and despairs of reaching the end of his journey. This is the dire fact of Gentile humanity perpetual from generation to generation, and universal from heart to heart. Let this fact be got rid of, or even modified, and the question will assume a different character. But this fact only becomes confirmed by experience, and increasingly illustrated by our acquaintance with the heathen. There is here no invention; there are no surmises, no grounds for theory. We have to deal with the multiplied facts of evil, wilfully practised, chosen and retained, notwithstanding all ordinary and extraordinary efforts at dislodgement.

If we were ignorant of the Gentile world, as we were comparatively a century ago, we might imagine that the Gentiles of the apostolic age, and those of this era, were not alike in moral character; that the dark lineaments sketched by a Paul would not find their originals in modern heathen; that his terms of condemnation must be mitigated as regards them, and consequently their hopes may be of a brighter cast. But let us hear our missionaries, read their contributions to our literature, collect the multitudinous facts from the four ends of the Gentile world; do they not all show that every word then uttered has its full application now? Is Scripture too strong as to their iniquities? No. The heathen themselves are witnesses. They tell us of their own sins. They reveal those of each other. They admit these very Scriptures are the searchers of their hearts, the revealers of their lives, and this very power is to them the most appreciable evidence of their divinity.

We are not forgetting that guilt is itself a relative idea, involving a knowledge of law. And on this very ground our convictions are deepened, for of the multitude of the heathen we may say, 'Verily, have they not known' the sinfulness of their acts? The African acknowledges that before the missionary came, he knew that the violation of such laws as are found in the decalogue, excepting that relating to the Sabbath, was sin. The Hindus never deny that theft, falsehood, adultery, are sins, but they excuse them by the depravity of the age, the decrees of fate, the necessity of committing them to sustain existence. Assuming the knowledge of law by the sinners of the Gentiles, the apostle Peter declares of them that 'they shall give an account to Him who is ready to judge the quick and the dead.'

Now, let the guilt involved in heathen life be estimated by us as we will. Our measure of it will be according to the mental standard we have formed of the Divine claims, and of human obligations; of the self-revelation of God in nature, in the economy of the human mind, and the arrangements of human society, and of man's capabilities of discerning that revelation; of the clearness of the voice of God in the living soul, and the susceptibility of that soul of attending to it; of the traditional knowledge that has come down from Adam, and the ability to distinguish and sever it from what of false is mixed up with it. When we have made large deductions, possibly much *less* than God himself will make, there will be still left a vast accumulation of guilt lying at the door of every individual soul, and with which every conscience, when quickened into life, will be for ever burdened.

But there is another aspect of this subject. Let us reduce our estimate of the heathens' guilt to the very lowest degree, admitting every extenuation that may be pleaded in arrest of judgment; still the fact of their moral unfitness for all holy and heavenly enjoyment remains. Assuming, for a moment, that there is no guilt—can its absence remove the fact of a morally corrupt nature—a nature loving evil and hating good? And whither do all the issues of such a nature tend but to misery? We may know nothing of the sphere in which they are to spend eternity; but we do know unto what heathen hearts and tastes and predilections tend. We do not know the bounds of their habitation in the world to come; but we do know that the congenialities of their souls are with evil, and against God, and we need to know no more to produce a conviction, as deep as it is solemn, that there is in their case the absence of all meetness for blessedness. 'Without are dogs, sorcerers, whoremongers, idolaters, and whosoever loveth and maketh a lie'; and this not merely by a judicial award, but by a moral necessity, which prevents them from entrance. We see that the great law of adaptation prevails in the natural, and we may be assured that it holds equally in the moral world. Birds for the air, fishes for the sea, beasts for the forest;—everything for the sphere to which it is physically adapted. So the good for the regions of goodness; the wicked for 'their own place.' Instead then of canvassing the precise amount of guilt, let us grasp the palpable fact of a depraved nature, and be assured that its issues, wherever they are found, must be in regions of wretchedness.

There is still another light in which the salvation of the heathen may be viewed. The question may be taken out of the region of disquisition, and be answered by an appeal to fact. The *possible* future salvation of the heathen is best understood by ascertaining whether any of them are partakers of an *actual present* salvation. Is there in Scripture any salvation treated of, save that which consists of deliverance from sin, in its dominion over the soul, and in its guiltiness toward God? Are not forgiveness and holiness linked together in the Divine mind, and found together in man's history? Are not the justified and the sanctified one and the same in the kingdom of God? Did not Paul believe his converts to be partakers of salvation, because he saw them washed, sanctified, justified, in the name of the Lord Jesus and by the Spirit of God? Can the heathen be saved hereafter who is not saved *here?* Can he become holy *beyond* this life, who has no principle of holiness imparted *in* this life? If so, it must be by another dispensation, of which no mention is made in the Scriptures. The question, then, narrows itself, Are the heathen saved in this life from sin? Do they become holy? Are they in any legitimate sense made partakers of a divine nature? Is there any redeeming power within them—any resurrection life from trespasses and sins? This, like all other facts relative to character and conduct, must be the subject of experience to themselves and to observers.

We have had within the last hundred years abundant experience, and of the most diversified kind. Our missionaries have lived among the heathen, eat and drunk in their wigwams, or in their mansions, slept in the encampment of the nomade tribes, and on the couches of citizens of heathen towns. The key to the heart and to the mental hidden experience of great bodies of people has been obtained—the living language, the index to all their thoughts and feelings, aspirations and experiences. Have the missionaries, then, found a heathen people or a small section of it *saved from sin,* its power and rule, abandoning evil, pursuing good, loathing falsehood, loving truth, developing any signs of deliverance from that to which others are subjected? Are there any clearly defined individual experiences? Did Morrison find a Chinaman, or Carey a Hindu, or Moffatt an African, or Williams a Polynesian, or Johnson a negro hungering and thirsting after righteousness, bearing the fruit of the Spirit? The author is inclined to advance to the utmost verge of hope on this subject. He is prepared — with regard to India from experience—to admit that there do sometimes here and there present themselves those who seem to desire deliverance from evil; who, as it were instinctively lay hold of the truth and disentangle it from falsehood; who evince some predilection for the good, in principle or conduct; whose eyes are open to discern much of the evil around them; who occasionally condemn it with their lips. Even from the casual congregation, suddenly convened in a Hindu village, never perhaps again to be seen and addressed, has stood out, here and there, one and another towards whom the evangelist was irresistibly drawn, and over whom his heart yearned, on whose brow candour seemed written, whose manner evinced seriousness, whose inquiries indicated a love of truth. But these cases, how few—units among tens of thousands; and from the nature of the case, how unsatisfactory; seeing there is so much of the seeming in human, and especially in Hindu character; and that those whom one is drawn to love, on occasionally hopeful appearances, are often further from the kingdom of God than those of a more repulsive standing. Nay, it has happened that those who had on the first hearing of the gospel excited most hope, have on a fuller acquaintance with it, developed the radical evil of their heart, and sunk in one's estimation below those to whom they had seemed superior.

There is another fact whence we may derive some consolation. From those who have been brought to Christ from among the heathen, have been some who had for previous years seemed to be under a Divine guidance. There have been manifestly the leadings of Providence, sometimes as marked as those which led Cornelius to seek Peter; and there have been also preparatory teachings and monitions which could not be referred to any other source than the Spirit of God. Instances drawn from these classes do not indeed necessarily show that there are spiritual processes in heathenism analogous to those which mark the dispensation of the gospel, but that, when God has a people to call out from heathenism by the ministry of the gospel, he prepares them by sundry methods to obey the call. Although the appearance of truth-seeking minds among the heathen, and the fact that those who do emerge from heathenism have been under Divine teaching prior to their hearing the gospel, may not justify a conviction, yet they may surely warrant a hope, that in the masses of vileness drawn from the vast sea of heathenism and to be cast away, a few jewels may be discovered and owned that shall shine in the diadem of Christ; that from the chaff which the wind bloweth away there may be gathered into the heavenly garner a few precious grains of wheat. Whatever elements of hope there may be in cases of either kind, let them be received; and whatever just ground of generalisation, let it be adopted. We can afford to dispense with no consideration that has a germ of encouragement, though at times the hope may seem to be against hope.

But how do these individual cases bear on the great question of the salvation of the heathen at large? Is it enough for us to know that a heathen *may* be saved without the gospel, in the presence of the indisputable fact that the heathen as a mass *are not saved?* Are we to fold our arms in the hope that the wind which bloweth where it listeth may breathe on some dead heathen soul, and place him among the sanctified, when, on looking around us, the generations of heathen are living and dying *unsanctified?* If we make a mere speculative possibility, or even a probable contingency, outweigh a multitude of patent facts, are we not trifling with the interests of imperishable souls?

Let us view this subject still further in the light of Scripture—a light to which, if we blind ourselves in this matter, we shall be left in utter darkness. First of all, let us consider it as illustrated by the genius, and scope, and bearings of the gospel. As regards God, it is an offer of justification, and a medium of sanctification. As regards man, it is a scheme of mercy, a plan of salvation. It is hence morally certain that the world to which it is addressed is under judicial wrath, and unsanctified, and therefore in a lost state. The offer of reconciliation involves rebellion; the promise of forgiveness implies wrath; the offer of justification involves condemnation; of holiness, depravity. The gospel otherwise would be an anomalous institute, its provisions would be unnecessary, and its preaching a solemn mockery.

Again, let us observe that the rejection of the gospel, according to universal admission, involves increased condemnation—that most abandoned sinners are represented as finding the day of judgment 'tolerable,' in comparison with those who reject the offer of mercy. How can we reconcile the wisdom and goodness of a dispensation exposing some to such increased condemnation, from a refusal of its blessings, unless there is a necessity for it, to the justification of others. If men without Christ are not in a lost state, wherefore preach him to them, when the moral certainty is that they will reject him, and incur increased condemnation? Where are the 'unsearchable riches of Christ,' and where is the 'grace' given to apostles of preaching them, to their almost certain rejection on the part of some, if the heathen are in a state to dispense with them; in other words, if they can be saved without them?

Surely, the gospel, coming with such tremendous penalties of unbelief, is no glad tidings to men, unless they are in very truth in a state of condemnation without it. We should scarcely wish to witness the flight of the 'angel having the everlasting gospel to preach unto them that dwell on the earth,' thereby increasing human responsibility, were we not assured that men without that gospel were exposed to God's judicial wrath. The certainty that to some the ministration of justification will be 'death unto death,' is only tolerable from the equal certainty that to others it will be 'life unto life.'

We can bear only to preach Christ crucified—a certain stumbling-block to the Jew, and to the Greek as certain foolishness—when we know it also to be to 'them that are called' the power of God, and the wisdom of God. We can consent only to increase the responsibilities of the heathen, when we consider that all would otherwise be without salvation. The only consolation in the certainty that by unbelief some will be 'lost' through the gospel, is that some are saved by it who would otherwise certainly be lost. That all are already condemned is a sufficient plea for offering salvation, although there may be involved the consequence of the increased condemnation of some.

Those who will be saved, will be so absolutely, and would not have been saved but for the offer of salvation in the gospel, and their acceptance of it.

Further—let us consider the terms of the original commission to preach the gospel. 'He that believeth shall be saved.' Is not the inference inevitable, that those who are without the gospel, are not amongst the 'saved.' If already saved, the belief of the gospel could not introduce them into salvation. Again, Christ enjoins that 'repentance and remission of sins should be preached in his name among all nations.' Can we forbear the inference that, apart from that name, and without that preaching, the Gentile nations are in a state of unforgiveness? Further, the Lord Jesus, when he gave his commission to Paul as a minister to the heathen, spoke of the objects of his mission thus: 'The Gentiles unto whom now I send thee, to open their eyes, and to turn them from darkness unto light, and from the power of Satan unto God, that they may receive forgiveness of sins, and inheritance among them which are sanctified by faith that is in me.' Let us remember these are not the words of a Jew viewing Gentilism from the stand-point of Judaism, and with the Jew's distinctive prejudices, but of One who viewed them from the stand-point of eternal truth, and intuitively knew what was in man—Gentile as well as Jew. The heathen are in these words declared to be internally blind, as well as in outer darkness, to be subject to the power of Satan, to be unforgiven, and unsanctified. This is surely a state incompatible with salvation.

Coinciding with the terms of the commission is the language in which it was carried out. The apostolic preaching was, 'Believe in the Lord Jesus Christ, and thou shalt be saved.' 'Whosoever believeth in him shall receive forgiveness of sins.' 'I am not ashamed of the gospel,' says Paul. What reason does he allege? 'for it is the power of God unto salvation.' This involves that those who are without the gospel are in the opposite state of condemnation. Agreeing herewith are the terms which relate to the conversion of the Gentiles. 'As many as were ordained to eternal life believed.' 'Then hath God also to the Gentiles granted repentance unto life.' The *spirit* in which the apostles fulfilled their ministry, also, testifies their conviction that the salvation of men depended on their instrumentality, and could not be effected without it. 'I endure all things,' says Paul, 'for the elect's sake,' that is, for the sake of those who, by their instrumentality, were to be called out of the mass. 'I am made all things to all men, that I might by all means save some.' It is here evident that men were viewed by him as not partakers of salvation, apart from their reception of that truth which he strove to present in the most conciliatory manner.

Let us further consider the language in which the apostles addressed the primitive converts. The apostle Peter writes to the scattered strangers of Asia

Minor, as those who were 'once not the people of God, but are now the people of God; who had not obtained mercy, but now have obtained mercy.' Paul gives thanks on behalf of the Colossians for the 'hope laid up for them in heaven,' and thereby leads us to infer that there was no hope for them ere they believed. He bids them 'give thanks to the Father who had made them meet to be partakers of the inheritance of the saints in light.' Their condition, then, was once the converse of all this. They were not meet, but most unmeet, and under the power of darkness. He tells them also that they were once 'alienated and enemies in their minds by wicked works.' He addresses the Ephesians as being 'by nature the children of wrath, even as others'; as having been 'dead in trespasses and sins'; as having had 'no hope, and without God in the world'; as once 'afar off'; as formerly 'darkness.' Language such as this could not have been applied to the converted Gentiles if they had been viewed as having any portion or lot in salvation. Yet these special passages are but illustrations of the spirit of the apostles. They might be multiplied, but we haste to the conclusion. Gratefully recognising the shades of moral character, and degrees of moral culpability, to be found among the heathen; laying hold of all that is encouraging that flows from the mercies of God; apprehending his adorable nature as love, and his holy exercises of compassion and long-suffering; and even soothing ourselves with a hope that there may be some from among the heathen who love righteousness and hate iniquity—we cannot shut out the conviction that the heathen world is a 'lost' world; that there are no mansions for the heathen, as such, in our Father's house; that they have no inheritance among the sanctified; that there remains for them no rest, as for the people of God; that as they are 'without God,' so are they without hope; that their admission into heaven involves the greatest possible anomaly, as repugnant to all that is true and good, and subversive of all that is stable in the Divine administration. Did not the moral Governor himself interfere—an impossible presumption—the very stars in their courses would fight against their entrance into the realms of light and glory; holy intelligences would shrink from the contact of the unholy, and all that is powerful in nature and gracious in morals would combine to purge itself from the 'uncircumcised, and the unclean.' It is a deeply rooted conviction of this character that has sent our missionaries to their labours, and keeps them there. All, in their several trying spheres, tell the heathen that they are willing to live and die in their midst that they may save some, who, but for their labours, would be lost. Closer than galley-slaves to their oars, the spiritual labourers cleave to their work, knowing that on it depends the salvation of their fellow-men.

From such a conviction, indeed, the feelings revolt, although the judgment assents. Difficulties rise up and threaten to overpower us. We tremble at the conclusion we have drawn, and are made to examine again our authority, and test our principles. And it is only when we find no alternative left than that of rejecting the scriptural authority, that we again fall back on our declared conviction, and say, 'Let God be true, though every man a liar.' It were no difficult task to explain away scriptural statements on one hand, and fritter away heathen responsibility on the other, till we made the state of the heathen infinitely less woful; but we should be cutting away from under our feet the very foundations of faith in natural and revealed religion.

There is one objection which we think it meet to answer ere we conclude this chapter. The universality of heathenism is, to some, the strongest ground of hope of the salvation of the heathen; or, rather, it precludes the idea of their condemnation. The fact of multitudes seem to modify individual responsibility, and to alter individual destinies. Were heathenism confined to an island, or some obscure part of a continent; were its subjects numbered by units and hundreds, rather than millions; were it an isolated fact in human history instead of its staple material; an occasional outbreak against Divine rule, rather than an organized rebellion; a casual anomaly, rather than subsisting by hereditary law and principle; conclusions would be drawn respecting the hapless few such as coincide with Scripture. But the multitude of destinies that are involved is supposed to vitiate the argument, and the conclusion is resisted. Look, say some, at China, with its hundreds of millions; and at India, with a moiety of the population of China; and Africa, equal, perhaps, to India; can these multitudes be 'without hope'? It is relevant to remark that Christians are found herein adopting the very same line of argument which the heathen do. They boldly say to the missionary, 'Do you declare that all these multitudes are lost? If so, we will cast in our lot with them. What they suffer we are willing to suffer. We will live the life and die the death of the unrighteous world.' How fallacious is the argument against future condemnation, drawn from the multitudes of the subjects of it. By what known analogy is it justified? Were the antediluvian sinners saved from the deluge by their multitude? Was not the fact that 'all flesh' had corrupted its way, the reason of the sentence, 'The end of all flesh is come before me'? Did the universality of sin in Sodom save it from fire from heaven? Was Jerusalem saved from destruction because of the myriads who had assembled in it as their last refuge? Does the fact of a densely crowded city save it from the earthquake?

In ordinary providences, do we ever find the Ruler of the universe stay his hand because of the number of transgressors;—sheathe the sword because of the multitude to be slain? Is it not in the Divine government a principle, that wherever the carcase of evil is, there are the eagles—executives of Divine wrath—gathered together? The question of heaven and hell is not one of majorities and minorities, but of personal transgression—forgiven or unforgiven. The inquiry is not as to the number of sinners, but as to the fact of their sins. Every one must give account of *himself* before God. 'The soul that sinneth, it shall die.'—The death denounced is not abrogated by the multiplication of the sinning souls. Even in civil governments, ordinarily, individual transgression decides individual destiny. Whether the prison-house is scantily tenanted or filled, each prisoner will have to stand at the bar. Whether the convict ship departs from our shores with a few convicts on board, or crowded with them, their penal destination is the same.

The argument drawn from universality of transgression ignores the relation of this world to other worlds, of man as a moral being to other moral beings. The universal sin of this world may be but an exception to the righteousness of the universe at large, as the criminals who fill our jails are an exception to the social virtues of the community. This earth may be but the prison-house of a few criminals, when compared with the almost infinite number of 'those who need no repentance.' And judgment on all these criminals of earth, however multiplied in our numeration, may be essential to the government of the vast aggregate of moral beings.

The argument to which we have alluded is, therefore, a treacherous one, ignoring the high probability, that the universal of this earth is but the fractional of the universe, and that the condemnation of this fractional section may be demanded by the high principles of universal moral government—principles of which we can form but the least estimate. Let us not by speculative principles, which are in antagonism to Scripture, destroy our heathen brother 'for whom Christ died.'

The universality of sin only corroborates the statement of the apostle John: 'We are of God, and the whole world lieth in the wicked one.' The fact was indisputable in his era. It is equally so now, and the issues are equally disastrous. We proceed to a conclusion.

From whatever position we view the heathen, there is abundant motive for evangelistic effort. Do we regard merely their condition in this life? They have little happiness, and much misery. They are the subjects of social oppression, or cruelty, or neglect—domestic discord, individual discontent; each soul is disjointed and ill at ease. Do we view them as travellers through this world to another? Then we see them benighted in utter darkness, wandering in the drear mountains of error, or in valleys filled with snares and pitfalls. Do we estimate them as moral beings? Then is the fleshly predominant over the moral, the worse principle over the good. The inner life, if there be a struggle at all, is overborne by the powers of evil from within, and the irresistible force of evil from without. Passion impels, fierce desires agitate the heart; ignorance and prejudice darken and pervert the mind. Do we contemplate them as subjects of a moral government, amenable to law? Then is every command in spirit or letter trangressed, every condition of reward violated, every penalty incurred. Are they probationers for eternity? Then are they at an infinite remove from making their probation sure, and securing the honour, glory, and immortality that shall be given to every one that seeks them. Do we view them in their spiritual relationships? Then are they in a state of alienation from the Father of Spirits, cut off from the source of life, separate from God, and God separate from them. Though 'in the image of God,' ordained to be like him, every feature of that image is gone, and in some we find not merely the likeness of the human, but the devilish. Are they redeemed by the blood of Christ? Then are they ignorant of the ransom and the ransomer, and, in that ignorance, void of faith, and, therefore, destitute of sanctifying power that shall make them meet for the inheritance of the saints. Do we track their course beyond the confines of this world? All is unutterably gloomy—no God, no Christ, no hope. As far as is revealed to us, eternity will open up no new dispensation, wherein to attain a righteousness before God, or sanctification of heart. The evil they carry with them is all-sufficient to constitute a hell. We know of no remedy for that evil in the world to come.

From every point of vision, we see enough to

'affect the heart.' All recorded subjects of lamentation are insignificant compared with this; all other grounds of compassion are feeble; all other incentives to action weak. There is enough here to make us raise our cries to heaven, and besiege it with prayers, as though we would take it by violence; to make us employ every resource for relief, concentrate every power, strain every nerve; nor desist from effort till the awful mass of human corruption be removed, and the whole heathen world rise from its death of trespasses and sins.

CHAPTER V.

THE SEVERAL FORMS OF ANTICHRIST.

The Jew: his opposition to Christ, and Christians.—Infidelity.—Worldly spirit.—Strong grounds of hope.—Mahomedans: their spirit towards Christ—Their relation to Missions: Offensive and Defensive.—The Moslem's future.—Corrupt Christian Churches: Characteristics of Apostasy.—Special aspects of Opposition to Christ.—Spiritual Lies and Counterfeits.—Church of Rome.—Other Churches.—Moral Relations of the above Classes.—Appeal to a Spiritual Church.—Hope for Jew and Gentile only in the economy of grace.

WE revert to the question of the second chapter—What is the aspect of the world towards 'Jehovah and his Anointed?' The division of mankind at the commencement of Christianity was that of Jew and Gentile—the Jew in his *nationality* opposed to Christ; the Gentile ignorant of him. Since then the Jew remains in his unique and uncompromising character, and hostile rejection of Christ. But a portion of the Gentiles has, in the lapse of centuries, come to occupy towards him certain definite positions. Many have believed on him, but multitudes who once received him have fallen away in their generations, occupying a practical antagonism to his person and the truth as it is in him. An Antichrist also, in the person and system of Mahommad early arose, and abides till now. Thus, as we find in heathendom an Atheism, Pantheism, or Polytheism, opposed to or ignoring 'God the only true,' so, apart from it, we meet with faiths and systems which either oppose Christ or practically supersede him. We devote this chapter to the consideration of the several classes by which these faiths are professed.

The Jew is still first, but in an eminence of opposition to Christ and Christianity. Modern Judaism has its prototypes in the spirit and character of the Sadducee, the Scribe, and Pharisee of the New Testament. The Jews evince the same unbelief, ask the same questions against Christ, oppose themselves by the same arguments to the gospel, resist the Spirit with the same stiff-necked pride, and count themselves unworthy of everlasting life, as did their fathers. Dissatisfied with all that Christianity presents of evidence, they still ask a sign; indignant at its doctrine, they still make it 'a stumbling block'; unattracted by its offers of present blessing, in redemption by grace, they seek that which is to come. The exclusive and arrogant spirit of their fathers is made intenser by the lapse of time. They still demand that the righteousness of God should be *their* righteousness; the kingdom of God, *their* kingdom; Messiah, the Prince, *their* prince. They will neither share a righteousness with God, nor salvation with the Gentiles. They occupy a position of confirmed enmity to the person of the Redeemer. The 'Lord's Anointed' is to them Jesus of Nazareth. The 'Son of God' is but the offspring of Joseph and

Mary. 'The Lord our Righteousness' is a Galilean. He whose name is 'the Truth,' was a deceiver. The 'Saviour' was one who could not save himself. They still murmur when told that Jesus is the bread of life, and ask contemptuously, 'How can this man give us his flesh to eat?' They insist that the true Messiah once come, abideth for ever. The prophecy that he 'shall be cut off,' is ignored. His 'lifting up' is to them still an enigma; his 'drawing all men unto him' is a mystery.

They hate Christ for his own sake; they hate him also for the sake of his disciples. Over and against their own persecution of Christ, is the historical fact that those who are Christ's have persecuted them. They hate the instruments of Divine judgments. The wrongs of their fathers, the multiplied woes of all their tribes, tortures, extortions, confiscations, conscriptions, banishments, deaths, rise up like mountains before their vision, and hide from their view whatever is benevolent and disinterested in the professors of the gospel. They have a scroll of history written inside and outside, with lamentations and woe. Their legends have transmitted Gentile wrongs, not to say that still in most countries they either suffer actual persecution, or sustain privations of rights and privileges. They view Christianity, then, as the religion of those who have done them evil. Nor in its actual developments do they witness aught to engage their affections. The mass of Jews located in the regions of the Eastern and Western Churches, come into contact only with corrupt forms of Christianity. Taught by repeated captivities, and divers judgments, to hate idolatry, they see professing Christians practising idolatrous abominations similar to those the prophet rebuked from the banks of Chébar. These they know to be hateful to Jehovah, as were the idolatries of Judah and her sister Israel. They view the disciples of Christ, therefore, as accursed of God, and seek no fellowship with them. Into their secret they desire not to enter. Even in Protestant countries the circumstances of daily life bring them into contact with earth-seeking Christians who manifest none of the qualities by which their own ancient worthies were distinguished. They see in them revived neither the world-forsaking faith of Abraham, nor the calm, steady piety of Isaac, nor the love and fervour of David, nor the patience of Job. They see little of Christ among Christians, and hence they see not that their doctrines are of God.

But the Jew is not only found in a state of opposition to the gospel, but to the law and the prophets. Many have sucked the breasts of the Gentiles only to imbibe poison, receiving as truth a semi-Asiatic Pantheism or the gloss of the neologist. There are infidel Jews, not a few, who see no glory in God's covenant, no truth in God's testimony, no foreknowledge in God's prophecies; to whom all scriptural truth is but a myth, and all the grand associations of their sacred history are but airy figments. Miracle is explained away; prophecy is reduced to wise conjecture. The foundations are destroyed. They need to be again built ere faith in Jesus can exist. They believe neither Moses nor the prophets. To such there is no appeal from the Scriptures that testify of Christ.

What tends greatly to confirm the Jews in unbelief, whether of Moses or of Christ, is doubtless their own worldly spirit. Jacob has become an Esau, selling his birthright for a mess of pottage. It would seem as though, having lost the kingdom of heaven, they were especially desirous to secure the riches of the kingdoms of this world; as though the privation of the spiritual inheritance had shut them up to seek one that is seen and temporal. Without a priesthood and temple, altars and sacrifices, they have made the world the God of their idolatry, and the people offer themselves a whole burnt offering to it. When a dweller amongst the civilized and wealthy, the Jew is absorbed by the love of gain, and seeks the literal fulfilment of the prophecy that enriches Israel with the 'riches of the Gentiles.' When he is ground down by tyranny, he is oppressed with severest cares and corroding anxieties for sustenance. Both alike operate on his soul, shutting him up in indifference to the Divine promises and their fulfilment in Jesus, blinding him to the excellence and glory of Christianity, obscuring all the glories of that kingdom in which Abraham, and Isaac, and Jacob, and all the prophets are to sit down.

Strong, however, are our hopes of Israel. They

are not cast off for ever. Their life is indeed *now* hid, but it is to be found in the future. Prophecy's brightest page is inscribed to them. Christianity itself unfolds to them a glorious future—'All Israel shall be saved.' We gather hope even from their spiritual depression. Signs are not wanting to warrant the expectation that the earnest spiritual Jews may yet, from their very despair, be led to Christ. Hope deferred, already makes their hearts sick. They may still cling to the promises, but it is with fear and trembling. The cry has sounded in their synagogues from century to century, 'Send Elijah the prophet,' but he has not come. They have waited for Messiah, till expectation is wearied; they remember him at their solemn feasts, and pray for his advent, but there are no signs of its approximation. They go forth in the market place to seek him, but they find him not. The surrounding Gentiles mock their expectations, and it would seem as though God mocked them likewise. No people are in sympathy with them, and Jehovah himself is turned against them. And this, indeed, is the very depth of their bitterness, the aggravation of all their woes. They have no proof of Jehovah's presence; no symbol of it meets their senses, nor does a sense of it abide in their hearts. No Shekinah as of old overshadows their mercy-seat. Every mark of former glory is gone, and nothing in God's providence as yet is fraught with hope. They could bear political oppression; they could submit to the barbarity of Mahomadans, or the cold indifference and hatred of Christians. They could brook to be a people robbed and spoiled, if they could only be assured of the Divine favour. They could raise their heads from the waves and billows which pass over them if they could only say, 'Jehovah of Hosts is with us, the God of Jacob is our refuge.' But they are unable to appropriate this language. The cloud in which he dwells is seen by them, not on the bright side, as by their fathers, but on the dark side, as it appeared to the Egyptians. No 'consolations of God' assuage their griefs; no soothing assurance, 'When thou passeth through the waters I will be with thee.' A Jeremiah in a dungeon, or weeping over Jerusalem in ruins, or a Daniel in captivity, are the prophets who supply them with words. Psalms of lamentation, deprecation of woes, or imprecation on enemies, supply them with sentiments and utterances. Yet, as we have said, in all this there is hope. The disappointments of eighteen hundred years are surely a ground of appeal to them to re-examine the foundations of their faith. Their apparent abandonment of God gives force to the suggested inquiry, 'Is there not a cause?' The non-advent of their Messiah emboldens us to charge them with the rejection of the true Messiah. All the admitted facts of their disconsolate history, their expatriation, their privation of a temple and a priesthood, and all the privileges that once distinguished them, save the possession of the 'oracles of God,' which, however, they no longer enjoy exclusively, furnish them with so many strong proofs that God has departed from them, and us with so many pleas for their turning to 'Him whom they have pierced.'

Nor do we conceive that their temporal depression is without hope. They are 'minished and brought low through oppression, affliction, and sorrow; bound in affliction and iron; their hearts are brought down with labour;' yet out of this very depression the Lord may gather them out of the lands to himself. Their wretchedness may induce them to listen to the voice of the Comforter; their oppression may urge them to hearken to Him whose yoke is easy and burden light; their exceeding poverty, especially in the Eastern nations, may be an incentive to seek imperishable riches. The remembrances of their past and present sufferings, will make them the more accessible to the disinterested love and patience of the missionary, who, in the spirit of the apostle, 'will to the Jew be made a Jew,' that he may save some. Setting aside speculation, we may affirm that Christian disinterested love will be God's method of saving the Jew.

'For with love,
Stony hearts will bleed.'

The Jews are, moreover, accessible above many other objects of evangelistic efforts. Five millions constitute an ample missionary sphere. Although as a people they may be scattered, finding a home in every land, yet they have their great centres. As though reluctant to lose sight of their fatherland, standing with shoes on their feet, and staff in their hand, ready at God's signal to 'pass over' into the land, still of promise—they are found in densest numbers and closest organization in the countries adjacent to Syria. Large communities have dwelt for centuries in Russia, Poland, Austria, European and Asiatic Turkey, Arabia, and Northern Africa. In almost all those places they are of easy access, and the local authorities to which they are subject offer no hindrance to their conversion. The Mahomadan thinks no worse of the Jew if he adds Christ to his list of prophets. The Pope himself, who debars the circulation of the Scriptures among Christians, allows the Hebrew New Testament to be distributed to the poor degraded Jews of Rome.

Another advantage is, that they practise no social exclusiveness, neither is there domestic seclusion. Families may be visited by the Gentile Christian, and children are often committed to the missionary's care. There is an absence also of a strong ecclesiastical centre of power and influence. No longer does the Sanhedrim 'judge any man' as in the days of old, and obtain a Pontius Pilate to carry out its unrighteous decision. Rabbis may denounce conversions, but their influence has narrow limits. Jewish excommunication is now a feeble thing. No civil power stoops to be the executive of Jewish persecuting law.

There is, moreover, intelligent mind whereon the evangelist may work; mind of high, if not the highest type,—which has produced a Neander and Tholuck, sustains much of continental literature, and embraces much of professional science. The several ancient types of mind coeval with the Jewish are deteriorated. Where is the Assyrian, with its high power of conceptions and formation of analogies? Where the Greek, with its philosophical and analytical tendencies? Where the Roman, with its juridical science, its powers of ethical disquisition and historical delineation? All these types have become, if not obsolete, yet degraded. The Jewish cast of intellect remains in its integrity. It has retained its vigour from a more or less intimate connection with the great intellect of the world—'the Father of Spirits.' There is an encouragement in this. Does Christianity appeal to mind? It is found in the Jewish race. There is indeed a cloud over that vigorous intellect, and still worse, a veil over that heart. Yet when it shall turn to Christ, that veil shall be taken away. Moreover, the Jewish mind is still able to take the lead in instructing and influencing others. It has didactic powers and persuasive force. When under Divine influence, it can yet furnish us a Paul and Cephas. Already one out of every sixty Jewish converts is a spiritual teacher of others. Missionary zeal may yet find its strongest centre in the Jewish heart, and salvation to the Gentiles go forth from Zion in the persons of Jewish evangelists. Israel's hope is not cast off. All that is needed to give the Jew liberty of knowledge, and of faith, and of confession of Christ, is 'THE SPIRIT OF THE LORD.'

If Judaism is the crucifier of Christ, Mahomadanism is his flatterer and betrayer. The Jew cries, 'Away with him;' the Mahomadan says, 'Master, Master,' and kisses, but betrays. 'He was a deceiver,' says the Jew; 'He was a prophet,' says the Mahomadan, 'but a greater than a prophet is Mahommad.' Whilst the latter is in advance of the former up to a certain point, his peculiar view of Christ, and sentiments towards him, are at an infinite remove from the truth. To him the *person* of Christ is merely the holy thing born of the Virgin. All attribution of divinity to him is reputed highest blasphemy against God. The *death* of Christ is not even to him an historical fact, being contradicted by his Scriptures, which affirms that Jesus never suffered death at all, but that the Jews and the Romans were blinded, and wreaked their vengeance on an ideal figure. The *atonement* of Christ as a doctrine is not even intellectually apprehended, much less is it believed with the heart unto righteousness. Typical sacrifices are not an element of the Arabian religion, and the great Antitype is denied. Ignorant of the moral attributes of God, of which their own low moral standing enables them to form the feeblest conceptions, and to which Mahommad himself was, in a remarkable degree, blind—having treated of the natural attributes of Deity in most glowing language, but excluded his holiness—they are not distressed about personal transgressions, and feel no need of atoning blood. Wherein they deem themselves possibly guilty, they claim as intercessors Abraham and all the prophets, in conjunction with Christ and Mahommad.

The regal office of Christ, his priesthood and intercession, his government and providence, have no influence on them, being viewed either as Christian figments to exalt Christ, or as being superseded by the offices of one greater than Christ. The virtue of the mission of Christ, according to their view of it, lay chiefly in its preparation for that of Mahommad, whom he is said to have foretold under the appellation of 'Paraclete.' The life and spirit of Jesus are the very opposites of those of their own prophet, and are incomprehensible by them. The genius of Christianity is, also, repugnant to them, as it condemns every feature of their moral character, and the practices which they indulge. The vices which Christ attacked and condemned are their virtues; the virtues which Christ inculcated are their vices. Retaining the characteristics of their respective races and their constitutional tendencies—the Arab, his love of rapine, with his hand against every man; the Kurd, his thirst of blood; the Turk and Persian, their sensuality and love of indulgent ease; the Tartar, his savage love of conquest—they have obtained the sanctions of religion for them all. Polygamy, so honoured as an institute in Asia, has been confirmed by the God of Mahommad; vengeance, and rapine, and blood are scriptural virtues if they are directed against unbelievers. No wonder that with such principles they are opposed to the religion of Jesus, with its monogamy, its forgiving temper, and meek forbearance.

Relatively to Christian Missions, Mahomadans occupy both an offensive and defensive position.

First. They question the basis of Christianity. They say, the religion has no ground-work. They attack the Scriptures as the *writings of men*, and as such constituting *no revelation from God.* 'This is the Epistle of Paul, this is the Gospel of Matthew; these are not the words of God, but of man. I cannot attach my faith to them.' Thus speaks the indignant Mussulman when pressed with Christian truth. The Koran is in his estimation, the writing not of Mahommad but of God; the veritable word having been brought down by the angel to Mahommad. Judging by this standard, they laugh at the faith of the Christian, attaching itself to writings whose authors were known, and 'lived and moved' as other men. The idea of a medial revelation from God is to them incongruous. Further, they attack Christianity as a spurious system. 'Its books,' they say, 'are not genuine; they have been corrupted; first, the Torat (law) by the Jews, and the Ingil (gospel) by the Christians.' 'Where is the true Ingil? where the veritable Torat?' 'Produce *them*,' they triumphantly exclaim, 'and we will believe them.' In detail, they reserve their special attacks for the fundamental truth of Christianity—the divinity of Christ. Professing exclusively to hold the unity of God in its eternal integrity, they reproach the appellation 'Son of God' as direct blasphemy. 'God has no son,' says Mahommad in the Koran; 'God has no son,' reiterates the furious Mussulman, as he hears the Blessed One called the 'Son of God,' and leaves the crowd of hearers with curses on the speaker. 'Whose son is Jesus?' asks the Turk, or Arab, or Indian, of the Christian, with the intention of confounding him in his answer, and loading him with rebukes for his faith.

But the deadliest wrath of the followers of Islam is directed against Christians themselves, making no discrimination between those who are genuine, and those who belong to that corrupt section of Christendom with which they may be conversant. They view them as idolaters unfit to live, as transgressors of both law and gospel by their superstitions, as falsifiers of the unity of God by their reverence of saints. The Arab thinks himself the better man, if he has shed the blood of a Christian. The Affghan gives thanks to Allah that an infidel dog is delivered into his hands. Nazarene blood shed in malice or by accident stains no Mussulman's conscience. He feels he has fulfilled his mission when he has relieved earth of the abomination of a Christian.

If we consider the Moslems in their position of defence, Mahommad is the central man to whom the law and prophets, and Christ himself, have pointed —'The desire of all nations'—'the Paraclete.' His law supersedes all prior law. His is the last mission. As the last prophet, he takes the precedence of all preceding ones. If pressed for a sign, they direct us to his conquests as the most substantial proof that God was with him; or they point to their scripture, and in the words of its author say, 'No sign shall be given to the infidel save the Koran.'

Evangelistic labours among these races have only recently ceased to be an impossibility, and even now are practicable only in certain parts. Mahomadans have still political power in such central positions as Turkey, Persia, Tartary, and Northern Africa. Though possessing little intellectual force, and exercising no influence peculiar to modern civilization, they are absolute within their own territories. He who dares breathe a word against Mahommad in Arabia, Persia, Bokhara, Affghan, and till recently in Turkey, or circulates books directly or by implication condemnatory of Mahommad, is exposed to the prompt vengeance of a fanatic mob, or suffers death by a judicial sentence. The Koran breathes no mercy, and its spirit has been too fully imbibed by its professors to allow them to show any. It is only where they are destitute of civil power, as in India, or forced from strong pressure of Christian power, as is the case of the Ottoman empire, that they can afford to be tolerant.

Yet for all these there is hope. Their political power is yearly waning. History is falsifying the chosen symbol—the crescent. The Euphrates is leaving the banks once so wide apart, and flows in an ever contracting channel ere it becomes finally dried up. And when the civil power is gone from the Mahomadans they have none other left them. When the sword is sheathed, they have no available argument. They lose, at the same time, the weapons of offence and defence. The Koran cannot bear analysis. Its morality cannot brook investigation. Their religious hopes are baseless. Let but the servant of Christ have an open field of discussion, and the people not be prevented from hearing by the terrors of death, and then, by the energy of that Spirit which convinces of sin, the Mahomadans will bow the knee to Jesus. Already, under such circumstances, has the gospel had its legitimate fruit, and in India, and Africa, and recently in Turkey, Christ has had from amongst Moslems his most sincere disciples. But prior to their evangelization, must be the resuscitation of Christendom. Our grand hope for their conversion is in the revival of Christianity in the East. We argue thus from the consideration that when Christians are turned to God and righteousness, the mission of Mahomadans will be at an end. They have been God's sword to punish corrupt professors, but when those shall be converted, wrath will be staid, and the sword thrown away. God will no longer *need* to employ such agents, and they themselves will become conscious of having no work to do, when idolatrous forms have ceased. We are justified also in this conclusion from recent facts. The appearance of genuine Christians in Turkey has done more to convert Mahomadans than any other agency. A living Christianity will avert the displeasure of God; it will also convert the hitherto enemies of Christ.

We advance to a consideration of the remaining forms of Antichrist to which allusion has been made. Side by side with Jewish hatred and Mahomadan treachery, is the corruption of so-called Christians. It is not enough that Jesus should be once crucified by the Jew, and put to open shame by the Mahomadan; apostate churches, called by his name, crucify him afresh, and put him again to an open shame. 'Anti-Christ' appears clothed in the garb of a Christian, and the enemy of God sits in the temple of God.

As there was an apostasy of Judah and Israel from Jehovah, so has there been a falling away of Christendom from Christ; the latter involving far more criminality than the former. The Jewish apostasy was from Jehovah the Sovereign, the Judge, the Lawgiver. The Christian defection is from Christ the Saviour, the Intercessor. The one is from law; the other from grace and truth. The one is from symbols, and shadows, and types; the other from the enduring substance — the everlasting Antitype. The latter is also more widely spread. Empires and nations, and tribes, are comprehended in it. It assumes also a worse type of depravity. As the worst corruption is of the best things, Christianity, the sublimest faith, and the purest life, has been debased into the most puerile creed, and the most corrupt life. Like Israel of old, these new apostates cause the name of God to be blasphemed, and, in addition, the name of the holy Jesus to be dishonoured. They have thus stopped the progress of the gospel of Christ more effectually than his enemies, by giving a false estimate of its nature. The marks of this apostasy are patent, and have been delineated in the Scriptures; idolatry and superstition, perversions of fundamental doctrines and corruptness of morals; perverse representations of Christ and salvation by him, whereby his person is dishonoured and offices obscured; the Scriptures couched in a foreign tongue, or wholly neglected; preaching scriptural facts and doctrines laid aside for ceremonies; and, as a consequence of all this, an absence of spiritual life, and a quenching of the Holy Spirit. The sovereignty of Christ is taken away by the establishment of other and opposing authorities within the church. His supremacy is abrogated by the priestly assumptions of clergy and hierarchies. His spirituality is obscured by the pride and pomp of a carnal sensuous worship. His atonement, 'once for all,' is falsified by the repeated sacrifices of the mass, and its perfectness by the declared need of penances before death, and purgatories after death. His righteousness is hidden behind the cloud of incense of human righteousness. His mediatorial office is annulled by the institution of mediators in the persons of the Virgin and of saints. His priestly character is set aside by the recognition of an earthly priesthood, able to forgive sins and pronounce absolution, and by supplication made to saints in an intercessory relationship. The Christ of such churches is not the Christ of the New Testament. The cross they glory in, is not his cross. His truth is darkened by superstition. They hold it in unrighteousness. And hence, they come short of his holiness.

There is an absence of spiritual discernment and spiritual taste. The churches, as such, have no spiritual life. As they have forsaken Christ, he forsakes them, walking no longer in their midst. Like heathen idolaters, they are given up to believe and make lies. The ecclesiastical systems of corrupt Christendom are indeed huge systems of shams and deceits, and counterfeits, which mock us with names of holy things, without any substance of them. We ask for the doctrine of Christ crucified—they show us crosses of wood, or stone, or precious metals. We demand the doctrine of grace, and they give us a law of works and human merits. We desire to witness the spiritual exercises peculiar to a church of Christ—they present us with empty forms of ceremonies, whose models are either Pagan or Jewish. Instead of worship rendered to a supreme Trinity, such as is required from those baptized in the name of the Father, Son, and Holy Spirit, we witness reverence and homage parcelled out, in their times and seasons, to the Virgin, and to saints and angels. We ask for practical religion, and instead of penitence they give us penances; for contrition of heart, genuflections and crossings. Instead of living faith, they give us dead works; for active love, they deal in traffic with God and men for indulgences; for love to all the saints, we have hatred against the really holy, who love the truth as it is in Jesus; for purity of heart they show us white apparel, or outward cleansings. We ask for Christian morals: instead of the new man, which is created in righteousness and true holiness, we have the old man, which is corrupt, according to the deceitful lusts. While, as far as concerns themselves, we have these substitutes for real godliness and faith, we ask for the gifts of God among them, which characterise true churches, and we are also presented with their counterfeits. For pentecostal fire they show us a material 'holy fire,' coming down from heaven; for the baptism of the Spirit, they present us with fonts, and sprinklings, and crossings; for the unction of the Holy One, which abideth on believers, they give us anointings with oil, and aspersions with salt; for the residue of the Spirit, they show us relics of saints. They have thus gone back to types and shadows, with all the beggarly elements of the world, seeking to be made perfect in the flesh, binding themselves with the very bondage from which Christ was revealed to make them free.

Let us regard these churches in detail.

First in a dire eminence, is the ecclesiastical system of Rome. None others can compete with it. It retains all its prophetic characteristics, and all its historical precedents. It is 'the man of sin,' as though sin belonged to and were centred in it. It still stands out as MYSTERY, in character; the mystery of cruelty, that has not yet been revealed; of licentiousness, that no day has brought to light; of hypocrisy, that no one has thoroughly unmasked;—as MYSTERY, in its organization, comprising and conciliating contrary doctrines, and harmonizing conflicting practices, retaining and cherishing within her bosom sects and schisms, believers and infidels;—as MYSTERY, in regard to the world's knowledge of her, unknown by those whom she beguiles, mistaken for what she is not, receiving homage, and power, and dominion, as a church of Christ, whereas she abides as the synagogue of Satan;—as MYSTERY, in all the vicissitudes of her history; now dethroned, and then casting down thrones; now a captive, and then leading captivity captive;—as MYSTERY, in her yet future, not as to the issue, which will be everlasting destruction, but as to the mode whereby it shall be effected. And, with all its phases of mystery, Rome is a revealed ANTICHRIST—in its doctrines, which rob Christ of his glory; in its worship, which virtually excludes him; in its hierarchies, which rob him of his eminence and authority; in its spirit, which opposes his Spirit; in its influences, which form the most effectual barrier to the kingdom of Christ which the god of this world ever raised.

What an immense falling away of Gentile Christians is presented by the Romish Church. This 'Lucifer, son of the morning,' what a host hath he drawn after him in his fall from heaven! The apostasies of the Jews from God throughout their whole history seem to dwindle into insignificance compared with the great apostasy which numbers millions, and prevails in most of the nations of Europe, a great section of the East, the whole of southern America, and a portion of Africa.

What is the relation of Missions to Rome? Do we seek to convert her? No. The Romish church cannot be said to be the object of evangelical Missions. The Scriptures give us no warrant to suppose that she is to be regenerated. Viewed as a great centre of ecclesiastical power and political influence, and a great mass of moral corruption, she is reserved for destruction. The 'man of sin' is 'the son of perdition.' When fully revealed, it is to be destroyed by the brightness of His coming. We do not pray for the conversion of Antichrist, but for his speedy destruction. Missions may be directed to every form of pagan error and abomination, but it would seem that the Spirit suffereth them not to be directed to that Babylon which is destined to sink for ever in the mighty waters. Yet have we a work to fulfil in relation to Rome. We have to take up the cry, 'Come out of her, my people, lest ye become partakers of her plagues.' God has a remnant which is to be called out. Labours should be abundantly directed to all professedly Romish countries, with the full confidence, sustained by all past history, that the holy seed shall be redeemed from them. Yet none should engage in such labours without a readiness to be 'offered up.' In urging forward to such an enterprise, we cannot but entertain the fear of adding to the list of those martyrs whose spirits already from under the altar, cry, 'How long, Lord, holy and true, dost thou not judge and avenge our blood on them that dwell on the earth?' We need, also, by our Missions to anticipate and thwart Rome in her aggressive movements on the world. She amazes us by her zealous enterprises—from the days of Xavier until now—the number of her converts, and her labours worthy of a better cause and better issues. Rome has been *before* us in China, where she counts her hundreds of thousands; in India, where she reckons a few millions; in Asia Minor and Syria, where she numbers a million of adherents; in the American Continent. She comes *after* us in the South Seas and Africa. Where, indeed, have we possessed Missions which she does not seek to supplant by her own?

The Greek and Russo-Greek, Armenian, Coptic, and Syrian churches differ from Rome, and from one another, in priestly orders and government; in laws and discipline; rites and ceremonies; yet present, each and all, an aspect of degeneracy from the pure religion of Jesus. They are more or less remote from the apostolic type of religion, according to the source whence they received their Christianity, the historical circumstances under which they have since passed, and the extrinsic influences which have been brought to bear on them. Still, while there is a diversity, there is yet a unity—the unity of ignorance of Christ the living one, who abides *in* believers as a quickening power, and who lives *for* them as a justifying righteousness. All of them, as churches, have resisted evangelical influences, especially the Russian and Greek. Where individuals have been enlightened by the word of God, and made a formal or practical protest against the superstition of their respective churches, they have been excluded from communion. The Nestorian church is the only one which has comprehended the light, admitting the true evangelist to share in its own ministrations, and forbearing to excommunicate the enlightened.

The Abyssinian church would claim special attention, as illustrating how low a church may sink in ignorance and superstition, when all foreign elevating influences are removed. Her religion is the very caricature of Christianity. Her ceremonies are a burlesque. She blends the rite of circumcision with the Christian institute. In her calendar, even Pontius Pilate and his wife can command a commemoration day, and Balaam's ass has a festival appropriated to it.

Would that truth did not constrain us to include a portion of Protestant Christendom in the great falling 'away.' Large sections of the continental churches that have protested against Rome, have yet denied the faith equally with her. Orthodox standards are overlaid with Christ-denying doctrines, and an abnegation of the person and work of the Holy Ghost. The liberty bought with the blood of martyrs is converted into a licentiousness of preaching damnatory errors, and introducing heresies and schisms. On one hand, infidelity in sentiment and indifferentism in heart, combined with unchristian practices, stand out in direct opposition to Christianity. To such, Christ is dead and buried, but not risen. His religion is sepulchred and its funeral dirge sung, as numbered with other religions long since dead. On the other hand, where he is professedly honoured, he *is virtually denied.* We ask for a living Christ preached from the pulpits, and we have the frigid morals of a system that cannot convert. We desire to witness a quickening spirit in the worship and life of Christians, and we witness forms so artificial as to reveal their insincerity, and conduct so destitute of holiness, as to demonstrate the absence of all fellowship of the Holy Ghost.

If the lapsed Israelites had cause to fear that their captivity would never return, saying, 'Our bones are dried, and our hope is lost,' and to compare themselves with the disjointed fleshless skeletons of the valley, there is deeper reason, viewing these several apostate churches from the point of mere human vision, to fear the continuance of their more lengthened and calamitous captivity. Who but an Ezekiel, authorized by the Spirit, would venture to say, 'Come from the four winds, O breath, and breathe upon the slain that they may live'? And who, but Jehovah himself, working by his Spirit, by virtue of the intercession of Christ, could quicken these dead ones, and open their graves and cause them to come out of their graves?

Ere we conclude this chapter, let us examine the moral relations of those classes who have passed in review before us, and inquire in what degree they appropriate the salvation of the gospel. As the characteristic of the heathen is that they are 'without God,' so may these be briefly described as 'without Christ.' Yet while this is their primary distinction, they are, equally with the heathen, though not in as broad a sense, 'without God.' We found this statement on the Scripture principle, that the knowledge of God comprehends the knowledge of Christ; that where the first exists, the other follows; and conversely, that ignorance of God is the cause of ignorance of Christ. Corresponding to the intimate relation between the Father and the Son, whereby the Father knoweth the Son, and the Son knoweth the Father, is the fact contained in the experience of those divinely taught, that he who knows the Father attains also to the knowledge of the Son, when externally revealed. The knowledge of either is, indeed, a sure starting point for attaining to the knowledge of the other.

The rejection of Jesus by the Jew had its cause in ignorance of God. He knew of him, he trusted in him, he had highest hopes from him, but his soul was not acquainted with him. He knew him not in his inner being, in his hidden life. Hence, he knew not Jesus, 'the brightness of the Father's glory and the express image of his person.' He was not 'of God,' and therefore heard not the words of God uttered by Christ. He was not 'of the truth,' and therefore did not 'understand his speech.' To them, therefore, Jesus said, 'Ye shall die in your sins.' What applied to the ancient Jew applies equally to others—without Christ—without God. That moral state of mind, those spiritual perceptions, those divine instincts which characterize one who has already known the Father, are in themselves a preparation and qualification for attaining to the knowledge of the 'only Begotten Son.' The rejection of Christ then evinces ignorance of God.

It is true that the modern Jew acknowledges God. The Mahomadan also makes him professedly the centre of his religious life, and repeats his attributes with glowing devotion. The nominal Christian makes the same profession. Yet we believe there is a grand defect in all this profession, a positive ignorance in all this knowledge. Wherefore? Because they know not Jesus. They are blind to the glories of the revealed image of the Father. They are then blind to the glory of God himself. In the case of all, to be without Christ is to be without God. Although, therefore, in their several degrees these classes have much advantage over the heathen, by being in possession of the traditional or written revelation of God, and some acquaintance with scriptural truths, yet in their Christless state they are on the outside of the kingdom of God, and need missionary efforts, as destitute of the essence of salvation.

We close with two remarks. To whom have we addressed ourselves? To the spiritual reader. From him alone we expect a sympathy with our subject, and to him alone we present our appeal. It is evident that the measure of our estimate of the world's spiritual loss is the consciousness of our own spiritual gain; that our sense of its wretchedness in its isolation from God depends upon our 'joy unspeakable' in our nearness to him; our estimate of their destitution, on our realization of the imperishable riches of Christ; our judgment of the dreariness of their state, on our bosom consciousness of the evil of sin, and the glory of redemption. It is only when seated in heavenly places, as risen and sanctified believers, that we can rightly judge the state of those who lie in the dark valley, dead in trespasses and sins. Jewish and Mahomadan unbelief will be apprehended by us aright, only when in the exercise of a living appropriating faith. The evils of the bondage and superstition of corrupt churches cannot be estimated unless we are enjoying the liberty of Christ and walking in his truth.

If the evil elements of which we have treated are found in ourselves, we are unable rightly to pity or abhor them in others, and there will be a corresponding reluctance to relieve. A supine and carnal church cannot appreciate the state of the world. It is ignorant of the standard of comparison, and is destitute of the needful inward contrasting experiences. Hence, Missions engage the sympathy of the few, not of the *many*. The ability to discern their glory can be possessed only by a spiritual church having the mind of Christ, the illumination of the Spirit. We appeal, then, to a spiritual church to estimate the wants and woes of which we have treated. We appeal from the reader, if carnal, to him as spiritual, and conjure him to view all the dark facts contained in these chapters 'in the light of the Lord.'

Our second remark is this. The apostasy of heathendom on one hand, and of the greater part of Christendom on the other, is so thorough, depravity is so great, prejudice so inveterate, that the work of regeneration manifestly belongs to the Lord alone. If there be no virtue now flowing from Christ in his exalted state—if no pentecostal Spirit to open hearts that are shut, and wound and bruise the obdurate; if no 'Paraclete' to convince men of sin; if there be no Head to appoint, and qualify, and direct his own servants; no active energy of an Almighty God; no special providence over all things to the church of a King on his holy hill of Zion; no abiding presence in the church — then is the task of evangelization utterly hopeless, and Missions are, of all things, most absurd in their pretensions, however benevolent in their idea. Then may we say of the world, there is no hope; and of ourselves, there is no encouragement. Then may we fold our arms and wait for the judgment. But there is ONE able to do exceeding abundantly above all that we ask or think! He wrought in the beginning of the Church's history. He worketh hitherto. 'He shall not fail, nor be discouraged till he have set judgment in the earth.'

CHAPTER VI.

MODERN APOSTOLIC MISSIONS.

Missions:—Their Moral Force.—Their Extensive Range.—WESTERN AFRICA:—Madeira.—Coast of Senegambia and Guinea.—First Converts.—Introduction to Inland Countries.—Prospects.—SOUTHERN AFRICA:—Early Labours.—Onward Progress.—New Era.—EASTERN AFRICA:—Abyssinia.—Exploratory Journey on the Coast.—MADAGASCAR:—Human Co-operation excluded.—The Agency of Christ conspicuous.

OUR apprehension of the moral and spiritual state of those who are the objects of evangelistic labours will enable us to appreciate the work of the evangelist, or rather Christ's work in him and by him. The force that resists, determines the power of the lever; the pressure it bears, the solidity of the fulcrum. The edge of the plough and the skill of the cultivator are tested by the hard unyielding nature of the soil; the skill of the helmsman, by the adverse power of the winds and waves. And so in human operations that have to do with human minds and hearts; the teacher is approved according to the intellect he acts on, the moralist in proportion to the depravity he seeks to rectify, the spiritual labourer according to the ungodliness and carnality of the heart he seeks to impress. Of what force and moment are the 'acts' of modern apostles? We may judge from the description already given of the moral and spiritual state of the world. What those 'acts' are; what difficulties have been overcome, and triumphs achieved, we proceed to specify from modern missionary annals.

'See,' said the apostle of Burmah, turning a globe and pointing from island to island and continent to continent, 'how the gospel light girdles the world.' And so it does, though not in an unbroken stream, nor with a uniform intensity. Mission stations are scattered over the world—here like solitary stars, casting a faint light on the thick moral darkness, and there like constellations almost entirely dissipating the blackness of the night.

If we view these stations as aggressive agencies on moral evil, then does the church occupy so many outposts in the realms of the great enemy by which they shall be able to overcome, and spoil, and make captives to Christ. If we view them as stationary repositories of truth, then are there so many centres whence offers of salvation may be promulgated.

The world lacks the bread of life, and storehouses are opened in every direction for its free distribution. It lacks a balm for its woes, and our Missions are so many dispensaries for its bestowal 'without money and without price.' The world is already more blessed, inasmuch as the elements of blessedness are found in it scattered far and wide.

NORTHERN AFRICA — the scene of so many triumphs in the early ages, once studded with flourishing churches, yielding its great writers, and illustrious teachers, and its martyrs, has yet to be made a missionary sphere. Lying, as it were under the shadow of Papal Europe, it has known Christianity only in its corrupted forms; and under the domination of Mahomadans, it is closed against genuine Christian effort. The Jews, however, who occupy the towns on its coast, have been the objects of missionary labour, and Scriptures are freely circulated amongst them.

Leaving this land of darkness, and following the track of the early discoverers of the other parts of that great continent, we arrive at WESTERN AFRICA. In one of its first discovered islands, whose perpendicular hills seem to rise at once from the depths of the ocean, have been witnessed triumphs of the gospel, not exceeded in ancient or modern times.

A pious physician,* as he ministered gratuitously to the sicknesses of the natives of Madeira, told them of the disease of sin, and of the Great Physician. He dealt with individual souls, and those souls were first inquiring, then convinced, then converted to Christ. Few had ever seen a Bible; all were ignorant of its contents. Its circulation among them excited attention, and induced earnest desires, first, to read, and then to understand. This led to the foundation of

* Dr. Kalley.

adult schools. In six years, more than two thousand attended them, half of whom became proficient readers, and able to search the Scriptures. In three years, the influence of the truth had spread so far and wide, from mind to mind and family to family, that the people, hungering for the bread of life, came in numbers to hear the Scriptures read and explained. The homes of many were distant, and the path lay over hills three thousand feet high; but distance and toil presented no obstacle. Sabbath after Sabbath more than a thousand assembled to hear of Christ crucified, till at length the number reached five thousand. What a scene was that—the physician with Bibles before him ready for distribution, preaching salvation by the blood of the cross—the people sitting in the open space near his house surrounded by the vine trees clustering with grapes, or on the ridge of a mountain rising perpendicularly above them, and valleys stretched out before them; and what a swell of voices was that which arose in the open air and was echoed by resounding hills, of evangelical hymns of praise and prayer. And all this in one of the outposts of Rome, where Romish doctrine alone had been heard for ages, and spiritual worshippers had never been convened. And such a result—the issue of private faithful labours without any ordinary aids. But Rome, ever thirsting for the blood of saints, now moved to avenge itself on those who in word or deed forsook her communion. The physician himself was interdicted, then imprisoned. Several of the inquirers were cast into prison; the walls of which resounded with the hymns of their new faith and ardent loves.

Let us observe the sequel. An evangelist,* with an exhausted frame, yet possessing undying vigour of soul, strong faith, and ardour of a first love, followed to take the place of the first labourer now silenced. The place was to his mind 'the forlorn hope of Christianity,' and he knew not but that bonds and imprisonments might await him. A brother forbidden to preach on pain of banishment or death—twenty-six native Christians shut up in prison, and one of them under sentence of death—thoughts of them would arise at times before him, and suggest a dreary prospect. But his heart was strong, trusting in the Lord. He proceeded to his destination, and the sheep at once found in him a shepherd. Affectionately did they commit themselves to his pastorate, and diligently wait on his ministration, assembling singly, or in small groups, to inquire the way of Zion, to reveal their experiences of scriptural truths, and to seek, from human instrumentality, light and strength. The zealous invalid received them cordially, and, like Philip or Paul, preached to them Christ, that Saviour whose all-sufficiency he had newly found, and preached him as the all in all of the sinner, and the fulness of the saint. The doctrine dropped as the dew; the same Spirit which had accompanied the efforts of the first labourer came down to bless these

* Hewitson.

new efforts, and souls were more abundantly drawn by the exhibition of Christ's love. They apprehended the salvation which is by Christ, in its simplicity and freeness; Christ became in them the hope of glory. Several were filled with joy and peace in believing. The terror of bonds and imprisonment did not deter them from confessing him. Even converts of the weaker sex declared themselves ready to die for the Lord Jesus! More than sixty converted Romanists, of whom there was hope that they were 'called to be saints,' soon commemorated the death of Jesus in a private room; no longer adoring the elements themselves, but Him whose broken body and shed blood were shadowed forth by them. As soon as an ingathering of souls into the kingdom of God had taken place, persecution assumed a virulent character. Converts were tracked, seized, and examined. Animosities broke out in families and villages, and threatened the lives of believers. Threats were uttered from the highest ecclesiastical authorities, to check and crush the movement, to suppress the circulation of the Scriptures, and root out the newly rising faith.

Viewing the gathering evil, and looking beyond to the Power that should make their wrath praise him, the evangelist exclaims—'They make war against the Lamb, but the Lamb shall overcome them, for he is King of kings and Lord of lords; they make war against the saints, but the saints shall overcome through the blood of the Lamb and the word of his testimony.' What was the effect on the minds of the converts? Did they fail? were they discouraged? Far from it. Their patience and fortitude were such as to amaze the evangelist himself. One after another was imprisoned for testifying against the 'man of sin'; yet still the word of God spread, and still were souls ingathered, and built up into Christ as living stones. Private meetings were held among themselves, for reading of the Scripture and prayer, and proved seasons of grace. Forestalling the evils that would arise to the scattered sheep, when the shepherd should be smitten, this wise 'watchman of Israel' instituted a special class for training a few of the converts in more grounded and accurate knowledge of divine things, who, after his departure, might be able to teach others the oracles of God. From them he appointed elders and deacons. Others, he sought to qualify for the direct work of the ministry in doctrine. They were in his judgment called by the Holy Ghost to that office. Thus had the work assumed that eminently apostolic type, the raising up of an indigenous ministry, and the Holy Ghost himself had made overseers of the flock. A church of Christ was not only called, but organized, in the very midst of Antichrist.

Clouds that had been long hovering burst, and the storm raged. The missionary, threatened with a legal prosecution, retired, not shaking off the dust of his feet, but entertaining a hope of speedy return. And now the converts were called to endure a great fight of affliction. They 'bore joyfully' the spoiling of their goods, were beaten, were thrust into prison. Some fled from their homes to the mountains, whither they were pursued by their enemies. At length, the persecuted ones, to avoid the strokes of priestly malice and the ruder assaults of the frantic people, took refuge on board a vessel in the harbour, and leaving their native land, sought a home elsewhere. And as that ship receded from their native shores, what a scene to witness the converts singing their hymns to Jesus, and praying for their persecutors, and those who had fallen back from their profession. Then, indeed, was the triumph of grace, not only over Rome, but over vindictive nature. As persecution waxed hotter and hotter, one company after another left Madeira, till more than eight hundred souls, bodily and spiritually, bade farewell to Rome for a settlement in the land of civil and religious freedom. Thus has Madeira furnished her 'Pilgrim fathers' to the American Continent. May their families become rooted and grounded in the faith, and yet send back to their brethren and companions the gospel which was delivered to them. In reviewing the work at Madeira, we may well take courage to labour amongst those who apparently belong to Antichrist, but whom Christ has chosen for himself, resting assured that Christianity has 'no forlorn hope'; that grace can lay hold of all, and Christ will be magnified in all.

Advancing southward, we come upon that bold coast with its towering headlands and promontories, far spreading, palm-covered plains, and high table lands, which we successively term Senegambia and Guinea Coast. The Gambia, Senegal, and Niger, besides smaller rivers, flowing over immense tracts, pass through wide estuaries into the Atlantic Ocean. Pagans and Mahomadans inhabit the villages or towns on the coasts, with a sparse population, but as we advance inland, and enter the valleys of the great rivers, we meet with populous towns and villages. The inhabitants belong to the great African families named after the famous African rivers, the Nile and Niger, or to mixed races. These are divided into tribes and families, under the rule of kings and chiefs, or under patriarchal government. Although fearfully debased by superstition, and sunk low in the moral scale of being, they possess many elements of civilization, extensively cultivating the soil, and producing rude but useful manufactures.

When first this sphere of missionary labour was occupied, there existed every conceivable discouragement. The Atlantic then was covered with slavers of the great European nations. Factories were built on the coast to receive the slaves brought from the upper countries. The traders were hostile to Missions, and more than once did they excite insurrections, and oblige the missionaries to withdraw. The aspects of heathen life were of the most revolting character. The tribes were hostile to each other, and wars and tumults prevailed. The kidnappers waylaid the solitary traveller, and organized bands waged war for the purpose of making captives whom they might sell. The climate was deadly, and nature herself seemed to combine with man to keep the missionary away from a place wholly given to murder and rapine.

The social life of the natives was one of extreme degradation; their religion was in the literal sense devilish—for the pagans were worshippers of devils —the practice of witchcraft destroyed social peace, and the arbitrary cruel measures taken to detect and punish them made each man an object of suspicion to his fellow. Numerous languages and dialects rendered converse difficult; the population being broken up in petty tribes and sections distinct from each other. Such difficulties were sufficient to deter missionary effort, had it not been actuated by undying Christian love; but though disasters followed upon each other till the hearts of good men were sickened, the work once begun was unweariedly prosecuted, and has never been abandoned. Sympathy with the wrongs perpetrated by slave dealers on Africans—pity for their extremely debased state, and latterly the great success reaped on the coast, have conjointly urged the prosecution of the missionary work in this part of Africa on every section of the church of Christ in Britain and America. As the result, Missions are now studded all along the winding coast, from Bathurst to the Cameroon Mountains, from the Gambia to the Gaboon. The great slave repositories, Lagos, Badagry, are occupied by the missionaries. The African lion has thus been bearded in his den. Portions of the Scriptures are translated into the rude dialects of the tribes of the coasts as well as the language of Yoruba.

The first decisive success was witnessed in the Christianization of the liberated negroes. These were re-captured by British vessels from the slavers, and set on shore at certain settlements in the Sierra Leone colony. Speaking different tongues, all strange to the missionary, and often to each other; in the utmost social disorder — wives without husbands, husbands without wives; children without parents, and parents without children—in the bereft state in which they had been kidnapped from their homes; with emaciated bodies, with former vicious habits increased by the disorganized state in which they had now found themselves; these hundreds and thousands, drawn up from the reeking holds of slave ships, formed a singularly unique section of humanity whereon to expend missionary labours, and test the great power of the gospel.

Faith alone would view the work as not hopeless; but faith itself could scarcely have formed large expectations, as their ignorance and vice rendered futile the first efforts employed. But what will not Christian love attempt; and what will not the Spirit effect, accompanying such attempts? The extremities of human weakness were made the occasion of Divine strength, and the utmost adverseness of circumstance was made the season of God's prosperity. Of these slaves, many entered into the liberty of Christ. They had never known that their hearts were black as well as their skins; but this knowledge was now attained under Christian instruction by the convincing power of the Spirit. Sable faces were bedewed with the tears of penitence, and knees were bowed in private and public prayer, and the sons of Ham entered into a greater blessing than many of tho sons of Japhet have obtained. Their amulets and charms were discarded; their fear of devils ceased; their viciousness of heart and life was rectified. One negro after another came with a broken and contrite heart to receive forgiveness from God; one after another experienced the melting power of the cross of Christ. Churches were formed with hundreds of communicants. No station where there was godly labour was without its blessing. The gospel vindicated its power of ruling over every adverse circumstance, and the experience of renewed souls was illustrated among a people who, from their original history and present circumstances, seemed furthest from the kingdom of God. Where sin had abounded grace did now much more abound.

This first success, great in itself, derived increased value from its bearings on the evangelization of Africa, and constituted a new era in the history of its Missions. These emancipated negroes had been snatched away from their several families and homes in the inland countries, hundreds and thousands of miles distant. Now that Christianity had refined their natures and given them closer affinities, they desired to retrace their steps to their native lands, with the double purpose of rejoining their friends, and communicating that precious treasure they had recently found. Acquainted with the people and languages of the inland kingdoms, they accompanied the European missionaries, aiding them most effectually in the attempt to gain an introduction for the gospel. Amongst the foremost were two African youths, set free in boyhood and trained under different sections of the church, who became ordained ministers, and led the way to their fatherland. An exodus is now taking place with a yearly increasing energy; not from captivity, but from liberty, to enjoy freedom in paternal homes and communicate a spiritual freedom to others. Emancipated negroes are finding their way from the darkest of all lands, South America, to their own inland African homes. As the result of this providential guidance, the chiefdoms of Yoruba have been entered, and Missions established which have gathered their first-fruits to Christ. Even the kingdoms of Ashanti and Dahomy, countries whose name has been a terror, and whose chiefs, or kings, have been the oppressors of their own people, and the scourge of their neighbours, have allowed the evangelists to take up an abode in their midst. A few years ago such a consummation could scarcely have been expected. Where the slave trade obtained its many victims, and mutual violence and treachery prevailed; where human sacrifices had attained to a monstrous profuseness, which made the capitals so many Golgothas; the man of peace—the harbinger of liberty is admitted, and in his hands are portions of Scripture, translated into their own tongues, declaring the reconciliation of God to man, and beseeching man to be reconciled to God. Hitherto the jealousy of chiefs, and the animosity of priests, have, in a measure, resisted the onward course of Missions; yet here and there congregations of faithful men have been gathered, many of the rising generation brought under instruction, the gospel freely preached, and by some eagerly believed. Small churches have been formed, which have exemplified true religion. In Yoruba, women who have believed have endured much persecution, yet have retained unshaken faith.

In the slave marts of Africa there has, indeed, appeared One whose form is known by many to be that of the 'Son of Man.' He has come and claimed one and another as his own redeemed; plucked them out of the hands of the great slave-holder, struck off their chains, and made them free.

Hope and faith point to a glorious future for Western Africa. The promises already travail with 'a glorious day of grace.' A voice has already said, 'Cry.' Many are preparing a highway for the Lord. The church of Christ has obtained a 'base of operations,' in the partially evangelized stations on the coast. Fifty thousand professed Christians, of whom a third are counted worthy of discipleship, constitute a nucleus of future churches; and if discipline and needful supervision be exercised, and spirituality maintained by their pastors, they must soon prove a spiritual power amongst the surrounding Pagan and Mahomadan people. The sons of the first converts offer themselves, and are trained for the ministry. A goodly number have already approved themselves as good 'ministers of Jesus Christ.' While there is such internal prosperity, liable, it is true, to be modified by the idiosyncrasies of the African mind, there are outward circumstances of the most hopeful character. The navigation of the great rivers has commenced, and communication is opened up with the dense population on their banks, some of whom, with a dim consciousness of their own moral necessities, and deeper convictions of the anti-slavery tendencies of the gospel, have demanded missionaries. Instead of scattered remnants on the coast, we shall soon have access to populous tribes; for a floating population, difficult of access, we shall have to evangelize nations with their perpetual homes. We can use the experience we have already acquired of reaching the African mind, and we have as aids those willing to be Christian colonists from the already converted negroes of the coast. The prestige of the white man as the destroyer of slavery spreads far and wide, preceding the steps of missionaries. Some of the chiefs have made treaties with Britain for the suppression of that abomination. Others are ready to follow their example. Ere its extinction, there may be 'a struggling gasp for life.' European nations may desire to patronize it under another form and name, but the spread of Christianity on the continent will effectually destroy it. It brings peace and good will amongst men; in its track follow civilization and commerce.

Occupying a commanding position, and within sight of slavery states, is Liberia—land of the free, with free institutions, free subjects, a free gospel, and an indigenous ministry. In possession of a large territory, affording abundant scope for labour and colonization, she is, we hope, destined to act an important part in the regeneration of the continent.

South Africa has been the scene of labours never exceeded in perseverance, self-denial, and strong endurance. Missions have passed through many phases, from the extremes of hopelessness to prosperity; now broken up, and now re-established; yet with all their fluctuations, they are, viewed collectively, waxing stronger and stronger, extending their outward range, and becoming inwardly consolidated. The first attempts were to convert the Hottentots, Bushmen, and Caffres; three as unpromising specimens of human nature as degraded Africa itself could furnish. The former were sunk so low in intellect and morals, so socially debased, that the civilized doubted their right to the *name* of men, and certainly denied them the rights and privileges of humanity. A great portion were kept in the most servile state, and debarred from instruction, first by the Dutch, then by the British Government. They were also exposed to grievous impositions, watched with suspicion and treated with a deadly hatred by the settlers. Those who retained their freedom dwelt in an almost savage state, preferring the chase to husbandry, nakedness to clothing, filth to cleanliness, the woods to dwellings. They knew nothing worthy the name of knowledge. No idea of the Creator existed, and to entertain it, or any of its associated ideas, when suggested, was to them difficult. Amongst such a people, in the presence of difficulties as extreme as could be found in any shape, did such devoted men as Schmit and Vanderkemp labour, stooping that they might raise them, dwelling with them in the jungles that they might induce them to dwell in villages, sharing the trials and dangers of an isolated position that they might obtain safety for them, braving the persecution of their own countrymen in order that they might obtain for them a double liberty. The earnest pleading of Afric's friend* with the colonial and the home governments secured at length liberty for the oppressed, and an impetus was given to the prosecution of African Missions.

The first successes had been on a narrow scale. They had vindicated the capacity of the Hottentot to understand the gospel, and his susceptibility, in common with other degraded portions of mankind, of being sanctified by the Spirit. They had also rewarded the extraordinary love and faith in which

* Dr. Philip.

the pioneers of Missions laboured. But now, divers striking providences showed that the path of Missions lay onward, and one missionary after another visited the tribes beyond, and found an introduction into more numerous and influential communities.

In this onward course, one river after another was crossed, and successive ranges of hills, with their table lands. Here and there, as chiefs might give permission, or tribes might seem disposed, would the missionary fix his habitation in the very midst of the heathen. Where the population was scattered, he would, with greater independence, lay the foundation of a settlement that should be the model of civilization, the centre of Christian influence, the nucleus of a Christian people, the congregation of families, the starting point of evangelization. Under the missionary's mechanical skill, and the industry of his newly-gathered people, the parched land is irrigated, and streams are made to flow in the desert, that the people may have sustenance. Houses and schools arise, and in prophetic language, 'The desert blossoms as the rose.' Many a 'vale of grace' in this way has beautified, and many a 'happy prospect fountain' has enriched, the barren plains. The South African missionary is a man that has known discouragements. The heavens above have, at times, refused to pour down the needful rain on which the lives of his dependent community have rested; the earth has refused its produce, or the murrain has seized the cattle, or a more ruthless invader has laid waste the whole settlement. The labours of years have been destroyed in an hour, and loftiest hopes have been at once laid low. The heathen, also, have by their heartlessness, and suspicion, and stolid indifference, made severe demands on the missionary's faith and patience.

They have looked on and wondered at the issue of such novel undertakings in their midst. During many a weary year have they failed to understand the missionary's motives, or catch the purport of his message. The doctrine of the Creator has been received by them as a curious speculation, rather than a fact; responsibility to him as as an invention of the missionaries; the judgment, and especially the resurrection of the body, as a fiction. Tribes professing independence, as the Batlapi, resolved that they would never bend the knee to 'King Jesus.'

Yet the work has been onwards. In this mission and in that, according to that viewless wind that bloweth where it listeth, one and another inquirer would come and desire to understand the 'Word of Life.' A nucleus, once formed, always enlarged; the spirit of inquiry, once existing, always spread; converts, once made, always induced others; and as the issue of a slow, steady progress, churches are now in existence amongst Griquas and Bechuanas which severally number hundreds of believing souls; whilst among Caffres and Zulus, Fingoes and Hottentots, churches have been gathered, of no mean number. At an early period, miracles of grace that have made friends wonder and confounded enemies, were wrought amidst the savage, hard-hearted, truth-despising tribes—miracles which produced an indelible impression on the men of that generation; the tradition of which has been transmitted from father to son, and the fame of which, spreading far and wide to remoter tribes, made them also willing to be taught, inspiring them with the feeling that this was the day of power of a conqueror to whom they also must, sooner or later, subject themselves.

Not the least interesting spot of Southern Africa is that whereon is raised the leper hospital of the Moravians. This people, whose mission, approaching nearest to the Spirit of Christ, seems to be to seek and save that which is all but utterly lost, to enter every forlorn hope, to occupy every discouraging field, to labour on the most sunken specimens of human nature; who seem to be most 'at home' where all is dreary, and to luxuriate where physical and moral barrenness are most conspicuous, have gathered together, for daily teaching and instruction, the paralytic, the leper, and the incurably diseased, of all classes, and making that curious congregation their special charge, seek to bring the sinner of the eleventh hour to the Saviour, and to fill the last expiring moments of disease-smitten men with penitence and faith, that shall open up a sinless and sorrowless eternity.

A new era of African Missions has been just inaugurated. As labours amongst the Hottentots of the Colony were but preliminary to evangelistic efforts among the northerly and more influential tribes, so these latter would seem but the precursors of other and far more important enterprises. As each station has been formed in the wilderness, it has pointed to a region beyond, and the missionaries having come to the term of known tribes, have been induced to find out the unknown. The traveller whose name is not only in all the churches, but in all scientific circles, with an adventurous spirit unparallelled in the history of travels, and with a faith not exceeded by any Christian enterpriser, has traversed the regions of Central Africa, laying them bare in their latitudes and longitudes to the geographer, and opening them up with their dense population of negro tribes, which inhabit the valleys of the large rivers, or skirt the lakes, to missionary enterprise.

The unmistakeable call of God has been heard bidding his servants advance from their small outposts to take the citadel of heathenism in Africa. A chain of Missions may be established from the mouth of the Zambesi to the western coast. What the traveller in Eastern Africa dared hope for, the establishment of a chain of missions from the estuaries of the Niger, Congo, and other rivers to their sources, may have its counterpart realized in the south, until at length Africa, opened to the evangelist by communication along her rivers and over her hills, both in the northern and southern portions, may receive the word of God in all her multitudinous tribes, and yet find the curse of Ham and Canaan removed in Christ.

EASTERN AFRICA is yet rather the land of hope than of success; like Canaan, which, although a land of promise, had to be spied out ere it was conquered. The Coptic and Armenian churches in Egypt have received a little light from the circulation among them of the Scriptures, and here and there are souls in earnest to know and live the truth. Still, as churches, the light in them is darkness, and missionary labours have yet to reveal any marked success. One grand hope for Egyptian Christians is the fact, that numerous readers of both sexes have been raised up by devoted labourers, and the Bible has free course. Cairo, and more recently Alexandria, are the centres of missionary effort. A few men of apostolic character sought to evangelize Abyssinia. They entered into a country almost barbarous, and witnessed a Christianity almost Pagan. Their effort to establish a mission was unsuccessful. Romish missionaries had preceded them, and excited hostilities to Protestant missions. But let us herein mark the providence of God. As soon as the missionaries were banished from that part of Eastern Africa, reluctant to give up the land, one of their number gave himself to the work of exploring the eastern coast, with the design of thence entering the interior, and founding a mission among the Pagan or Mahomadan tribes.

We follow the footsteps of a Krapf and a Rebbman in those regions, with amazement at the men, and adoration of Christ in them. Few can speak like them of dangers by sea and by land, of unrelieved solitariness, of journeyings in valleys and on mountains, whose name and locality had been hitherto unknown. Now they coast the shore in some native craft, the best procurable, but scarcely safe for voyaging; and now they travel many a weary journey on foot. By night, they hear the howling of wild beasts; by day, they are exposed to attacks from merciless robbers. We follow them with an increasing interest, now separated, and now in company, to Usambara, to the Jagga country, and to Ukambani, with the immediate object of opening up to the church permanent spheres of labour.

One successful exploration is the call for another, till tribe after tribe and people after people are discovered. They dwell among them in closest association; sometimes unutterably distressed at the sins and abominations they witnessed; at other times filled with an overpowering compassion of their godless state. Again and again does fever lay either traveller low, and threaten to remove them and destroy their Mission at the same time; but an imperative necessity sends them onward, as soon as physical strength will admit, and Krapf lays the foundation of a Mission among the Wonicas, with words that bespeak a soul rising above all circumstantial difficulty: 'The Mission *must* be commenced, and should death or life result to me, I can now have no regard to sickness whatever.' When prevented from journeying, they apply themselves to the framing of vocabularies of the barbarous tongues, or translate into them portions of Scripture. Difficulties yet confront the East African Mission which nothing but a faith and perseverance of the same type as that evinced by these first explorers can overcome. The climate is deadly; chiefs are capricious; the people are mostly sunk in vice and inertness; and there are few external motives to induce them to seek instruction.

Meanwhile, during the prosecution of all these exploratory journeys, and these repeated attempts at opening up Africa from the coast, Abyssinia, the lost hope of more than fifteen years, is again opened to Protestant Missions, and the original labourer returns. The Jesuit is banished by a self-constituted monarch, and the Protestant missionary is allowed to take his place. Jerusalem itself has also proved a centre whence to send a small company of men, who, with meekness of spirit, calm boldness of heart, and an all-conquering faith, seek to subdue the land to Christ. From another point, also, has Abyssinia been entered. At the time when the Western evangelist was debarred an entrance, God raised up servants from the East. Two Abyssinian youths, placed by their father under the instruction of missionaries in Bombay, were there taught and converted to Christ. Their hearts' desire was to revisit their native land, where spiritual darkness reigned, and there to diffuse the light of life. They were committed to the grace of God and sent as evangelists. They have founded a school, and discreetly distribute the Scriptures in the Amharic tongue, and by a holy example are seeking to diffuse the gospel. The history of Christian Eastern Africa has yet to be written. Its records will, we trust, soon tell of successes corresponding to the zeal and self-denial of its early evangelists.

Ere we leave the African continent, let us turn our eyes to the island of MADAGASCAR. This is the household word of British Christians; and few are the Mission stations where its name is unknown. Her martyrs have already a fame, wherever a Christian literature exists. Their endurance is an example by which the missionary of other lands strives to strengthen his own weak ones, and brace them for conflicts. We do not point to this island so much as the scene of 'Acts of the apostles,' as of the direct working of Christ himself. There has been more of God and less of man there than elsewhere. The beginnings were bright and hopeful. Royal favour had patronized the Mission; a few converts had enrolled themselves. Parts of the word of God had been given to the people in their own tongue; a rising generation was receiving in the schools the first principles of Christianity. A reverse, which was not a reverse, takes place. Political change ensues, and the head of the Government is opposed to Christianity. Missionaries are banished, Bibles seized, schools suspended, converts scattered. The church is ready to say of Madagascar, 'Her glory is departed.' Not so. God has removed men that he may reveal himself. He puts human instrumentality far away, that he may draw near. He creates a blank all around him, that he may freely move in it himself. Ere he resuscitates the souls he has chosen for himself, he will send far off all seeming co-workers with him, that the excellency of the power may be of God and not of man. He had allowed his servants to lay the foundation, but himself will build the structure, and there shall be no sound heard of axe or hammer. He will put aside his general principle of instrumentality, lest his people should deem him dependant on it, and show that, whilst he condescendingly allows believing men to convert sinners and establish saints, he can and will, when he sees fit, dispense with them. He will prove, also, to a gainsaying world, that truth, applied by the Spirit of truth, is still, as of old, omnipotent, and that human weakness needs only to be brought into contact with his strength, to overcome the world and endure all things. He strengthens the converts, and they are enabled to resist an imperious woman's will, as opposed to God's righteous law; they suffer unto death for the truth of Jesus, or are bought and sold into slavery, and suffer bonds and imprisonment.

The terrors of a Diocletian age pass over them; or rather, the history of the first three centuries of persecuted Christianity seems repeated and condensed into a few years of experience of the Madagascar churches.

The threat and design of the Government are to extinguish the new religion, and to erase the name of Christ from the books, and consciences, and memories of the Christians. But all is in vain. The blood of the martyrs becomes the seed of the church. God raises up converts to succeed those who have suffered. In the solitude of glens, they meet and pray. Bibles are secreted from enemies, and on every precious opportunity are its promises read. Believers are multiplied. Persecution gathers, and not scatters; strengthens the cause, rather than weakens it. The British churches are distressed at sad rumours, and make strong intercession. Above the cries of suffering martyrs they hear a voice, saying, 'Be still, and know that I am God.' They fear lest sufferings should extinguish the infant band of believers: Christ is seen strengthening with all might, calling out and adding saved ones to his church. Again, they essay to send British evangelists, but they are prohibited from settling: the Lord himself goes on to propagate his own religion without them, shewing his own word to be imperishable seed, and his own Spirit to be an all-quickening power. After a lapse of years, wherein no European labourer has trodden the soil for the purpose of preaching, the church, though bereft of hundreds of disciples, is still multiplied, strong in faith, and patient in endurance. Christ has walked in the midst of her. She has not been moved. Destitute of teachers, the Malagasys have had the

Great Teacher; without fixed ordinances, they have enjoyed One who is better than ordinances. Whilst we are writing, a relentless persecution is going on, and our hopes of calm and peace are disappointed. The cruel tangena is yet applied, and the spear still transfixes the witnesses of Christ. Of such a history—dark yet bright, terrible yet joyous—what shall be the future? Will not the cries of those under the altar be heard, and persecutions arrested, and the future of the people of Madagascar be that of holiness to the Lord?

CHAPTER VII.

MODERN APOSTOLIC MISSIONS.

LANDS OF THE BIBLE: — A Pioneer's Statement. — Formation of Armenian Churches.—Chain of Missions.—Interesting Facts.—Elements of Encouragement. — NESTORIAN MISSIONS: Their Success.—DESERT REGIONS. — INDIA: A Sphere Well Known —of Multiplied Labours—of Faith and Patience—of Triumphs —of Hope.

WE have hitherto treated of countries, all whose associations with the gospel are but of yesterday. We have now to treat of lands whose religious records are as ancient as history itself, in which has originated our own religious life, and whence we have derived a name and place among the royal nations and holy priesthoods of a regenerated world. We refer to the lands of the Bible—of patriarchs, and prophets, and apostles; of a heathendom whence Abraham was called, and a Christendom whence were gathered the primitive churches,—lands by whose rivers or on whose mountains prayer has been wont to be made, or sacrifices to be offered; whence truth has sounded and resounded; and, more than all, where the Spirit of Truth has effected his mightiest triumphs, and Christ had earliest disciples, as the dew of his youth.

A pioneer of Missions,* in the extensive regions washed by the Mediterranean, looked with an anxious eye for a hopeful sphere of labour. All around him was thick darkness. He saw lands trodden down by the Moslems, and the remnants of old eastern churches as much politically enslaved as they were in spiritual bondage. The idolatry and superstitions of so-called Christians, the unbelief and hatred of Jews, and the pride and wickedness of Mahomadans, forced from him the statement—'In whatever way I come in contact with the minds of men in this country, it seems like walking amongst the scattered walls and fallen columns of its ancient cities. All is ruin, confusion, and desolation. It is an open valley, full of bones, "they are many, and, lo! they are very dry."' How should a genuine church of Christ be formed in such lands? Religious innovation was resisted by the Turkish power, whose centre was at Constantinople, and whose offshoot was in Egypt. The Patriarchs ruled their respective sections of Christians with a sway second only to that which Rome exercises, inflicting both ecclesiastical and civil penalties. Souls seemed barred 'under the ribs of death,' in a sepulchre within a sepulchre. Society seemed shut up in the bonds of destiny, to retain that specific form, Mahomadan, Jewish, or Christian, in which it had been moulded for centuries.

The missionary traveller looked around in hope, but that hope found nothing outward that could

* Rev. Pliny Fisk.

sustain it; it could only exist while the soul looked to the Divine promises. For a work which seemed thus beyond compass, only two or three labourers were in the field. Within thirty years what a change, and that change what a harbinger of other and still greater changes.

Let us in few lines trace the gracious process. A few missionaries from across the Atlantic first directed their attention to the Jews in Western Asia, and hoped that a remnant might be found among them. As of old, however, the Gentiles were ordained to eternal life, and believed. The word of God, circulated among the Armenians, was the grand instrument of vivifying the dead. The errors of their own church were by it revealed—the sin of their own heart laid bare; the righteousness of Christ was made known by the convincing Spirit of truth; and a few, chosen and true, took up their cross and followed Christ. On one hand, they had to meet Turkish persecution, and on the other, to face enemies from their own ecclesiastical communion. They were hated of all men for the name of Him whom they had apprehended, but they seemed to attain at once to the eminence of faith—submitting to the loss of their goods, separated from their families, and at length excommunicated. Mutual sympathy, and the necessities of their position, led them to form a distinct community. A holy joy in Christ distinguished their early gatherings. The unction of the Holy One rested upon them. They found the true baptism.

They enjoyed the true spiritual presence of Christ in the eucharist, and fruits in outward life ensued corresponding to such a fellowship. Gradually churches were formed here and there, and a native pastorate raised up. Spiritual influences were radiated from these centres. The word of God was studiously read, preaching eagerly listened to, and believers were multiplied. The providential interference of Him who is Prince of the kings of the earth, gave these new communities, under Turkish rule, a civil and ecclesiastical status, as Protestant Christians; and, with this new organization, sincere inquirers hastened to connect themselves. At this early period, what is the issue? In connection chiefly with those Transatlantic brethren referred to—but inclusively of other brethren whose missions are addressed primarily to the Jews—a chain of mission stations girdles the regions of Asiatic Turkey, extending from Constantinople westward, to the borders of Persia, and from Erzroom northward, to Jerusalem on the south. Central stations, or their outposts, are scattered over the ancient regions of Asia, Mysia, Galatia, and Phrygia, Syria, and Mesopotamia. They skirt the banks of the Hiddekel and Euphrates, and crown the summits or lie in the valleys of Ararat, Lebanon, and Hermon. With the boldness befitting those who take possession of a land in the name of Jesus, our American brethren have arranged their missions in four great centres, with their subdivisions—Armenian, Syrian, Assyrian, and Nestorian. These are occupied in force by more than a hundred American labourers, whose efficiency is doubled by the aids of native pastors and evangelists.

More than a thousand genuine believers united in fellowship from a community of five thousand Protestants, congregated in above forty churches in this sphere of labour, attest the reality and extensiveness of the work of God. There are historical incidents involved in this rapid progress of the truth in these regions, which present us with a renewal of past scenes, a repetition of ancient facts. In the birth-place of Paul, a Christian community receives the testimony of his epistles. In the city of Lydia, one of the seven churches, are found Protestant brethren and sisters, whose hearts are opened to receive Christ. In Ur of the Chaldees, is a native church, wherein the faith of Abram is renewed in the home of his childhood. Jonah, calling to repentance, is again heard in the region of Nineveh, and the gospel resounds on the banks of the Tigris. Antioch again witnesses believers of the same type as those she first called Christians. In Damascus, a congregation of Jew and Gentile celebrate Christ's ordinances in a way that strikingly contrasts with the superstitious observances of the Syrian churches, and wins the respect and confidence of the Damascene Mahomadans. In the street called 'Straight,' there is a depository whence Syria may obtain the Scriptures of truth in all the languages of her tribes. The old Phœnician city of Sidon has its congregation of Christians, and young men are found reading the Scriptures in the spirit of the Bereans. Tyre has sent its deputation to the missionary, asking for some man of God to come and instruct them in the way of life. In the missionary residence near the summit of Mount Lebanon, looking out on the 'Great Sea,' do Syrian youths study European sciences in conjunction with the sacred Scriptures. In the villages at its base, divided into mission districts, the gospel spreads more freely than in other parts of Syria. At Beyrout, a church is gathered, and Arabs listen to the gospel, while females, hidden by a veil from strangers' gaze, listen unseen to the word of life. The Samaritan women again hear the word of the Messiah by the well of Jacob, and the men ask his servants to 'abide with them a few days.' As there is a dew on Mount Hermon, and the cedar again thrives on Lebanon, so the glory rests on Mount Zion, where a few, comprising Jews and Gentiles, meet in holy fellowship, young disciples learn the same lessons as were taught to Timothy, and Christian benevolence seeks to heal the sick of all names and creeds. The birth of Jesus finds its readers in Bethlehem, and the words of Christ in the synagogue are read in Nazareth.

Viewing this vast field in connection with the Syrian Missions of other brethren, not an element of encouragement seems lacking. First, an earnest demand for the sacred Scriptures extensively prevails, always a forerunner of enlightenment and conversion.

The press scarcely keeps pace with the demand. Arabs and Turks, Armenians and Greeks, with Syrian Christians, in their own tongues, and the characters familiar to them, read the wonderful works of God. The incorruptible seed is scattered far and wide by winds adverse or prosperous, by the storm or by the breeze. Now a few persecuted ones, forced to flee, introduce the Scriptures into new localities; and now a solitary preacher, unbidden by man but loving to spread the truth, carries them into Eastern hamlets and homes. Those Scriptures have shed a light that is as the dim twilight, yet is the precursor of a morning. They have prepared a way for the Missionary, removing prejudice, informing the mind, predisposing the heart, and often leading to practical results in the abandonment of unscriptural practice. Regions where the Bible has found an entrance are those in which the evangelist knows the way of the Lord is preparing.

Again, there are indubitable marks of Divine agency, apart from human instrumentality, and beyond its range. God is raising up apostles from beyond the organized churches, even as he raised up a Paul, or Apollos. In one place we find a Kurd chieftain, formerly a Mahomadan, preaching the gospel to his countrymen, and making from them disciples, ere he has heard a human teacher. In another region, a Syrian preacher brings over a whole village to Protestantism by the doctrine of Christ crucified, ere he himself has seen a Protestant congregation. The missionary in Damascus receives six of his disciples with a letter from their teacher, asking for instruction as to the Protestant order of religious services, and requesting a visit. He is entreated by the missionary to come and visit him. He enters Damascus in all his native, untutored wildness, to visit the missionary, and from his own narration, and the testimony of others concerning him, he forces on the missionary the conviction that he is God's chosen vessel, as 'the apostle of the Hauran.' The Kuzzelbash, beyond the sphere of direct evangelistic effort, are open to receive the truth. A few of their number receive a Turkish Testament, and, in the face of severe persecution, profess faith in the Redeemer. They declare that the adherents of this new faith already number a hundred souls. Another people, the Kurds, east of the Euphrates, hitherto a wild, untractable people, many of them hereditary robbers, have already received some portion of that gospel light and influence which are radiating in adjacent countries.

An indigenous ministry, characterized by self-denial, vigour, intelligence, and piety, is already raised up, and the willing liberality of native churches goes far to support them. Young men offer themselves with a devoted spirit to the seminaries, for ministerial instruction. The ordination of a pastor from among the Armenians after the simple model of scriptural appointment, attracts more than fifteen hundred witnesses, whose minds are solemnized by the simplicity of truth, and hearts beat high with hopes of the glorious future which God is opening up to their long benighted race.

Further, external difficulties are in a great measure removed. Persecutions, formerly so rife, are diminished. The Jewish excommunication has lost much of its terror, and rabbis persuade rather than threaten. The anathemas of dignitaries from among the Greeks, and Druses, and Maronites, strike only the ear. Thus an effectual door is opened to multitudes to hear the word of God, and profess the true faith.

The best of all is, the work in its latitude and bearings is not distinguished by the marks of a mere ecclesiastical, much less sectarian or political movement, *but of a deeply religious progress*. The Spirit of God works, convincing of sin, and testifying of Christ, and churches consist of 'living stones,' who are themselves built up into Christ in all things.

The Mahomadans are amazed as they witness a purer form of Christianity rising up in their midst; they lose their former arguments against the religion of Jesus, and are drawn further to inquire. The heavy pressure of intolerance is also partially, if not wholly, withdrawn, and a way opened for their public confession of Jesus.

God is thus showing that from the Eastern churches he has not hid his face, nor cast them away from his presence, nor taken his Holy Spirit from them. That Spirit, as though these lands were still the heirs of peculiar blessing and delightsome to himself, is dissipating the darkness of centuries, protracted from the time when the candlesticks were judicially removed by the Heart Searcher of the churches, and Christ again 'walks in the midst of the seven golden candlesticks.' If asked by believer or infidel for a sign of the Lord's presence in his church, we point to Western Asia. Nowhere have the providences of Him who is head over all things to the church, been more conspicuous; nowhere have there been more marked exemplifications of his grace.

What an interesting portion of the history of Missions in Western Asia is presented us in what has taken place among the Nestorians. These people, few in number, scattered over the hills of Kurdistan, or in the Persian valley; oppressed at different times by Persia, by the savage Kurds, and by the Turkish Pashas; enjoying the sympathy of none, objects of jealousy to all, from the measure of liberty and independence they have ever claimed; retaining a purer faith and more scriptural practice than others of the lapsed churches; less corrupted by tradition, and less fettered by their ecclesiastical organization; manifesting more candour and accessibility to the truth; repugnant to the Romish missions, yet fraternizing more readily with the evangelical teachers, opening their churches to their preaching, placing their children under instruction, studying the Scriptures given to them in the Syriac tongue by the missionary translators; allowing of innovations on their own ritual or religious practices when proved to be corrupt—they present already, as the fruits of short but energetic labours, the aspect of a saved nation; rescued, if not from political annihilation, to which probably their enemies would have reduced them, yet redeemed from an eastern barbarism and from dense ignorance of Christian truth. They are risen and stand upright, to call His name blessed in all their families and future generations. A people who constituted the last refuge of evangelical truth in the East, are the first to receive it back, after it has departed for a while; and those who were the most earnest missionaries of central Asia in the middle ages hold out hopes of again resuming their long neglected mission. To such ends have labours been performed by the Western evangelists, and what rich rewards have already been given to them. We see Grant, the physician of Utica, the first missionary explorer of the snow-covered ranges of Kurdistan, visiting the Nestorians in their rude mountain homes, giving sight to their blind, healing their sick, winning for himself and for his cause a way which no ordinary agency would have opened up. He dwells with them as his own people, joins in their religious worship and commemoration of Christ's death. He thus wins their confidence and love, and makes a way for the truth and those that shall follow his steps. We witness the equally self-denying, though not so exciting, labours of those who dwell by the lake Oroomiah, pursuing their work of education and preaching, whilst exposed to the suspicions and jealousies of Persia. We observe with interest the season of communion, when Nestorians, hungering and thirsting after a purer fellowship than they can elsewhere enjoy, meet to commemorate the death of Jesus, under the presidency of those who first taught them the way of life. Nor can we mark without delight the indubitable operations of the Holy Spirit in their schools, bringing Nestorian girls to receive the Saviour into their hearts in faith and love, converting the school into a sanctuary, and making even secular instructions to be lessons of the school of Christ. And we trace the footsteps of those girls, as they leave the missionary school and family circle, and themselves become centres of instruction in their own families and neighbourhoods, frequently founding schools themselves for the women who in youth enjoyed no similar privileges. What a conviction of their having received the Holy Ghost must pervade the heart of the missionary who looks on this charge and counts the greater number of them pious. And what a spirit of piety must exist in those youthful disciples, whose simple record of their own meetings is, 'These are blessed seasons, for they are sealed with the Holy Spirit.' Verily, though this Nestorian people be least among the thousands of the Eastern churches, yet among them has He undoubtedly appeared whose 'going forth is from everlasting.'

We pass over countries on which we would fain extend remark. ARABIA is not yet 'Araby the blest,' from the possession of the gospel. Mahomadan fierceness and intolerance have there a stronghold, and the Christian traveller's life itself is not secure. Yet missionary zeal has not passed it by. We see the missionary* leave his home at Constantinople, and by way of the Red Sea, reach the Arabian coast; then braving the dangers of a journey among proud and superstitious and murderous Moslems, he seeks out in the inland parts his own countrymen after the flesh, gives them the Arabic or Hebrew Scriptures, converses with them of the Messiah in social gatherings, comforts them in their oppressed and disconsolate state, and directs them to Jehovah as the God of their fathers and their God—precious opportunities, stealthily enjoyed and obtained only by arduous efforts and suffering, and only to be continued for a season. His life is now in jeopardy from robbers and now from Sheiks; one buffets and another swears to kill him, but the servant of God passes through the midst of them unhurt.

Persia will not receive the evangelist. The voice of Martyn and Wolf was heard there, and the labours of one and another distributor of the Scriptures have been witnessed there. To the Jews also has the gospel been offered in needful secresy, but the land is as yet intolerant of all that opposes the false prophet. Turkestan has received the Christian missionary only as 'he that tarrieth for the night'; the blood of Christians has been already shed in Bokhara, and no evangelist dare abide there. The

* Rev. H. A. Stern.

fiercest spirit of hatred to the Christian '*infidel*' is found in AFFGHANISTAN. The vast regions of TARTARY are as yet sealed against mission settlements. Russia westward and China eastward unite in barring all intercourse to the rude tribes under their governments. Many and glorious have been the attempts made to open up a highway for the gospel, but the 'times and the seasons' which the Father hath appointed have not yet disclosed themselves.

Passing over these lands of desolation, whose very darkness is palpable, and whose shadow is that of death, we enter INDIA—the 'high place' of the field of Missions — the sphere on which are centred the thoughts and aspirations of all evangelical Christendom. This country, or rather, this range of countries, this swarm of nations, and storehouse of religions, possesses all conceivable elements of interest, now joyous, now sorrowful. Let us attempt to present them in detail.

India is a well-known sphere. We may safely say that no two hundred millions of human souls in all their important aspects and relationships are so well known to the Christian church as the people of India. Although there is still much further knowledge to be desired, much has been attained. It is known geographically, for its vast extent has been mapped out, its villages and lands surveyed, and the electric telegraph traverses its length and breadth. It has no *Niles* nor *Nigers* whose sources we have to discover, nor large sandy deserts to be explored. The valleys of every river are studded with towns and villages from their estuaries to their mountain sources. The small regions yet unexplored are scarcely the habitations of men. It is known ethnologically, for its nations and tribes are classified; socially, for the castes which form the framework of their social existence are known, and their distinctive peculiarities are noted; morally, for we have become conversant with their fundamental character, habits, and principles as developed in private life, and in their conjugal and family relationships; and above all, it is known religiously, for the religions of India, as practised by the people, in all their folly and wickedness, have been diligently studied, and their original sources have been carefully investigated. The severe study by learned Europeans and missionaries, of the ancient languages Pali and Sanscrit, and the Zend of ancient Persia, have opened up the contents of Shastras that had usurped an unparallelled influence, and the fruits of years' researches are made available for future missionary labours. When Zeigenbalg began his work, he vainly offered a large sum to his Pundit to transcribe the Vedas. No native would then make known the contents of those sacred books, but now they are for the most part patent to the English reader. The more refined Hindus, when charged with apostasy from 'God the only wise,' and the supplanting of his worship by the hosts of mythology, fell back on these ancient writings as the repositories of their pristine faith, and declared themselves as not needing Christianity. The partial translation of the Vedas has driven them from this refuge. In those books, invocations of air, earth, sea, and even the moon plant, take the place of the adoration of the Supreme God.

Again, the Védantas, which were also cited as of divine origin, and containing a system of worship of the Supreme, have been analysed, and found to be only a refined Pantheism. The Puránas, the sources of all the popular religions, the records of the births and renowned acts of the gods, these have also been studied, and some of them translated. The Brahmans boasted of their antiquity; European scholars find them, from astronomical calculations, and still more decidedly from strong internal evidence, to be of modern origin. They asserted their unity, we find the several Puránas to be contradictory of themselves, and of each other; having been composed to favour the worship of particular deities, and their authors contending against each other with all the virulence of sectarian hatred.

The common people, when pressed with the sin of idolatry, had represented their religious worship to be symbolic, or addressed to the representatives of the Supreme Being; we expose it, by their own authorities, in its literalities, its undisguisedness, its grossness, and deformity. As a religious system, we show the nothingness of Hinduism, and lay bare its hostility to the being, character, and perfections of

God. All had united in declaring the divinity of every line of their bulky volumes; we show, from internal evidence, that they could not have proceeded from God, whilst they are entirely destitute of external evidence. Such knowledge of Hinduism, however difficult to obtain, and repulsive when obtained, is of extreme value to the evangelist. In possessing it he occupies a high standing point. By evincing such knowledge he gains an access to the people. He places himself on the same platform as themselves, and a link of something like sympathy binds them. He thus wins a hearing he might not otherwise obtain, and secures a confidence which else would be withheld. He does not stand before them as a wilful, prejudiced assailant, but as a patient student, and, because of his research, able to give a reason for his unbelief. They see that if they worship ignorantly, the missionaries do not ignorantly assail; but, on the contrary, know what they affirm, and what they deny. Thus, by the oral and written exposures of their religion, is the prestige of Hinduism, as a thing unassailable, gradually dying away. Its sanctuary has been violated; its veil has been rent. Confidence in it cannot be restored. The Hindus already feel they must seek other defences of their religion than their Shastras.*

* The reading of an 'exposure of Hinduism' has a marked effect on a Hindu congregation. The statement of facts well known, but which need only to be presented in their moral relations to secure condemnation from them—the exposures of the bickerings and

Another element of knowledge, that is, perhaps, of still more value, is that of the Hindu heart. It is this which has made Hinduism what it is: the Hindu spirit has produced the letter of his religion; and, in learning that prolific source of all that now reveals itself to the senses, we become acquainted with the origin of that which we seek to destroy, more than by knowing the dead letter of the Shastras. That heart was not to reveal itself in a day, nor to one missionary. It required a collective experience, and a process of time, and an accumulation of circumstances, and a variety of events, to unfold itself. Nay, its depths have not yet been sounded. But we have obtained an acquaintance with much of its deceitfulness, its treachery, its subterfuges, and evasions, its reserves and compromises, its hiding-places and defences; and such knowledge is precious. By its means we are better able to apply ourselves to the work of conversion, and to guard, and watch, and tend those who are converted.

Hinduism is not the only religion thus laid bare.

quarrelings, jealousies, and adulteries of their gods, and the several monstrosities and contradictions of the Shastras, their false theories, and erroneous expositions of scientific fact, excite a keen interest, quicken sluggish consciences, and suggest doubts that will never be quenched. Some are, of course, vexed and maddened, as they see the veil drawn from their filthy idols; others are ashamed and confounded; while some few are led to see that no basis is left in their religion for any secure hope, no path opened up in it that leads to glory, and honour, and immortality, and that the true origin of their faith is to be found in the cupidity of Brahmans, and the zeal of sectarian founders.

The Parsees had spoken 'great swelling words of vanity' respecting their Zoroastrian faith, ensconcing themselves behind a set of writings whose author no one certainly knew, and whose language no one could decipher. A Wilson was raised up to study the language, to unravel the Scriptures, and to reveal them as polytheistic and puerile. The Mahomadans also spoke vauntingly as to the inspiration of the Koran, and the human origin and interpolation of the Christian Scriptures. A Pffander was raised up to defend the Christian religion, and carry the warfare against Mahommad into the Mussulman camp.

Further. *India is a sphere of widely-extended and diversified labours.* All sections of evangelical Christendom have concurred in sending their messengers to this land. Even our Western colonies* have given their first instalments of the debt they owe to Christ in her evangelization. The extent of population, accessible at all points, the protection of a Christian Government, and, more than all, the encouraging statements and heart-stirring appeals sent to Europe and America, by labourers in all parts of that wide field, have served to rouse and concentrate attention, which is itself the harbinger of future blessing to India. The results of this collective interest are to be seen in the Missions which form a connected chain from one end of India to the other—a chain, whose links are, indeed, far apart from each other, and here and there a great gap ensues which makes us

* Canada and Nova Scotia.

think we have lost the range, but which, nevertheless, takes a bold sweep, and is strongly consolidated. If we enter India from Central Asia, we find at Peshawar—the extreme northern limit, the very outpost of British Indian territory—a Mission to races but recently come under influence, hitherto proud of their own isolation from the other religionists of India, and which is also hopeful as a centre of evangelization to the Affghans. Punjab—the 'land of five rivers,' of which this station is the boundary, is partially occupied by well sustained missions. In the Himalaya range, even at a height of ten thousand feet, and in a region of perpetual snow and glaciers, is a mission occupied by a small energetic band of Moravians, eager from this centre to act on the Mongolian and Thibetian races, dwelling on the further side, otherwise inaccessible. In the table land is another mission, designed to act on the hill tribes in their native wildness and simplicity, and at the same time to diffuse some gospel light into Chinese Tartary. The missionary traveller has entered the vale of Cashmere, distributed Christian books to its inhabitants, and spoken words of truth to its despotic monarch; and ascending thence, has visited the Thibetian Lama in his mountain monastery. Descending the valleys of the Ganges and Jumna, along the table land of Hindustan, we find missionary stations in the large central towns which line or encircle their banks, till we reach their estuaries in the sea of Bengal. Leaving central India, an almost uncultivated field, and advancing southward along the high table lands, or skirting the eastern and western coasts, we meet with Missions occupying central positions, scattered, not profusely, but still with a liberality that gladdens the heart, until reaching the extreme promontory we cross over into Ceylon, and there find the evangelistic work strongly rooted and freely progressing. Over this vast area, more than four hundred European evangelists are distributed; here, as solitary labourers attacking the weaker parts of heathenism among a rural population, or in small aggregates, so as to act on heathenism as found consolidated in large towns; now acting in the undivided character of gospel preachers, on a people accessible in no other way, as neither requiring nor willing to receive education for their children; and now laying a foundation for the christianization of another generation, by indoctrinating youth in that gospel to which their parents are unwilling even to listen. Whilst most of these labourers are messengers of the European or American churches or societies, a few are found here and there sustaining no such connection, supporting themselves by secular occupation, or receiving casual bounty, while few and far between are some labourers who, in the spirit of the Haldanes, whilst they pursue their own labours, maintain fellow-labourers from their own pecuniary means. This band is strengthened in number, and still more in power and efficiency, by some hundreds of native evangelists, themselves witnesses of the power of Christianity, and living evidences that though it be so novel and exclusive a religion, it may yet be received and practised by the natives of India.

If in *labour* there is blessing, then is there ample blessing in store for India; for *there* are 'labours more abundant,' sometimes divided according to exigency and the adaptation of individuals, but often necessarily concentred in one missionary. There are labours in literature, commencing from the time when the scholar, ardent to speak the language of the people, and willing to give kingdoms for the acquisition, first learns its characters, and unskilfully articulates its words, to the time when his painfully acquired powers are employed in translating or revising the sacred Scriptures, or composing tracts and books of biographies and histories, hymns and psalms, for children and for sages, of didactic exposition or defensive argument, or refutation of falsehood, or, if need be, in editing the periodical that may meet with the perusal of those who would not read a Christian book. A single Tract or Bible Depository in India, what abundant testimony does it furnish to these labours, with the tracts or Scriptures in multiplied languages, composed and printed in the several missionary institutions, evidencing that though the curse of Babel is not removed, and though no linguistic miracle of pentecost characterises modern Missions, faith and prayer, with labour, suffice, in a very short time, to open up a way to the minds and hearts of people of strangest tongue. Again, there are labours in education, ranging in its character from the elementary instruction of vernacular schools, to the literary and scientific instructions of collegiate institutions; and in the objects it embraces, from the orphan children cast in providence on the missionary's care and tutelage for body and soul, growing up under his eye with every tendency to heathenism checked, and a frequent early development of Christian character, and early gathering into the kingdom of God, to the youthful members of a theological class, in training for the holy ministry. There are the labours of the pastorate—the watchings after those so apt to stray, the seeking out of those departed, the warning of the unstable, the teaching feeble converts publicly, and from house to house, the nursing and cherishing of babes, the edification of young men in Christ, and the comforting of the aged. There are labours of preaching; in the school and sacred edifice, in the tent and in the house, in bazaars and from the threshold of shops, under the shady tree and on the steps of temples, by the banks of rivers and in the dharamsalas,* to the small casual congregation which a missionary's voice may collect, or to the dense thronging masses of a Hindu festival. There are labours in itineration—from the transitory visit of adjoining places, to a prolonged period of visitation by land or water, of large districts with towns and villages thickly studded, and a population that seems innumerable; directed towards tribes and people of the most opposite character, of varying

* Places where travellers alight—found in every town and village.

social positions and conflicting religions. Now the missionary finds out the hill tribes, lowly in their own estimate, deeming themselves sunk so low as to be beyond recovery, detached from Hinduism, without a literature or priests, who seem grateful for pity, and are ready to lay hold of any uplifting hand; and now he engages in discussion with those who are wise in their own eyes and eminent in their own righteousness. There are also labours far from insignificant, of controversial discussion, when on set or casual occasions the missionary has to contend, single-handed, against proud, bigoted, wrathful opponents, defenders of their own system and opposers of Christianity, or answers charges against the gospel by the medium of the press.

India is a sphere of unequalled perseverance; where faith and patience have had their severest trials in long delayed success, and almost overwhelming disappointments, where hopeful converts have fallen away, appearances most prosperous have become adverse, measures fraught with expectation have become fruitless in results, and the almost realized has issued in nothing at the very term of its seeming accomplishment. If India has not yielded fruit to God in extensive conversions, it has done so in the holy calm endurance of its evangelists, 'who have borne, and had patience, and for His name's sake have laboured and have not fainted.'

As regards man, their voice has been as a whisper in the thunder, lost to sensible appreciation, in the tumult of scoffers and blasphemers; their wisdom has been deemed foolishness, their entreaties have been mocked, their expostulations derided. They have gone forth bearing precious seed, but their sowing has been on scarped rocks, and they have not returned with their sheaves with them. Scriptures have been read, or given to read, but few eyes have been enlightened to see the wondrous things contained in them. There have been no 'sons of peace' to receive the peace they breathed; no children of blessing to ask for the blessing they offered. A gulf that has seemed interminable, has lain between the Hindu heart and their heart, and debarred its sympathies; and all this because of the distance of that heart from God.

As regards God, the prayer of these labourers has been—'But thou, O Lord, how long?' But that prayer has been answered only with blessings in the soul of the suppliant, with no apparent fulfilment of the petition itself. Such have anticipated, or responded to, the sentiment of Judson respecting India and Burmah. 'They will tire out the weary and faint hearted, and send to their homes all but the few who have put their hands to the plough with a grasp that no discouragement, nor death itself, can unloose; but who bring up their children to the same work, and swear them at the same altar.' But these labourers have not been tired out, nor have they discouraged other combatants. If they have fallen in the warfare, it has been with an upraised standard. They have seen the triumph afar off. They have bequeathed their work to their sons, and left behind them the record of its glory—a glory visible to faith, both in the dark present and the bright future.

An inquiry into the paucity of conversions in India will not be here irrelevant. We are accustomed to resolve the non-acceptance of Christianity by the Hindus into the socio-religious institute of caste, which fetters its subjects by the intertwined bonds of social and religious life, and inflicts secular penalties, as well as threatens those of worlds to come; by a literary, aristocratic, and widely diffused priesthood, and more still by the nature of that complex religion which we term Hinduism, laying hold, as with the power of an enchantment, of all the faculties of their nature, and moulding them after its own image. Such and other extrinsic causes which are assigned, do not seem wholly to resolve the difficulty. Is there not a more potent cause in operation? Is not Hindu *character* the greatest obstacle to the gospel? Although that character has been itself wrought out by these extrinsic circumstances, yet its direct power far outweighs them. It has two primary distinctive elements—falsehood and self-righteousness—not to be parallelled in the whole world of human character, ever prone as it is to such vices; a falsehood deeply ingrained into the moral system as a principle, and ever operating as a habit, and a self-righteousness, in whose sight neither heaven nor earth is clean, and before which all other men are impure. If he that is of the truth hears the voice of Jesus, what aspect must he bear towards it who lives, and moves, and has his being in lies. To prove the truth of Christianity is not to win your way to the Hindu mind. For truth, as such, he has no appetency. The love of the *principle* is absent, he cannot love the thing itself. Again, a mind encircled with its own associations of righteousness and merit, either personal or appropriated, shrinks from that gospel which declares there is none righteous, and concludes all equally under sin. And here, is not the fact illustrative of this remark, that those people or races who have received Christianity, have been those in whom these vices did not exist in the same concentred degree—the devil worshippers of the south, sections of the rural population, and of the aboriginal mountaineers?

But independently of the natural operation of these elements of Hindu character in preventing the reception of the gospel, is not this very character peculiarly repugnant to the Divine Mind? Does it not, more effectually than all other causes, resist the Holy Ghost, and cause Jehovah to withhold those gracious influences which descend elsewhere? And thus, instead of referring the absence of converting grace to the sovereignty of God, may we not more justly refer it to the justice and holiness of God, withholding blessing from those who, being false in heart, and the children of religious pride, do not simply, as others, love darkness rather than light, but love darkness as darkness, and hate light as light?

Forming this estimate of native character, do we not see a blessing, as well as a curse, in the extraordinary outward difficulties to the conversion of the Hindus? Is there not involved in that whole range of obstacles, a trying, and proving, and purifying process, whereby only the sincere and humble are enabled to enter the church of Christ? Hindu character being as it is, the adverseness of Hindu circumstance, is perhaps not the great evil which it is frequently considered. The two stand together. The one necessitates the other. If we regard the future interests of India, the delayed success of our Missions is not, therefore, without its elements of gratulation. Estimating rightly the deceitfulness of the natives, and the necessity of holy beginnings in a work which is to progress for centuries, and in its issues to last for eternity, we say the trials of converts have not been too many; the force of external circumstance has not been too adverse. By these means, painful, yet necessary, the foundation has been laid of a church pure and truthful, that has in some measure given the heathen an idea of a heavenly religion. The power of Christianity has been seen in the sacrifices it has constrained its professors to make, and its graciousness in their renewed characters. A new thing is seen in the land, a community who speak the truth, and strive to live conformably to it. Hence Christianity is a holy thing in the midst of the people. All this has been dearly bought by the personal sufferings of converts, and by the hope deferred of labourers; *but it is well bought.* India will be all the purer for it. Its future evangelization all the more real; its renewal in the image of Christ all the more complete; the conquest over Satan will be all the more decisive. Were this questioned, we might cite the history of parts of India where hindrances were few, conversions rapid, caste retained its hold, and, as a consequence, a low inoperative Christianity was introduced, that had scarcely energy to transmit itself to the next generation, and certainly impressed on its professors no principles of truth and purity, so that their descendants have, from the corruptness of their conduct, become a byeword equally among the heathen and European Christians.

Such traits of faith and patience have also their instructive lesson to the church at large. They have taught us the necessity of a more apprehensive faith, a more entire devotedness to the work on the part of those who engage in it. In the great evangelistic work there are degrees of qualification needful to overcome difficulties which vary in intensity. Ordinary faith and patience cannot effect that in India which might be wrought elsewhere. It is there that Christians have need for unusual grace and extraordinary endowments. The 'devils' of Hinduism can only be cast out by 'prayer and fasting.' The church will be tried and proved, and what is in her heart will be revealed to her ere she inherits the promises. We shall need all the encouragement of other Missions, as well as that afforded by the Divine promises, to sustain us in a warfare which will doubtless be protracted. We have engaged in no such warfare yet; all other spheres are but a section of this; and all difficulties gathered from the wide world are not comparable with what a single Indian district presents. The church has been and will be taught the omnipotence of evil and its own powerlessness, when viewed apart from Christ, whose sole agency will be so clearly evinced in the successes which shall appear as to exclude all glory in man.

Further. *India is a scene of evangelistic triumphs.* These are all the more real in their nature, that they are so partial in their extent. We estimate the triumphs of the gospel, first, from the *cast of mind* which it has subjected. It would seem as though Satan had apprehended, or rather, brought down with him from his native heights, the Christian idea of consecration—body, soul, and spirit—to God, and sought to work it out in Hindu experience, only directing that consecration to himself. The principle that religion is the all in all of life; the centre of social conduct, of private duties, of hopes and aspirations, fitted to control every thought and emotion, and to fill up days, and minutes, and seconds with its glorious self, has been elaborated by the 'god of this world' in the entire economy of Indian life, but wrongly applied in all its references, and inverted in all its relationships. Instead of God, he has enthroned himself, by means of mythological representatives, as the centre of religious worship. Instead of moral works, he has substituted ceremonial; instead of spiritual, he has introduced carnal; instead of heart-purity, bodily and material cleansings. Thus the

Hindu deems himself a consecrated being, while all his acts, tested by truth and righteousness, are desecrate. There never was a soul so full of religion, yet so destitute of it; so apparently holy, while so essentially unholy; so conversant with names of all that is good and true, and so ignorant of realities; grasping dark shadows and holding no substance. One dwelling in their midst has given from experience this graphic testimony: 'There is a whole universe of falsehood built up in the mind of the Hindu. There is a heaven, an earth, a hell of falsehood. There is a supreme deity, three hundred and thirty millions of gods, angels, heavenly choristers, Titans, devils, hobgoblins, and spirits. There are a number of distinct mansions in heaven, and each of them is furnished with its appropriate inhabitants, and characterized by peculiar occupations and pleasures. So, too, there are many hells. All these regions are mapped out in the mind of the Hindu, as the geographical divisions of the earth exist in the mind of a European. Humanity is all seen falsely; with distinctions of caste as well defined as the distinctions between the different genera of animals. The idols are to them real beings; animated, intelligent, and powerful. They themselves have passed through thousands of births, and have thousands more to pass through. Their body, soul, and spirit is God; and there is no thought of their heart, however vile, that God is not the author of. All is false, all is perverted; from one end of the universe to the other, from the throne of God to the lowest abyss of hell, there is nothing whatever that they know aright.' Let the reader place himself as far as possible in sympathy with such a mind, and as he faintly realizes its real character, let him remember that over many such minds thus perverted, found in all sections of Indian society, has the gospel triumphed. They have received the true ideas of purity and righteousness; obtained a true appreciation of personal sin and guilt, of Divine justice and mercy; and, above all, have been made partakers of a spiritual life and renewed in the image of God.

Or, take another cast of mind—the Buddhist or the Pantheistic—the one incased in rigid unbelief of the first principle of the Divine existence and government, the other bewildered in the mazes of an indiscriminating faith, converting all substances and being into that of deity. Christ has triumphed over them. Further, let it be remembered that minds of such complexion have been converted *singly.* The law of mutual influence in social or domestic life, is, in regard to Christianity, almost inoperative. One by one are our converts made. Believing husbands have not often sufficient influence to persuade their own wives to embrace the faith. The work of conversion has to be performed in each case as though no other case existed. The same ground has to be fought and won over and over again, and as in Indian warfare, isolated forts to be stormed and taken. Whilst this fact adds both to the difficulty of conversion and of retaining conviction, it enhances the triumphs of the gospel. To believe what and when others believe demands no strong exercise of faith. To believe what all others disbelieve, and what all others reject, demands a mental vigour, and a moral courage, which nothing short of a Divine inspiration can impart. Every single Hindu converted from his former faith is, then, as great a miracle of divine power and grace, as is to be found in a world that has been no narrow theatre of such displays.

In another type of mind which has been evangelized, we see illustrated the same power of the gospel, although by a different operation; we mean that of the demonolater. Devils have been cast out of his intellect, which apprehended no other object of reverence than what was also an object of fear; they have been cast out of his body, which had been given up to possession, and they have been exorcised from his soul, whose emotional susceptibilities had all been taken captive. Love has overcome fear, hope has banished dread. The apprehension of the living God has put to flight the demons of imagination; a sense of his power has enabled the convert to defy 'the powers of darkness,' and a knowledge of his will has made him renounce 'the works of darkness.' What Brahmanism could not do,—exorcise the devils of the aboriginal population, but in its impotence patronized them and grafted their worship on their own system, has been effected by the gospel. Nor is it without significance, that the largest section of

Indian converts has been from this class of religionists. The Missions of Tinnivelly and Travancore, which, with their evangelized villages, their strongly established Christian institutes, their large numbers, and compact organization, have gained for themselves a primary distinction and encouraged others to perseverance, are among a devil-worshipping people. The devil temples have been rased to the ground to furnish a site for the worship of God; devil rites and ceremonies have given way to the simple service of Christ; and in the most literal sense, Christ has with the finger of God cast out Satan and divided the spoil with the strong.

Again, the gospel has triumphed over the constitutional character of the Hindu. The defects which still exist must not allow us to ignore the good effected. The Hindu has passive strength, but not active; he is strong to bear, but weak to act; destitute of moral courage. The gospel has put energy into him. Out of weakness he has been made strong. In the day when he has called, God has answered him and '*strengthened him with strength in his soul.*' The timid, starting soul, which trembled before the taunts of men, puts on courage and goes forth to act as an assailant. Though unused to independent action, having solved personal responsibility, and thought, and purpose, into his caste and priesthood, the Hindu has been by this new power braced to personal independent effort, and that antagonistic to those before whom he once bowed down. The history of many native evangelists supports these remarks; also the records of the persecutions of native Christians. Though tempted, they have abode faithful, and evinced a readiness to die rather than deny Christ. The Christians of Barisal, when falsely accused, in order that they might renounce their faith, said, 'We are Christians, and do what you will, we shall be Christians still.' 'O judge,' said one of them, holding up his bonds before the magistrate, 'I am not a dacoit or a thief, or an evil doer, but because I am a Christian, I have been bound with these bonds.'

We have hitherto viewed the subject only in the light of individual conversions. Let us now consider it as illustrated in the fact of Christian churches. The formation of a church is far more repugnant to Hindu society than the mere conversion to the Christian faith of the individuals who compose it. In that very degree is illustrated the power of the truth. Could Christianity be content to have isolated disciples; were there not the divine precedent of formation of distinct communities; were it not a principle of our Lord to *add to the church* the saved ones; we are assured that the nominal conversions to Christianity in India would soon astonish those of largest expectations. It is the *church* that is the stumbling-block of India rather than the *cross;* or, rather, it is the violation of caste involved in this institute, that constitutes the heaviest cross. The church is in spirit and letter the opposite of Hinduism, and its very defiance, a fragment severed from the mass of Hindu society, a disruption of caste, a standing protest against it, and destruction of all past associations. To become a member of it involves an incalculable self-sacrifice of feeling, while the sight of it fills the supporters of heathenism with indignation as an abomination, and with fear as a sad omen for their future. It seems to say, with a prophetic inspiration, 'Your glory is departed.' Thus every Hindu who joins the church of Christ, has not only to brave the general sentiment of his people, but to overcome his own principles and tastes which are in sympathy with theirs. Yet all has been overcome, and side by side of a Christian profession is church membership. More than three hundred churches, whose members vary in number from a few converts to one or two hundred, and whose aggregate is more than eighteen thousand, drawn from a nominally Christian community of six times that number, are found studding the plains of India;—congregations of worshippers, families of newly constituted relationships, collective witnesses for Christ, walking in divine ordinances, whose members not only desire to be Christians, but to embody the fact in a visible perpetual institute; not willing to cast scattered rays but to form themselves into centres of gospel radiance; serving as nuclei of future inquirers, as centres of evangelization, as the basis of future operations.

From what has been advanced it will readily be perceived that the full triumph of the gospel of Jesus over Hindu mind and heart are appreciable by no sensible test. Recorded conversions, certainly, constitute no criterion. The number of converts to the truth of the gospel is far greater than the number of those who profess it. Multitudes exist to whom Christianity is a truth, but who do not publicly embrace that truth, nor yield themselves to its legitimate influence. There are indisputably hundreds and thousands not identified with our native churches whose genuine conviction of the truth and claims of Christianity entitle them more to the appellation of 'Christians,' than multitudes of professors in Britain. Their intellect has been enlightened, their judgment has been convinced, though their heart may not have been won over. Still, the triumph is of great value, as far as it goes, as not only illustrative of the power of the truth, but as gradually creating, by means of such convinced minds, a new sentiment in India, forming a new social conscience, and thereby depriving the heathen systems of their wonted power, and imparting to the succeeding generations new moral susceptibilities.

Further:—*India is a sphere of boundless hope.* There is hope from the past. Where are all the prayers that have ascended from purest lips and holiest hearts? Have they been dissipated by the winds that wafted them, and ceased to be? No; they are all registered before God. Where are all the labours of the past? Are they gone—with the days and hours which witnessed them? No; they are also 'before God.' 'He is not the God of the dead, but of the living.' The Great High Priest will turn them all to due account. They shall re-appear in blessings in India. There is hope in the present. The fact of the agency already at work, and constantly increasing, is one strong ground of hope. Believing that every godly labourer is called of God, and is Christ's gift, we receive the aggregate of labourers there, as Christ's own pledge that he will convert the people. The fact of his sending them proves that he has a design: can that design be less than the calling out of 'much people' to himself? Nor are the hopeful elements to be ignored, which arise from the great company of godly men whom Christ has raised up in European society, mostly occupying influential positions, and who would seem to be a pledge of future blessing to the land. Nor again, should we be heedless of the measures now in progress to secure the dominance of Christian principle in the government of the people, and the abandonment of all official countenance of the religion of the country.

But there are hopes founded on intrinsic, as well as extrinsic, circumstances. We have hope from the constitution of Hindu mind. That mind, now at all points so opposed to truth, needs but to be touched by the finger of God, and it becomes in harmony with it. The very habits and associations which have made it inimical to the gospel, will, under Divine teaching, secure a strong desire for, and appreciation of, the gospel. For, what are the prominent religious ideas of the Hindu who is earnest in his religion? Salvation and deliverance. These are the poles around which his mind ever revolves. Deliverance from the delusions of the senses, the deceits of the world, the passions of the body, the ocean of sin, the myriads of births, the depths of hell, is the ruling, absorbing idea of his religious life. Now the gospel is a deliverance. Christ is a deliverer. The Hindu aspirations for deliverance need but to be rightly directed by the Holy Spirit, and he embraces Christianity. What a mass of religious thought and association is also found within the Hindu mind — comprising the attributes of deity, the relations of man to a 'true teacher,' a 'substitute,' an 'intercessor.' Let the sentiments be diverted from their false objects, and Christ becomes the 'desire' of this nation. The author keenly feels the force of this argument. He has known Hindus whose minds, under Divine influence, apprehended with *ease* evangelic truths, and whose moral constitution seemed penetrated with them; to whom, not only the gospel seemed adapted in every way, but who themselves, by past associations, seemed adapted to the gospel.

Further, we draw hopes from the constitution of Hindu society. Here again, social influences, now keeping the entire mass compact, and preventing individual desertion, thus barring even the entrance of the gospel, need only to be rectified, and they become the greatest auxiliary to its progress:—mind transferring its own impressions to other minds, friend helping friend, and brother teaching brother, 'know the Lord.' The consolidated mass that now resists innovation will, when its own conscience is on the side of Christianity, allow an entire impenetration. Thoughts all suggestive of hope crowd on us, when contemplating the character of Hindu mind, and the framework of Hindu society. When we think of the plastic nature of the Hindu, a fact which the god of this world has hitherto turned to his own account, moulding it in every conceivable form of evil, both in principle and habit—of the teachableness of Hindu childhood, and the readiness with which they learn their own tongue, with its facile character and simple principles—when we take into account the mild susceptibility of womanhood, and the extensive ramifications of closely bound family relationships, the compactness, also, of the village system, and the consolidation of society in large towns, with all the habits of intercommunication near and distant; when we remember the readiness with which the entire mass ever receive and transmit influences, and propagate sentiments; when we see a Christian native agency already existing, able to teach others, and possessing a host of appliances in Scriptures, and books; the conviction is irresistible that whenever from any cause there be a popular diversion towards Christianity, the teaching and learning will be so multiplied, in the study and in the school; the preaching and hearing so intensified, the social converse so frequent and so diffused, in the market and on the journey, in the house and by the wayside, that multitudes will come under strongest evangelistic influence, and souls be gathered in with a rapidity that shall make Zion ask, 'Who are these that fly as a cloud, and as doves to their windows?' Blessed are ye labourers, whoever you are, and wherever your term is fixed, and lot is cast, who shall reap the waving harvest of India's plains and hills. But no less blessed in the kingdom of God are those who preceded you, weeping as they sowed, and returning empty. They shall look down and rejoice together with you, in an unutterable sympathy; or, if they await 'the restoration of all things,' then meeting you in holy companionship, they who have sowed, and you who have reaped, shall rejoice together.

CHAPTER VIII.

MODERN APOSTOLIC MISSIONS.

ASSAM.—BURMAH: Its Associations.—First Era.—Second Era.—Third Era.—SIAM: Its Past and Present.—CHINA: Its Religious History.—Missionary Plans.—Chinese Character.—Mission Results.—Special Work at AMOY.—China's Future.—INDO-CHINESE ARCHIPELAGO: An Arduous Sphere.—A Few Successes. SOUTHERN SEAS: Former Condition of Inhabitants.—Night of Toil.—Work of Jehovah.—Methods of Divine Procedure.—Native Evangelists.—Christianized Islanders.

THE small region of the valley of the Bramaputra, called ASSAM, has not been neglected. It was early coveted by the Burmese missionaries as a medium of introducing the gospel into China. Its own people have been also objects of interest—the Assamese of the plains, and Nagas who occupy the hills. Amongst them already are small churches formed, and the Assamese read the Word of God in their own tongue. The work is but initial, yet hopeful. Brahmanism has a feeble hold over those who profess Hinduism, while the hill tribes are wholly free from its influence.

BURMAH—what shall we say unto thee? What exquisite associations are blended with thee in the hearts that love Missions! Whatever is poetic in feeling, and pure and sublime in imagination, ardent in a Christ-like affection, is recalled to our memories and hearts when Burmah is but named. Where has more self-denial been evinced, more striving unto blood, more enduring unto death? And where has woman earned to herself greater renown; or, rather, where has she brought more glory to her Lord and Saviour? The heroic in action, the courageous in enterprise, the ardent in affection, the purely human elements in sweet concord with the divine, have all been largely illustrated in Burmese Missions. What sacred lessons have been learned by the church of Christ from these records! What a holy flame has been kindled in many hearts from the sorrows and endurances of the first labourers! What encouragement has been furnished by recent successes! We feel that the soil of Burmah is sacred for the steps that have trodden it. The ground is hallowed by the dust that sleeps there.

Look at the first era of Burmah's spiritual history, with the personal and relative sorrows of the first missionaries, their hard, and, to the eye of sense, almost fruitless labours. Think of Judson in Ava and Rangoon reiterating the truth of an eternal God in his zayat, or in the market place, or the palace. The Buddhists deny it, and tell him none will credit it. He tells of the one Christ, a Saviour, an Intercessor; they laugh at it, and say there can be no remission of sin. The converts who come out singly, are exposed to persecution and death under the despotic monarch, himself the slave of Buddhist priests. This goes on year after year. Fellow-labourers come out, but some are forced to return, or the grave is opened for those who would turn many to righteousness, but die in the attempt. The churches of America are discouraged. They wonder at the paucity of results, and point to what is going on in other more fruitful parts. The missionary answers, 'Let us go on, and you will hear of us.' A quarter of a century from the earliest commencement, when missionaries were sent from Serampore, has come to its close, and a small room is capacious enough to hold the church of Burman converts.

But a second era dawns. A man becomes a 'chosen vessel' of the Lord, who is to do a work at which Christians shall be astounded. By race, a Karen, he is the slave of a Burman, of rude habits, of untutored mind, dull to stupidity, without an element of learning. His passions are ungovernable;—of the seed of Barabbas, his hands are stained with the blood of more than thirty victims. This man comes under Divine teaching and receives the truth. His conversion can scarcely be credited by the Burman church, and his baptism is delayed. As soon as it has taken place, God's word is in his mouth, and he desires to proclaim it abroad to his own people. These are scattered in their native wilds, and are most difficult of access. The Burmans rule over them when in the plains, like the Egyptian task-masters, and they are, therefore, forced to make their homes the 'munition of rocks.' Whilst such an agent, chosen for the work of evangelizing this people, illustrated the exceeding riches of Divine grace, the people themselves were equally illustrations of the Divine providence and fore-knowledge. Heathen, yet not heathen; for ages living among and serving a people with a literature and an established priesthood, yet influenced by neither; holding religious truths, and occasionally uttering them in the form of songs, and proverbs, and legends, infinitely beyond all the speculations of Brahmans and Buddhists; possessing, also, a code of morals whose source must have been not far from the oracle of Sinai, and historical legends, which had their origin in primeval history; 'scattered and peeled,' yet in their captivity looking according to traditional teachings to a brighter era, when their captivity should return, and they should sing the song of redemption both temporal and spiritual; so seclusive in their habits as to avoid the highways, and rivers, and harbours, and keep themselves from all intercourse with foreigners, and from such seclusion remaining unknown to ethnology, yet looking to the advent of the white man from the West as the medium of their redemption, who should by means of *the Book*, instruct them in the worship of that Jehovah to whom they uttered their occasional song of praise; scattered over the hills, extending from the spurs of the Himalayas to the southern extremity of the Burmese provinces, and occupying the valley of the Irrawaddi up to the proximity of China, yet retaining a bond of national union, and cherishing reminiscences of their former greatness as a people, they were, in every way, 'prepared of the Lord,' and the few missionaries who had been struggling for existence in Burmah, and contending for Christianity with an obdurate heartless Buddhism, had been sent to 'make them ready.' But the pioneer is one of themselves. A Karen must be the first missionary to the Karens. Kothabyu, a fool of fools, and servant of servants, is given a commission like that of Moses. Slow of speech, he is sent to this second Israel in Egypt. The people, with more faith than their prototypes, received the word in love and obedience. From this evangelist, this word commends itself as the word they had as a people waited for. In company with him a few return, and for the first time see the white man with *the Book* in his hand. Then does Boardman go forth and seek to overtake the work. Like a true shepherd he seeks out the Karens as so many sheep from the wilds of Tavoy. With a delicate constitution and sickly frame, he braves the malaria of the swamps, crosses the rapids, ascends the rocky eminences, and baptizes his converts in the mountain streams, till mortality is swallowed up in life. His wife takes up his work and braves the same dangers. She gathers the Karen women together and teaches them Christ. She holds classes of the children, and, in the absence of all other aid, she sends not back the *men* who have come from afar to hear the new and living word; but, urged by a necessity which knows no law, and actuated by a spirit, to observe which is a Divine order, she yields to the necessities of untaught but thirsty souls, and in congregations smaller or larger, preaches to them Christ. Judson, also, the lone widower, leaves for a while his engrossing translations, and visits the mountaineers. And as he breathes a purer atmosphere than that of the Burman plains, and finds his frame invigorated by it, and has his soul refreshed by contact with unsophisticated minds, so strongly contrasting with the Buddhist soul and intellect on which he has been operating for years, he feels himself in a new world of being. Then it was that, substantiating within his whole soul the presence of the Omnipotent God—so grandly symbolized by the stupendous rocks around him—and glancing at the possible, if not certain, future history of Karen Christians, of which he now witnessed the first beginnings, he used the words of one of England's greatest prophets, 'The best of all is, God is with us.' The work goes on. Mason, and Vinton, and Kincaid—all honoured names, and not exclusive of others—sow fresh seed or gather a portion of the ripening harvest, and in this second era *thousands of Karens were introduced into the church of Christ.*

But a third era begins. The Karens are yet the Burmans' bondsmen, and, as such, are fearful of embracing Christianity. The work has been rapid, compared with that of other missions, yet slow in comparison with the wishes of the Karens and their preparedness for the truth. Churches formed in Burmese territory are liable to be scattered.

Missionary efforts must be conducted with caution and secrecy. A still further interference of that Providence who has already done wondrous things, will be welcomed. War breaks out between the British and the Emperor of Burmah. The conquest and annexation of the southern portion of the empire ensues. Amid the dying tumult of a war scarcely concluded, some Karens press forward, and ask, 'Where are the teachers; the Karens demand them.' They had been praying for them, and had taught their children to join in supplications. British protection is now offered to all who choose to occupy the appropriated territories. The Karens hear of it, embrace the offer, and simultaneously place themselves under Christian instruction. Those who had never seen the face of a white man, receive their teachers, as sent of heaven; and though they had only heard of the glad tidings, without hearing the message itself, many, who were without teachers, strengthen their application for them, by first of all building a place for worship and a school. Christianity stands out before the people as the religion they have been destined to embrace—the long-waited-for confirmation of their desires, and the fulfilment of ancestral prophecies and longings. Great, now, is the multitude of preachers and of hearers. Many labourers now come from the west, and Missions are established with an amazing rapidity. Karens are baptized in hundreds. 'The kingdom of heaven suffereth violence, and the violent take it by force.' God raises up pastors for the newly-gathered churches from amongst themselves, and schools are instituted for a native ministry. The Karen nation has already yielded its hundred thousand of willing learners, ready to be gathered into the kingdom of God. That the people are not wholly evangelized is from want of men to overtake the work. The reaping has followed so closely on the sowing, as to render an adequate supply impossible. The Burmans remain as they were, being gathered only by units into the church. The first have become last, and the last first. Already do they sustain their own pastors from among themselves, and establish their own schools. At one meeting, convened for the purpose of ordaining a brother from among themselves, are present no less than forty Karen pastors. After the labours of only nineteen years, fifty churches of one district resolve to support their own native and foreign ministry. Here may be truly appropriated the prophecy—'A nation shall be born in a day.' Well may one of their own evangelists say, '*The records of every month are enough to awaken songs of praise to the God of Missions in the bosom of the most slumbering church.*' Were there a romance of Missions, what could the boldest imagination have sketched more striking than the truths of the Karen mission? Had there been a believing, praying church, acting up to the fulness of faith, could it have apprehended in prayer, more than God has granted? Could it have *thought,* could it have *asked* more abundantly than God has actually given? What most glowing page of prophecy has not here its counterpart, in the page of Karen history? 'Before Zion travailed she brought forth children.' British Christians, if introduced to these newly-gathered people, would be constrained to say, 'Who hath begotten us these?'

And shall there not be a fourth distinct era? Has this nation, so rich in an indigenous ministry, no ulterior destination? May not her evangelists go forth to Siam and Burmah and India or China? Why not? Let the work become consolidated among them, which, if God's blessing still continue, will not be a very lengthened one, and the nation who was a 'servant of servants,' may yet upraise the neighbouring races, higher in civilization, yet sunken in idolatry.

SIAM, also, connecting Burmah with China, the highway to its borders, and receiving thence a portion of its inhabitants, the stronghold of Buddhism, which is upheld by a government, which, though despotic, deems itself the servant of the Buddha (Gotama), has become the scene of evangelistic labours. The history of the labourers has been a chequered one; without the thrilling incidents that have occurred in Burmah, but full of labours like theirs, and severe endurances. They have at times pursued their evangelistic work, exposed to imprisonment and banishment, and debarred from appropriating any dwelling place. When in the extremity of circumstance, an English consul was raised up to interfere on their behalf and by special provision of a treaty to secure their comforts and the liberty of their Missions. And now Siam may receive the gospel before Burmah. The ideas of the West have already found an entrance to the palace of the Siamese Cæsars. They have learned the English language and read English intelligence, and study English sciences, and have sent their embassies to France and England. We may hope for a new era, the downfall of Buddhism and the establishment of Christianity.

THE EMPIRE OF CHINA now challenges our attention. For its evangelization many hearts have been enlarged, and prayer has been made continually for it. Efforts, also, have been unwearied, and valuable lives have been expended. The Chinese, in their inquiries for religious truth, were for ages as those 'mocked;' for bread they received 'a stone.' Their own indigenous systems, Confucianism and Tauism, are modified forms of atheism, lacking all religious inspiration, and incapable of affecting the heart. These barren systems of mere thought and reason have doubtless moulded the Chinese character, of which also they are the products. The people have been no less cruelly 'mocked' in the foreign religions which have been introduced. They sent an embassy to the west to inquire after the new divine teacher, probably THE INCARNATE WORD, of whose glory some rumours may have reached China. The Buddhists of India met them, presented Buddha as the object of their desire, and Buddhism as the religion of blessing. Returning with them, they found an easy introduction into China, and established that atheistic system which has endured till now. Thus, in the striking language of a German writer, 'The light of heaven was converted into the phantasmagoria of hell.' Romanism, also, found a large introduction into China, but gave them no Scriptures, and offered no pure Christianity. At length God had mercy on them, and raised up true prophets, who have kindled a flame of light and heat, which none shall extinguish. The faith was great which sustained a Morrison for years, labouring at his Chinese dictionary, or with his colleague Mylne, translating the Scriptures in the hopes of their labours being ultimately useful for the evangelization of a people at the time shut out by edict from evangelistic labours. Nor were those of 'little faith' who laboured in the Malacca Straits or the adjacent islands, upon the offscouring of a Chinese population, in hope of an ulterior entrance into China. And according to the faith of these few solitary labourers has it been. The door has been partially opened, and every moment is increasing the probability of a full and effectual entrance. Meanwhile, how many adventurous spirits from Britain and America have hasted to take possession of the land, and prosecute labours in those 'ports' which are opened to them. Restrained as they are by compacts and treaties, we see them use all the advantages they possess. Wisely adapting themselves to their peculiar position, some of them spend whole months in their boats, sailing up the rivers or canals, which like a net-work intersect the land, visiting the towns and villages which so thickly skirt the banks, dispensing the bread of life, and then passing on. Or they abide in hired houses in places not distant from their central stations, as long as Chinese toleration will permit, and receive all who come to hear of the kingdom of God. In their own fixed localities, part of their number exhibit the benevolence of Christianity, and thus win a way to the heart for the reception of Christ, by healing the sick, whilst others proclaim the gospel in the peculiar dialects of the place. Schools for male and female Chinese youth, supplement their labours. Christian women have in them found an ample and encouraging scope for their efforts.

What is the aspect of the Chinese in relation to Christian Missions? With their voluptuousness and earthly mindedness; less fettered by a creed than the Hindus, but more by lust and passion; without faith, yet full of all credulity, regardless of all moral and spiritual realities, reckless of all interests that are not proximate and visible; these people are not open to an easy impression from a religion which demands a spiritual susceptibility, a principle of faith, and an appetence for something that is beyond the sphere of sense. Their hearts are like their temples, which are devoted with equal readiness to secular and religious purposes, where devotion and pleasure, seriousness and fun, are in strange proximity. They lack *soul*, and have no love for the religion of the 'single eye' and the 'pure heart.' No wonder that the progress of the gospel amongst them has not been the march of conquest. But China has not withheld her converts to the grace of Christ. The strong man armed kept the Chinese mind in the bonds of sensual sloth, but a stronger than he has led captivity captive. The Confucianism, or Buddhism, or Tauism, and more than all, earthly mindedness, which characterise the Chinese, have been supplanted, in not a few souls, by the doctrine which is from above. As elsewhere, so in China, all classes have received the truth. The learned graduate has become a scholar in Christ's school, and the poor illiterate has assumed the same position. Misery, physical and moral, has brought its seekers after rest and consolation, into the Christian church. The poor forsaken opium eater has felt that, in his last extremity, there was one help, and that was in Christian fellowship; there was one Saviour from his sin, and that Saviour was Christ. Some of the converts have been mere sojourners in the place where the grace of God has met them, and taking back the truth into their own districts, spread the religion of Jesus where no missionary could enter. In one or two places, which have been favoured with Divine influences, the signs of the presence and aids of Christ have been most manifest. In Amoy, missionaries who had laboured elsewhere without success, have within a short period seen the power of grace in the conversion of the wicked. Nearly four hundred Chinese, within a centre of small radius, are witnesses of Christ, and form a collection of churches. The work has there assumed deeply spiritual characteristics. There is, first, the unity and love of the brethren, a marked spirituality of mind, fitting them to be the channels of grace to their people. There are spiritual inquirers who come face to face in quiet converse with the missionary, and lay bare their hearts, full of spiritual solicitude. There are also earnest converts, faithful disciples, 'living epistles,' cultivating mutual affection, and feeling holy love to the Lord Jesus. Those favoured to be God's instruments in this work are forced to declare 'the blessing is greater than there is room to receive it.' The solicitude of inquirers is more than they can satisfy; their spiritual necessities are beyond their capacity to minister to them. It was fitting, in the early ages, that there should be an 'Ephesus' in Asia and a 'Corinth' in Greece, which, by the numbers and intelligence of their converts, should form fitting centres of influence, diffuse an extensive knowledge of Christ, and give a tone to the future Christianity of their respective lands. So has it been deemed fitting, under the same administration of the Omnipresent Christ, that there should in China be an AMOY, which should exhibit Christianity as an embodied institute, in a spiritual Christ-loving church.

No difficulties need now be started regarding Chinese evangelization; they have been already combated. There is no room for questions as to the set time for Sinim. God has shown that his own time has come. Let but that unchristian and antichristian trade in the poisonous drug of India be abolished, and thereby a great argument for unbelief be removed, as well as a source of physical and moral evil, incalculable in extent, dried up, and the church can confront all obstacles with a triumphant hope.

How readily China may be not only open to the gospel, but prepared to attend to it, and her vast masses be converted into thronging congregations of gospel hearers, and the studies of her wise as well as ignorant, rich as well as poor, be in a day concentred on the Scriptures of truth, has been amply exhibited to us by the wonderful providence of God in the strangely blended political and religious movements of the last few years amongst the Chinese themselves. The spread of Christian truth in China—what a prospect for herself—what a prospect for the world! Its population colonizing so many parts of the earth, and threatening to overpower or absorb feebler races by their numbers, may be God's instruments in converting the islands of the Eastern Archipelago, and even the dark parts of South America. *Already are Christian Chinese labouring in Singapore, Australia, and California.*

THE INDIAN ARCHIPELAGO, to men merely *reasoning,* not acting from command, would have seemed to be beset with insuperable difficulties. Some of the islands are equatorial in position, of fiery temperature, inhabited by barbarous aboriginals or their savage conquerors, or by a migratory population. These comprise all grades of human nature, and amongst them are found the relics of all religions. As the islands themselves seem to have been tossed up and scattered promiscuously in mid-ocean, so people and tribes, governments and religions, are found in pell-mell confusion; Malays and Chinese, Dyaks and Javanese, Arabs, Siamese, and Macassars, Battas and Papoos, constitute a motley mixture, whilst the religions of Buddha, and Brama, and Mahommad are found in strange proximity with sundry forms of aboriginal superstition. Missionary zeal has not shrunk from labour in such a sphere as this, though local difficulties have been more than ordinary, climate has been deadly to many frames, and worse still, Missions have been left without needful aids from home. Men have been found who counted not their lives dear unto them, ready to explore the unknown jungles of Borneo or Sumatra, and to settle down and labour there in order to regenerate the barbarous and densely ignorant population. In the first island, a devoted labourer took up his abode among the Dyaks, who approve their right to marriage by the heads of human victims, and make peace-offerings of human skulls to evil spirits; to whom piracy is legitimate trade, and slaughter becomes a sport. He studied their language, reduced it to writing, translated a portion of Scripture, composed and printed hymns, framed a vocabulary, and pursued his labours till struck down by disease. Gospel light is now dawning in that island. Under British protection, now established in a portion of Borneo, the natives have partially come under Christian teaching. The other island has acquired a painful interest by being stained with the blood of those devoted men Munson and Lyman, who with joyful hearts plunged into its wilds, far from all civilization and protection, and then fell by the hands of savages. They went to their deaths with holy joy and confidence in future success of their Mission, with an absence of gloomy presentiment of their own fate, reminding us of the victim going willingly to the altar, with gay colours and garlands on its neck.

Persevering labourers are found in the Loochoo islands, hoping to obtain an entrance for the gospel in Japan. Here and there in the stations of the 'straits' is found a solitary labourer. The Dutch islands have received most attention, and have yielded most fruit. Java, on which much labour has been expended, has at length yielded fruit largely to God in large Christian congregations. One who had laboured long and patiently, ere he left the sphere, could rejoicingly say, 'I have lived long enough to see His kingdom come!' Viewing this vast sphere as a whole, the work is only in its beginnings, and in order to success must certainly be prosecuted with more vigour. Some few first fruits from the races which have been the objects of continued labours, have been reaped. The Dyak has received the 'sincere milk of the word,' and the Malay has had his fierceness tamed by the peaceful doctrines of the gospel. Do not these islands demand evangelists from China and India, and Burmah? From such centres they have in the past been proselytized to false faiths. May they not now claim from them the true?

Who shall describe God's work in the SOUTHERN SEAS? Prophecy has become history: the isles have waited for and received his law. Separated from the great continents, dispersing further and further from an original centre, divided and subdivided in their tribes, tending to greater and greater isolation till they bordered on extinction, retaining fewest possible primeval traditions, losing all knowledge of a Creator-God, obliterating moral distinctions, discarding shame, with natural affections, if not extinct, ready to die out—the denizens of these islands illustrated two principles; first, how human nature may lose its normal characteristics, when in an unsocial state, isolated from great families of nations and central repositories of legendary truth; and, secondly, how deeply depraved it becomes, even to the very verge of devilish, when it wholly departs from God. Volumes must be read to give us an idea of how near hell was to earth in these islands, or rather how the elements of hell were blended with those of earth, and were gradually assimilating them to themselves. It may be doubted whether intestine wars, and infanticide, and evil practices would have allowed the population of these islands long to exist. Amongst such people, did men fix their habitations, for Jesus' sake, witnessing sights that may not be pourtrayed—hearing what is unutterable—and enduring what none could endure, save as seeing Him who is invisible. In their several isolated locations in the ends of the earth, privileged with only occasional correspondence with Europe, and receiving precarious supplies, they wept and prayed, longed and watched, for the advent of Jesus, THE MAN, to restore these men to their own human image, and Jesus, THE GOD, to renew them after the Divine likeness. In some great centres, as Tahiti, New Zealand, labours were diffused over years without success; the object of the missionaries was misunderstood, their character unappreciated; not a custom of heathenism was abandoned, no sympathy was secured, no heart was impressed. Their very position was precarious, and abandonment of their stations all but problematic. Their night of toil was like the wintry night of northern latitudes, where the sun is below the horizon for months, save that, in their case, it was illumined by no stars shining coldly but clearly. All the light and heat they found in that live-long night was within their own homes and hearts. Now they are exposed to violence, now constrained to silence, now forced to flee, because of the encroachments of war, or the loss of some protecting chief, and frequently constrained to labour for subsistence. Thus were they made to feel, and, through them, the church at home, that nothing but an

Almighty providence could open a door, and nothing less than Almighty grace could give them an effectual entrance. And when faith was ready to fail, and knees were unsteady, and hands hung down—when man seemed strongest to oppose, and God seemed most inert—He took up his own cause, and laid bare his holy arm in the sight of the heathen.

We love to see Jehovah 'sitting on the circle of the earth,' and 'taking up these isles as a very little thing'—these isles, so great in geographical extent, according to our standard, and whose moral obstacles to genuine conversion seemed so insuperable—with his noiseless power affecting men's minds, now by hope, now by fear, and now by some other sentiment, undefined, it may be, yet potent—opening for his gospel a way, by providential visitations, varied as the circumstances of the islands and the character of the people, and making for his grace a channel in human hearts and affections—unimpeded by the pride of intellect and confirmed resistance of his Spirit, which have marked the semi-civilized and self-righteous people of Asia, and which have hindered his operations among them. With what majestic ease does he turn the hearts of those on whom the very entrance of the missionary depended, and now of the people who had tumultuously opposed the truth. Again, we see him, at some critical moment, cast his shield of protection over the missionary. And the Divine agency—how conspicuous it is rendered by the numerical feebleness of the human instrumentality, producing results of which no adequate solution can be furnished apart from himself. And this especially, when foreign primary agency has been absent, and a few from amongst the newly-converted ones have been the only instruments.

In tracing the methods of the Divine procedure in thus making all things new, we witness varied operations. Here he operates on individuals directly by his quickening Spirit; there, on people collectively by some preparatory visitations. In the former case, we observe the penitence of heart and the exercise of prayer—apart, in the bush, and in the mission family—and the belief in Christ which characterize other conversions. One and another inquirer comes to long-despised and insulted teachers and says, 'What shall I do to be saved?' Convictions then spread from heart to heart, deepening as they are multiplied. The natural conscience of a people seems resuscitated, and iniquities which the missionaries themselves had never known are spontaneously confessed. Special striking conversions evincing the great power of Jehovah, the irresistible might of his word, hasten the conversion of the multitude. He touches the hearts of blood-thirsty chiefs, and they become as lambs. He takes those stained with deepest guilt, and they become in the eyes of all the people 'purged with hyssop and whiter than snow.' Where sin unutterable abounded, there grace did much more abound. Depravity, which awes even those who hear of it, and makes them feel as though within the gates of hell, loses its awful magnitude by comparison of the greatness of the grace which triumphs over it. But in many cases the Divine operations have been of a different character. Jehovah has acted at once upon a people, and thus prepared them for the gospel. He has impressed them with a sense of his own supremacy, and the vanity of their gods. His providence has so arranged times and circumstances, as to furnish them with some sensible proofs of their worthlessness. They are, it may be, when put to a specific test, unable to deliver from the pestilence, or the tornado, or famine. Or, it may be, that priests, long trusted, are impotent to afford some specific relief, and call on their gods in vain — to their own discomfiture, and the annihilation of the faith of the people. The sentiment of the nothingness of their deities then forces itself on them with the power of an intuitive truth, and casting indignantly their idols into the sea, or burning them in the fire, they come crying, 'Teach us, we would know Jehovah, and Jesus the living and true God.' They have sent messengers to intreat the missionary from afar to visit them. The mode in which intelligence of the missionaries, and the God whom they serve and proclaim, has been diffused, has strikingly evinced the Lord's providential agency. From some chance voyager driven from his course by adverse winds, or from some of their own people conversant with recent converts, or from the direct visit of one or more such converts, have they first heard of the 'God of gods,' and of the physical and moral benefits flowing from his religion, and no sooner have they received such tidings than they have been filled with desire to receive the teacher and enjoy the whole train of his benefits. Or again, it may have happened that Jehovah has *put in them his great fear,* and thus prepared them for the truth. The destruction of idols, discomfiture of priests, and the confusion of the enemies of Jehovah, have had on the minds of some of the islanders an effect analogous to that which Moses describes as produced on Edom, Moab, Palestina, by the passage of the Israelites over the Red Sea. 'Fear and dread fell upon them; by the greatness of His arm they are still as a stone.' 'The chiefs are afraid; the mighty men—trembling takes hold of them; the inhabitants melt away.' In either case the march of the missionary has been a triumph. Idols have been kept from destruction only that he might witness it on his arrival. They have put away heathen evil before they have known the Christian good. They have built houses before there was a teacher to inhabit, or erected a chapel before there were worshippers.

It has also not seldom happened, that the striking illustration of some distinctive characteristic virtue has turned the hearts of multitudes, as the water-courses from their channel. A Christian people have been successful in a defensive war, and their vanquished enemies are expecting death at their hand; they are magnanimously pardoned for the gospel's sake, and then, for the first time, the iron enters their soul. They are melted by the exhibition of sparing mercy. They attribute it to an almighty power and a divine goodness. They will then also yield themselves to so subduing a power. Or it may be, as in the case of king George of the Friendly Islands, that a chief by his profession of Christianity has drawn on himself the opposition of numerous chiefs; but their confederacy becomes broken, and they are exposed to his vindictiveness. He gives them their lives and liberty. They resolve to make his God their God, and they kneel at his family altar, and enroll themselves disciples of the new faith.

The most conclusive evidence that God is with us in our Southern Missions is in the number, and character, and successes of the native evangelists. Babes in spirit, yet with a manly heroism; fools, yet wise; weak, yet strong; they have given themselves to a work which none could covet save from love to Christ and to souls, and none could prosecute without the presence of Christ. They have but just been rescued from grossest vices to go and dwell with those who still practise them, separated from the wicked, to go and live and die in their midst. They have tasted of the sweets of truth, and liberty, and holiness, only in order to communicate them without delay to others. Their social enjoyments have been experienced only to make others partakers of them. We think the young islander renouncing home, to dwell amongst an unreclaimed people, the depths of whose degradation he best knows, exposing himself to the loss of that he has but just acquired, shutting himself out, it may be, for years from the visits of a missionary, and the protection afforded by them, and all this with the frequently recurring experience that some are barbarously killed and eaten by those whom they have sought to bless, is one of the sublimest spectacles connected with Missions. Whole groups of islands have been converted by native agency; a people raised up and prepared for the foreign evangelist to be baptized and formed into organized churches.

Thus, by 'divers manners,' has God glorified his Son in the islands of the Pacific. In the language of an islander, addressing his own people, 'No sooner was the gospel call given, than they came flocking to the Saviour, from the East and West, and North and South.' That which God himself deemed impossible, regarding mere human agency—that a nation should change its gods—he has made actual by his own agency. In Madagascar he was heard to say to the churches: 'Be still, and *know* that I am God.' In Polynesia he has said, '*Come and see* the works of the Lord.' There the 'plowman has overtaken the reaper, and the treader of grapes him that sowed seed; and the mountains have dropped wine, and all the hills have melted.'

And now that God has thus worked and made a way for us — now that he has removed former abominations, and created 'all things new' — we love to draw near and contemplate regenerated

Christian man in these islands in his distinctive races. The throng of worshippers keeping holy days; the Sabbath schools; the training institutions, with young and ardent souls seeking and gaining sufficient knowledge of heaven and earth to qualify them for becoming teachers or evangelists; the missionary gatherings, where native eloquence gains its first inspirations, and native generosity affords its amplest proofs; these, and such as these developments, attest a Christianized people. Nor can we fail to take an interest in all that follows in the train of the direct holy influences of the gospel;—the newly rising civilization; the expansion of commerce; the acquiring of refined tastes; the drawing upon new resources; the new civil constitution; the moral code, after the Sinaitic law; the institutions of liberty, framed from the Anglo-Saxon model; until a people, asserting the rights of a Christian humanity, claim a place in the great paternity of nations, and challenge the respect of long established political powers. Such developments we see carried to their furthest point in the Sandwich Islands, already recognized by those who colonized them as a Christian people; occupying a religious position higher than most of the old Christian communities, as having a fourth of their population partakers of church fellowship, able to support, with little help, the whole of their ministerial agency, and taking a lead in missionary enterprise to regions beyond. New Zealand, also, would seem on the eve of attaining a similar position, already reckoning twelve thousand members of churches, and almost all her youth able to read. The Feejeean islands stand out as most conspicuous illustrations, first, of the long suffering and forbearance of God, and then, of the 'exceeding riches of his grace.' Those, full of all unrighteousness and malice, have submitted in thousands to Christian instruction. Even chiefs, on whose heads rested murders on murders, till we are amazed that the Divine vengeance allowed them to live, now live a new life in Christ. The paucity of labourers alone keeps back the whole people from declaring Jehovah to be their God.

There is a dark aspect as well as a bright one, in which all these Missions may be viewed. Here and there spiritual life decays and first love waxeth cold. Artificial tastes threaten to overpower the 'new creature,' and worldly desires to quench the Spirit. Such facts are but natural to human nature in all its conditions, and constitute a demand on the church of Christ for more extensive supervision, deeper spirituality in her teachers, and stronger supplications to her God and Saviour.

CHAPTER IX.

MODERN APOSTOLIC MISSIONS.

AMERICAN INDIANS:—Interesting Associations.—Adversities of past Missions.—Present Missionary Operations.—Phases of Missionary Life.—Blessed Results.—The Indians' Future.—Indians of South America.—WEST INDIES:—Unique Experiment.—Trials of Early Labourers.—Negro Conversions.—Fruits of Emancipation.—GREENLAND AND LABRADOR:—Peculiarities of the Work.—Progress.—AGGREGATE RESULTS OF MISSIONS:—The Work Progressive.—New Phases Developed.

WE now approach the American continent. Who has not rich associations with the American Indians—the Hurons and Oneidas, Delawares, Mohicans, and others? We know them from the romance in which genius has given them an earthly immortality. We know them from their international history, which is itself the wildest romance, whose chief elements are mutual wars, hereditary animosities, and horrid vindictiveness. We observe with wonder their patient endurances, noble darings, contempt of death, and more than Roman stoicism. We watch with interest the national assembly, where each speaker's soul is set on fire, and kindles others as he speaks. We hear from them forms of speech indicted by the spirit of nature—utterances now smooth and flowing as their rivers, now rapid as their falls, and now descending

11

as their cataracts, and illustrations gathered from all that is significant in their native scenery. We follow them from that assembly on their errand of destruction. We hear the war cry, we see the tomahawk and spear, and we mark tribe with tribe, or nation with nation, contending in an all but exterminating warfare. In their track we find women and children massacred, villages burnt down, settlements laid waste. We know them also too well from their connection with British and French history, and the 'American war,' when men, swift to shed blood, were chosen as allies by either civilized power; and war, always terrible, had its horrors increased tenfold by such bloody alliances. But we have also associations with them of a different kind, the very contrast of all that is natural to them. We have seen from their number trophies of redeeming grace. Under the teachings of Eliot, and Brainerd, and Zeisbergen, they learned to put on Christ, and were admitted into the great family named after him. The warrior laid aside his scalps, and put on mercy and compassion. He that had never shed a tear wept from a sense of sin, and knees that had never been bowed were now humbled in prayer and praise. Lands were redeemed from the wilderness, converted into plantations for the sustenance of Christian Indians, who gathered around the missionary in hamlets or towns.

'Let no dark cloud rest on the work of the Indians; let it live when I am dead,' were the dying words of the Indian's apostle Eliot. But a dark cloud has rested on the work, more or less lowering, ever since these words were uttered. The transplantation of the people has often broken up Missions; the breach of treaties, in the letter or spirit, has induced suspicion, and hindered the advance of Christianity. Stations once flourishing have become languishing from the introduction of intemperate habits, and in some places the fructified field has become a desert. The races have died out, or the churches have become extinct. 'Where are they?' we might ask of Eliot's people—of once flourishing churches of the Moravians, and of other earlier or later Missions. Had the 'red men' suffered less wrongs from the white men—had the western races who encroached on their domains developed the law of Christian love, rather than selfishness and guile—especially had they refrained from tempting them with ardent drinks, inciting them to all evil—and still further had the church prosecuted its first labours in its first love—had there been more Eliots, and Mayhews, and Brainerds—this people would, doubtless, ere this have been evangelized, and the 'nations' themselves would have retained their integrity, not as now, scattered into fragments; at any rate, churches would not have become desolate. But as it is, those under Christian influence form a great minority, and, after a lapse of two centuries, Indian barbarism is found skirting the domains of Anglo-Saxon civilization, and heathenism lies at the door of Christianity. Yet missionary operations are doing much to redeem the past, and certainly no other agency promises to remove the 'dark cloud.' The only rays of hope for the future are those which gild our evangelistic prospects.

What an immense area these people occupy! Although the chief nations, or tribes, as the Chocktaws, Cherokees, Chippeways, Delawares, are centralized in a territory *for the present* their own, reserved for them by compact; yet sections are found westward of all the territories of North America, till we last meet with them in a scattered state, occupying Rupert's Land. The numerous sections into which they are divided show their tendency to subdivisions, and give some solution of their ever-diminishing numbers. As this field of missionary labour is wide, so is it a difficult one. Scattered over prairies, occupying woodlands skirting the lakes, or centring at the forks of the large rivers, subsisting by the chase, refusing the arts of civilization; many of them still in all their original wildness, and entertaining jealousies and hatred of the white men who have supplanted them; they constitute a sphere of self-denying labour often repulsive, but nevertheless possessing its peculiar elements of interest, and in a most encouraging degree successful.

We behold the missionary, whether from America or Britain, leaving the homes of civilization, and plunging into the wilds of an Indian forest, dwelling with the Indians as his own people, sleeping in their wigwams; if need be, following them in their migrations, unwilling to let them go from him, that he may bring them to Christ. If his labours are prosecuted among a scattered people, he erects a dwelling in the wilderness, where he may instruct the children whom parents, distant on their needful excursions, may have committed to him, and where he may also receive the Indians, on their temporary and fitful visitations, for instruction in Christianity. Near that dwelling he persuades his earliest converts to abide, and, abandoning the chase, to secure by industry a produce from the soil, a supply in seasons of dearth. Others follow their example, and gradually families are gathered around the missionary, and a Christian settlement of order and stability is seen in the desert plains, with its busy schools and well-attended sanctuary. In the prosecution of his missionary work, we see him go forth to distant settlements, where the nuclei of congregations are to be found, facing the wintry blasts, riding over the frost-bound plains, or crossing the frozen rivers; or, where operations are further advanced, and he has made a way for the gospel, we witness the Indians themselves visiting him in his own home, paddling, if it be summer, over the rivers, or shooting down the rapids, or crossing the ice in winter, from distances of more than a hundred miles, to keep holy day unto the Lord. Tales outvying all romance, of self-denial and heroism of the missionary, and of faithful attachment of the Indians to the gospel and its teachers, are connected with the rivers and plains which form the diversified region of these aboriginal Americans.

As the result of faithful labours, we witness nearly *sixty churches gathered from these people of the wilderness, comprising more than twelve thousand members.* Large tribes, as the Choctaws and Cherokees, have renounced heathenism, with its conjurations and evil spirits, its polygamy and infanticide, its murderings and plunderings, and acknowledged Jehovah as their Sovereign, Christ as their Saviour. The village and the town have arisen, with their central objects, the school and the church. The simpler arts and the more ready comforts of civilization, an infant literature, an indigenous ministry, a written civil constitution, a legislative assembly, a regular system of judicature, are found among these people. And this—wrought, not by influences of political states, nor prelections in law and civilization, but by the man of God, book in hand, and grace in heart, and Christ with him, preaching, as John in the wilderness, 'Repent,' and, like him, crying, 'Behold the Lamb of God, that taketh away the sin of the world.'

We behold, from many other tribes, churches formed of holy men and women, manifesting signs of conversion, the same in kind as are witnessed in the churches of the white men. The letter of the moral code of Christianity is observed, and its spirit is imbibed. Instead of fearing evil spirits, or having shadowy conceptions of a good spirit, they now look up to the Father of the spirits of all flesh, and call him, 'Abba, Father,' in Christ. They are distinguished by a diligent attendance on the means of grace, often amid serious difficulties from inclement weather and great distances. We have seen already, from their number, catechists, and pastors, and missionaries raised up, whose devoted conduct has justified an appointment to the ministerial office. We may say, with Peter, 'God is no respecter of persons, for in every nation he that feareth the Lord, and worketh righteousness, is accepted of Him.'

What of the future history of these Indians? Pressed from behind by the ever-surging wants of Saxon migration and conquests, which have already expatriated them from ancestral homes, and threaten to deprive them of their present resting places, till they reach the very shores of the Pacific; subject also to want and famine, from the inadequate supplies of rivers and forests; unable to train their offspring; the subjects of severe diseases, of which they do not know the remedies; or abandoned to vices which diminish population—these people are threatened with extinction. Some of the tribes have already died out. The language into which Eliot translated the Bible is no more spoken. The rivers, and valleys, and hills to which their forefathers gave their names, and whose regions were occupied by them, know them no more. It would seem as though they must eventually share the fate of the aboriginals of the Indian islands. This tendency to extinction, however, where it has arisen from themselves, has been in the absence of the gospel. The reception of it, with its conserving power, arrests the destructive influences existing. Families and tribes have been saved by locating themselves in fixed habitations, and applying themselves to systematic industry. Were the gospel to become more widely influential, it would doubtless redeem whole tribes from the threatened extinction. But, supposing that the law of extinction is one not to be overcome—that an early close awaits the career of the Indian Missions—are the wisdom and beneficence of our operations brought into question by the fact of the evanescence of the races who are the objects of them? No. If these races are, by a providential necessity, to die out, be it so; yet is our duty clear. The Saviour, ere a dying thief perished from the earth, gave him an imperishable place in the paradise of God. We would do the same for these dying races. If their names are to be erased from the great record of earth's tribes, and peoples, and tongues; ere the decree go forth, let us see to it that their names are written in the book of life. If they and their doings are to cease to be a part of human history, we should be the more diligent to give them a place in the records of heaven. If they are to be expatriated from their ancestral or recent homes, let us be the more solicitous that they obtain a seat in the New Jerusalem.

The Indians of South America have not been forgotten. Where they are within reach of our influence, as in the British Guiana territories, Christianity, true to her nature, seeks to find them out. The Missions to the negro expand themselves so as to comprise the Indian, and one and another labourer has sailed up the Essequibo, or entered the jungles, to preach Christ to those widely scattered people. Nor without success. Some few of the Indians of those districts, young and old, male and female, have pressed into the kingdom of God. The tribes further south, under papal jurisdiction, are beyond the reach of Protestant effort. It was to open up a way for them, and introduce the gospel to those who seemed beyond hope, that the heroic Gardiner performed extraordinary labours, and rather than abandon his mission of love, settling at the Southern extremity with his companions in faith and tribulation, he embraced a desperate hope, the issues of which were starvation and death. Patagonia may ere long give her first fruits to Christ.

THE WEST INDIES, viewed in their special relations to the past, challenge no ordinary interest. The experiment of evangelizing slaves had its numerous precedents, but never were slaves evangelized under such circumstances. There was an unwonted depravity and anti-Christian principle in the slaveholders, an irreligiousness and licentiousness in the slaves, and a power of local circumstance that seemed to remove both from the influence of the missionaries. The captain of a merchant ship, on arriving at the latitude and longitude of Jamaica, trying to descry it with his telescope, expresses his expectation of one day looking for it in vain, saying its deep iniquities are enough to sink it into the ocean. On the arrival of missionaries, stringent laws were enacted against them, and every obstacle thrown in their path. Dutch, Spanish, English planters abhorred the gospel and its messengers, as hell abhors the light and joy of heaven. Their one resolve was to keep the slaves in slavery and the ignorant in ignorance. But the might of endurance and the irrepressible power of faith enabled the servants of God to overcome, while God, in faithfulness to his promises, brought to pass the discomfiture of the enemies of truth and righteousness. Where shall we meet with a greater self-abandonment than was manifested by those early labourers? Though none actually became slaves to win the slaves, they had the spirit to do so, had it been necessary, and they actually endured as such. Exposed to the bitter hatred and opposition of the planters, objects of suspicion to the colonists, bearing the charge of every insurrection of the slaves, or the spirit of insurrection which they might manifest, with names cast out as evil in the islands, and misrepresented at home, sometimes imprisoned and saved from violent death only by the fear of retribution from Britain, these early founders of West India Missions *bore the reproach of Christ*, probably more than any other body of missionaries, and must ever have an eminent place in apostolic annals. The only sympathies they enjoyed were those of slaves who dared not express them openly; their only encouragements were drawn from their repentance and faith, which they could only secretly avow; their joys were derived from religious exercises, liable to be broken up by masters who revelled in iniquity and to whom cruelty was a luxury; their rewards were the blessings of those who acknowledged they owed all that was precious to the missionary's love and zeal. Never had Christian love such a part to act; never were disciples of Christ more faithful unto death, 'through good report and evil report, as deceivers and yet true.' And what fruits they reaped! what miracles of redeeming grace were witnessed by them! How was Christ glorified in these slaves, washed, sanctified, justified. There was an offer of spiritual liberty, and the poor bound and oppressed ones grasped it. There was a Father's heart of love revealed, and the outcasts from all love and sympathy save that of their teachers, rejoiced in such a loving Father in heaven; redemption through Christ was preached, and a Saviour's love thrilled the hearts of those sons of Canaan with joy unspeakable, and full of glory. The gospel commended itself to them as glad tidings; its breathings of mercy were what they needed; its promise of glory soothed their sorrows, and made them sigh for rest from earth and earth's tyrants. They saw the door of the kingdom opened by Christ, and by faith they entered in; dropping the chains of slavery only when the bonds of mortality were severed, and experiencing their first freedom in heaven itself. In the woods or swamps, or in their own huts at night, we see the little bands learning the first elements of English, or reading the Scriptures, or hearing them from one of their own number or from the missionaries, or uniting in prayer, real and heartfelt; the terror of the lash, and even of death, hanging over them, in case they were discovered by their masters. Now and then they receive accessions to their number from the very men set over them to watch and punish. Grace constrains them to join the little band, and endure the lash rather than inflict suffering on those under them. Christ was often in their midst in these social meetings, as was manifest from the tears and groans of penitence, the strong cries for mercy, the supplications for the Spirit. And, further, how many gifts and graces of the Spirit characterized these slaves of men, but freedmen of Christ! What reminiscences yet linger of their ardent prayers, their zeal for souls, their truthfulness, their strong social affection, making its bitterest sacrifices for the gospel's sake, their meek prayers for enemies, and efforts for their good, their undying attachment to their friends the missionaries, their faithfulness unto death to the Lord Jesus! And when their emancipation was effected, and freedom came, as God's own gift from heaven, what multitudes were gathered into the church of the Firstborn! Then gratitude brought its richest offerings to the Lord's house, and for a while money's chief value was felt to be its subservience to the gospel, and the glory of the Lord who bought them was the absorbing motive of action. Then did the fearful and straitened churches arise and put on strength; they lengthened their cords and strengthened their stakes, and congregations were numbered by thousands. Many have since been the drawbacks, numerous the backslidings, and the generation that has succeeded is, in some respects, unlike the one preceding it; but viewing these Christians as men, and the work, however Divine, like all other work, not unmixed with human elements, we still recognize multitudes as a worthy section of a redeemed humanity. Looking at their churches, many of which are self-sustaining, comprising an aggregate of not far from one hundred thousand members, and having in connection with them probably double that number of attendants on public worship, their indigenous rising ministry, their first messengers sent to their father land, or to the Indians near them; their institutes for training pastors and evangelists, we see indisputable marks of the presence of Christ in their midst. And the work still progresses. In Surinam, Moravian missionaries have recently administered baptism in one year to *two thousand slaves,* many of whom approved themselves as enjoying the liberty of the gospel.

Ere we close this sketch of Missions, let us glance at the Mission settlements, of world-wide fame, of Greenland and Labrador. The work of a hundred years still abides, and with the same characteristics. There are still the Herrnhut of a century ago, and the Nain and Hopedale and Hebron of a later era. Devoted men, of a similar stamp to the original founders of these Missions are raised up, and the labours of a Christian David and a Jens Haven, are renewed in this generation. They still endure privations, occasionally alleviated by British generosity, which sends fuel to cheer their dark dread winter; are constrained to say in some severe seasons, that all creatures given for the comfort and nourishment of man in those regions, would seem to have perished. Brethren and sisters are still frequently engaged in ministering to the bodily wants of converts throughout a season destitute of supply, and thus save the perishing. Trials and mercies are still blended in their history, and lamentation often follows hard on, or is the predecessor of, gratulation. Disease and famine sometimes prevail to diminish spiritual hungerings and thirstings, yet, on occasions, physical destitution is a season of spiritual blessing, while no earthly trials are able to separate the converts from the love of God which is in Christ Jesus our Lord. *More than three thousand souls* in these regions—so separate from the great hives of people, so distant from ports of commerce, and shut out from all but Christian love—enjoy the instructions of the Moravians. Tokens of His presence who opened the heart of the first Greenlander to receive the truth, are not wanting. Men like Kairnac are now and then converted, and hoary sinners like Taglavina testify of converting grace. These Missions, in their arctic dreariness, and on the very confines of regions where physical existence is impossible, stand out as witnesses of what Christ's love will do in the hearts of teachers, and Christ's grace can effect in the dark cheerless souls of the taught.

We close these imperfect sketches. We have taken only the more extended spheres of labour, and have omitted reference to home and continental Missions. These latter, conducted in Holland, France, Germany, and parts of Italy, have reaped their reward in souls saved from rationalism, infidelity, or Popery. A cyclopædist of Missions computes as the result mostly of modern labours an aggregate of *two hundred thousand church members, from a nominally Christian population of above one and a half million of souls,* under the spiritual oversight of sixteen hundred foreign missionaries — statistics necessarily incomplete, and doubtless far below the actual fact. Let us add to this blessed aggregate, the multitudes who have within this period been gathered into the kingdom of heaven, and what a glorious result has been already secured. What the seer of Patmos saw only in prophetic vision, we partly realize in fact, for Missions present us with the *sight* of a great multitude out of all nations, and kindreds, and people, and tongues— a part of that innumerable host who will one day stand 'before the throne and before the Lamb, clothed with white robes and palms in their hands.'

But while we write, time is falsifying our statistics. God's word is not 'bound.' We may draw lines and fix present limits, but the Spirit is not circumscribed by them. His grace is not quiescent. The wind bloweth where it listeth, and its sound is often so gentle that we can take no note of it. The Sun of Righteousness stays not his course, but has no sooner visited one people with his rays, than he ascends and irradiates other meridians. The angel is flying with the everlasting gospel from one end of the heavens to the other, and, as we observe his descent, and the delivery of his message in one place, it is only to mark his speedy flight to places beyond. The science of Missions, unchanging in principles, is ever multiplying its details, and accumulating its facts. The panorama of the church's history is ever widening before us, and new scenes are pourtrayed thereon. Germs of new nations are being planted in the earth, whilst old nations and people shift their political relations, and present different aspects to the church of God. Australia is becoming a centre of evangelization to the islands of the Pacific and the Indian Archipelago. Closed ports are everywhere being opened, and seven-leaved gates of nations are unbarred. In China, the great powers of Europe are demanding unfettered commerce and amicable relationships. An American squadron seeks to open a door for commerce with Japan. Armenia no sooner receives the scriptures of truth, than Bulgaria stretches forth her hand to take them, and European Turkey holds forth the promise of such fruits as have been reaped in Asia. Men shift the bounds of their habitation, but the gospel pursues them. Chinese, unwilling to be taught at home, are found by the missionary in California and Australia. Hindus, unwilling to abandon idolatry and caste in India, are encouraged to do so at Mauritius and even in the West Indies. Romanists of Ireland wait till they reach America to break the spell of Rome. The material already prepared of Scriptures and their living preachers, is creating fresh material in a progressive ratio. Conversions already effected become additional centres of converting power. Many wearying preparatory processes are finished, and the results attained will be more than we ask or think. Progress is the law of Christianity in her early history. The readiness of a people to receive the gospel often bears a proportion to the strength of past resistance. The virgin soil is the more productive that in its indurated state it almost blunted the sharp edge of the gospel plough. After twenty years' labour in New Zealand, eight disciples only were gathered. In a little more than ten years were gathered nearly three thousand. Every accession from the kingdom of Satan not only leaves that kingdom weaker by the loss, but enfeebles it by adding power to the hostile array which is made against it. At home the missionary spirit pervades new circles, and obtains fresh advocates. What pens are now writing—what hearts are now yearning—what souls are now praying —'Thy kingdom come'? Not only do the promises, but the facts of modern evangelism, 'travail with a glorious day of grace.'

CHAPTER X.

OBSERVATIONS ON THE PHENOMENA OF MISSIONS.

Principle of Selection of Stations.—Expansive Spirit of Missions.—Appositeness of Locations.—Unity of Evangelistic Means.—Oneness of Result.—Dark side of Missions.—Lack of Success.—Appeal to Facts. — Qualifying Considerations. — Missions dependant on *Command.*—Comparison with Apostolic Missions—With the Progress of the Gospel at Home.—Expenditure of Material and Life.—Answer.—Nothing lost to God—Nor to the Individual—Nor to the Cause of Evangelization—Nor to the Church—Nor to the World.—What is Lost.

THIS general survey suggests some important remarks. The missionaries seem to have located themselves irrespectively of those considerations whereby men are ordinarily influenced. The healthfulness or unhealthfulness of climates, the proximity or distance of places from the centres whence missionaries proceeded, the civilization or uncivilization of the people, their peacefulness or lawlessness, the friendliness or hatred of their governments, political or commercial advantages, have certainly not controlled, however they may have modified, the location of Missions.

The Briton, or American, or German, goes and settles at the very antipodes of his native land. The balmly isles of the European Archipelago, the salubrious, though tropical, isles of the Pacific, have not been coveted as such, more than the Eastern Archipelago, with islands lying on the equator. Neither the miasmatic vegetation of Sierra Leone, nor the marshes of Demarara, nor the snows and ice of Greenland, have been repulsive to missionaries, under the influence of their own peculiar motives. The healthful table lands of India have not been so desired as to leave the alluvial sickly plains deserted. Missions have been planted, alike where civilization in any form or shape has existed, or where unparalleled savageism has threatened to destroy the messengers of mercy. The wild tribes of Borneo and Celebes have been sought out as freely as the civil Chinese. The tenants of the wilds of Canada and western bounds of the United States have been cared for as freely as the semi-European Greeks or Armenians. Impetuous and blood-thirsty Affghans have had the gospel preached to them, as well as the passive and helpless slaves of the West Indies. Missionaries have been content to labour under the hostile governments of Siam and Burmah, as well as under the protection of the Christian government of India; to preach the gospel in the sanguinary chiefdoms or cruel despotisms of Ashantee and Dahomey, as well as at Cape Town, in Shoa and Gallia of Eastern Africa, as well as in the English or Dutch colonies on the same coast. There seems to have been *one* principle of selection —that as the carcase for the eagles, the prey for the spoiler, the market for commerce, so the *souls of men* for Missions. The prominent fact of Missions is, that evangelists are traversing the wide world in quest of *men;* men lost, but to be sought out and saved.

It is this principle which explains the expansive character of our Missions. If missionaries first locate themselves on a coast, they soon strike into the interior; if on an island, they soon seek to compass a group. The known and occupied becomes a station whence to explore the unknown, and occupy destitute parts. The sympathy with the heathen brought into exercise by the practical work of Missions has been unlimited and irrepressible. Williams is at Raiatea, and on the slightest intimation goes to find out Rarotonga. The Friendly Isles are made a centre whence to convert the Feejeans. Carey is in Bengal, and translates for Nepaul, and his colleague studies for China. Judson is located at Burmah, and, widening his horizon, he appeals home for Arracan, Siam, and China. Sierra Leone is made the starting point for inland Africa. Even when no hope of an immediate establishment of Missions has existed, our Christian travellers have explored unknown regions as pioneers of the gospel, to find out where, and in what circumstances, man exists, so as to furnish data whereon the church may act, the richest legacy they could bequeath. In this way has Krapf traversed Eastern, and Livingstone Central Africa, and Gardiner a part of South America, to prepare a highway for the gospel. In sympathy with the Adorable One who claims the spirits of all flesh as his own, our modern missionaries have said, 'All souls are ours,' for conversion, and instruction in righteousness. No limit is affixed, or, if prescribed by authority, it is not observed. The most expansive of all territorial conquests is that which is in the name, and for the glory of 'the Prince of the kings of the earth.'

Another thought suggested by this survey is, the appositeness of mission stations, in the absence of any central local authority. The world is in a sense occupied by Missions, which, as à rule, are *where* they should be, but without one presiding mind, or ecclesiastical organization, or concert between organizations. There has been a central authority, a controlling wisdom, a superintending power, but we seek it in vain in any visible form or organization. We cannot say, it is *here*, or it is *there*. The evangelists themselves are of all nations on the earth, and of all names in the church. The several societies have, in their selection of stations, acted in a great degree independently of mutual control or guidance, forming their own judgment from facts patent to all. Yet it is indisputable, that the most central and advantageous positions have been occupied for the ulterior object of converting the world. Some positions have resulted from those providential arrangements, which, from our inability to refer to respective causes, we call accident, as when the landing of two heathen youths from the Sandwich Islands in the United States was the occasion of exciting an interest in their race, and led to the establishment of the most successful Mission in the world; or necessity, as when Judson, prevented from pursuing his labours in India, found only a solitary ship in the Madras Roads, going to Burmah, and, therefore, was shut up to the alternative of going thither, or abandoning his mission to the East; or, again, as when Dr. Coke, accompanied by missionaries whom he desired to land in Nova Scotia, was necessitated by heavy weather and a leaky ship to touch at Antigua, where Christian slaves had been supplicating for messengers of the gospel, and was thus induced to plant amongst them the earliest West Indian Mission. Other Missions have originated in special calls, when messengers have come from a-far, entreating for God's servants to come over and help them, as when some Hottentots in South Africa, earnestly desiring a missionary, set out on a journey of some hundreds of miles to Cape Town, and met on the road a missionary just arrived from the Cape, in quest of a heathen people beyond the Orange river, to whom he might preach the gospel. Or they have owed their establishment to specific impressions, analogous to those made on the apostle's mind by the vision of the man of Macedonia, and which we can refer only to Him who controls all minds, and influences all movements. As when Jens Haven, hearing that the first missionary had been murdered at Labrador, 'felt a strong impulse to go and preach the gospel to that very nation, and became certain in his own mind that he should go to Labrador,' and notwithstanding such impression, after he had been located in Greenland and studied its language, he heard a voice, saying, 'This is not the place where you are to stay, for you shall preach the gospel to a nation that has heard nothing of the Saviour'—words which were thrice repeated, and on which he ultimately acted with marked results. Other spheres, again, with no special attraction, have been chosen merely from the fact of being unoccupied. That the people of any place could say, 'No man careth for our souls,' was deemed sufficient argument for sending to them the gospel. Yet from all this diversity of causes, the simple result is manifested of a world, or the world's greater portion, bearing on its surface, ready to act on myriads of souls, apposite centres of gospel truth and power. If Britain is said to have a command of the ocean and of the world, by her possession of numerous maritime fortifications and harbours, the church of Christ has already a command of the world by her great missionary centres, whether on the continent or on the ocean. In this result, manifested at so early a period —a result that proves that the church possesses the true apostolic spirit, since the several classes of evangelists, rather than make Christ known where he was known before, and thereby build on each others' foundations, have abstained from crossing each others' lines we behold the foreknowledge and arrangements of the one Mind—the source of all evangelistic principle and the centre of the church's direction. It is He who has said to his servants, 'Come,' and they have come; 'Go,' and they have gone. It is He who, being head over all things to the church, and having all authority in heaven and on earth, has so controlled minds, and so disposed the elements of nature—so arranged times, and seasons, and circumstances, and so moulded events—as that the locations of Missions justify themselves as *well* chosen.

Another thought suggested, is the unity of evangelistic means employed by missionaries, notwithstanding the diversity of characteristics of those who are the objects of their labours. Estimating the difference of culture, both mental and moral, between the Brahman youth of Calcutta and the North American Indian; the Calmuc and the Chinese; the Javan and the Greek, the nomade of the desert tribes, and the inhabitants of Turkish towns, we might expect that men seriously designing to make Christians from such divers classes, would supply different means—would have their esoteric and exoteric doctrines; their inner and outer circles of discipleship; their preparatory and initiatory processes. Yet, if we examine the working of Missions, we find in a diversity of measures, a striking unity of means—the utterance of gospel truth. That truth may be taught in the class at school or college, to passers by or to the stated congregation; it may be uttered in its brief simplicity, or illustrated by allegory; but gospel truth—one and the same—is that which is alone used, and on whose use all hopes of success are based. Brainerd, in the

Indian's wigwam, uttered just the same truth as Duff in the Calcutta Institution. Moffatt, in the kraal of the Bechuana, says just the same things as Hewitson in his private room to the Portuguese of Madeira. Mylne, in China, uses moral suasion of exactly the same character with the Chinese, as Vanderkemp with the Hottentots. All are uttering one *truth*. The teachers explain, but do not modify. They do not add to or detract from the one message, though they illustrate it according to the capacity of the hearers. And thus their unity one with another is also an identity with the first apostles. What Paul testified—that men 'should repent and turn to God, and do works meet for repentance'—is the testimony of our modern missionaries. In seeking to secure an obedience to the faith, they adopt no philosophizing plan, commending themselves to human systems rather than to men's 'consciousness as in the sight of God.' There is no substitution of the 'wisdom of man' for the 'foolishness of God,' nor of the 'power of man' for the 'weakness of God.' Whenever there has been such an attempt, it has always failed. Never was an agency more unique than that employed in Missions. Never were means to an end more identical in their nature. The argument is strengthened by the consideration of the diversity of mental attainments of the agents employed—from the unlettered potter and carpenter who first went from Moravia to the West Indies, to Buchanan, head of the Fort William College. With all national and particular predilections suggesting different methods, they are each and all shut up to the adoption of one—the presentation of the gospel message, 'Be ye reconciled to God.'

No less evident is the oneness of result in the case of the converts themselves. The moral and spiritual effects of missionary labour are, amongst all people, essentially the same. Those who acknowledge themselves to be under the influence of the word of God, and are recognized as such, and counted worthy of the fellowship of saints, manifest the very same phenomena, irrespectively of all diversities of culture and past association. The hearts of all become alike; their spiritual natures are affected in the same way. There is in kind, though not in degree, the same contrition of heart; the same faith in a Saviour; the same love of the truth, and of those who know the truth; the same hatred of sin and thirsting after righteousness; the same desire to see God, and join the assembly of heaven. They are evidently members of the same family and partakers of the same nature, under the same Divine teaching. This unity binds by mutual ties the converts of every part of the missionary field, and places them on the same platform with the entire Christian church.

Missions present dark as well as bright sides, and particular phases vary according to the stand-point of the observer and the idiosyncrasies of temperament. The cloud of glory that rests over them, if viewed from the side of unbelief or worldliness, is only a dark mass. It is also shorn of its brilliancy if contemplated under the influence of false preconceptions, and analogies that are inapplicable.

The most popular objection is that which upbraids the enterprise with a lack of success, either in its numerical results of conversions, or in the moral and spiritual standing which the converts occupy. The objection ignores the facts of Missions, and is mostly urged by the ignorant and indolent. To these facts we appeal, as already presented in this work. It may be founded, also, on a partial view of Missions; one or other unfruitful sphere being made the basis of an unjust generalization. Let it be remembered that the field of Missions is the world, and that sphere must be viewed in its entireness, not in a particular position. What have been the results of evangelistic efforts *on the whole*, and relatively to the numerous races and people to whom they have been directed? In the presence of an extended productiveness, we can draw no conclusion from a partial sterility.

But, laying aside the facts of extensive success, it behoves the objector to consider—In what a world does he make this objection, and respecting the operations of what religion? The world knew not *Him*. It were, therefore, no wonder, had it, to the present day, not known his messengers. The world crucified him, the guiltless One; we need not be astonished were the history of Missions thus briefly written:—Men of God went forth to labour, but were cast out as evil and killed. Again: Of what a gospel is this objection made? One, which when uttered by the guileless lips of Jesus himself, made its converts only in units, not multitudes. Three years after *his* preaching, and miracles, and all his benignant influences on the minds and bodies of men, no more than one hundred and twenty disciples dared to meet for prayer in the upper room; and this, notwithstanding the preparatory process of the Law and the Prophets, and the more proximate ministrations of John the Baptist. The objection is based upon a misapprehension of the position of *truth* in this world, and the office of its messengers. Truth, is like its Lord, 'despised and rejected of men.' It has ever been militant on the earth, but never a universal conqueror. It has often to struggle for its existence in a world of falsehood; or, rather, the God of truth has often to put forth his energy to maintain for it a habitation among men. By the law of its being, as hitherto developed, it blesses and suffers; heals and is wounded; it calls and is rejected; testifies and is disbelieved. It stretches out its hand to a disobedient people. It has gained a sufferance on the earth, but has never been enthroned. It has won for itself a way, not gained an apotheosis. It is to prevail, but never has prevailed. *Its* times and seasons are in the Father's hands. It has taken hearts captive, not peoples—it has ruled over individual spirits, not aggregates of men. It calls out a people from the Gentiles rather than the Gentiles themselves. It ministers to a little flock, and gives to them the kingdom.

Further: Is the objection before us carried to a practical issue? Is it insinuated that we should suspend Missions? Do our objectors forget that we have received an unconditional command to prosecute them; and that, consequently, as the presence of success does not constitute their obligation, so its absence does not annul it?

But there must be some standard by which the objector is mentally testing the work of modern Missions, and pronouncing it lacking. What, then, is the object of comparison? Is it the work at home? Is he beguiled by appearances of Christian England, in the nineteenth century, expecting that Mission spheres are to become conformed to it? Does he forget the lengthened processes in providence and grace which have been required to bring the churches in this nation to their present numbers, influences, and moral and spiritual position? How chequered has been their history, how frequent their trials, ere they have been able to occupy their present standing! What multiplied instructions, what diversified means of grace, what holy examples, what purifying and disciplining measures, have been in operation to place them where they are! And, moreover, what numerous concomitant influences of civilization, national temperament, civil liberty, social customs, institutional advantages, have helped to work out those moral phenomena whereby British society in this age is distinguished!—which influences are mostly lacking in the heathen world. Can any one expect the converts of thirty or fifty years' history to present the same spiritual phenomena? 'Let us judge righteous judgment.' But, to retort the charge, is not the analogy, when justly presented, *on the side of Missions?* Has the heathen portion of England been the scene of successes at all comparable with those which have been realized abroad? Or, on the contrary, has not the progress of the gospel at home been much slower than that of many missionary spheres? Within thirty or fifty years, what institute of the heathen society of Britain has been abolished? Which of her idolatries has she given up? What national form of iniquity has ceased? What terrific 'social evil' has been expurgated? What classes of men who pander to iniquity, and minister to moral corruption, have died out from want of employment? Apply the question to any given spot, to a county, or the kingdom. Alas! for her gin palaces, her dens of iniquity, her gambling-houses, destroying more than perish by the human sacrifices of Africa, or the self-immolations of India. Do they not yet stand before us in all their cruel strength, towering pride, and baneful influence? But, within the same period, whole groups of islanders have discarded every public form of iniquity, and abolished every institute opposed to the gospel.

By what other analogy does the murmurer against Missions seek to justify his objections? Is it that of the apostolic age? Our answer is, that we often deceive ourselves in the estimate of the early progress of Christianity, and transfer the realized aggregate results of the second and third centuries to apostolic days. Taking in the end from the beginning we attach to the one what only belongs to the other; we ascribe to years what was the work of centuries, and consider instantaneous what was really protracted. Seeing Christianity enthroned in the age of Constantine, we forget the awful and reiterated persecutions prior to such an era; in the fact of her crown, we are apt to forget the cross which she bore for such a protracted season; in the final patronization of Christ's religion by philosophy, we lose sight of the period during which it was its bitterest enemy; and, in its final adoption by the multitude, we forget how long their virulent cry was, 'Take the Christians to the lions.' Slow, gradual, and partial were the first advances of the truth. Long, wearing, and severe were the oppositions of its enemies. Every inch of ground gained was, indeed, a step to future progress and easier conquests; but, in the early conflict, every inch was fiercely contested, and gained only by 'striving unto death.' When the aged Peter wrote, it was to *strangers scattered* through Pontus, Galatia, Cappadocia, Asia, and Bithynia, *not to those provinces converted to the faith.* When Paul wrote his epistle, it was not to Christian Rome, but to *a few Christians in Rome.* He made converts in most towns, but he left the towns *heathen.* He left no church at Iconium, or Lystra, or Athens, to whom he could write one of his immortal epistles. What was the state of Judea when he bade it a final farewell? On the occasion of his voyage and memorable shipwreck, was Syracuse converted to God, and had the Cretans become truthful? Was the ship, whose sign was 'Castor and Pollux,' owned by one not an idolater, or manned by Christian sailors? Did the wrecked apostle find Melita a Christian Island? Was Appii-forum a Mission out-post? When he was beheaded, or Peter crucified, what temple at Athens, or Corinth, or Rome was shut from want of worshippers, or from the priests having become Christian presbyters? Such results did take place, but how long a time first elapsed! When they glorified God in their death, no institute of Greek or Roman paganism had been abolished. The stoa of Zeno had not been vacated. Epicurus had not lost his bands of admirers. Platonism still enrolled its disciples. Seneca did not introduce Christian morals into his ethics. The rule of 'gods many and lords many' still dominated, the schools of a false philosophy were still frequented, and the rites of superstition still prevailed. The dying apostles looked by faith only to the final subjugation of heathenism. The success of modern Missions, tested even by apostolic history, is, then, far from discouraging. And wherein the great advantage lay with the apostles, that fact has its own ample solution, without detracting from the merits of the humbler position we occupy. They had powers which we have not, and a faith which we have not; added to which, the Spirit, whose office it was to 'justify' Christ to the judgments of men, and glorify him in their hearts, was poured out in an abundance by the recently ascended and glorified Redeemer. Yet, notwithstanding all our deficiencies, which are grievous, and none more so than in the class of objectors, who are hinderers of the work, none who have marked the progress of the truth, as evinced not so much by actual profession of converts, as by the large increase of moral convictions, the enlightenment of conscience, the preparedness to believe, have ever felt discouraged. As a rule, the oldest and most experienced missionaries, those who can compare the past with the present, who can count the steps and measure the ascent of past progress, are most hopeful. Those who view the work through the haze of distance, whose judgment is clouded by the obscurity of reports, and who are testing by false standards, and especially the heartless and speculative, are most replete with dissatisfaction.

There is an objection of another form. It arises from a painful, and oftentimes selfish and Christ forgetful sense of the expenditure which is involved in Missions; of time, talent, feeling, money, life. Many say in heart, and a few with the mouth, '*Wherefore this waste?*' There is at times much of the spirit of Judas, as well as his very words, in this inquiry. But it may be urged, from a less culpable state of mind. Who has not, at times, whether in the constituency or directorship at home, or in actual labour abroad, *felt* with poignancy the severe loss, especially of life, which is occasioned by Missions? What sad mementoes of the past are the cemeteries of Calcutta, Constantinople, Sierra Leone. How frequent the tidings of bereavements and separations. We admit all the facts urged, only a fraction of which is known to Christians generally, but we deny the conclusion drawn from them.

We admit *the expenditure* of Missions, in its widest sense, to be great, but we deny *the waste*. The ointment poured forth is costly, and it might be given to the poor; but it is best used as it is. To the question before us, we answer by pointing to all that has been realized in Missions, in the regeneration of man, in the glorification of God.

An infinitesimal portion of what has been effected would be a reward fully compensatory of all that has been expended. We quote the words of an eminent minister at the commencement of American Missions: 'I solemnly aver, that were there but one heathen in the world, and he in the remotest corner of Asia, if no greater duty confined us at home, it would be worth the pains of all the people in America to embark together to carry the gospel to him.' Viewed in the light of the Scripture, these are sound words. But, further, when will professing Christians learn that the value of every thing, and every person, is in its subjection to the will and subservience to the glory of God; that there is nothing precious which is not made so by his use of it, nor aught wasted which has had the remotest connection with him; that the despicable standards of earth are not to be applied to spiritual objects; that the perishable affords no measure of the imperishable interests of souls and eternity?

Guided by these principles, we affirm that in the evangelistic work, as indeed in every work of faith and labour of love, *nothing is wasted.* To sense and reason much seems wasted. The money changers declare much money has been wasted—it was expended on utterly unproductive materials. Those who value time apart from eternity—and life irrespectively of immortality, declare many valuable lives wasted. Those who view sacrifices of feeling, disruption of ties, social sorrows, and domestic distresses, without their connection with the glory of God, and the joy and exaltation which will succeed them, declare that much of what is sacred in human interests is wasted. But, no; nothing is wasted. Every fragment is put into its basket, so that nothing will be lost.

First, nothing is lost to God. Every act of faith has honoured HIM—every labour of love has been a sweet smelling savour unto him. He has been glorified in the self-denial, and consecration unto death, of his saints. A world of professors—'Lord, Lord,'—is nothing to him, compared with one who has *done* his will. Every life has, in its premature end, been precious in his eyes as a whole burnt offering. All costly sacrifices of feeling, or interest, or relationships, are so many oblations which yield 'a sweet smelling savour' to him.

Nothing is lost to the individual; either as

regards present grace or future glory. What sanctifying influences have been exerted by missionary labour and circumstance on the labourers themselves! By the discipline of missionary work have been trained the most exquisitely gracious souls that earth has ever known, who were here burning and shining lights ere they were translated to the heavenly hemispheres to shine as stars for ever. When were last words breathed by a holier heart than that of Martyn? But how much was that holiness matured by his missionary experiences. When was a more matured spirit emancipated from the tenement of suffering than that of Judson? But how large a share in this sanctification is to be ascribed to the disappointments, struggles, and trials of his missionary career. If we compare his earlier with his later life, we see the marked influences of all his endurances and conflicts as a missionary. Bitterness of solitude, the peculiar heaviness of domestic losses, the dreariness of spirit in the absence of manifest results, all have tended to imprint the seal of holiness on the missionary's soul, and to make him, ere his departure from earth, a holier man than he would have been without such influences. The Indian evangelist, as he stood on the ruins and desolations of his Christian settlements, exclaims, 'My heart hath much ado to hold up my head; it doth daily lead me to the Everlasting Arms, where alone is my hope and help; the world is a place and state on which I will lean no more.'

As nothing is lost to character, so nothing is lost as regards personal glory. Every act of faith is registered, every labour of love is ready to be requited. Every sorrow has entered HIS ears; every tear is treasured up; every loss is recorded. 'They that turn many to righteousness shall shine as the stars for ever.' With peculiar force are the words of the Redeemer applicable to the faithful missionary. 'Ye are they which have continued with me in my temptations, and I appoint unto you a kingdom, as my Father hath appointed unto me.' He that would not allow the labouring ox to be muzzled, that he might eat the fruit of his labour, will not leave the labouring spirit of man without a commensurate reward in heaven.

Further—Nothing has been lost to the great cause of evangelization. The prayers and labours of the departed, every hallowed exercise of thought and feeling, every expenditure of energy, fruitless though it seem, has its important bearing on the coming of the kingdom, in hastening, or maturing, or extending it. Like the deep and rapid river of France, losing itself beneath the rock and reappearing after a while, everything done in the sphere of Missions, however for a while lost, will eventually reappear. One soweth and another reapeth. Those who bestow no labour gather the harvest of the preceding ones who *did* labour. The influx of the Karens into the kingdom of God—had it no relation to the first labourers in Burmah, who lived and died without knowing them? Had the fifteen years of fruitless labour of Hans Egede, in Greenland, no connection with the afterwards fruitful labours of the Moravians? Had not all the desultory efforts of the two first Chinese missionaries important bearings on the evangelization of all China? Had not the brief spaces of labour, and the shortened lives of the first Sierra Leone missionaries, a part in the consummation of the extensive conversions that have since ensued? And all this, not only by the relation of cause and effect, whereby spiritual agency, in all its parts and sections, is so bound together, as that each is causally essential to the other, and all are concerned in the final issue, but by that medial relation to God whereby he blesses some for the sake of others, and in the sphere of Missions shows his graciousness in answer to prayers long since offered, and in requital of labours long since performed, but which have abode before him as a memorial. Does not God view this work as a whole, and is not his blessing dispensed *in consideration of* past as well as present labours? Is not the warmth and fruitfulness of noon the sum of all the solar influence from early dawn? and are not autumn's fruits the issue of the bracing spring and genial summer, in conjunction with the labours of those seasons? Yes, we are entering into others' labours, and others shall enter into ours. Those who have gone before us, and departing said, 'We have spent our strength for nought'—we are reaping what they sowed, not the fruits of our own hands. And thus there is a link binding labourers together, as well as conjoining labours, and in one harmonious company, *he that soweth and he that reapeth shall soon rejoice together.*

Nor is aught lost to the church. Holy examples kindle her own zeal, raise her spiritual standard, rouse cold professors, take away her reproach cast on her by the world for supineness and carnality, and show the power of her Christianity. A fund of experience has been obtained; lessons of rebuke have been received, counsels of wisdom have been treasured up. If her missionaries' lives are short in years and days, they are lengthened by their moral power, the labours condensed into them, and energies expended. Their deaths are not losses. An evangelist dies, but his death effects more than his life, in drawing others into the missionary work. A Colman in Burmah dies, and Boardman and his wife are raised to an intense zeal. Lyman and Munson in Sumatra perish by hands of violence, but their death arouses Lowrie to give himself to the work. He dies by the hands of pirates, and the news thrill many a heart, and induce others to join the missionary band. Harriet Newell falls an early sacrifice to anxieties and privations, and a Harriet Winslow is roused to follow her. In the spiritual warfare the standard is caught from the hand of him who falls, and raised aloft, and thus Christ's standard-bearers cease not from the earth.

Nor is anything lost to the world, which, spite of

its alienation from God, has its sympathies with the heroic and sublime, the disinterested and self-sacrificing, and can discern the constraining power of Christian principles, although itself a stranger to them. It understands the argument of self-consecration better than all logical evidences, and yields itself to the influences of earnest men, who love their fellow men. And withal, let it be remembered that all of sanctified human life that is lost to earth *is gained by heaven*; that those spirits which so adorned the missionary circle, and shed such glory on the church, being translated hence, are mixing with seraphs around the throne, and exchange earth's toils for heaven's labours and rest, which are ever sweetly conjoined.

Operations of unscriptural plans have been lost; attempts to civilize apart from evangelization have been lost. The labourers lacked the power of Christ to sustain them, his love to constrain them, as well as the outward blessing to crown their efforts. Plans carried out in a sectarian spirit have been lost; they lacked the unction of the Spirit. Works of personal ambition and greed of fame have been lost. Works carried on in impatience and unbelief, in a covenanting and bargaining spirit, made dependent for their continuance on the reward of fruits, these have been lost, and will again be lost. All expenditure of wood, hay, and stubble has been lost, but not an ingot of gold, not a bar of silver, not a single precious gem has been lost, in the endeavours of Christ's servants to build up the world-wide fabric of a Christianized humanity.

CHAPTER XI.

CHRIST IN THE MISSIONARY 'CALL.'

Analysis of the Phenomena of Evangelism.—Prerogative of the Glorified Christ.—Bearing of Individual 'Call' on the Formation of Missionary Societies.—Objects of the 'Call.'—Manner of the 'Call.'—Principles on which Men have Embraced Missionary work.—Obedience to Command:—Moravians—Carey—Judson.—The highest Expression of Self-consecration.—Recognition of the Glory of the Work:—Rhenius—Mylne.—Compassion for Souls:—Johnson—Knibb.—Relative Usefulness:—Macdonald—Grant.—Christ in the Operation of all these Principles.—Counter Supposition.—Summary.—'Call' of this Book.

An analysis of the phenomena of Missions presents us with three constituent elements: First, the agency; secondly, the 'effectual door;' and thirdly, the results. In each of these we see the presence and energy of the Lord Jesus Christ. He it is who by his grace creates and sustains the agency; he it is who opens up by his providence the sphere wherein that agency may be employed; he it is who by his Spirit produces results in the conversion and sanctification of souls. In other words, he 'calls' the missionary, gives him a field of labour, and secures the fruits of his labour. We devote this and the ensuing chapter to an illustration of the power and grace of Christ in the missionary agency.

He, whose name, as revealed to the ancient

church, was 'The Messenger of the Covenant;' who manifested himself in the ineffable glory that overshadowed the tabernacle, and shone forth between the cherubim; whose Spirit dwelt in the prophets, and spake by them; who when on earth called unto himself his disciples and chose from them 'apostles,' has 'in these latter days' the undoubted prerogative of sending into the world, as his own ambassadors, the ministers of his gospel. As the Father sent him, so he now sends his servants. His own commission is carried on in the persons of his disciples. That universal power which is given him in heaven and earth has scope for exercise in the Mission of apostles, whose 'acts' consequently originate in himself. He 'calls' them. They are his. To him they owe their evangelistic being, and position, and fruits. He is their source, their authority, their life. And here at the outset it is worthy of remark that the organizations now existing for *sending* missionaries mostly originated in the specific 'call' of individuals *to go.* The church at large did not first lay hold of the missionary idea, and apprehend the privileges of the work. It did not first lay down the axiom of the duty of sending, and then seek for individuals whom it might send. No, the first 'call' of Christ was to individuals. As in Scripture, so in modern missionary history, the voice of Jesus was not *send*, but '*go* into all the world.' A sense of individual obligation to go, spreading far and wide, originated the sense of obligation to send. Missionaries were not the result of the felt wants and uttered appeals of the church, but the sense of obligation of the church has itself been the result of individual calls. Men first exclaiming, 'Woe unto us if we preach not the gospel,' have produced a corresponding conviction in the church, 'Woe unto us, if we send not the gospel.' In America, Judson and Mills, with kindred spirits, presented themselves to the churches, and said, 'We *must* go to the heathen; we *dare* not repress our convictions;' and hence the organization of the American Missions. So unprepared were the churches of America for the missionary movement, that some signatures were struck off from the list of those who with Judson addressed the 'Association,' lest the number of youthful candidates should *alarm*. Cold and reluctant was the consent of many of the brethren. The general voice declared the undertaking fanatical, and many drew back from it. Although the line was not so clearly defined in Britain, yet is it true of it, viewing the rise of the evangelistic spirit in its general history, that a missionary church did not create missionaries, but missionaries, receiving their call and commission from Christ, created a missionary church. Dr. Coke, so successful in kindling a missionary spirit among the Wesleyans, himself traversed the globe as a missionary. Carey, ere he roused the Baptist churches, felt his individual obligation to go. Some of the founders of the 'Missionary Society' were themselves desirous of becoming the earliest missionaries. Thus the excellency of the power is of

God, and not of man. In the call of individuals, in making them willing, and thus fitting instruments in awakening the church itself to a sense of its obligation, we see the presence and agency of Christ.

Various are the modes in which Christ uses his prerogative. He calls *whom* and *by whom*, and *when* and *where*, and *as* he will. 'Who will go for us?' may be heard from him by the rapt prophet in the temple, by an Ezekiel on the banks of the Chebar, or by an Amos in gathering his sycamore fruit. 'Follow me,' may strike the listening soul by the 'Lake of Gennesareth'; or at the 'receipt of custom,' or on the high road to Damascus. When the learned are not ready, he calls the unlearned, and endows them with his own wisdom. When the ordained ministry are not prepared for his service in so arduous a work, he calls men from the plough and the sheep-cote, the loom, the forge, the factory, the shop. Many called to the work have had to say like Amos, 'I am no prophet, nor the son of a prophet.' When Britain's sons would not consecrate themselves to this service, he took his 'choice vessels' from the little cantons of Switzerland or the villages of Germany. He has raised up a ministry for foreign work which may be termed *unique*. Many of those whom he has chosen, but for that peculiar call to the missionary work, would never have entered the ministry at all. Nay, farther, many are in the home ministry who would not have been introduced into it but from the primary dedication of themselves to foreign labour.

The 'call' may come like the rushing mighty wind of the upper chamber, or like the still small voice heard by Elijah in the cave. It may come with an irresistible conviction, or it may be the issue of a long painful process of judgment. The heart may yield to it after a struggle, or receive the first intimation with a joy unspeakable. It may bring with it an overwhelming display of Christ's glory in the work of redeeming souls, exciting intense desire to promote it by personal instrumentality, or it may transfuse into the heart a melting sympathy with human woes, such as made Jeremiah exclaim, 'Oh that my head were waters, and mine eyes a fountain of tears.' Its accompaniments may be indignation and zeal for the Lord of Hosts, or love and compassion for the multitude of sinners.

The 'call' may be direct or indirect. Jesus may speak to the soul in such a tone that it may rest assured it is not the voice of a stranger; or, there may be a chosen medium of his utterance—a friend, a stranger, a pamphlet, a book, a sermon. As the arrows of his quiver are many, so are the methods in which he collects and places them there, as well as the uses to which he assigns them.

Those who have been manifestly 'called' of God to the missionary work, who have not only retained the conviction of the fact throughout a life-long career, but made their calling and election sure by a holy, consistent, and often evidently successful course, have been constrained to embrace the work by different principles, according as they might view it from the stand-point of obligation or privilege, duty or taste. It may have presented itself to them in its relations to the world, to be saved by its means; or in its relation to God, to be glorified thereby; or in its relation to themselves, as affording scope for their spiritual tastes, and the exercise of their divinely bestowed endowments. But we discern in all these different operations concurring in one result, the personal agency of Christ.

In attempting to classify the principles on which men have acted, and the feelings by which they have been affected, we do not intend to signify that these are so distinct from each other as never to be blended in the same individual experience, but that in distinct minds will be found the operation of specific truths, or specific aspects of the same truth; so as to call into exercise different states of mind, predominating over the rest, and sufficiently characteristic to distinguish one missionary from another.

First, some have embraced missionary work in simple obedience to the command, 'Go ye into all the world and preach the gospel to every creature.' Perhaps the greater number of missionaries have been actuated by this principle, recognizing in Christ's own words the broadest, most appreciable and convincing call. A personal obligation to fulfil the last injunction of Christ has been made to them a first truth, an axiom of life. Providential circumstances without, and the voice within, have concurred in one utterance to the soul—'Thou art the man.' They have thus interpreted the terms of the evangelistic plea—souls to be saved—a gospel to save them—a command to the church to dispense that gospel, which cannot be neglected by any one member save on the grounds of a personal or circumstantial inability, as distinct from want of predilection, or a positive unwillingness. They have felt that the thing to be proved is not why they should go, but why they should not go. The command has been the primary argument; exemption from the application of which has to be made clear to the conscience. Christ has stood out before them as a 'Lord' and 'Master.' His command has come to their judgments and consciences, with all the freshness of yesterday's utterance, and all the vividness of a living, personal authority. Moravians seem especially to have acted on this principle. In it we see a solution of the missionary character of their entire church. They deem themselves as a church established to carry out the commands of Christ, of which this is the foremost. Hence they stand ready to fill up the numbers, when failing, of those already in the field, or to enter on new stations, whenever providential circumstances, or the voice of the brethren, call them to do so. Whether they have had to select spheres suitable to qualifications, or to obtain qualifications suitable to spheres, they have felt their work, as a church, to be to preach the gospel to every creature, as fulfilling the law of Christ, as answering the end of a church institute. They have not waited for any special inward call, in the presence of a general command. Christ's will has been their sufficient warrant for evangelistic labours. With this obligation resting on their conscience, no impediments have sufficed to make them abandon their work. Neither poverty nor climate, hatred nor indifference, scorn nor persecution, nor even lack of success, have checked their onward movements. We adduce one or two individual illustrations of this principle:—

A Baptist minister, supplementing the scanty support furnished by his small and poor church, by either the avocations of his former trade, or scholastic efforts, yet finds time, and cultivates a heart, for attention to the *world's* wants and woes. He constructs a rude map of paper sheets pasted to each other, draws with a pen continents and islands, fills up the spaces with an account of their religion and population. Like Humboldt, he knows and cares for no less than a whole world. Like him, he scans each parallel of latitude, and meridian of longitude. But with what a different eye and soul! Man is the sole object of his study. His false religions make his heart bleed; his need of the gospel touches all his sensibilities; and, from the narrow compass of his present sphere, he longs to hasten to his relief. He tells his scholars of the geographical position, physical aspects, and resources of foreign lands; but, underneath his outer lessons to them, he is revolving those lessons in which a Divine love has instructed him. There is present to him by night and day one great idea—obligation—his Saviour's command *ought* to be obeyed; as a Christian, his *duty* is to take or send the gospel. Carrying out this idea, he writes on '*The duty* of Christians to attempt the spread of the gospel among heathen nations.' At the religious services, he is ever descanting on the same subject. At the ministers' meeting, he urges that it is '*their bounden duty*' to evangelize the world. He offers himself to fulfil the duty which lies heavy on his conscience. The Baptist minister of Moulton is the CAREY of Serampore. Christ has called him to an Indian career of usefulness.

An American youth, of vivid imagination and towering ambition, who has drunk deep into the spirit of the world, and sought to become acquainted with it in its several phases, whose strongest argument against the Bible was that it would not allow him to enter with zest and enjoyment in a career of worldly ambition, was, by a gradual illumination of the Holy Spirit, converted to Christ, and immediately dedicated himself to the work of the ministry. His literary and political ambition is now supplanted by high and holy thoughts, pure principles, and spiritual ends. His glory and honour are now concentred in one point—the glorification of Christ. In this impressible state of mind, itself the work of the

Spirit, the gift of Christ, he reads Buchanan's 'Star in the East.' A new train of thought is excited. The deep fountains of feeling are opened. Missionary labour appears to him attractive. It seems, to his sensitive mind, to combine the very essence of romance and charm of poetry, with all that is noble in principle, benevolent in philanthropy, and devoted in religion. This temporary excitement, and these first extravagant feelings, dissolve the fascinating charm of home, and make the thought endurable of abandoning wonted pursuits and animating prospects. But this excitement passes away. It is but the morning cloud and the early dew. But that cloud passed not away without pouring a blessing on the soul over which it hung, nor did that dew dissolve ere it had rendered fresh and fragrant the spirit on which it rested. A strong desire to prosecute inquiries, and ascertain the path of duty, remains behind. The thought has been originated, the idea entertained; the principle yet needs to be imparted, and He who has man in his entire keeping, with all his natural susceptibilities, was about to impart that gift also. The young student is deeply meditating the subject in the solitude of the woods that skirt the Theological Seminary of Andover. Viewing the work from the human stand-point, he sees naught but thick darkness. He has no precedent to guide him; no missionary has gone before him to show the practicability of the measure he contemplates. The field of heathen labour is distant—how shall he reach it? The climate is unpropitious; he may fall an early victim to it. The inquirer is disheartened. Had he not better give up the idea—not urge it forwards to a conclusion, fraught with probable fatal consequences? No. *That 'last command'—the undying oracle—comes home to his heart with a power and clearness that bespeaks its utterance as direct from heaven:* 'Go into all the world, and preach the gospel to every creature.' He listens to the still small voice. He appropriates it as a command to himself. His doubts are dispersed. His wavering mind is resolved. On that very spot he determines at all hazards to obey, for the sake of pleasing the Lord Jesus Christ. In those moments, so precious to himself, to the church, and to Burmah, it is, according to his own confession, not faith that predominates; it is not love that is the paramount feeling; it is the sense of obligation, the spirit of obedience. He returns to his college room a missionary in heart and purpose. The student to whom we refer was JUDSON, the apostle of Burmah, the founder of the first church of the Burmese, and translator of the Scriptures. Among his fellow-students, of sympathy with himself, were RICHARDS and MILLS. When we consider that the gathering together of these kindred minds from different places, at this critical juncture, was the occasion of the formation of the first American society for the conversion of the heathen, we cannot but see with increased clearness the all-wise, all-gracious government of the Lord Jesus Christ.

Others have embraced the missionary work as the highest expression of self-consecration—a principle of which, as Christ is the object, so is he the author. Hence, dedication to the missionary work has been often the first-fruits of conversion. Love to Christ, and this work, have been consentaneous. The first consciousness of forgiveness has been followed by an unreserved surrender of body, soul, and spirit to God, and the specific form of consecration has been to the work of an evangelist. The newly justified soul, in the fruition of its unutterable peace, conscious also of the first-fruits of the spirit within, and having an earnest of future glory, referring all these unspeakable gifts to the free grace of God in Christ, hastes to devote itself to Him who has thus received him into his covenant, and sealed him an heir of salvation. A work like this, so identified with the Divine glory, in such harmony with the Divine will, having such holy heavenly issues in time and eternity, has presented that very sphere of action, and seemed to afford that scope for all his spiritual faculties which he so much desires, and he eagerly presses forward to embrace it. There is no altar so broad and deep to receive his whole burnt-offering as that of the evangelistic service. Prospective trials, sacrifices, self-denials, only make the work more attractive to him, as furnishing a better test of his sincerity, a better proof of his love. In its endurances, he can shew how ample is his love to his Redeemer; in bearing its crosses, he can testify how sincere is his attachment to Him who bore the cross and shame for him. The question, then, with him is not, *Must* I go? but, *May* I go? not, Is it my duty? but, May it be my privilege? The surrender has not been the yielding to an imperious necessity, but the grateful acceptance of a proffered gift. The office and the gift are viewed, not from the standpoint of law and obligation, but of the riches of grace, and a glory that excelleth. 'Oh, that to me,' has been his language, 'this grace may be given that I should preach among the Gentiles the unsearchable riches of Christ.'

Consecration to this work often takes place from a sense of the *glory* of the service. The distinction apprehended by faith, of a messenger of the Lord, a prophet of the Most High, a minister of the New Testament to the heathen world, stands out to the sanctified loving soul, as ineffably glorious. The office as conferred, the work as committed, the functions as appointed are invested with a dignity and grandeur which are shadowed only, not expressed, much less parallelled, by any human glory and dignity. The glory of the similitude of the evangelistic work to that of Christ has also affected the soul, and won it over to a dedication to Missions. The office of a missionary has been desired as the nearest approximation to that of Christ in its abasements and humiliations. It was this very glory which attracted Paul. 'That I may know Him and the power of his resurrection, and the fellowship of his sufferings, being made conformable unto his death.' The glory of the work, in its surpassing *results*, has likewise constrained the heart — the glory of winning souls to Christ, and thereby enhancing his joys, pleasing the Father, filling all heaven with praise. These principles find appropriate illustrations in the following sketches:

A Prussian youth, at seventeen years, is converted to Christ. He receives him into his heart as 'the Son of Man who came to seek and save the lost.' He yields himself unreservedly to him, as saying to him, 'Follow me.' His faith is that of obedience. He knows the Saviour as one whom he is henceforth to *follow*. His first resolves are to dedicate to him body, soul, and spirit, for the practice of righteousness. This youth, at his uncle's house, reads the reports of missionary societies, especially those of the Moravian brethren. He reads of Greenland, and the West Indies, and the idolatry of the East. The words of the Saviour, 'Follow me,' which he had made the rule of his new spiritual life, now come with special application to his soul. He is resolved to rise and follow him into the field of missionary trial. Relative objections are raised, and his feelings, for a moment, yield to the claims whereby relatives would keep him back. 'It is indeed folly to forsake mothers, brothers, and sisters, house and land, and go into foreign countries.' But his soul returns unto its rest. Rallying from a temporary surrender to temptation, he prays that Christ may cause his light and love to shine in his heart, and make the extension of his kingdom above all things precious to him. Continued thought and prayer show him his own unfitness; he recovers from the chilling impression by laying hold of the assurance of the apostle: 'I can do all things through Christ, who strengtheneth me.' He is dismayed by the thought of breaking all relative ties, but is consoled by Christ's words, 'Whosoever loveth father and mother more than me is not worthy of me.' In a short time every scruple is gone. He seeks to be trained as an evangelist, and finds all he desires in the pious seminary at Berlin. There, among the breathings of his soul, ere he was finally ordained, we find recorded the following prayer, 'O my Saviour, anew do I devote myself to thee; take, receive me as I am; give me Thyself, thy Father, and thy Holy Spirit; and sanctify and cleanse my heart from all darkness; finish thou the office of my Redeemer; and fit me to thy work, according to thy image in love, meekness, and humility.'

The man thus called was RHENIUS, who laid the foundation of the Tinnevelly mission, saw a church of hundreds raised from devil worshippers of South India, and left behind him a work, which in its now expanded form is unrivalled in extent, and whose issues are connected with the future history of evangelized India.

We subjoin another example of self-consecration:—

A shepherd lad, fulfilling as a hireling his worldly calling in the wilds of Scotland, is converted to God.

Until thirteen years of age, his heart is thoroughly averse from religion, reading the Bible only with reluctance and impatience, dreading as death the visit of his parish minister, uttering the common oaths, and seeking to invent new ones, and looking forward to his sixteenth year as one in which he might obtain a worldly fame for an adeptness as 'a vain and trifling youth.' He at length undergoes deep and fearful struggles of mind, during which he would gladly, in order to avoid exposure to the righteous judgment of God, have been transformed into a stone, or one of the fowls of the mountains, which were flying over his head. He finds a place of prayer only in the sheep-cote where the sheep are penned in the cold winter night. There he kneels, on a turf which he has placed in the damp and foul soil. In such a place, for *hours* in the dark night, he confesses to the God who heareth in secret, and implores forgiveness. Whilst watching his sheep by day, he reads religious books on the brow of the hill, and converses by their means with the departed martyrs and confessors of Christ in Scotland. The kindlings of sympathy with the good, and true, and beautiful, are excited by a Divine power, and though his soul has scarcely as yet found rest, as one justified by faith, he entertains the hope that he also may be honoured by God to confess his name, and bear testimony to the truth. After long groping his way in the thick darkness, he emerges, under Divine guidance, into the light of the knowledge of Christ, as a Saviour giving eternal life to as many as believe in him. Possessing peace and joy in believing, he consecrates himself to the Triune God, in the stillness of the valley, amidst the everlasting hills, to be ruled, sanctified, and saved by him. And now a holy zeal for the salvation of others is kindled, never to expire. He beseeches sinners, he prays for and with them; he writes tracts for the young, and with intense interest reads missionary records. The glory of God, and the salvation of souls, becomes so absorbingly the theme of thought and prayer, that the morning star often finds him where the evening star had left him, on his knees before the Lord, unconscious of the lapse of time, while realizing the divine glory, the wonders of redemption, and the solemnities of eternity. For some years he prays for the kingdom of Christ as a 'private Christian,' not entertaining the idea of personally engaging in the blessed work. Whilst lying on the hill side, just above his cottage, reading the 'Missionary Magazine,' the first strong desire to go far hence unto the Gentiles rises within him, a desire that never left him. He would then lay reading, weeping, praying, and longing for wings, that he might fly with the apocalyptic angel to preach the everlasting gospel. He communes at midnight with his pious schoolmaster on the state of the heathen world. An incident gives intensity to his feelings, and makes him put his thoughts into action. He hears of a friend becoming a missionary; the following question was immediately suggested to his mind, Will this man's salvation involve more of the riches of forgiving grace than mine? He is assured none can owe more to Christ than he does. He will then express that obligation. He will seek the advice of Christian friends with reference to his personal duty. They encourage him to apply to a missionary society. He appears for examination, a shepherd lad with his Sunday apparel, fresh from his native hills, before learned doctors in a university town. They express doubts respecting him. They see in him nothing indicative of future promise till they hear him *pray*. His close converse with the eternal God reveals the depth of his piety, the fervour of his love. They then encourage him to hope. They bid him go home and re-consider. He does so. He again appears, and is accepted. The shepherd lad becomes Dr. MYLNE, the second missionary to China, colleague of Dr. Morrison, the translator with him of the sacred Scriptures into the Chinese language.

Many have embraced the evangelistic work from deep sympathy with the wants and woes of men. A world in its wickedness and alienation from God stands out before the mind, with the vividness of a present reality. No occupation so engrossing as to lead to forgetfulness of it; no possessed joys hide its sorrows; no cares so overwhelm the mind as to cover this care. Every religious experience, whether joyous or depressing, only serves to deepen the solicitude for the heathen; the former by contrast, the latter by sympathy. A sense of their own nearness to Christ brings to their minds the distance of the heathen from him; their own forgiveness makes them realize more fully their condemnation; their own experience of an indwelling Spirit suggests the awful reality of unsanctified souls; their own glorious prospects, the unutterable gloom that hangs over the future of others. Life, with all conceivable joys, would to them be no life, were it debarred from doing good in the rescue of such Christless souls. Death would have its highest note of triumph at the close of a career of humble efforts to save others. Influenced by such considerations, men have sought the missionary's office, with the eagerness of an unquenchable passion. To tell them of a certain speedy death in their course, would be no hindrance to their design. Life has to them one value—that of saving souls. Let them have an opportunity of doing this *where their efforts are most needed*, and they will bless heaven for the boon, whatever of dark and distressing may be attached to it. The following sketch illustrates these remarks:—

A German mechanic, one of the twenty thousand who are found in the metropolis of Britain, mostly without God and Christ, under the pressure of poverty, is urged to seek Divine help. When despairing of comfort, a remembered text of infancy, 'Call upon me in the day of trouble,' inspires him with hope, and stimulates him to repair to the throne of grace. At the German church in the Savoy, he hears a missionary preach from, 'Come unto me, all ye that are weary.' His weary soul is brought to Christ. The lack of the bread that perisheth has been the occasion of making him seek the imperishable bread which the Son of Man giveth. In less than three years afterwards, a period filled up with efforts of a youthful holy zeal, to bring first his wife and then his fellow men to the love of the truth, he attends a public meeting in Fetter Lane, wherein missionaries are set apart for heathen lands. By one of those powerful and enduring impulses of which God alone is the author, and the seal of which is their subsequent fruitfulness, he is filled with an unspeakable sense of his own privileges of adoption and grace, and the contrasting perception of the misery of the Godless and Christless souls of the heathen. '*Oh, could I but go and help them, and tell them of Jesus, how gracious and merciful he is to sinners! I must see others go, but shall I never go?*' Such are the utterances of his heart. But domestic difficulties confront him, also a sense of his own disqualification for the work. Still he exclaims, 'Lord, to thee nothing is impossible; here am I, send me.' He tries, however, to quench the newly excited desires. 'Mountains of difficulties' arise before his mind. His reason cannot surmount them. The privilege of a call to go forth to the heathen is for others; not for *him*. As soon as he reasons thus, a dark cloud overshadows his mind, he loses his own wonted peace in Christ, and is again constrained to cry out, with a faith that removes mountains, 'Lord, to thee nothing is impossible, here am I, send me.' He feels that nothing else than the Lord's service can make him happy. Still, the final decision is suspended; and desires are suppressed. The mental darkness now becomes worse than ever. His heart seems within him like a heavy stone. He hears the word, but feels himself insensible as steel. He cannot utter a word in prayer. At length, the prisoner of hope is to be set free. With extreme reluctance he goes to hear a godly minister. What are the words of that evening's exposition? '*If once a desire is laid in the heart by the Holy Spirit, if it be to the holy ministry or any other office, that desire will never be quenched. The individual may try again and again to quench it, but he will never have any rest, till it be accomplished.*' 'Have not I then resisted the Holy Ghost, for I have sought to quench this desire again and again?' Such is now the alarming suggestion to his soul, and he is filled with anguish and horror. That word of God, the strength of so many weak, and solace for so many afflicted souls, comes home to his heart, 'My grace is sufficient for thee.' He is encouraged. He applies to the minister who preached. He is not allowed by him to despair of success. He is introduced to a missionary society. The mechanic and his wife, now converted, and willing to share her husband's toils and successes, are accepted as schoolmaster and mistress for Western Africa. He is appointed to Sierra Leone, the grave of missionaries, and populated by liberated slaves in the lowest scale of vice and heathenism. Again, a thick darkness comes over him. It is dissipated by the promise, 'I will bring the blind by a way that they knew not.' He is encouraged, and goes out with his life in his hand. After a few months' labours, the schoolmaster finds souls under his simple teaching crying out, 'What must we do to be saved?' He preaches to them 'Christ crucified.' Without the external call, the solemn ordination to the office of an evangelist, he is fulfilling the work. The Lord has not waited for the church's commission to be entrusted to him. He has made his own call effectual. Soon, however, the schoolmaster becomes an ordained preacher of the gospel. Ere he closes the ministry of seven years, his call has been substantiated in the conversion and sanctification of hundreds of degraded Africans. His epistle from Christ has been written on their renewed hearts. A flourishing, civilized and Christian colony long bewailed the death of their missionary JOHNSON.

A youth is standing before a compositor's case. A letter from a missionary is put into his hands to be printed in the Society's journal. It is from Java, written by a missionary, who, filled with hopes for the conversion of the Javanese, declares himself willing to live and die amongst them. The sentiment affects the heart of the pious youth. He treasures up his first desires to give himself to missionary work. The youth in after life converses with his brother on

Missions. Each fans the other's flame. Both dedicated themselves to the work. So strongly formed is the purpose, and so earnest the desire of one of them, that on being told that native teachers were being raised up, he bursts into tears, and exclaims, 'There will be no work left for us to do.' Of these two youths, the one ran a short but glorious course in the West Indies, the other was WILLIAM KNIBB, who gathered spiritual children from the degraded slaves of Jamaica by thousands, and was a grand instrument in procuring their emancipation.

To others, the conviction of a 'call' to missionary life has been the issue of a calm dispassionate judgment of the relative claims of a heathen world. A soul already consecrated, and engaged in God's service, has looked on the world with the inquiry — Who most needs me? where shall I be most useful? how can I use my talents most advantageously? On one hand are the claims of home, with its masses of semi-heathen population, but with a comparative abundance of labourers, its multiform modes of doing good, without the delay of learning a language, or the contingencies of a foreign sphere, or the painful consequences involved in expatriation. On the other hand are the claims of the heathen, for whose souls so few care, and amongst whom so few are competent, if willing, to conduct a Mission. The issue of the comparison of claims, is the conviction that Christ would have them go and labour among the latter. Such a conviction may have been furthered by a consciousness of adaptation to one sphere rather than the other, whereby the talents intrusted by the Lord of all, may, in home-labour, be comparatively useless—such as the faculty of learning languages; the capacity of physical endurance; the possession of a spirit of enterprise; capacity of adaptation to foreign scenes and modes of life and habits of thought. These have all justly had a weight in deciding the man of God as to his sphere of labour. By the operation of such a principle we have been furnished with some of our best missionaries.

The pastor of a Scotch church, with closest family and social relationships to his father-land, and wide sphere of labour in London, is oppressed with a sense of the claims of the heathen world. The missionary feeling which he entertained at the time of his youthful conversion, but which was suppressed, has only been brought into active exercise by the practical labours of the ministry at home. The missionary principle and feeling have already made him preach in the open air, and frequent the hovels of the outcasts. But he is desirous of labouring where he is most needed. The absence of the self-denying spirit of the church grieves his soul. The coldness with which the stern yet melting appeals from India are received excites his ardour, and he presses forward to fill up the gap from which so many keep aloof. Many are the alternations of his mind—sometimes elevated by hope, at others depressed by fear. He importunately seeks direction, and tries to form a judgment free from fleshly bias and personal predilections. He thus records the decision: 'I seem to have determined to go forth as a missionary. I say *seem,* because I can scarcely realize even the decision of my own mind. As an act of my own will, it is now decided, and I have taken God to witness upon it, with this single petition, that if I am labouring under a mistake or delusion, he will rectify it and deliver me. *My soul has been easily, freely, yet irresistibly drawn to its determination this forenoon.* I am calm and composed, as ever in my lifetime. There is nothing in my view but a simple act of obedience to Christ. I seem to myself *as a mere cypher, taking its place where the cyphering hand would have it to be.*' Tears, entreaties, and remonstrances confronted him, but the claims of a perishing world, and of a dying Saviour's love, were impressed on his soul. The fact of his already existing charge is brought with force, both by the presbytery and the people themselves, to divert him from his purpose. With a conscience void of offence, he thus solemnly declares to them the basis of his resolution: 'I declare to my brethren that *I believe in my conscience this to be a call from the Lord Jesus Christ,* and that, therefore, it is my duty to obey it, and go forth as his missionary servant to foreign parts.' In the life of MACDONALD, the teacher of Hindu youth in the Assembly's Institute, we see that call verified.

A young physician in Utica, of the United States, one who when a child had listened on a mother's knee to her missionary tales of Brainerd and Eliot, is induced in adult age to ponder the claims of Missions. He is useful and honourable in his profession, an elder of the church, a Sabbath School teacher, reputed a 'friend of the poor,' securing the confidence even of those who are enemies to his faith; he has parents and two children of a departed wife, and is surrounded by just such a class of associations, as, while it makes this world dear and attractive, binds to that particular locality which is their centre. His heart is affected by conflicting claims, and for awhile judgment is suspended. Why should *he* go, when it is the manifest duty of others, less attached by bonds of nature, and social ties? Why should he renounce actual usefulness for a contingent good? The calls of the heathen world are loud and pressing —it is a grievous thing that others do not attend to them. Christ's commands are imperative, and woe to those who ought, but do not go. But am I not free? Am I not where God would have me to be? Such are the musings of his pious heart. He prays. He examines himself. He canvasses his own and others' objections. 'Others *might* and ought to go, but they do not go. Their negligences will not excuse me. I cannot let millions perish because others do not give them the bread of life.' He decides the matter by the question, '*Can I do more at home or abroad for the conversion of the world? Where am*

I most needed?' This question is not difficult of solution. At home he would not be missed. Others will occupy his place. Abroad, he may relieve one hundred fold more misery, perhaps save by his medical skill the lives of missionaries of inestimable value. His opportunities of doing good at home yield to those a foreign field affords, in which he might be the only spiritual guide to thousands who would never otherwise be reached. The church which he leaves, also, will be blessed for and in his loss, according to God's compensatory economy. His children may be committed to others who will act on his behalf. His parents, and brethren, and sisters, are not dependent upon him. Such are his thoughts. A meeting of the Board of Missions is appointed to be held in his own town. He attends. A report is read. Persia is mentioned in it—its spiritual claims—the details of missionaries already labouring there, their trials and griefs, their joys and successes. A chord of his heart vibrates. It is the central one which gives the peculiar tone to all the rest. To Persia his heart is directed. He singles out the Nestorians, an ancient church, but now corrupted from the ways of Christ. He reads the works of missionaries who have been in the field, ponders their rousing exhortations to their father-land; he also studies such works as may make him acquainted with the country. He then expresses the full, final decision of his judgment and his heart, love and duty conjoined, to the Board of Missions. '*As I ponder the worth of the soul, and see millions going to the awful retributions of eternity, my heart grieves that so few heed their cries, and I am ready to exclaim, "Here am I, send me." At Jesus' call, and sustained by the blessed assurance, "I am with you always," I stand ready to go, in the face of danger and death, to any part of the world under the dominion of the prince of darkness.* What though I tear away from children and all the endearments of home, wear out life amid toil and uffering, and find a grave among strangers? Only let me be the means of salvation to some lost sinner, who shall meet me in heaven, and I shall bless God for it through eternity.'

The man who spoke thus was Dr. GRANT, whose name is connected, as long as history endures, with the mountain Nestorians, who performed harassing journeys in Mesopotamia and Kurdistan, threading the deep gorges and scaling the snowy heights of the latter region, who laboured in season and out of season, among the Nestorians of the hills, or of the Persian plains. His body lies on the banks of the Tigris, but his spirit and his works have remained. His memory is blessed; he secured for himself, among friends and foes — and he had no foes but such as were of Christ—a testimony that he was a man of God.

In these several methods, and by the influence of these several principles, we see the Lord Jesus calling his servants, as his 'chosen vessels,' to carry his name to the several sections of the world. That agency cannot be hidden by the several instrumentalities employed to draw them forth. There is, indeed, a power of truth, but it is only as applied by him. There is the force of distinct motives, but only as presented by him. There is the influence of principles, but only as made to operate by him on the heart and conscience. Do his servants enter on the work in obedience to his express command? it is because he impresses it on their consciences. The outer call to missionary work already exists, indeed, in the word, but his Spirit brings it home to the soul. The mere outward word becomes an inward conviction. The general command becomes particular and personal. There is an operation by the Spirit of Christ analogous to that whereby the outward and universal call of the gospel to sinners becomes an effectual and personal call to believers. There is nothing new, but the old outstanding truth is impressed on the conscience and converted into a principle of action. Selfish human nature would refuse to appropriate the injunction, and would resist the application of a command addressed to none by name. But Christ gives the inquirer the spirit of candour and truth and impartiality. In the case also of the affections, there is scope for the agency of Christ. Who so sanctifies the heart as to make it covet missionary work; who so raises the spirits of a man, so quickens his spiritual sensibilities, so draws them to God, as to induce a self-consecration; who presents the glories of the Divine service in a manner fitted to charm and absorb the soul? Who but He who appeared in the temple to Isaiah, or passed by and shewed the skirts of his glory to Moses, or spake to Elijah in Horeb? Again, do his servants become evangelists from the principle of sympathy—man with man? It is he who is the author of that sympathy. It is a part of his nature, and is itself imparted by him.

Let us make a contrary supposition to that we have defended. Imagine Christ to cease to 'call,' and who else could speak with sufficient power? Let him forbear to 'draw,' and who would be drawn to so arduous a work? Let him fail 'to constrain,' and where would be found in the range of personality or of principle sufficient motive to 'constrain' a selfish nature to such deeds of self-denial? The creation of the ministry, whether for home or foreign labour, is his special prerogative; and, with respect to the latter especially, there is nothing in the wide world of motive save what is derived from his word; nor is there any *person* of sufficient influence to present that motive, save himself—the living, ever-present One. When we see the Northampton mechanic going forth from his limited sphere to translate the Scriptures into the language of India—the Cambridge wrangler resigning his worldly honours and 'departing far hence to the Gentiles,' to contend with the Brahmans of India and the Moolahs of Persia—the Rugby student called from his college to lay down his life in the conversion of the Telugoos—the American physician leaving Utica to take his medicinal art in conjunction with the gospel of grace, in order to secure a position among the fallen churches of the East—the German warehouseman abandoning his occupation to become the spiritual father and civilizer of hundreds of negroes in Sierra Leone—the compositor leaving his 'case' to go forth and further the double emancipation of the negroes of the West Indies—the student of Andover, with his wife, the delight of a new England home, going forth to enlighten Burmah—cases which are multiplied year by year, with as striking providences and as effectual issues—we have an evidence of Christ's personal presidence in the evangelistic work. The missionaries are but the executives of Him who is King in Zion. In the disposition of their minds, the inspiration of their souls, the arrangement of their circumstances, we see him 'high and lifted up,' and his glory fills the living temple of the church.

Reader, is there no 'call' to you in this book to the evangelistic work? Do all the facts of the heathen world brought before you, its sins, and miseries, and woes, present and future, constitute no 'call' to go and relieve them? Do all the past successes attending the labours of those who have gone forth to the Gentiles, constitute no 'call' to you to go and join them in their labours, that you may joy in their joy, and triumph in their victory? Do the examples furnished of those who have obeyed the voice of Jesus in his word and providence, and to whose mission he has affixed his own seal, constitute no 'call' to you to join the holy band?

Feeble as is the instrument before you, throw it not away; imperfect as are the statements, discard them not. There may be in all that has been advanced a call to *you* from the Lord Jesus. He may design by this book to urge missionary work on your conscience. If so, in the words of Judson, '*Resist him at your peril.*'

CHAPTER XII.

CHRIST IN THE MISSIONARY CHARACTER, ENDOWMENTS, AND COURSE.

Sympathy with God — Its Developments — Christ its Author. — Sympathy with Man—Its Origin in Christ.—Gifts and Graces. —Christ keeps his Evangelists from 'The Evil.'—Missionary. Discouragements—Christ Sustains.—Fiery Trials—Christ Upholds.—Joyous Experiences of Missionary Life.—Christ in them. —Missionaries 'the Glory of Christ,' in their Mission and Character.—Honour conferred by Christ on the Church.

In the call of men to the evangelistic work, we behold the energy, and wisdom, and grace of Christ. We witness them equally in their gifts, and graces, and numerous endowments. First, the spirit and genius of missionary *character* indicate Christ's self-communicating grace. There *is* a missionary character which may be considered normal, diverse indeed in details, and varying in forms, yet essentially the same. We need not now 'a priori' statements of what missionaries ought to be, and must be. We have the matter-of-fact knowledge of what missionaries have been, and yet are. A missionary biography which did not develope certain characteristics, would be pronounced deficient, and the original of it a failure. There are specific lineaments which belong to every genuine apostle. They are present to our minds when we talk of them. Their presence excites no amazement; their absence would be to us unaccountable. There has been constituted, and actually developed, a certain fixed type of character. Now as that type has its antitype in Christ himself, the original Messenger of the covenant, the Sent of God, the Apostle and High Priest of our confession, so is it the product of Christ. The formation of the peculiar habit of mind is *his* formation. It is a manifestation of Christ, and shows the intimacy of the bond between Christ and Missions.

Let us resolve the missionary character into its distinctive elements. It assumes its peculiar form from the nature of the office, which has a double relationship. The ambassador of God is in relation with the God who sends, and with man to whom he sends. As in human embassies, so in the divine, there must be a sympathy with the source of authority and investiture by whom the embassy is established, and with the prince and people amongst whom the embassy is conducted. The missionary must be in moral sympathy with God. He must also be in sympathy with man. The perfect harmony of the twain was alone in Him who comprehended the twofold nature of God and man. His divinity placed him in closest mental oneness and moral sympathy with God. His humanity brought him at all points, sin excepted, into close identity with man. None could respond more fully to the entire counsel of God. None could so fully take on himself, and bind up his soul and being with the circumstances and interests of humanity. That heart of

Jesus, which was the centre of Divine sympathies, pulsated, also, to every human interest and affection. Hence he was the perfect Apostle. His embassage was fulfilled with an entire reconciliation of Divine claims and human interests; of God's justice and man's guilt. He pleaded with man for God. He pleaded with God for man. He secured a reception of God's authority in the heart of man. He secured the remission of man's transgression in the heart of God. In the human ambassador these elements are never found in perfect harmony, or in the same relative proportion. On their due adjustment depends greatly the success of the missionary. But we do see in all true servants of God these two essential characteristics. We see, first, a sympathy with God—his dishonoured law; his violated justice; his character ignored or despised; his glory unknown: and, secondly, a sympathy with man—his ignorance; his wickedness and consequent wretchedness here, and exposure to woe hereafter. These two sympathies form the very basis of missionary character, and modify all its developments. According to the intensity of either of them, and the proportion of the one to the other, will be the individuality of the missionary.

Let us observe the operation of these two habits of mind. First, their exercise of sympathy with God. Their spirit is moved at heathen ignorance, because thereby God's glory is obscured; at heathen errors and superstitions, because his truth is falsified and his great and terrible name is dishonoured; at heathen idolatry, because the glory of the Incorruptible is changed into corruptible things; at heathen sins, because God's law is violated; at heathen's ignorance of the gospel, because Christ is thereby not known and loved as a Redeemer. One grand motive, therefore, of prosecuting missionary labour has been to make God's glory known to men—glory in the works of creation, in the wonders of providence, and especially in the economy of redemption. To communicate this glory, even in its elements, or in its dimmest intimations, such as the feeble intellect and darkened heart can receive, has been an object pursued with all the intensity and perseverance of a passion. How many, like Vanderkemp, have cheerfully stooped from heights of science and literature, to teach the rudest mind the first principles of God's truth? To make God *known* and *honoured* as the Creator and Redeemer of men, they have willingly left society with all its endearments, and made themselves the hermits of the forest or the rovers of the wilderness. They have felt that in the enlightenment and sanctification of souls, the richest honour will accrue to God; that in the conversion of the heathen, the Divine character and perfections will be gloriously illustrated—the object of study to angels and men now, and in the ages to come. The very degradation of the heathen will illustrate the grace of Him who rescues them—their ignorance, his enlightening power. The more foul their stains, the more precious will be the blood that cleanseth; the deeper they are steeped in iniquity, the more illustrious the power of grace that saves. 'Oh how his name would be glorified,' exclaimed one of the most saintly of women, and the most earnest of missionaries, 'by taking them (the Hindus) from their social, mental, and moral degradation, and making them joint heirs with himself to a heavenly inheritance; by at last clothing them in white robes, with palms in their hands, and giving them mansions in his Father's house.' This desire that God may be glorified in the heathens' conversion, has been an undying flame, burning bright on the altar of the heart. The missionary, whilst sympathizing with man in his translation from darkness to light, knowing that in Christ the convert is enriched with an inestimable blessing, also feels that God himself is glorified; that in receiving a new worshipper into his temple, a new child into his family, a new subject into his kingdom, his glory is enhanced for ever and ever; that Christ sees of the travail of his soul in the converted heathen; that an accession is made to his blessedness and joy; that a new gem sparkles on the many-crowned head of him who is King of kings and Lord of lords; and that in the fruitfulness of the believer the Father is glorified, and the Son. And what has oftentimes been the missionary's consolation under a sense of personal weakness and inefficiency, and sinfulness, but that in and through all this, his God will be glorified; his Divine strength illustrated in his weakness; the richness of grace made manifest in his sinfulness; the excellency of the power rendered all the more conspicuous by the frailty of the vessel of earth? Whence, we ask, this close soul-sympathy of the evangelist? Is it not from Him who is one with the Father, who resolved his own will into the Divine will, and subjected all his purposes to his glory? Does not Christ, abiding in the evangelist, give him his own spirit of oneness with God, and thus qualify him as an ambassador of God—fitted to beseech men in his own stead?

Let us now observe the operations of a sympathy with man. The missionary, in an humble, modified sense, like Christ, takes on himself the nature of man; that is, he so transfuses his own soul into their wants and necessities, and so allows them to be partakers of his thoughts and feeling, as well as recipients of all that he has to bestow, that he is one with them. He takes and he communicates. In a sympathetic, and, as far as may be, a practical sense, he takes their sins, and carries their sorrows. He takes of theirs what he can bear; he gives them that which they will receive. He is a vicarious man, willing to endure all things for the elects' sake—'to fill up that which remaineth of the sufferings of Christ;' parting with comfort, home, and oftentimes wife, children, health, life, that others may be blessed. Whilst he says with the apostle, 'My heart's desire and prayer to God is, that men might be saved,' he is also constrained to say that he could be anathema for their sakes. If by virtue of his sympathy with God, he says, 'I delight to do thy will, O God,' his sympathy with man constrains him to say, 'Yea, and if I be offered up upon the sacrifice and service of your faith, I joy and rejoice with you all.' How often, when told that death will be the certain consequence of continued labours in some particular sphere, has the missionary, giving utterance to feeling rather than guided by judgment, said, 'Then let me die here; rather let me *die* in my work, than *live* away from it.' And how often has death sealed the decision, and the missionary's last consolation has been that, like Jacob, his body would be buried in the land of promise, where his personal labours could no longer be prosecuted.

How warm have been the affections of missionaries to the heathen objects of their charge! It may be that sojourners in the same land are looking after its resources, estimating produce and cargoes; or that travellers through it view nature's beauties; but he sees MAN. The tenant is to him more than the house, the labourer more than the field. Distanced from him though they are in civilization, and degraded below him by vice, they are near to him by the link of humanity. The land is precious for their sakes; the very dust of the earth is sacred, as the dust of their dwelling-place. Man, in all his vileness, is still more glorious to him than nature in all its purity and gorgeousness. His love hides 'the multitude of their sins'—it rises above the indignation and anger which their wickedness induces; it constrains him to stay in their midst, when their indifference or hatred would compel him to depart. His language has been, 'How can I let thee go?' He can bear the taunts and scorn, the rancour of their spirit, and the bitterness of persecution, because he is bound up with them by the 'cords of love.' It is interesting to observe the partiality of missionaries for the people amongst whom they labour. Each, whilst he bewails their evils, yet, in the true spirit of love, finds in *his* people some virtues which others do not observe. The labourer among the negroes detects their intellectual powers, moral susceptibilities, and amiable qualities. Timid females, labouring among the cannibals of the South Seas and the Dyaks of Borneo, yet point out their redeeming qualities. The 'wild, untutored Indian' is the object of *more* interest to the missionary living among them than civilized Hindus or Chinese. He can take their infants in his arms, and sleep in their huts, feeling that he is within the wide enclosure of a common and beloved humanity.

Love—love—love: it is this that has made the men of God strong to endure, ingenious in devices, fruitful in measures, unwearied by opposition, forbearing in provocation, hoping all things, believing all things. If missionary labour be accounted for by enthusiasm, it is the enthusiasm of love stronger than death. This love has manifested itself primarily in an intense solicitude for the salvation of souls, not expending itself in utterances, nor sighs, nor tears, but in self-sacrifice in all its forms, of ease and comfort, of fame and honour, of feeling and interest. Missionary life is replete with acts of devotion to souls, and derives thence its greatest charm. The youthful missionary from Moravia would follow into the wilderness any of his Indians who forsook their first love. One of them had fled from the settlement a hundred miles. The missionary finds him in the forest, and tells him that it is in vain he flies; were he to go two or three hundred miles, he would still pursue him. The Indian replies, with a contrite heart, 'Does Buttner remember me still! are you come merely to seek me?' and, like Peter, weeps bitterly. The missionary writes to his fellow-labourer, 'Rejoice with me, for I have found the sheep which was lost. Jonathan (the Indian) is again become my brother. My heart followed him wherever he went, and I thought I must go and seek him, though he was hunting in the woods at a great distance.' Oh, how much of the mind of Christ in this! The dying Eliot, in his ninetieth year, when sensibilities are ordinarily chilled, looking back at numerous disappointments from man, the treachery of some and neglect of others, and thinking of his own infirmities, exclaims, 'Alas, for human nature! I have lost everything; my understanding leaves me, my memory fails me, but *my charity holds out still;* all fails, but thou livest and endurest for ever.'

This love it is, which has incited missionaries to a hearty interest in all that pertains to man. Whilst supremely solicitous for the salvation of souls, they do not stand out as spiritual beings isolated by their very spirituality from the generality of men, with all their common and minute interests. All that is human has attracted these men of 'broad philanthropy.' Like Christ, inasmuch as in them lies, they console the widow or the bereft, they heal the sick, they feed the hungry, they assuage all sorrow; for they know not human nature in one, but all its aspects, and interests, and necessities. We may remark, that herein has lay much of their success. The man who, like Christ, takes human nature to himself, him will human nature take to itself, to him attach its faith, and lay itself open to his instructions. But the question arises, Who is the author of this love? Who kindled this philanthropy? It is too pure to have originated in aught less than a Divine source. It is of God—of God in Christ—the Man Christ Jesus. It is *his* philanthropy—a beam of his own love, that brought him from heaven to earth. The philanthropy of the missionary bears the impress of Divinity. There has been witnessed a philanthropy without Christ, but not of *this* type, and without this holy anointing. Christ and Missions are then identified, in that the very principle of love, which is the constraining motive, is of *his* imparting.

We proceed to trace Christ in the endowments of the missionary. Early writers on Missions were assiduous in specifying missionary qualifications. They sketched their ideals of the missionary; told us of the endowments needed to sustain the office. Perhaps few have read such descriptions, without the consciousness that the ideal was beyond realization. So it was, as represented by them, but we submit that the real missionary, as made by Christ, has far transcended the ideal missionary, as made by man. In the former, there has been found not only the warmth and vigour of life, but a naturalness, a humanity, a symmetry, which are found lacking in the latter. We have less of the angel, more of the man 'in Christ.' What is wanting of the seraph is compensated by the abounding elements of the saint. Our missionaries have been men of like passions with ourselves, weeping as we weep, and rejoicing as we rejoice; sustaining the same relationships and feeling with us under like circumstances of loss, trial, separation, but all 'in Christ.' They have been also men of practical habits, vigorous action, mingling largely with earthly things and interests, associating intimately with man, moving and controlling him, but all 'in Christ.' They have lived in Christ; Christ has lived in them. His life has been manifested in their mortal flesh. In their mental endowments we see Him, the *Eternal Word*, in whom are hid all the treasures of wisdom and knowledge. He has wrought *by* them, he has spoken *in* them. By fellowship with him, they have learned languages, so as to wield them with power, and with a rapidity of acquirement that has almost compensated for a supernatural gift; they have translated the words of the Spirit into languages refined or barbarous; they have taught with power and demonstration, now mighty to convince, now strong to refute; they have swayed men's minds, and been to them 'as the mouth of God;' sometimes controlling the boldest spirits, and awing the most fearless, as well as commending themselves to the heathen's consciences. The prophetic and apostolic endowments, as evinced by an Elijah, or a David, or a Paul, have been witnessed in the more eminent missionaries of modern times. Schwartz will bear a comparison with Samuel, Eliot with Elijah, Judson with Paul, Hewitson with John, Mylne with Amos, Macdonald with Peter. Laying aside miraculous endowments, the elements of natural character, which distinguished God's ancient servants are found in those of a more recent age, whilst special gifts of power and energy, of zeal and love, fitted for influencing the spirits of men for high and holy ends, have been shared by both. Whence came those gifts but from Him who 'calls' and makes able ministers of the New Testament? If we speak more particularly of graces, then is Christ no less conspicuous in those he has conferred. There has been illustrated in missionary lives a *humility* which has led its subjects in their greatest exaltation to pronounce of themselves that they are 'less than the least of all saints'; of their works, that they are not worthy of record or reward—'I recal those words,' said Eliot, after he had written somewhat of himself; 'lie low, thou child of the dust'; whilst Carey would have no epitaph, save that as the chief of sinners he rested on an Almighty Redeemer; also a *prayerfulness*, whose power with God has been evinced in the manifold blessings which every act of prayer has brought down on the missionary charge and interests; a *meekness*, which has enabled the possessor to abide

> 'Calm in the sufferance of wrong,
>   Like Him who bore their shame;
> Calm 'mid the threat'ning, taunting throng
>   Who hate his holy name';

a *contentment* which has rendered willing to be unknown, even in the doing of a work worthy of filling the earth; to be *where*, and *as* God would have, although repugnant to every natural sensibility; a *gratitude*, all whose utterances were praise for least results and feeblest grounds of hope; an *unction* which has penetrated the natural qualities, and seemed to render the whole man instinct with grace. These wells of water springing up to everlasting life—whence their springs? from the throne of God and the Lamb.

We trace Christ also in the missionary course. By whom have our missionaries been kept from the evil that is in the heathen world? We know that before the seductive influences of heathen society, the enervating influences of climate, and the depression of the nervous system, a debased moral standard, the absence of social restraints, have often fallen the youth, and strength, and vigour of European colonists. Nothing but what has been godly and Christian has been able to stand against the insidious or openly hostile powers of evil. What, then, has kept our missionaries? or, rather, WHO has kept them? HE, who when on earth guarded his disciples from the evil, and then at his departure committed them to his Father. In this warfare how few of the mighty have fallen! How seldom have we been called to deplore the stumbling, much less the fall, of missionaries. But this preservation has been the effect of a sustained spiritual life. There has been life in the midst of death. A fire burning on the altar with no earthly sources to keep it alive, or, if dying out, to revive it. Removed from ordinances of religion, and the quickening influence of kindred minds, whence have they drawn their light, their comforts; whence has their faith been strengthened; whence have their graces been revived? See we not herein Christ, the ever-abiding One? It does not militate against such a conclusion, but rather confirms it, that the missionary cause has had its backsliders and its apostates. We have had sufficient experience that no solemnity nor publicity of vows can preserve them from violation, no professions can suffice to sustain those who make them. There are a few names blotted out for ever from missionary records—blanks that no one fills up—that are to human memory as though they had not been, whose portion is silence, whose works have no chronicler. There has been a —— by covetousness seduced from the narrow path of missionary devotedness; a —— forgetting his first love in the beguilements of luxurious ease and fascinations of popular applause; a —— making shipwreck of faith itself, falling away by unhallowed fellowships. If these stars fell, what keeps the others in their spheres? the others who, compared with the faithless, are as the fixed stars of heaven, compared with the meteors that shoot athwart our path. Is not the answer found in the fact that Christ holds them in his right hand?

Further—we see the grace of Christ in sustaining our missionaries under discouragements. If other trials are as the iron that enters into the soul, discouragement of the kind peculiar to missionary labour is as the ploughshare that cuts deep furrows into it. And what missionary, constitutionally sanguine or phlegmatic, who has laboured long, has not been forced to say, 'They ploughed deep furrows.' Who has not found, like Martyn, the conversion of the heathen to be a far more arduous and protracted work than had been imagined? Who has ever overestimated the difficulties of winning souls and turning many to righteousness?

There are discouragements from heathenism negatively considered. Its region is like the wilderness of *Sinai*, 'a land of darkness, and of the region of the shadow of death.' He who dwells there feels he is *alone*. God is not known. There is no one to testify of him; there are none to acknowledge him. No customs recognise him, no institutes honour him, no day is consecrated to him. The heathen have consented to banish God from their understandings, hearts, and homes. There are discouragements from the wickedness of heathenism which wounds every sense, pains even the understanding, and afflicts the soul; from obtuseness of intellect, where heathen mind has not been exercised, and its perverseness where it has; from the immensity of the work in connection with the number of combined agencies for evil, the strength of opposition against good, the mastery of the devil over every individual mind, and over society in all its forms. But the severest discouragements are from the apparently feeble effect of the word itself. The strength of evil does not so much discourage as the weakness of good. There is so little energy put forth by the Spirit: so little seen of 'God coming out of his place'! He seems 'behind the thick cloud.' His delays go far to exhaust the patience of his saints, and justify the tauntings of his enemies. Truth, though ultimately to prevail, is temporarily in a state of humiliation. The word of God, though 'a hammer to break the flinty heart to pieces,' is in its present effects, and local influences, an inert thing. The believer could bear to find *himself* weak; he could take to himself the blame of paucity of results, but then the word itself, as preached or published, heard or read, *that* appears weak, and is upbraided as such. The human testimony is unconvincing, but then the testimony of the Spirit, why is not that forthcoming? Incessant activity needs to be blended with sufferance, and perseverance in labour to be conjoined with waiting in hope; and this is a severe trial for human nature that reckons time by days and hours, rather than by thousands of years; that links sowing and reaping with no very long interval, in its mental associations and strongest expectations.

Under such feelings, one of God's labourers, pursuing his 'monotonous' course of instruction of Hindu youth, monotonous only because of the absence of inquiry after God, and love of truth, says, 'How hopeless seems the result of preaching to the students of the college. They are encased in prejudice, in spite of knowledge and conviction; they are living against their consciences, and rearing up refuges of lies to shield themselves against truth. *O Lord, how long wilt thou try us thus? If the trial must continue, strengthen our faith, lest we fail and come short.*' As the evangelist of youth, so of adults. Macdonald's words are but the echo of hundreds of hearts, similarly oppressed by the unbelief of the heathen.

The question forces itself on us, whence have God's servants derived strength to persevere amid so much discouragement? They are but men, whence did they obtain a patience more than human? In the unbending will and unimpressible heart of the heathen, the unpropitious circumstances of their life, combined with all the helps which the god of this world can afford to those who serve him, we see more than enough to discourage the man of God, and make him abandon his work in despair, unless his faith be divinely supported, and his perseverance secured by the energy of ONE who strengthens him. When we think of Hans Egede, with all his high hopes in going to Greenland, called to labour amongst them for many weary, dark, cold years, without seeing one heart changed, enduring scorn and derision from his countrymen at home, who heard of his failure, as well as the cold contempt of the ungrateful Greenlanders—when we look at the Labrador missionaries, who experienced from the Esquimaux a confirmed opposition, and came in contact with inveterate habits of evil, that resisted the gospel, and made the labourers as those who 'beat the air,' and yet pursued their labours—when we see Ziesberger going forth into new regions, to found new settlements for his Christians, as soon as the old flourishing ones had been levelled to the ground by the savage Indians—when we cast an eye at Judson, who touched the Burman shore with as sanguine expectations as ever dwelt in human breast, gathering his Burman church by units at long intervals, and finding the small band so scattered and deteriorated on his return, as to necessitate its reorganization—or when we consider the perseverance of the missionaries of Tahiti or New Zealand, or, indeed, of all the first missionaries in their new spheres, meeting with bitter reversals of preconceived ideas, frustrations of well-laid plans, failures of hopeful characters, and yet going on and on in their work, till death called them away—the conviction is forced on us that they derive their strength to pursue their work from Christ himself, who has said, 'Lo! I am with you alway, even unto the end of the world.' He has stood by his servants, and guided them by his eye. He has infused energy into the faint, repressed impatience, sustained faith, and, knowing that they are sifted as wheat, has prayed for them, that their faith fail not. And thus these labourers have more than conquered over the dispiriting power of circumstance, through Him who hath loved them. The experience expressed by one labourer is indeed verified in the case of all; 'When at home I used to say, Jesus Christ will sustain me in all times of trouble. Now I can say, Jesus Christ *does sustain me.*'

Under this influence they have seized and held fast the great principle of personal fidelity. They may have entertained exaggerated expectations, misinterpreted prophecy, misjudged history, but they have maintained *faith,* and rightly understood *duty.* Disappointment of the bitterest kind, on account of the nobleness and endearment of the cause, the absorption of the soul in its issues, has come on them, and threatened to paralyze them. But, in the presence of Christ, the Jonah-like spirit that sent forth its wailings has been hushed into a calm. They have been taught that the work is God's, not theirs; that they are his servants; that he is the repository of his own glory; that his kingdom will come in his own way; his will shall be done on earth by his own management; that his servants have to fulfil their duty and to abide his time, to execute their commission and leave its issues, to sow the seed of the kingdom, and look for the harvest in due season; that they have, in fact, to await the resurrection morn when a crown of righteousness is prepared for those who are faithful unto death.

It is Christ who has given them an exhaustless patience—patience when the intellect on which they worked has remained dull and stolid beneath their efforts to mould it; when the heart they have sought to impress has maintained its unyielding character, and refused to receive any moral impression; when the drear monotony of circumstances has suggested the stillness of the regions of the shadow of death; patience, amid the contradiction of sinners, the questions of fools, the blasphemy of the ungodly, the plots of foes; patience in God's seeming delay in the establishment of his own kingdom, in the church's lack of sympathy and realization of the work and its difficulties. 'The God of all patience,' has been with his servants, and said to them with power, though gentleness, '*In patience possess ye your souls.*'

What a beautiful illustration of the sustaining grace of Christ in discouragement is furnished by the African missionary. He has just taken up his abode in a barren and miserable land, where there is no grain, nor in the absence of water for irrigation any means of cultivating it. His mission is to a people characterized by jealousy and suspicion; the chief under whose protection he has placed himself, once a savage murderer, and now an immature Christian, not to be confided in; himself solitary, without a soul near to sympathize, or to whom he can pour out his heart. With the spirit of a David who said, 'I have set the Lord always before me, he is at my right hand, I shall not be moved,' he kneels upon the bare granite rock and pours out his soul to God, or reclining on one of the large masses of stone, in the stillness of the evening affording the utmost contrast with the noise and turmoil of an African kraal, he strikes the instrument of one who had already finished his missionary career, and tunes it to one of the church's sweetest songs—

> 'Awake, my soul, in joyful lays,
> And sing thy great Redeemer's praise.'

Who stood by? Who indicted the prayer? Who gave the spirit to strike the chords? Who taught the heart to make melody, when nature herself in its rugged wildness and dreariness seemed to repel joy? Was it not Christ?

The same truth of Christ's presence is further illustrated by the fiery trials through which many of our missionaries have passed. In these fires of affliction, there has been with them one whom we cannot fail to recognise as the Son of Man, unlike all others in his sustaining energies. There is the fiery trial of special danger or distress arising from the heathen. We see one of the early missionaries of New Zealand exposed day after day to the violence of the savage natives. Alarms by night succeed the visible dangers of the day. Now they point their muskets, now grasp their spears, and are restrained only from murder by an invisible hand. At length the Mission premises are burnt down, and the missionary and his wife are forced to flee for their lives. One of the daughters of America —a land rich in her spiritual heroines, takes up her abode among the Karens long anterior to their evangelization. Her dwelling is in the hut of a dissolute savage man, the only shelter procurable. She is miles distant from her fellow labourers. The heathen set the house on fire—thwart her efforts and place her life in constant jeopardy. The faithful one pursues her labours till a jungle fever arrests her, and she is called to a land where 'the wicked cease from troubling and the weary are at rest.' The Feejean missionaries dwelt for years among a people where every sight was horrid and every sound was distressful. They were forced to witness the dreadful feasts of cannibals, or the slaughters of wretched victims of cruelty or passion. Now they haste to intercede for widows doomed to be strangled, or victims set apart for sacrifice. Now they rescue children abandoned by ruthless parents. Who can estimate the trial of having one's *home* amid such scenes? Could they have pursued their labours unless Jesus had been present with them? Again, we see a missionary and his wife dwelling in Ashanti with the object of opening a door for the gospel. The place where they dwell is an Aceldama. The bodies of those sacrificed are found lying in the streets like carrion. The town seems occupied by fiends rather than men. And yet, though moving in such scenes, they are enabled in their own privacy to sing,' Saviour whom our hearts adore.' Was that Saviour distant? or, rather was not his presence that which made existence tolerable in such a habitation of cruelty and wickedness? There is the fiery trial of *temptation*, when, taking advantage of adverse circumstance or a depressed nervous system, the enemy comes in like a flood, and fills with suggestions to unbelief; or when the soul, shut out from all congenial associations, and lacking outward objects whereon it may exercise its powers, turns on itself and creates imaginary grounds of distress. Such were the temptations of the Moravians, who, discouraged by the unbelief of the Greenlanders, were almost consumed by painful solicitude as to their original call from Christ to prosecute their mission, and were filled with the most distracting suggestions. There is the fiery trial of *bereavement*, when solitude among the heathen that had been shared by another, becomes undivided, and a dreariness oft described, but never realized save by similar sufferers, steals over the soul. There is the fiery trial of *separation*, when, the conjugal or parental ties are severed by the unkindliness of climate or necessities of circumstance. There is the fiery trial of *personal sickness* and inactivity, when all around calls to action. There is the fiery trial of *abandonment of one's sphere*, a second expatriation far more painful than the first, an exilement from a land and people to whom tenderest ties bind. In the midst of all, is the Saviour found, binding up broken hearts and calming troubled spirits. And in that they live, we see the life of Christ; in that they prosecute their work, we behold his manifested presence; in that they abide in their holy calling, notwithstanding all things *against* them, we see the proof that he abideth the same, 'yesterday, to-day, and for ever.'

But we see Christ in the light and joyous experiences of missionary life, as well as the dark and sorrowful. It is the Sun of Righteousness that makes their daily path radiant; as well as dissipates the occasional darkness that settles over them. The missionary life is indisputably a happy one—nay, the happiest on earth. We might have imagined it to be so, anterior to experience, from the fact of its containing so many of the objective elements of the life of Christ; instructing babes, relieving sorrows, receiving sinners. A life approaching as far as the nature of the case will admit to his, would, we might imagine, have been characterized by many of his experiences, receiving from the Father a special seal, which should testify of his approbation of it; a seal which should kindle a joy unspeakable, and strengthen assurance. We might also have formed such an expectation from the explicit promise, 'There is no man who hath forsaken houses or brethren, or sisters, or father, or mother, or wife, or children, or lands for my sake and the gospel's, who shall not receive a hundred fold more in the present life, and in the world to come life everlasting.' And are such expectations confirmed by the facts of the case? All testimony from all sections of the missionary sphere agrees that missionary life is full of blessedness. 'Welcome! Joy!' said Eliot, looking forward to his future; but these words were but the echo of his experiences during the lengthened term in which he had served Christ. There is joy in missionary labour *as a principle.* It is prescribed of God, it is his method of conversion. Man must be converted by man. The evangelist is a fellow-worker with Him 'who worketh hitherto'; his work is *under* him who is the Head, and *with* him who is the active living One. There is joy in labour *in the detail;* joy in Scripture translation, for the labourer is thereby scattering leaves for the healing of the nations, opening up the river of the waters of life; joy in original composition of tracts or books for the heathen, for he is giving the first elements of a literature baptized with the Spirit of Christ, redeeming a language from its past desecration to idolatrous purposes, leaving the impress of truth behind him, in scriptural forms, that shall influence many minds when the place that now knows him shall know him no more. There is joy in *preaching,* for he is uttering the living words whereby men may be saved. Is that preaching to a casual assembly? precious seeds may be taken by one and another, and scattered over some fruitful soil. Is it to a fixed congregation? line upon line, precept upon precept, multiply the means of conversion. Is it, for the first time, in a town, or village, or district? then may it be an era in the future history of that people—the very beginning of their evangelization. There is *joy in teaching,* for the teacher is moulding impressible minds of youth, with the elements of Christian knowledge, and securing a generation that shall serve the Lord, and not follow the gods of their fathers. There is joy in *ministering* to the bodily wants of the heathen, for he is practically teaching them the gospel he preaches, and showing forth the benevolence of Christ.

There is joy in labour, even when unsuccessful; for he is 'a sweet savour in Christ, in them that are saved, and in them that are lost.' If none believe his report, yet is it honourable to Christ, that he should utter it; if all resist the truth, yet is it fitting that truth should have its standing advocate; if all are against God, the more incumbent on him to act as a faithful witness.

But who shall tell of the joy of successful labour? When a single heathen conscience shows signs of life—when one or two precious incorruptible seeds have germinated and appeared in the blade—when there is an earnest eye fixed on the speaker, and a look of sincerity, and a question of solicitude, 'What shall I do to be saved?' What joy did the Tahitian missionary feel when he heard the first native pray under the bush; or the Greenland missionaries, when the inquirer forced himself on their attention as they were reading of the sufferings of Christ, and said, 'How was that? tell me that once more, for I would fain be saved too?' 'These words,' *says the* missionary, 'the like of which I had never heard from a Greenlander, penetrated through my very marrow and bone, and kindled my soul into such an ardour, that I again gave the Greenlanders an account of our Lord's whole life and death, while the tears ran down my cheeks.'

Let this work of conversion be carried on to its issues—the sanctification of the soul. Let the missionary see the gradual but effectual influence of the truth renewing the soul, one lineament after another, into the image of Christ; the old form of corruption dying away, and the new man in Christ assumed; and thus let him receive the seal of the Spirit in his labours, and who would not be a participator of his joys? If this individual work become general; if the missionary be a Rhenius, who saw a people gathered out, schools of hopeful youth established, souls gathered into churches, native evangelists raised up, and the kingdom of God, whose primary seat is within the soul, yet assume a local habitation and a name among the heathen; or if he be a Williams, and witness marked providential interferences attest to himself and to the heathen the supremacy of Jehovah, and his blessing on the Mission, so that enemies are discomfited and the true friends of Christ take courage; his heart shall indeed be filled with the richest joy of earth. The heart has bounded with delight at the mere imagination of the heathen, who dishonour Him and serve other gods, turning to and adoring him, the only God and Saviour; but the sight has at times been too much for human nature. It has touched every sensibility to the quick. The missionary has been scarcely able to sustain his excess of joy; and sensible that life's great end has been accomplished, that time has given its grandest blessing, and this world his utmost bliss; feeling its links to earth relaxed, and itself prepared for translation, has found an appropriate utterance in the words of the aged saint, 'Lord, now lettest thou thy servant depart in peace, according to thy word, for mine eyes have seen thy salvation.' These were the words of Boardman, as he reclined on the banks of the stream where many Karens were baptized at once by the hands of another. He felt life's great end was fulfilled, and his cup of blessing was overflowing. Brainerd, gathering his first-fruits and harvest simultaneously, after a day's labour with his converted Indians, says, 'My soul, that had longed for this hour, was transported with joy. How I grieved to leave the place. Earth, cover thou not my head yet awhile! Though the thoughts of death are sweet, I would fain stay while this great work advances.'

There is *joy in suffering and privations.* The apostolic experience is renewed. 'As the sufferings of Christ abound in us, so our consolation also aboundeth *by Christ.*' The less of earth, the more of heaven. The absence of human sympathy only challenges the more of Divine sympathy, and fits the mind to receive it. The less of the treasures of nature, the more of the riches of grace. The fewer streams, the more accessible the fountain, and the more willing is the soul to draw from it. The losses are made up by an all-compensating Saviour. He has to make good his promise of compensation to those who have forsaken all for him, and he does so. Grant, widowed and bereft of his children, loses his keen anguish at his losses in a short communion with Christ on one of the hills of Kurdistan, and there confesses that his Saviour makes up for all, giving the hundred-fold that he had promised. 'I rejoice,' says the missionary so often quoted, 'even when many weary days and nights roll over my head, in perils by the heathen, in perils by the wilderness; when the tempest beats upon me, and I have nowhere to take rest.' One, who saw only the labours, without the successes of missionary life, on his fatal voyage to Sumatra, says, 'And why can a missionary be happy? Because God fulfils his promise: "Lo! I am with you alway, even unto the end of the world;" and also, "according as thy day is, so shall be thy strength." In our little boat of eight tons, managed by Malays, who are rather indifferent navigators; in our little cabin, partitioned off by mats, in the back part of the hold, with not room sufficient to stand upright; amid all the smell of bilge water and stores, with our chests on each side for sleeping and writing places, and a clean mat spread on the floor on which to eat our rice and chicken broth, for want of room to place a table, *I was never more happy, if I except the few first hours after I opened my eyes in the kingdom of Christ.*' In the presence of such experiences, we are constrained to remark, that the missionary is an object of high and holy emulation, but not of pity; of deep brotherly sympathy, but not compassion. We need not commiserate him, as unknown, for he is well known; as dying, for behold!

he lives; as chastened, for he is not killed; as sorrowful, for he is always rejoicing; as poor, for he is making many rich; as having nothing, for he possesses all things. We see Christ's joy fulfilled in them.

Let us suppose the element of positive joy to be excluded from the missionary's life; that the heathen rage and the people imagine a vain thing; that his labours are unsuccessful; that there are no spiritual children who shall speak with the enemies in the gate; that there is no one to stand by him when he is in difficulties; that he is neglected from home, as well as discouraged in his sphere; yet a peace will be found to steal itself, like a balm, over his hours of discouragement and seasons of disappointment. That peace, whence? It is Christ's peace.

Yet the main life of missionaries is in the future. They are prisoners of hope—they pierce through the dark clouds of the present. They look not at, but *o'er* and *beyond* the gloomy hills of darkness, and see afar off the brightness of his rising. The missionary traveller,* in a land where is no convert, no mission, nor desire for the truth—where to sight all was dreariness in nature, and in human character, and society—ascends one of the lofty mountains, and, looking over the whole land as one of promise, in faith and hope, commits its people, in all their generations, to the Lord Jesus Christ. This hope, so strong and undying, and so widely felt, whence is it? From Christ. He who, when on

* Krapf.

earth, grasped the future as well as the present, lived in it and for it, who was baptized unto suffering with the clear consciousness of emerging from it, and bore the cross with the full prospect of the crown—who saw the abundant fruit which was to spring forth from the single corn of wheat;—he has transfused *his own hope* in the hearts of his servants.

We have seen it abundantly illustrated, that Christ is the missionary's glory. We conclude with the remark, how appropriate to evangelists is the Scripture appellation, 'Glory of Christ.' They are so by manifesting his glory in their mission. The Divine mission is perpetuated in them; the Divine economy is carried out by them; the Divine energies are transmitted through them. Christ was the glory of the Father, by his labours, by finishing the work which he had given him to do. Missionaries are the glory of Christ in the same way, though in an infinitely humbler degree. They make known Christ in his offices of salvation. They lead a lost world to him. They instrumentally 'open the eyes of the Gentiles, and turn them from darkness to light, and from the power of Satan unto God, that they may receive forgiveness of sins, and inheritance among them which are sanctified by faith in him.' They are his sowers, to sow the seed of the kingdom; his fishers, to catch men; his builders, to hew and fix stones for the habitation of God through the Spirit; his shepherds, to bring those that are not of the fold into his fold, that they may find pasture. Christ sees in them the agents who, by the Spirit, carry on his work, secure the travail of his soul, and bring on the harvest of the world. They are also the glory of Christ in their *character*. As *his* living epistles, they are read; as *his* living witnesses they are believed; as *his* living examples, they are followed. The Son of God dwelt in the cloud; in it he enshrined his glory, and was therein occasionally visible. But now that glory is enshrined in his saints, and most visibly in those that serve him, like Paul, in their sympathy with his sufferings, death, and resurrection. The departed One is yet present in them; the absent yet re-appears. He reproduces in them his own character, those features which more particularly distinguish him as a Saviour—his love and sympathy. Christ is preached to the heathen, in his perfections as well as his work. Those perfections are shadowed forth in a dim but faithful outline, in the person of the preacher. They are thereby enabled better to comprehend them. The eye assists the ear. From the human developments they can more easily understand the divine. From a survey of the moral character of those who are Christ's, they can better apprehend Christ himself. Evangelists are thus Christ's witnesses, not merely orally, but visibly, tangibly. The heathen see that Christ's glory is not an impossibility, for it is in a measure actually realized in them. His life is not a fiction, for there is a reality before them, which, however it come short as a copy of the original, *shows that original to have existed.* Those who said of Martyn, 'he was a man of God,' were better able to comprehend the glory of God himself. 'I should think that Christ was like that man,' said an Indian convert of a minister, 'he is so meek, and loving, and gracious.' He felt that from an hour's communion with him, he knew more of Christ than he had done before.

Nor does the faithful missionary less manifest the glory of Christ, in relation to the universal church. The church has already heard with wonder of the grace manifested to her messengers, and has learned to glorify Christ in them. A wisdom and judgment have been evinced, which attained maturity without much time for growth; a strong will to carry out the plans and purposes of the mind, and as strong a spirit of endurance to bear opposition, and confront discouragements; humiliation amid all calculated to exalt, and elevation amid all calculated to depress; strength to pursue an arduous work, or to bear a grievous disappointment; faith to hold on their way without sight, and contrary to sight; hope in circumstances that would indicate despair, in the absence of all earthly consolation and solaces; an unction when no human hand applied the oil; a fervour lighted up from the altar of no kindred heart, a peace that passeth understanding in severest tribulation. These have been and are evinced in every mission, if not in every individual missionary. Whence came they? From Christ. In all their gifts and graces he is seen.

Thus, Christ their glory, and they Christ's glory, the highest honour is conferred on the church, whence they were called and separated. The whole body of the faithful derives glory from the glory of these, its members. The love, and grace, and condescension of Christ to his church, are evinced in his choosing from amongst her members, and not from his heavenly hosts, those who shall add to her numbers, enlarge her borders, strengthen her stakes, and thereby perpetuate her existence on the earth. *Zion is* enlarged by her own children. They are the builders of the walls of Jerusalem.

CHAPTER XIII.

CHRIST IN THE 'EFFECTUAL DOOR' AND SUCCESS OF MISSIONS.

Christ's Providence for Missions—In Missions—Spiritual Results from Christ.—'Manner of Entrance' of the Truth.—Agency of Christ therein. — Converts' Apprehension of Christ. — Dying Experiences.—Christ the Author of such Faith.—Converts' Character.—Source in Christ.—Pentecostal Effusions.—North Americans.— Negroes. — Bechuanas.— Fingoes.— Armenians.— Nestorians.—Cingalese.—South Sea Islanders.—The Spirit of Christ.—Concluding Remarks.

As in individual conversion, providence and grace work together, and concur in a common result, so in the great work of evangelization. For this great purpose, Christ is appointed 'Head over all things,' has 'all power given unto him in heaven and in earth,' is 'exalted a Prince and Saviour,' has 'power given him over all flesh,' is 'King of kings and Lord of lords,' is set as 'King on God's holy hill of Zion,' has the heathen placed under his rule, with authority according to the Father's decree, to 'rule them with a rod of iron, to dash them in pieces like a potter's vessel.' He exercises this universal supremacy, this absolute rule for the church, to give eternal life to all whom the Father has given him; to call them out, to deliver them from their enemies, to give them a conquest over the world, and all powers of earth and hell.

The multiplied ways in which he to this end exercises his control over men's hearts and earth's events; the vast purposes he plans, and causes his agents consciously or unconsciously to carry out; the modes in which he regulates and overrules political events and social developments, human thoughts, inventions, discoveries; making all things, even the counsels of his enemies, to work together for his own pre-ordained ends of evangelization, are beyond the scannings of our feeble minds. Those which may be more distinctly discerned, would require a volume for their scantiest illustration. We do not here attempt the task, however fraught with interest, yet cannot forbear to specify some few of the more striking exercises of his providence in their relation to Missions. First, his providences *for* Missions are manifest in having made us acquainted with the world to be evangelized. We know the world as it was never known before. The meridians and parallels of latitude are extended over a real globe, not an imaginary one, as in the days of the apostle. Ptolemy's geography and a modern 'Atlas,' how different in their relation to Missions. The Romans' knowledge of the world, when Britain was an *ultima thule,* and the European's acquaintance with all its continents and islands; how different their bearing on the fulfilment of the great commission. Moreover, we know the nations, and tribes, and peoples, and tongues, which occupy the length and breadth of this world; their characters, customs, institutes, and religions. Comparing the knowledge of four centuries ago with that of our own, we see the advantageous position we occupy for going unto all nations and preaching the gospel to *every creature.* But further, we see Christ's providence in the fact that this world, so well-known, is at length made traversable; in its seas and oceans, spite of storms, whirlwinds, rocks, or sands; in its continents with its deserts, mountains, and rivers. As a whole, and for immediate evangelistic objects, the world is a compassable one. In these respects we can say of the apostles, relatively to our own times and advantages, that 'without us they could not be made perfect.' It is only in these latter days that we are enabled to understand the terms of the original command, the breadth and length of their meaning; and also it is only *now* that we are enabled by the facilities of locomotion to carry it out in its literality. But in order to such a simple result, what sciences have been originated, and what applications made of them; what discoveries have been made, and practical results elicited from them; what a multiplicity of motives and interests have been brought into play on the part of man; and, connected therewith, what a series of providences, what revolution of wheel within wheel, on the part of the providence of Christ.

Further,—this world so known and so traversable, is, at most salient points, accessible to the church. When Missions were first earnestly prosecuted, the

South Seas afforded the most eligible sphere, as that most easy of access. The world was then shut. Now even China is opening to the missionary. But to this end what a series of conquests, or of treaties; what diplomacies, what commercial enterprises and successes; what emigrations and colonizations. And in all this, has there not been manifested the providence of Him who has power over all flesh?

Nor do we see less of Christ's providence in the characteristics of those to whom he has evidently committed the work of evangelization. The Teutonic race, with its capacity to rule mind, to teach and influence other races, its bold enterprising spirit, capacity of endurance, powers of invention, love of emigration, and above all, its knowledge of the truth as it is in Christ, has been prepared, through a series of centuries, for this great work. The Saxon offshoot threatens to compass the globe. No one can have read the biographies of American, German, and British missionaries, without perceiving how eminently adapted they were, by the qualities of race, the physical, and moral temperaments of their respective peoples, for the evangelistic work.

Equally with this providence *for* Missions, is his providence evinced *in* Missions. The history of this would be of equal extent with that of Missions themselves, of which it is, like Israel's cloud, the guide and glory. It has been already treated of incidentally; a fuller illustration is beyond the compass of this book.

We advance to the more special object of this chapter—the illustration of Christ's presence and energy in the success of Missions. It is he who not only calls the missionary, and makes a way for his utterance, but so carries that utterance to the heart as that faith ensues. Do the heathen hear the things which are spoken to them? It is because the Lord opens their hearts. Do they become obedient to the faith? It is Christ who makes them so. Are saved ones added to the church? It is the Lord who adds them. Is a congregation gathered from a heathen people? it is because the hand of the Lord is with those who utter the truth. Is a church founded? It is because Christ builds it, and the gates of hell are not able to prevail against it. Is there a pentecostal effusion of Divine influence, so as to awaken multitudes to cry, 'What shall we do to be saved?' It is the Lord who pours out that which we see and hear. These general statements are illustrated by a consideration of the 'manner of entrance' of the truth among a heathen people, the faith and character of the individual converts, and the circumstances of conversion. The very method of introduction of Christianity in a heathen land, involves a difficulty insuperable by all but Divine power. What is that method? The operation of truth on individual minds—with no other aids and means than are afforded by the truth itself. The word of God has to be apprehended by a single mind, communicated thence to other minds, till a mass is pervaded by the truth. We might have expected a different order in the Divine economy; that leading minds, or ruling authorities would be first affected; great centres of thought and power revolutionized in favour of Christianity; and then, by force of example, influence, and authority, a people made willing to hear, and prepared to obey. We might have imagined an arrangement whereby every monarch should be a Constantine, every chief a patron, every presiding genius converted into a witness; that the scribes and pharisees of every people, and the rulers of every Sanhedrim should first believe, and thus facilitate the faith and obedience of the common people. But how far is such an imagination from fact. Ordinarily, all that is potent, and commanding, and influential, is *against* the newly taught religion. Every mind must, therefore, believe *for* itself, and *by* itself, differently from, and contrary to all others.

Now, what is to gain over these individual minds, to make them obedient to the faith of Jesus. Who shall win a way for a faith that contravenes all existing faiths, opposes all prevailing habits, enjoins a renunciation of all previous religious ideas, a denial of self in its religious as well as its carnal forms; a faith, moreover, the possession of which involves the loss of what man holds dearest, and draws on the professor what he deems most terrible. Once let Christianity exist, let there be precedents of faith, let there be living examples of practice, and thus the new religion become a fact, and the doubtfully practicable made a reality, and the question assumes a different character; but the outset is the difficulty of which we now treat. Let nuclei exist, and men will gather around them; let schools be attended by a few, and scholars will assemble; let churches and chapels exist for converts, however few, and the number of worshippers will increase. But the beginning of all, the first influences, the gathering of the first few learners, the baptizing of the first few converts; *there* is the difficulty, of which all conversant with the heathen world will say, 'With man it is impossible.' So deep was the sense of this impossibility that the worldly at first pronounced that Missions, especially to the East, would be a failure; and even now, many ignorant of the power of God, declare the heathen *cannot* be converted.

Christ removes the difficulty of which we are treating. He does so by securing individuals' faith in himself. The heathen receives Christ, and for his sake, Christianity. He loves a person, and communicates of that person to another. Nothing is more conspicuous in the process of conversion of a heathen people, than that individuals at first apprehend Christ. They are converted *to him*. Their faith lays hold of him, and their affections go forth towards him. They distinctly recognize him as the Saviour—his atoning work; his priestly intercession; the grace which is through him; the promises which are in him. Christ stands out before the converts in his personality as a living ONE, present to them. 'They know in whom they have believed.' He assumes in their minds a position distinct from and above other Christs, who have been hitherto the 'end of their faith.' In receiving this 'One Lord,' they also discard all other 'lords.' This one Saviour casts out a multitude of saviours. This one Expiator supplants their confidence in other expiators. They do not balance systems and accept the superior one. They receive a person—a living Saviour. Christianity is nothing to them, save that it is the religion of Christ. They first apprehend him, then receive his religion. They become obedient to the *person*, then receive his 'mysteries,' and attend to his commands. In the wilderness of South Africa, Dr. Vanderkemp's first convert, a Hottentot woman, expressed her conversion to the faith by saying that she incessantly prayed to Jesus to reveal himself to her and teach her what she ought to know. His overflowing heart rejoiced, that in such a place and with such a woman, *he could converse confidentially of the mysteries of the hidden communion with Christ.* The confessions of the first Burman convert were, 'Besides Jesus Christ, I see no way of salvation. He is the *Son* of God, who had no beginning and no end. He so loved and pitied men that he suffered death in their stead.' One of the first converts of the Moravians in North America, himself once the most depraved of a very depraved people, says, '*Even when asleep, I dreamed of the blood of Christ shed for us.*' The early converts of Brainerd discovered *vehement longings after Christ to save them.* 'Of forty assembled, there were scarcely three who could refrain from tears and bitter cries.

They all as one, seemed in an agony to obtain an interest in Christ.' Of one of the first, he says: '*She seemed to be filled with love to Christ*, and afraid of nothing so much as to grieve Him whom her soul loved.' The Greenlanders, it is well known, when converted *at all*, were converted *to Christ;* not to a faith but a person. The first convert from their number, when invited by his own people to a dance in celebration of the rising of the sun from below the horizon, replied, '*I have now another kind of joy, because another sun, even Christ, is risen in my heart.*' When the early Hottentot converts of the Moravian settlements were lying in groups on the bare ground under the effects of a raging epidemic fever, the missionary and his wife who visited them were cheered by the earnestness with which they listened to them conversing on the love of Christ; they seemed to forget their own sufferings whilst contemplating his, and expressed themselves resigned to his will, grateful for his love, and hopeful of his reception of them into glory. One of a kindred race in prayer, with a faltering voice and a heart too full for utterance, exclaims, 'How can we ever love Thee as we ought to do for thy love to us?' The first negro converts of Sierra Leone are characterized thus: 'They dwell in love, and *live a life of prayer and praise to Him who loved them and gave himself for them.* The hearts of many of them seem to be full of the love of Christ the whole day, and when merry they sing psalms.'

The faith and love of converts to Christ have evinced themselves in their endurances. His sufferings, death, and resurrection ever stand out before them as *facts* fraught with motive, encouragement, solace, hope. They appeal to them as known occurrences; speak of them as events apprehended by their minds, and operative on their affections. The convert suffering bodily agony, thinks of the agony of Christ, and from the comparison, which he feels defies comparison, draws a motive to patience. The Esquimaux woman, forced to ascend rugged hills with a heavy burden day after day, bethinks herself of the load which Christ bore on his way to Calvary, and feels encouraged to proceed on her weary way without a murmur, saying in the retrospect, 'Yes, he was very near to me then.' For his sake, as one who is 'precious,' to whom they 'have come,' and whom they know, in whom they abide, they endure joyfully all manner of wrong. They bear the cross of daily trials; it may be of mockings and scourgings. They count not their lives dear unto them. The Malagasy women offer up their lives without hesitation, rather than deny Him whom their soul loveth. The Hindu has become a martyr for the faith of Jesus. The negro died under the lash, rather than dishonour Christ. The Karen 'died the death of Jesus' for the sake of Jesus. The South Sea evangelist goes with his life in his hand amongst wicked men, for the sake of the Lord Jesus. The newly-converted Armenian suffered the fearful bastinado, rather than deny the faith he had embraced.

If the dying hour be a great revealer, then will it betray the falsehood or weakness of the convert's faith, or it will afford additional evidence that the 'root of the matter is in him.' When flesh and heart fail, then will he show whether or not God is the strength of his heart and his portion for ever. What, then, is the character of the dying hours of the converts? The Hindu, who in his heathen state, when on the brink of death, would be full of apprehension of going before Yama, the judge of the infernal regions, or becoming a disembodied evil spirit, doomed to wander in misery, or to take some incarnation of brute, or vegetable, now sees Jesus; desires to die to him as he has lived in him. We hear one of these brethren, in his dying hour, thus addressing his family, who were yielding to the distractions of sorrow, 'You need not sorrow and weep for me. Neither my place nor rest is in this world. God has not made us for this world. Will you send me away, not with joy, but grief? Will you be the occasion of hindering and grieving me? and will you not leave me to pray to my Saviour, in whom I trust in this hour of death? Oh! let me alone!' The Esquimaux, who would fear either annihilation or departure into gloomy, ice-bound regions, or to be tormented by the evil spirit, sees HIM 'as mighty to save.' His presence smoothes his dying couch, his smile lights up the grave. Arranke, the once savage and murderer, now a Christian, falls sick. His heathen wife bewails his approaching death. 'Wilt thou leave me, my husband? Wilt thou leave thy two children, and go to that dim country of shadows?' 'Weep not,' replies the dying Christian, '*I go to that Redeemer who loves men so much.*'

A pestilence sweeps over the Moravian settlement in Labrador. Of the little band of believers, one after another dies, till the extinction of the whole is threatened. So numerous are the sick and dying, that none are able to minister to their wants. The missionaries could do little else than bury the dead. But what of the state of mind of those departing under such a trial of faith, as though God had rejected them, or as though that Christ, whom the missionaries had preached, and whom they had believed, had forgotten them? 'They all declared,' is the testimony of the missionaries, 'that they rejoiced in the prospect of seeing HIM face to face who had redeemed them from the power of sin and the fear of death. Parents were separated from the embraces of their children, and departed with joy.' Had they failed to apprehend Christ in life, could they now so clearly view him in death? Was not their dying faith the consummation of the faith they had exercised in life, and God's seal of its sincerity? An Indian of South America, once a conjuror, now a Christian teacher, grieving that his ignorance and weakness prevent his seeing Christ more fully, when told that his illness is likely to be fatal, with an eye glistening with joy, exclaims, 'I will settle my affairs, and think only on Jesus; for since I knew aright what HE has done, I have ever wished to be with him.' The South Sea islander, calm and composed in the prospect of death, says, 'Christ is my resting place; the fear of death is removed; I have taken leave of all things, and am waiting and praying for the Lord to take me.' The dying negress of the West Indian island says, 'My only hope is in Jesus, my Saviour; in him death or life is welcome. I call upon him sincerely, with my whole heart; he will take me. I know my sinfulness, but his precious blood has atoned for my sins.' A Bechuana woman in her dying hour thus addresses her friends and neighbours: 'I am going to die. Weep not because I am going to leave you, but weep for your sins, and weep for your souls. With me all is well, for do not suppose that I die like a beast, or that I shall sleep for ever in the grave. No; Jesus has died for my sins. He has said he will save me; I am going to be with him.' A young woman of another tribe, two hours before her death, assures her spiritual teacher, 'Ah! I love the Lord with all my heart! with my whole heart I cleave to Thee, and thou wilt come and dwell with me. This is my consolation. In joy and pain my soul depends on thee, with humble confidence, thou Rock of my salvation.'

We need adduce no other testimony of the fact that, to the modern heathen converts, from all sections of the missionary sphere, as well as to the strangers whom the apostle Peter addressed, are applicable the words, 'Whom having not seen, ye love; in whom, though now ye see him not, yet believing, ye rejoice with joy unspeakable and full of glory.'

We ask, whence this vivid apprehension of Christ, this vision of the Invisible, this felt nearness of the distant One? Whence the conviction of Christ as a real person? Whence the trust expressed in him, in his revealed character and offices? Are we referred to the testimony of the missionary, or that of the book he brings with him? Let us underrate neither; but neither will suffice as a solution of the question. What is the testimony? First, of the fact that one named Jesus, eighteen hundred years ago, lived in Judea, a country unknown to most of the heathen, and, though mighty in word and deed, died on the cross; secondly, of the doctrine that through his death God is reconciled to man—that they who believe in him are forgiven, justified, and shall receive the Holy Spirit. Will this testimony of itself, unsupported by any higher testimony, win for itself conviction? We trow not. Its effect will be, according to the peculiarity of the mind to which it is given, a stumbling block, or foolishness. To those who have assumed the position of believers, the whole array of external and internal evidence by which the missionary testimony is supported, will commend itself. But we are treating of unbelievers, and those, mostly, whose habits of mind are little accustomed to investigations of evidence; all whose immediate interests are against the testimony, and all whose personal, and ancestral, and social prejudices, are against it likewise. What is to carry conviction to their minds? How is that Christ of whom the missionary testifies to become to the soul of the hearer a living reality, a present person? How are the facts to become substantiated to his consciousness? How are the doctrines to be clothed with the power of living truths and operative principles? Apart from a Divine agency, the conversion of the heathen to the faith of Christ is of all things impossible. If the preacher of the gospel were uninstructed in the truth of a Divine agency, his actual experience would force on him the doctrine, and a contrary supposition would shut him up in utter despair of success. No words can express the intellectual, moral, and circumstantial difficulties which lie in the way of a single heathen's conversion to Christ, be he a Hottentot void of intellect, or a cultivated Hindu. That any conversion does take place is a standing miracle, an evidence of the truth of Christianity itself; or, rather, as bearing on our argument, is the proof of Christ's self-manifestation to the soul of the heathen; an evidence, therefore, of his presence and operation in Missions. The Spirit, which is the spirit of Christ, which he sends from the Father to testify of himself, and glorify himself in the hearts of men — he bears a conjoint testimony with the missionary; and that testimony, united, yet to be distinguished—apart, yet mysteriously blended— wins the heart of the heathen to the obedience of Christ. Whether we consider the Father as shining into the heathen heart, to give the light of the knowledge of the glory of God in the face of Jesus Christ; or the Spirit, as glorifying Christ, by taking of his and showing it to the soul; or Christ himself, as the light of the world, appearing to the soul, the result is the same, the manifestation of Christ, so as to secure faith. It were in vain that the newly taught soul felt after Christ if haply it might find him, were not Christ *near* so as to be found; that the outer testimony existed unsupported by the inner witness; that, in fact, man should reveal Christ, did not Christ reveal himself. Missions are, then, successful because Christ is in them.

We have seen Christ in the faith of the convert. Let us now behold him in the character which is developed by him as a new creature. The classic fable of the power of music on animate and inanimate nature has been realized in the moral influence of Divine truth on the heathen heart, and the prophetic figures have had their ample verification in the changes that have come over heathen society. The changes have been beyond comparison; they have transcended conjecture; possibly exceeded hope. We have collated testimony, and did space permit, might here adduce it, from all missionary spheres, unanimous in asserting a moral regeneration of the members of the several churches. In putting on Christ they put off the corrupt deeds of the old nature, and are transformed in the spirit of their minds. The fruits of the Spirit, which are invariably produced in those who believe, are fruits of righteousness and true holiness.

Now, whether we view these converts as receiving the promise of the Father, 'I will dwell in them and walk in them;' or, as built up in Christ 'for an habitation of God, through the Spirit;' or Christ himself dwelling in them and they in him, and thus bringing forth fruit; the truth is the same, that Christ is the author of this renewed character, and consequently that he is in Missions. He now dwells in the churches of China, or India, or Africa, even as he once dwelt in the churches of Asia. From him they receive their graces and maintain their life.

'Look at me,' said a Hindu convert, a native preacher; 'I was once full of sin; all unrighteousness dwelt in me; some of you are witnesses how I lied, and deceived, and cheated. But when I knew Jesus Christ, I learned to hate sin and fought against it. It was strong and difficult to overcome, but Christ gave me strength; one sin after another was slain, and I am hoping soon to be without sin.' The solution was truthful and wise. Let it stand for all his brethren. 'All things which belong to the new creature are of God.' Christ is the renewer of the heathen heart, by his Spirit that dwelleth in it.

The Lord Jesus is no less conspicuous in the manner of conversion of the heathen, than in the faith and moral character which are the result of conversion. It would be interesting to show how frequently a people have been converted, when their teachers had began to despair of success and had perhaps temporarily left their mission. But we limit our observations to those Pentecostal effusions of the Spirit which we witness at different periods in almost all Mission spheres. The same phenomena are manifested among people of different mental characteristics, of varying past associations, and widely diverging from each other in their social circumstances. There is an energy which is diffused through many minds at the same time, arousing, alarming, convincing. Those under its influence suddenly evince earnest desire to know the truth, deep compunction on account of past transgression, are inconsolable as long as they are unconscious of having found Christ, and obtained in him forgiveness and peace, and full of joy when this blessed gift has been obtained. The effects which remain after the more direct energy is gone, are a decided triumph over past sinful associations and habits, and the manifestation of righteous principles and holy conduct. We propose to refer to spheres of labour where such operations with their results have been indisputably enjoyed. And first we quote the well known experience of Brainerd in the conversion of the Indians. Never has there been a work more decidedly of the Spirit and less of man. That man was indeed mighty with God, and prevailed for the outpouring of the Spirit; but his power with man, dependent as he was on an interpreter, was more than ordinarily feeble. Yet with all this feebleness, what did not Christ accomplish by him? 'I discoursed,' says he, 'to the multitude on that sacred passage, "Yet it pleased the Lord to bruise him." *The word was attended with a resistless power; many hundreds in that great assembly, consisting of three or four thousand, were much affected, so that there was a very great mourning like to the mourning of Hadadrimmon.'*

On another occasion, when a band of sixty gathered round him, he tells us, 'The influence of the Divine truths was great; they all, as one, were in an agony of soul, as I discoursed on the love and compassion of God, and the more I invited them to partake of that love, the more their distress was aggravated; yet it was solemn and affecting, being shown by deep sighs and tears, and the softness of those hard and cruel natures. I could but perceive how their hearts were pierced with the tender invitations of the gospel when there was not a word of terror spoken to them.'

Of a totally different sphere, that of the negroes of Sierra Leone, at an early period, the missionary testifies, 'There has arisen among the inhabitants of this settlement, not only a longing after the bread of life, *but also a continued inquiry after the way of salvation.* From another place the testimony is, 'A spirit of prayer is poured out on the people in a remarkable manner, so that we find as we pass through the streets, on returning from evening school, that almost every house is become a house of prayer.' The heathen also in and near the colony were at a much later date simultaneously influenced by the Spirit of God to surrender their idols and seek religious instruction in the knowledge of the true God. The missionary writes, 'The idolaters of Sierra Leone are casting their idols to the moles and bats. The kingdom of Satan is falling like lightning.' In South Africa, the work has been at one and another station urged on by the same energy of the Spirit. After the terrible and protracted discouragements of the Bechuana Mission, the Spirit was poured out from on high. Those who had scorned to weep, now cried out for pardon from a holy God and Saviour. The dull and indifferent became thoughtful and intent inquirers after salvation. Prayer and singing took the places of idle talk and licentious conversation. The house of God was thronged and became a Bochim from lamentations of conscience-smitten souls. One exclaims, 'I seek Jesus;' and another, 'I am feeling after God; I have been wandering among beasts of prey; the day has dawned and I see my danger.'

At the Moravian settlements in South Africa, unbelieving farmers, who had resisted the missionary work, were won over by this same Almighty Spirit, and thus prepared to be effectual helpers of the Lord. The missionary, in recording the work of grace, says, 'Our churches have been filled with attentive hearers, our schools with crowds of children, and both churches and schools have been filled with the hallowed presence of the Spirit of God, who has wrought a marvellous change in the hearts of many, both old and young.'

The Fingoes, newly delivered from the bondage of the Kaffres, and assembled in thousands at the Moravian Mission station, came under these marked influences. No place of worship could receive the concourse that assembled to hear the word of God. Services were conducted in the open air. Multitudes listened to the preachers, as though they felt it to be the 'word of this life'; deep emotion filled their hearts, which expressed itself, now in weeping for themselves, and now in tears of commiseration for their unbelieving parents and relations.

In Asia, among the lapsed churches, has been a marked Pentecostal power, 'as in the ancient days.' The Holy Spirit has from time to time infused amongst the Armenians the spirit of earnest inquiry, opened hearts to receive the truth, shed a precious unction on the souls of believers, excited to holy exercises of soul, and induced believing and persevering prayer. Under his gracious influence, whole communities have been won over to embrace the truth, so that in a few years Christianity has become a *power*, not to be ignored either by the ecclesiastical heads or the civil power.

The same Spirit of grace has, in like manner, operated on the Nestorians—a people, none of whom when first known to the western churches, gave any evidence of genuine piety, and who now number hundreds of sincere spiritual disciples. The work has extended mostly from the young to adults. The former—scholars in the Mission seminaries—

were visited with deep solicitude for their own souls, until they received Christ into their hearts, 'the hope of glory.' The sacred flame spread to parents, whom the children visited, or to families of the surrounding country. Within eight months of one of these gracious visitations, not less than one hundred and fifty, amongst whom were several ecclesiastics, found justification and peace at the foot of the cross.

He who ordaineth praise out of the mouth of babes and sucklings, glorified Christ in the hearts of many of the scholars in the Mission seminaries in Ceylon, who simultaneously gave themselves to Christ, and, together with converted adults, were received into the church. 'Two of the most pleasing features attending this work,' say the missionaries, 'were its quickness and depth. Conversion almost immediately followed conviction, and the depth of feeling was manifested by uninterrupted prayer and praise in their general meetings, social circles, and private rooms.'

The history of the Karens has been that of repeated outpourings of the Holy Spirit, from the time when Kothabyu first preached to them.

The islands of the Southern Seas have been the scenes of the same Spirit's effectual operations. They have been manifest, as we have already seen, in preparing people for the messengers of truth; by decided influence on men's minds, exciting expectations and desires, and infusing fear and hope relatively to the word of Jehovah. But no less have there been exercised those *quickening* influences under which dead souls arise from their death of trespasses and sins. The Son of God has uttered his voice, and they that were in their graves of moral corruption heard it and lived—not by units but by hundreds. Such a mode of operation was needed where the sphere was so extensive, islands so thickly scattered, groups so distant from each other, and labourers so few; and the need has been supplied by Him who is able to do exceeding abundantly more than the church has asked or thought. The Sandwich islands have enjoyed pre-eminently these spiritual influences. Though none were admitted to church fellowship without evidences of real conversion to God, so greatly did the word of God prevail, that in one year the Lord added five thousand to the church, and in the succeeding year ten thousand more. In twenty-three years from the commencement of the Mission, including the time of preparation for preaching, more than *thirty-eight thousand* had been enrolled as disciples of Jesus.

The Friendly Islands were visited by the rushing of a mighty wind which shook the hearts of the obdurate, filled wicked transgressors with strong compunctions, and induced wide-spread strong desires to enter the kingdom of God. At Vavau, one of the stations, the work is thus described:—'On that day, we believe that not fewer than one thousand souls were converted; not now from dumb idols only, but from the power of Satan unto God. For a week or two we were not able to hold the schools, but had prayer meetings six times a day. We could not speak five minutes, before all were in tears, and numbers prostrated before the Lord, absorbed in deep concern about salvation. Frequently their words were "Praise the Lord! I never knew Jesus until now, now I do know him. He has taken away all my sins; I love Jesus Kalaise." Some were so filled with joy that they could not contain themselves; but cried out for hearts to praise the Lord. *This has not been like the dew descending upon the tender herb, but as the spring-tide, or as the overflowing of some mighty river; all the mounds of sin have been swept away; the Lord has bowed the whole island to his sway.'*

Of another station, the testimony of another missionary is, 'In the morning we repaired to the house of prayer as soon as it was light. The Lord made the place of his feet glorious; the stout-hearted began to tremble; there was a mighty shaking among the dry bones. As soon as service began, the cries of the people commenced. What a solemn but joyful sight to behold! *One thousand individuals bowed before the Lord, weeping at the feet of Jesus, and praying in agony of soul!* I never saw such distress—never heard such cries for mercy or such confessions of sin before. These things were universal, from the greatest chiefs in the land, to the meanest individuals, and of both sexes, old and young. The Lord heard the sighing of the prisoners. He bound up many a broken-hearted sinner in that meeting, and proclaimed liberty to many a captive. We were engaged nearly the whole day in this blessed work. *I attended four services and witnessed hundreds of precious souls made happy by a sense of a Saviour's love, on that day and the preceding evening.* As the result of such and similar awakenings, five hundred of the natives are now preachers of the gospel.'

The Feejean islands, so abandoned to all crime that no Christian would have dwelt there but from obedience to Christ, has been visited by the same blessed Spirit which maketh all things new. Of one of these revivals the evangelist's record is as follows:—'Business, sleep, and food, were almost entirely laid aside. We were at length obliged almost to force some of the new converts to take something for the sustenance of the body. Some of the cases were the most remarkable I have ever heard of; yet only such as one might expect the conversion of such dreadful murderers and cannibals would be. If such men manifested nothing more than ordinary feelings when they repent, one would suspect they were not fully convinced of sin. They literally roared for hours through the disquietude of their souls. This frequently terminated in fainting from exhaustion, which was the only respite some of them had till they found peace. They no sooner recovered their consciousness than they prayed themselves, first into an agony, and then again into a state of entire insensibility. The results of this work of grace have been most happy.

The preaching of the word has been attended with more power than before the revival. *Many who were careless and useless have become sincere and devoted to God.* The experience of most has been much improved, and many have become by adoption and regeneration the sons of God.

Such testimonies might be multiplied. Are any inclined to say of these witnesses, what on similar grounds was said of Peter and the apostles, 'These men are drunk with new wine—the wine of enthusiasm and extravagant hopes?' They can well meet the charge and vindicate their own calmness and impartiality of judgment; and pointing us to the substantial effects of these pentecostal seasons in the renewed lives and characters of converts, they may address an unbelieving church in the language of Peter, '*This is that which is spoken by the prophet Joel, And it shall come to pass in the last days, says God, I will pour out of my Spirit upon all flesh,* and your sons and your daughters shall prophesy.'

Reviewing all that has passed before us, which is but a section of the work of God; considering the different places and circumstances under which these works have been wrought, the diversity of character and temperament of the agents, their connection with different sections of the church; allowing, therefore, of no solution from anything of constitutional habit or modes of action peculiar to the agents themselves or those who sent them;—can we shut out the conviction that *the Lord Jesus, being exalted at the right hand of God, hath poured out this which we now see and hear?* Reason itself can admit no other solution, as at all adequate; while faith finds every doubt and difficulty removed in a glorified Christ sending the promise of the Father. These ingatherings of souls show that He who makes his disciples fishers of men, is standing on the shore, and having bid us cast our net into the sea, has also by his omnipotence secured the draught.

We close this chapter with two remarks. First, in a personal Christ we see the secret of the power of Christianity, and its wonderful adaptations. A *person* can be received by all, literate or illiterate, savage or civilized, a child or sage. A code would demand study, a system a large comprehension. A theology might require a sustained intellectual effort. A being can be apprehended by all. The historical man, although a God-man, who lived and moved on this earth, who, as an Atoner and Intercessor, is the object of faith and hope, is the man to whom humanity can and will attach itself. There is no person, past or present, in the wide domains of heathen history, to compete with Christ. No claims ever put forth may be set by the side of his, no character sustain comparison with his, no work be placed in the same category with his. 'He is a rock. His way is perfect. A God without iniquity, just and right is he.' The power of Christianity in laying hold of human hearts is in Christ.

Hence, also, in an ever-living, present, and operating Christ, we see the secret of the undying life of Christianity. Its success is in a living Christ. He is the source of its operations on human hearts, its sustained influence on society. He liveth; his religion lives also. Systems grow weak when their founder is departed. The withdrawal of the imposing genius of the living person, who originally established them, is a shock which no human schemes of religion ultimately recover. Mahommad's death was the death of Mahomadanism. Although his mighty spirit, being the spirit of war and rapine, has for a time pervaded his religion, yet it must ultimately die out. No genius can be transmitted to endless generations. But Christ is alive for evermore. 'He is the same yesterday, to-day, and for ever,' in the reality and sensible presence of his adorable being. He may at all times, and by all, be known, understood, felt, loved. His genius and spirit depart not from the earth. He is with his people 'always, unto the end of the world.'

CHAPTER XIV.

EVANGELISM IN ITS RELATIONS TO CHRIST.

Recapitulation—Christ in Missions prosecutes his own Mission—Secures the Objects of his Redemptory Work—His Travail and Glory.—Christ in Missions an Encouragement—A Rebuke—A Motive—Missions to be Prosecuted for Christ—In the Mind of Christ.—Under Christ.—Promise Fulfilled.—Conclusion.

WE recapitulate what has been demonstrated in previous chapters. Christ is in Missions. His impress is on them. His presence pervades them. They are, in principle and detail, identified with him. He is their originator, the source of their power, the spring of their life, the author of their success. The men are his, by an awakening call; by a personal commission; by convincing credentials. He gives them moral power; furnishes them with needful gifts; and sustains them by his grace. The providential arrangements whereby spheres are opened up, people rendered accessible, and events concur to secure a welcome for his messengers, are *his*. Lastly, the success is his. Understandings enlightened; wills subdued; hearts purified; souls washed, sanctified, and saved; and from converts themselves, a band of evangelists raised up—this is all *his*. We recognize herein not merely a doctrine, but a fact. We realize it not only by faith, but sight. It has been said of certain great men that their biography is the history of their age; so closely bound up is the one with the other. In like manner the life of Christ, as now revealed, is the history of Missions. The one is identified with the other. Let us view the fact in its twofold relation. First to Christ himself; secondly, to the church.

First, Christ in Missions—prosecutes his own mission as the sent of God. By their medium, he prolongs his own days on the earth. He was the Minister of the circumcision, and also the Apostle of the Gentiles. He who sent him, said of him, 'It is a light thing that thou shouldest be my servant, to raise up the tribes of Jacob, and to restore the preserved of Israel. I will also give thee for a light to the Gentiles, that thou mayest be my salvation unto the end of the earth.' His direct personal mission to the Jews was carried out when in the flesh, but his mission to the Gentiles was to be accomplished by the medium of other agents. He never fulfilled in person those prophecies which embraced all men. His mission was to the world, yet he abode and laboured only in a small section of it. He was the light of the world, yet never did he move from the confines of Judea. He was Apostle of the Gentiles, yet did he say of himself, 'I am not sent but unto the lost sheep of the house of Israel.' By whom, then, can he fulfil his mission? By his disciples. By what medium? That of Missions. The bodily presence is removed, and the personal mission ceases; but the spiritual presence abides, and the mission is still prosecuted. Evangelism is not a supplement to the mission of Christ, but a continuous fulfilment of it. In the person of his disciples, he is 'set for salvation to the ends of the earth.' By them he speaks to all men. The world still has Christ as its apostle in the person of faithful missionaries. He is still the light to enlighten them, reflected from living men who are his representatives. His own mission from the Father is carried out from age to age among all nations, in the person of ambassadors. 'As the Father hath sent me, even so send I you.' 'As thou hast sent me into the world, even so send I them into the world.' Believers have not merely their own individual mission relatively to Christ, but they fulfil Christ's mission relatively to the Father. That mission, the subject of so much prophecy, and the source of so many blessings, cannot be reckoned by his human life nor temporary ministry. In this sense, 'who shall declare his generation?' The believer takes up what he laid down, or rather receives the commission by transfer from Christ. When his evangelists preach, he speaketh in them; when they instruct, he is still fulfilling his office of the first Teacher; in all their journeyings in quest of souls, he is seeking and saving that which is lost; even in all their offices of love, healing the sick, and relieving human miseries, he is fulfilling his vocation of carrying men's sins and bearing their sorrows.

Further, Christ in Missions—secures the objects of

his redemptory work. That work, viewed in its relations to God, was a finished one. 'I have finished the work which thou gavest me to do.' 'God was in Christ reconciling the world to himself.' 'It is finished,' said the Redeemer on the cross. 'By one offering he hath perfected for ever them who are sanctified.' But this work, so complete in itself, so accepted by God, so efficacious to the remission of sins, *is unfinished relatively to man.* It needs to be made known in order to be believed, and to be made effectual in them that believe, to forgiveness of sins and renewal of the heart unto righteousness. Whilst, then, in its divine relations Christ's work cannot be supplemented, it needs to be *carried out* in its human relations. Relatively to man, that work is nothing, if unknown and unapplied. Nothing for the production of repentance; nothing for the introduction of faith, and procuring remission of sin; nothing for his sanctification; nothing for his glorification. The work of Christ needs to be made known in order to the realization of its holy influences, and the attainment of its ends of salvation. Hence, as soon as the mystery of a redeeming God, and a dying Saviour, which had been hid from ages and generations, was revealed in the person of Christ, *it was made manifest to the saints;* not by them to be retained still a 'mystery,' but to be communicated far and wide to all who knew it not. As soon as the secret was evolved from the recesses of the Eternal Mind, it was henceforth to be buried in no other mind, but by medium of believers to be unfolded to every one. 'The unsearchable riches of Christ' were no sooner given, than they were to be preached to the Gentiles. The life and death of Christ, as facts, have to be announced. The propitiation effected by it has to be declared. The willingness of God to accept sinners is to be proclaimed. There are links in this chain, one of which may not be broken. The whole depends for its efficacy on the continuity of its several parts. Christ personally and directly wrought out redemption, but he brings it nigh to men by an instrumentality. Independently of all agency, he brought in everlasting righteousness; but he makes it available only by his servants. Alone does he work out salvation by his blood; but he proclaims it by others. His own history constitutes the facts of evangelism, and the basis of its doctrines was laid in his death; but the evangelism itself must be accomplished by men. This work is not his directly and personally, nor is it that of the Holy Spirit, which is the special glorifier of Christ. His province is to *apply* the word uttered, to give the increase to that which is actually sown; to create and bless spiritual agencies from the midst of Christ's disciples. Again, Evangelism is not the work of angels, whose office is to minister to those who are heirs of salvation, not to preach to those who are under condemnation. No other agency exists than that of Christ's disciples.

It is, then, by the provision of Missions that Christ sees the travail of his soul, and is satisfied. They bring the atonement nigh to souls, and souls nigh to God. They proclaim the fountain open for sin and for uncleanness, and souls wash therein. They are the agency by which the Spirit acts for Christ; the testimony in conjunction with which he testifies and reveals Christ. By their means, those given of the Father come to Christ. By them his voice reaches those that are afar off, and his 'ensign' is lifted up and attracts from the uttermost parts of the earth. They communicate that knowledge to people and tribes, by which he 'justifies many.' They are his instruments whereby he makes war, and conquers, and 'divides the spoil with the strong.' By their ministrations of the incorruptible word whereby souls are born again, he sees his seed; by them, though absent, he prolongs his days; by them the pleasure of the Lord prospers in his hand; by them the rod of his strength goes forth out of Zion; by them he rules in the midst of his enemies.

Missions also are the media of Christ's glory, both as regards the manifestation of it on earth, and its realization in heavenly places. The prayer, 'Father, glorify thy Son,' in its application to this world, can be effected only under the present dispensation, by the medium of Missions. They spread abroad that word which testifies of Jesus. They publish his character and works, and offices, and make known his glory. The heavens which he made as the eternal WORD OF GOD do indeed shew forth his glory; but it is not perceived; their voice is not heard, their utterance unheeded, nay, their testimony is turned against Christ; the work of his hands being glorified instead of himself the Maker. His people, also, reflect his glory, and by holy lives, and loving acts, give the world some glimpses of his holiness and benevolence. Let Missions cease, and, relatively to the world, the Sun of Righteousness is eclipsed. His glory can only be seen through the medium of the evangelistic work.

But further, Christ's personal glory is realized only by this medium. Above the glory derived from material worlds that are his own, above that rendered by principalities and powers that are subject to him, will be the glory accruing to him from his holy ones redeemed from amongst men. Of his 'many crowns,' that crown will have a peculiar glory which is studded with the jewels of redeemed spirits from this world of sin, and his most glorious princedom shall be that of ruling over the once alienated but now reconciled and grateful hearts of the children of men. But what shall bring to pass this glory? Not the mighty armies of earth, nor the mightier hosts of heaven, but the evangelistic work. Not to the angels that 'pour out vials of wrath,' nor those that 'fight with the dragon,' is it given to announce 'the kingdoms of this world have become the kingdoms of our Lord and of his Christ.' The instrumentality he hath chosen, for such a consummation is that of his gospel preachers. That glory, which was the joy set before him, and for which he endured the cross and despised the shame, is substantiated by Missions.

Let us now view the fact that Christ is in Missions, in its relation to the church.

First, Christ in Missions, is an encouragement. As the Christian, conscious of the seal of his calling and election, prosecutes his career of duty and privilege with courage, zeal, and love, so let the church, assured of the seal which the Lord has impressed on Missions, pursue the work with courage, earnestness, and calm confidence of victory. The warfare in which we are engaged is not ours; he is with us. In the van of the evangelistic tribes of Christian Israel, is the Lion of the tribe of Judah. The Angel of the covenant that dwells within the cloud goes before and fixes our encampments. The shout of a King is in our midst. The processes and issues, labours and rewards, suffering and glory, cross and crown of the evangelistic work are his—to arrange, allot, and dispense. Let labourers have this confidence, and let them evince it. They will thereby weaken and subdue their enemies. When they see us conscious of a Divine invisible presence, which leads and sustains, they will take alarm, and make submission. The sense of the Invisible is our best defence; it is also our most effective weapon of offence.

Christ in Missions, is a rebuke. A neglect of Missions formerly involved a dereliction of duty, a transgression of commands, a want of apprehension of the promise; but now it involves blindness at events, the want of perception of a presence, a failure to apprehend Divine powers and energies. A former treason against principles has therefore now added to it a treason against facts. Christ is in Missions; where, then, are the multitudes who are called by his name? Are not the servants where the Master is to be found? Have they forsaken him and fled as the disciples in Gethsemane? Do they refuse to stand by him, as the treacherous friends of Paul in Rome? Christ is in Missions. Why go not his disciples out to meet him, to fall into the lines of the host marshalled under him?

Christ in Missions, is a motive. Think of the mighty influence on the human heart of a person, as distinct from an abstract principle. What no reasoning could effect, nor array of motives, is secured by a person. In a person may be comprehended all that is cogent in authority, constraining in love, powerful in influence. For a person may be made every sacrifice; to him may be rendered the most absolute and self-denying obedience. A principle may command the understanding and influence the heart; but a person rules the entire man, subjugates every sense, seizes the imagination, engrosses the passions, controls the undivided life. No power is at all comparable with that of a person, a living being meeting another at all points of his moral nature. The power of Christianity is in a person; Christ is its Alpha and Omega; hence, its power over human hearts, its world-wide adaptation and conquests. So the power of Missions is in a person. He is the motive to join in the work. Around this Person, then, let the church gather all that is rich in resources, powerful in talent, devoted in love, faithful in obedience. If Christians will not love Missions for their own sake, let them love them for Christ's sake. If they will not aid them for the good they produce, let them do so for the sake of Him who is in them. If they can refuse to them a costly sacrifice, yet let them not refuse it to *Him*; if they can withstand all other arguments, yet let them not turn away from Him who pervades Missions with his adorable presence. We plead not now for missionaries—they are merely the servants of Christ; nor for missionary societies—they are the appointed agencies through which God's faithful ones act, and direct the sacred work. We plead for Christ himself, whose command and sanction, presence and aids, have made Missions what they are. By all the manifold obligations which bind the soul of the reader to him, by all his mercies received and hopes entertained, by all his profession and vows of consecration, we charge him, as in the sight of God, to engage according to his ability, be it great or small; his talents, be they few or many; his property, be it scanty or large; in this work of Christ.

We proceed to deduce a few practical principles from all that has been advanced.

I. Let us prosecute Missions for Christ. As he in infinite consideration identifies himself with them, so let them in grateful zeal identify themselves with him. As he is their original, so let him be their aim and end. As they have their life *from* him, so let them have their life *in* him. As the rivers of Evangelism issue from the throne of God and the Lamb, so let them flow back to it. Let us disclaim subsidiary motives, mixed principles. Let the eye of the Christian be single. Let the whole body of Christ be full of light.

Missions for Christ is the only worthy principle. To prosecute Missions, whether as personal agents or as sustaining the agents by temporal resources, for lower objects than the Object—Christ, is to ignore their true character. Missions for church or sect is an unworthy and Christ-dishonouring cry. To pursue this glorious work in the spirit of proselytism, to spread our own sentiments or inspire our own spirit; to enlarge our borders and strengthen our stakes *as ours ;* and to break forth on the right hand and on the left, that *our* seed may inherit the Gentiles, is to stoop to the position of the sea and earth-compassing Pharisee, and come fearfully short of the end of Missions. In this work, we dare not have a divided aim—a double purpose. Every aim and every purpose must be found 'in the face of Jesus Christ.' We are dependent on the Spirit for every item of success. That Spirit honours Christ. He honours not by his regenerating influences churches and sects, as such, nor the interests of any organizations. His office is to glorify Christ. 'Missions for commerce,' may exclaim the man who sees their influence in exciting a demand for the products of civilization. We dare not take up the cry, for the Spirit on whom we depend, glorifies not commerce but Christ. 'Missions for civilization,' is the cry of a semi-evangelized section of the church. No, the Spirit is poured out from on high to convince men's souls of sin and draw them to a Saviour. He will not move from his holy place to crown efforts for such an end, however good in its appropriate objects and by its appropriate methods.

Missions for Christ is the only adequate principle. It is only as we labour *for* Christ, in sympathy with him and for ends having relation to him, that we can apprehend the work itself in its due relations. Missions must ever be meagre in spirit, and feeble in action, that merely regard man in his physical and even in his spiritual wants and woes. They cannot meet these woes in their length and breadth, unless first made to coincide with the mind of Christ, and to be directed to him. It is only as we view them from the stand-point of Christ that we can understand them, and put forth adequate efforts to their renewal. If our principle be Missions for man, we may come short of Christ; but if it be Missions for Christ, we are sure to reach man, in his universality, for Christ is identified with such. Guided by this principle, we shall extend our labours to the lost souls at home, as well as abroad; to the debased races, as well as the elevated; the rude as well as the civilized; all whose nature Christ assumed; all for whom he died; all with whom he has a sympathy, as the great representative of humanity. This principle will admit of no partiality, no predilections; it is as broad as earth, as comprehensive as human nature itself, as expansive as the mind of Christ. This is the only principle that can convert a *world.*

Missions for Christ is the only permanent principle. The world in its shifting forms of evil, its virulent enmity, its heartlessness for good, its uniform indifference to truth, may wear us all out, as it has undoubtedly sickened many labourers. Philanthropy of purest kind may become disheartened, at the contemned rejection of its proffered offices. Unbelief may prove too much for the proclaimer of truth. Hatred and opposition may make the hands fall and knees bow down. This principle never wears out, and we can never wear out while under its influence. The campaign which is entered on for Christ will last out till the end. He who serves him as a good soldier to please him, will not doff his armour. The metal that is tempered in the love of Christ will never be broken nor shiver to pieces.

Or, again, the novelty of the missionary enterprise will pass away, and the church may grow weary of her protracted efforts. Time will rob subsidiary motives of their present power, and weak principles will vanish away. The now exciting details of heathenism will soon be as a tale that is told, and fall like lead on the ears of satiated hearers. Or, the work itself may be protracted beyond our utmost expectations, and lengthened delay may utterly discourage us. The evangelistic work is only in its infantile beginnings. As yet, only one out of eight hundred millions of heathen are converted to Christ, whilst a large majority of the human family have not even heard him. The work in the East will probably extend over centuries. Why not? The Roman world did not yield to Christianity till after that period. Arguing from analogy, we may expect at least the same time for China and India, ere the knowledge of the Lord shall cover those lands. We want, then, an undying principle, one that shall be perpetuated from generation to generation, living when all else is dying. It is found in Missions for Christ. Labour for him will endure as long as love and the spirit of obedience hold out. These principles abide in the church for ever. Believers will always love him, though unseen, and obey him as their Lord. The weakness of our labourers has arisen, partly from the want of strong apprehension of this principle; the coldness of our support and sympathy with them has been the measure of our lack regarding Christ.

Missions for Christ—is the principle to which is attached a righteous reward. When the Redeemer shall see of the travail of his soul in a redeemed multitude; when he shall rejoice over them with singing; when he shall present them in his triumphal display before his Father, in the presence of thrones and dominions, powers and principalities — not as captives, but ransomed, not prisoners, but emancipated ones;—these labourers for Christ shall share in that glory and dignity, as having been his instruments in bringing these ransomed sinners home. When he shall divide the spoil with the strong, they shall receive a portion of the share. When he takes possession of the joy that was set before him, they shall not be excluded from participation with him. The glory of redeeming and glorifying souls, which is peculiarly his, by virtue of his vicarious sufferings and justifying intercession, he condescendingly shares with them by virtue of their obedience and sympathy. As they have known the fellowship of his sufferings, so shall they have the communion of his joy.

II. Let Missions be conducted in the mind of Christ. Think of its comprehensiveness, as known by his sacrificial work. The world's unity, to his thoughts and feelings, was not broken by the multiplied diversities of race, grade, circumstance, nor by the successions of generations, nor distances of time or space. The countless myriads of past and future, distant and near, were contemplated by him as one whole. With that whole he has identified himself, and for it he has made an offering. 'He tasted death for every man.' Again, think of that comprehensiveness as known from his evangelistic work. Although his Mission was to the lost sheep of the house of Israel, yet with an outgoing of heart that revealed its natural force and tendencies, he dwelt at times on the outskirts of heathendom and raised up the fallen Gentile. His most signal miracles, most striking condescensions and commendations, had relation to those who were not of the seed of

Abraham, nor partakers of the covenant of promise. A despised Samaritan woman and Syrophenician outcast, were regarded equally with a 'master of Israel.' And when the proselytes from heathenism to the purer faith of Judaism stood before him at the feast, the representatives of the whole heathen world, and first fruits of the Gentiles who should seek 'to see Jesus,' he saw with a glance, and realized with an exulting though for a moment depressed and troubled heart, the 'much fruit' from among the Greeks, as well as the Jews, those afar off as well as those that were nigh, which should spring forth from his divinely appointed death. And further, how comprehensive his directorship of Missions, when, for so small a population as that of Judea, he appointed besides his own select twelve, other seventy, who should go two by two into every town and city where he himself should go. And lastly, how comprehensive the terms in which he gave the command of evangelism, 'Go ye into all the world, and preach the gospel unto every creature.'

In this comprehensiveness, then, let Missions be prosecuted. Let the church seriously design to compass the world, and form her purposes and plans as though the thing were practicable. Let her not look, as unbelieving Israel when on the borders of Canaan, to the giant-like forms of evil, or their numbers which withstand, but rather at the Lord of hosts, who fights for her. Let her not even ask with unbelief, like Philip, as she contemplates her own feeble resources,

'What are these among so many?' Rather, let her rest in the confidence that He whose very touch is consecrating, and whose use is fructifying, can take and 'bless' the few resources she offers to him, and multiplying them, just as she faithfully employs them, can make them available to the full comprehension of the work.

But in order to this end, it is evident that undeveloped resources need to be brought to the light of day, and presented to Christ; that agencies, which are now scarcely thought of, need to become substantiated; that organizations, scarcely ever employed, need to be brought into vigorous action. *Individuals* must take up the work. Each man in Christ must act as a *man*, not as a babe. The individual must not be solved, as he is so frequently, in the church, or the missionary society. Why do we so seldom hear of a *Groves* leaving his profession, and for Christ's sake going to Bagdad or India? Of a *Start* labouring and supporting labourers amongst the heathen? Of an Aldersey, going out and labouring for years, on her own resources, in China? How few are the Barnabases who, having land, sell it and become fellow labourers with apostles.

Again, *is not the evangelistic work one for churches as churches?* Are not they the peculiar organizations which can apprehend such a work? Will it ever be really overtaken whilst institutions of Christ's own founding are content to solve themselves in a general society? We are not regardless of the fact, that small churches cannot take up the work efficiently;

but we are quite sure that an immense number of churches, at home and in America, are able severally to conduct their own Missions. The advantages of such management are evident, if we consider the ease with which they are convened, their compactness and order, the strong sympathy of which they are susceptible, the ready measures of which they are capable, their personal knowledge of the missionaries whom they would send forth, the facility of fraternal correspondence with them, the solicitudes for them which would be exercised, the prayers and strong cries which would ascend on their behalf in circumstances of trial and difficulty, and the praises which would ascend when those prayers were answered. In all these particulars we see how exquisitely adapted they are to send and sustain missionaries, and *to foster infant churches affiliated to themselves.* 'May the time soon come,' says Judson—and we would have the words resound throughout Christendom—'when no church shall dare to sit under Sabbath and missionary privileges, without having one of their number to represent them on heathen ground.'

Further, is there not need of a more diversified agency? Our sphere of operation lies among all classes of mind, all grades of social being, and in all possible outward circumstances: we want a varied, and by its very variety an adapted agency. There is scope both for the learned and the unlearned. The intellect of the world must be met by the intellect of the church. The various works of literary composition and translation demand high powers. But there is a vast amount of work which can be performed by men of honest hearts, taught in the school of a divine wisdom, though not endowed with the gifts of human culture. The church must take and appropriate all that the Head of the Church sends to her, without testing them by her own conventional standards. A Johnson from his warehouse converted hundreds of degraded negroes, and a Mylne from the sheepfold translated part of the Bible into Chinese. Let not these cases be considered as extraordinary, and affording no precedent for the church. It is Christ's prerogative to 'call things that are not, to bring to nought things which are.'

Another remark suggests itself—Why has there been no colonization for Christ? Fathers of families go forth for their children's sakes; young men that they may found families. When do we hear of men going forth for the gospel's sake? Why do not Christians *settle down* in some heathen land, when practicable, in order to bring souls to Christ?

Further, let Missions be prosecuted with the same mind of *self-renunciation* which was also in Christ Jesus. Here is the great lack, for which nothing can compensate. We augur little for Missions in the absence of such a spirit. All that has hitherto been greatly done, and well done, has derived its quality from this likeness to Christ.

The office of the church, as Christ's body, is, as we have seen, to implement his Mission, to 'fill up that which is behind,' whether by holy character or active labour or passive suffering. There is therefore a needs be, an economic necessity, somewhat analogous to that whereby Christ himself suffered, for the self-emptying and humiliation of his people. Paul, in expressing his desire that 'he might know Him and the power of his resurrection, and the fellowship of his sufferings, being made conformable unto his death, did not place himself beyond the legitimate experience of other members of Christ, or speak that which ought not to be coveted alike by all. Is not that church which is his body, and by whose means he pursues his own Mission, designed by him to 'be conformable unto his death'? Are the members to suffer one with another, and not with their Head? Is practical sympathy and identity of experience to be confined to Christians in their mutual relations, and not to comprehend Him after whose name they are called? Have we studied aright the redemptory economy in all its processes from the foundation of the world till the salvation of the last soul, if we exclude Christ-like labours and sufferings on the part of believers? We know that the vicarious sacrifice of Jesus was needful; rendered so by the moral exigencies of the divine administration, by the immense difficulties which lay in the way of forgiveness of sin and the bestowal of the sanctifying Spirit. Are we wrong in saying that there is also a necessity for the church to pray, labour, and suffer in its own due degree, and appropriate relationship?

Those prayers in answer to which the Lord of the harvest is to send labourers into his harvest—those labours which are to bring the word of salvation nigh to souls—those sufferings which are endured for the elect's sake; these are all indispensable according to God's redemptory economy, viewed in all its parts. We cannot fail to observe, that there is a necessity for a self-renouncing church, arising from the nature of the work, the obstacles it presents, the malice and hatred of those who resist the Holy Ghost; but there would seem to be a necessity lying far behind this, arising from the entire economy of redemption, under which apostles '*are set forth* by God *as spectacles to the world*, to angels and men'; whereby life works in others only by death working in them, and the life of Jesus is not made manifest, but by the workings of death in their mortal bodies. If believers fail to recognize their vocation, and fall in with this necessity; to occupy their proper position to Christ and take up their appointed ground relatively to the world, refusing to fulfil their legitimate function and accomplish the ministry they have received from the Lord Jesus; do they not therein mar God's work, and in the only practicable sense defeat God's purposes? In their way and according to their measures, are they not hindering the work of redemption? nay, do they not destroy those for whom Christ died? It was by fulfilling his work relatively to the Father, in doing his will, when sacrifice would not avail, that Christ became our Redeemer. Had he not drunk of the cup which the Father put into his hands, none could have partaken of salvation. Jesus saw it was so; after a short struggle he apprehended the necessity; he bowed under it; he acquiesced in it. 'Father, if this cup may not pass away except I drink it, *thy will be done.*' He took the cup and drank it off to its dregs. We see and feel all this; we commemorate it as the source of our salvation. The church of Christ must also drink of the cup he puts into her hand, and be baptized with the baptism wherewith he would baptize her. If, unlike her Lord, she refuse that cup and avoid that baptism, the world cannot but suffer loss.

III. Let Missions be conducted under Christ. Let them have his direction and rule, as well as be in harmony with his principles. Christ, either personally or by his Spirit, is the director of missionary efforts. It is he who opens doors of Missions and shutteth them. He directed when and where the apostles should labour. He took the control of times and seasons and places of the evangelistic work, as well as commissioned the men. The day of Pentecost was *his* day, as the Spirit of Pentecost was his Spirit. Philip would have gone on his way, had not the Spirit told him to go and minister to the returning Ethiopian; and would have gone still further with his newly made disciple, had not the same Spirit withdrawn him from the spot. Christ directed Peter to Cornelius, and Cornelius to Peter, as well as poured out on the assembled friends the gift of the Holy

Ghost. The hand of the Lord laid the foundation of the first Gentile church at Antioch. He bade Paul and Barnabas to be there ordained to the work which he had appointed. He prevented the fulfilment of their intent to plant their Mission in 'Asia.' He suffered them not to enter Bithynia. In the visions of the night, he it was who induced the apostle to go over to Macedonia; thus himself introducing the gospel into Europe, and making the Western regions a repository and safeguard for it, against the time when it should become corrupted or lost in the East. Paul, with a mind shaken by severe conflict with the Jews, would have left Corinth, had not Christ said to him, 'I am with thee, and no man shall set on thee to hurt thee; for I have much people in this city.' Christ directed his appeal to Cæsar, having arranged that as he had testified for him at Jerusalem, so also he should bear witness of him at Rome.

Thus, we see that if the apostles had schemes of their own, they were laid aside on the slightest intimation of his will; their measures were carried out only on the invocation of the Holy Ghost. Do not our missions, in all their schemes and plans of operation, need more of this apostolic spirit? Do we cast ourselves sufficiently on the Spirit's wisdom, and commit ourselves fully to his guidance? Or, is it not too much a practical habit with us, to lay down *à priori* principles, and carry them out, notwithstanding all appearances and all probable consequences? Is the paramount question with us all, 'What is the mind of the Spirit?' We may be sure that the Spirit, who as the Paraclete, is the teacher of the science and guide in the practical work of Missions, *has a mind* respecting every evangelistic work, in every place and by every agent. He cannot ignore anything that is for Christ, and according to the will of Christ. Are we then solicitous, as we should be, to know that mind, and to carry it out when known; to abandon our own designs when they seem to militate against it? Are openings, when presented, entered into *fully, determinately?* Are places providentially closed, recognized as such, and our labours directed elsewhere? No Missions have been more successful than that to Burmah and Western Asia. In both cases the missionaries acted on the principle we advocate. When the door was open among the Karens, they diverted their resources from the Burmese, and applied them in that direction. When the Jewish Mission in Turkey did not prosper, and the Lord opened the door among the oriental Christians, they abandoned their own ideas and established Missions among them. It would be profitable to shew where this valuable principle has been violated, and to make specific applications of it to the several Mission spheres; but we forbear. While it is good to be able to say, 'We have the mind of Christ,' the assurance is of no less value, 'We have the Spirit of God.'

It is by the observance of the conditions we have here urged, that we shall receive the promise, 'I am with you alway, even unto the end of the world.' The fulfilment of that promise is the only hope of

Missions. In our past experiences the presence and operations of Christ have been the 'all in all.' Without him we can do nothing, has been the conviction wrought out by painful trials and severe rebukes. The experience of the past is our guide for the future. We must have Christ with us, in order to a diligent prosecution of the work at all, much more to obtain success. No natural strength of will, stedfastness of purpose, fund of acquirements, intellectual or moral, will sustain the work; no resources of mind, no material treasures, however profusely lavished, will avail. We shall prosper only as he prospers us. We can afford to renounce all acquired advantages of dominion, political influence, commerce, sciences, but we cannot afford to part with his presence. We may lose all our prestiges of power and wisdom, but we cannot do without the prestige of that name, and the power and wisdom of that presence, before which even devils are subject to us. We may joyfully sacrifice all, if need be, in order to gain Christ. But we cannot sacrifice the presence of Christ for anything else, possessed or unpossessed. We repeat it, in our warfare with principalities, and powers, and spiritual wickedness in high places, as well as with the powers of this world, we must have Christ. Every missionary now in the field, but for the certainty of Christ's being with him, would give up his work, or, continuing it, would be 'of all men most miserable.' Still more, if we may speak of comparisons, will that presence be needed in the future history of Missions. The work is only begun. Satan's strength is not yet put forth. Souls have been redeemed from the god of this world, but not the mighty masses. The 'confused noise and garments rolled in blood' scarcely as yet characterize our warfare; they are reserved for our future advances. Outerworks only have been taken; strongholds have as yet to be stormed. As we have yet to urge our warfare and to reap our victories, so have we to experience the effects of success in the increased virulence of our opponents, the marshalling of their combined forces, their protracted wiles, and sudden violences. Persecution will arise, as in days of yore, fierce and terrible, from those who 'worship the beast;' the malignity and fury of the followers of the false prophet will be expended on those who believe in him whose very name they hate so mortally—the Son of God. Infidelity also will arouse itself for its last contest against faithful witnesses for God and his Christ.

In whatever light we regard the work, we need Christ with us, giving unanimity to churches and societies at home; shedding a holy unction on labourers abroad; infusing fear into his and our enemies; sending the 'promise of the Father;' bringing forth judgment unto victory.

'THY KINGDOM COME; THY WILL BE DONE.'